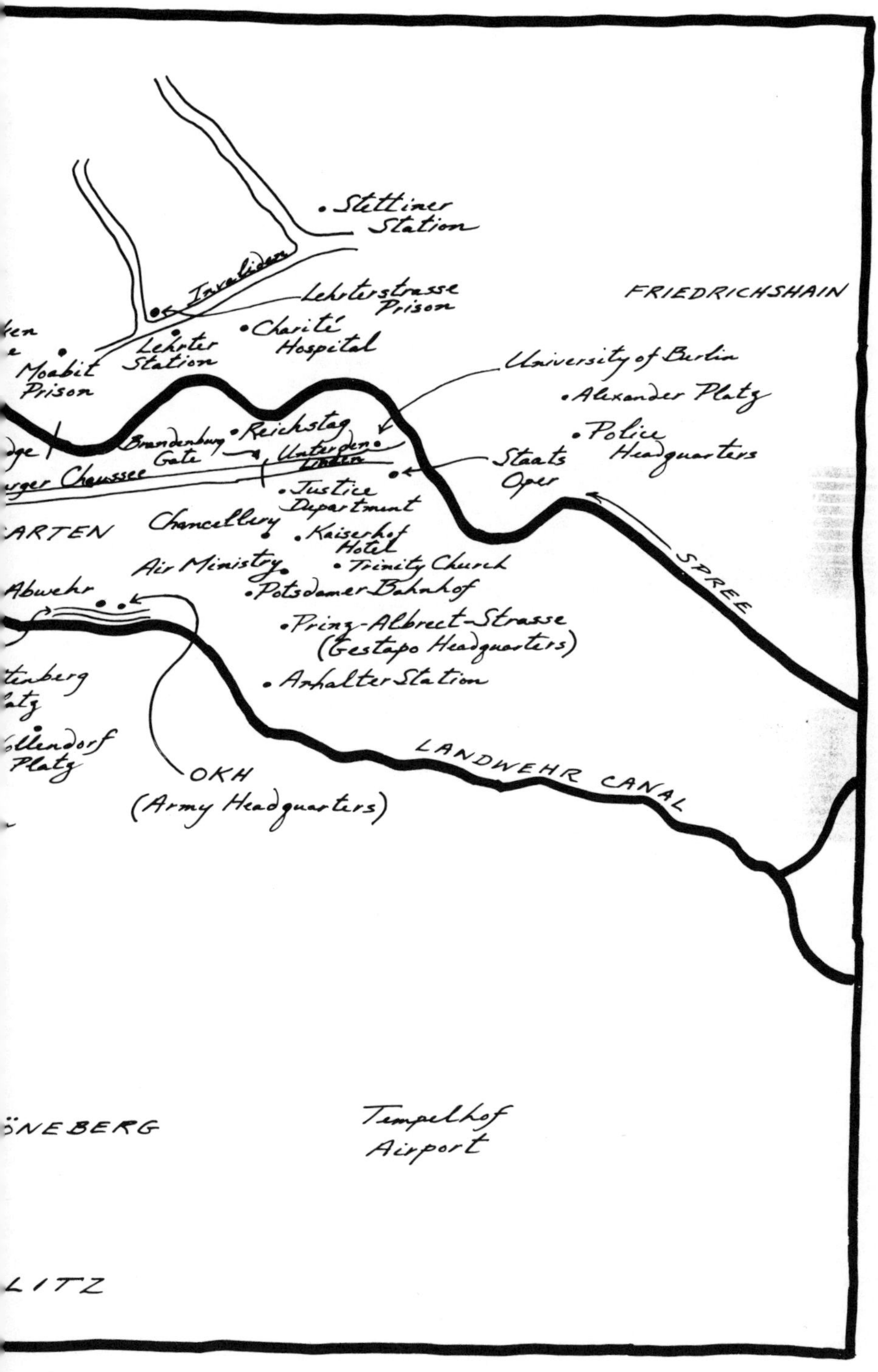

Stettiner Station
Invaliden
Lehrterstrasse Prison
Lehrter Station
Charité Hospital
Moabit Prison
FRIEDRICHSHAIN
University of Berlin
Alexander Platz
Police Headquarters
Reichstag
Brandenburg Gate
Unter den Linden
Staats Oper
Justice Department
Chancellery
Kaiserhof Hotel
Air Ministry
Trinity Church
Abwehr
Potsdamer Bahnhof
Prinz-Albrect-Strasse (Gestapo Headquarters)
Anhalter Station
SPREE
LANDWEHR CANAL
OKH (Army Headquarters)
Tempelhof Airport

THE CUP OF WRATH

THE CUP OF WRATH
The Story of Dietrich Bonhoeffer's Resistance to Hitler

by
Mary Glazener

FREDERIC C. BEIL

SAVANNAH

Library of Congress Cataloging-in-Publication Data
Glazener, Mary, 1921–
The cup of wrath: the story of Dietrich Bonhoeffer's
resistance to Hitler/by Mary Glazener
p.   cm.
ISBN 0-913720-71-2 (acid-free paper)
1. Bonhoeffer, Dietrich, 1906–1945—Fiction. 2. World
War, 1939–1945—Underground movements—Germany—Fiction.
3. Theology. I. Title.
PS3557.L387C85 1992 813'.54—dc20 90-941 CIP

Manufactured in the United States of America

First Edition

For O.W.

From the hand of the Lord you have
drunk the cup of his wrath.
The chalice of trembling
you have drained to the dregs.

—Isaiah 51:17

Let this cup pass from me;
nevertheless, not my will
but thine be done.

—Matthew 26:39

Preface

Unlike the typical historical novel in which fictional characters play out their lives against a historical background, the characters in this story are real people and the scenes depicted are based almost without exception on actual events in their lives. There was no need to try to create exciting events. They were already there. In fact, there was so much to tell that the difficulty lay in deciding what to leave out. The characters have their own names, with the exception of two—Elenore Nichol and Hugo von der Lutz. With fictional characters a novelist is free to make of them what he will. On the other hand, working with real characters and real events places a severe limitation on the author. Depiction of the men and women who people this kind of story becomes, of necessity, an interpretation of all that the author has learned about them. So I cannot claim that you are about to meet the real Dietrich Bonhoeffer. I can only say that in these pages you will meet the Dietrich Bonhoeffer who over the years has become real to me.

This endeavor depended on the help of many people, first and foremost my husband, O. W. Without his help and support it would have been much harder to complete this work. As the chapters were written I sent them three at a time to Germany to Eberhard Bethge, Bonhoeffer's friend and biographer, and his wife, Renate, Bonhoeffer's niece, who out of the goodness of their hearts read them and gave me their valuable criticism. Another close friend of Bonhoeffer's, Franz Hildebrandt, in Edinburgh, Scotland, read the first half of the manuscript and gave his comments until his death in 1984.

I also owe a debt of gratitude to the other Bonhoeffer people I met on my two trips to Germany in 1977 and 1979: Bonhoeffer's three sisters—Ursula Schleicher, Sabine Leibholz, and Susanne Dress; his sister-in-law, Emmi Bonhoeffer; his students—Jochen Kanitz, Winfred Maechler, Otto Dudzus, Albrecht Schönherr, Reinhold Rutenik, Karl Stefan, and Werner Koch; and his friends—Martin Niemöller, Elisabeth Bornkamm, Julius Rieger, and Anneliese Schnurmann in London. I had already visited Bonhoeffer's fiancée, Maria von Wedemeyer Weller, in Boston; and in Germany I visited her mother, Ruth von Wedemeyer; her brother, Hans-Werner von Wedemeyer; and her sister, Ruth-Alice von Bismarck. In New York I talked with Maria's younger sister, Christine Beshar. In addition, I spent several hours with Harold Deutsch, author of *Hitler and His Generals* and *The Conspiracy Against Hitler*. Dr. Deutsch is a leading authority on the German Resistance, having been a U. S. Army intelligence officer in Germany following the war, when he interviewed many of the players in this story, including some of the Nazis.

Someone told me once that "the most important thing is to have a good editor." In that I have been blessed with Mary Ann Bowman Beil. Her toughness, expertise, and unflagging commitment to excellence were always balanced by a willingness to listen to my arguments, even when it meant more work for her. I thank her very much. Earlier I had the good fortune to have George Core, editor of *The Sewanee Review*, give me his critique and his encouragement. He continued to help as I tried to cut the manuscript to a manageable length. Readers (a necessity for this writer) who helped were my husband, O. W., my daughter, Joy, and also Bob Hill, Patrick Murphy, Roger Lovette, Aida White, and Randall Greene of Greene Communications. I must add a thank you to my computer doctor, Elaine Pearsall, of Clemson University. When something went haywire (which always sent me into near panic) she was always there to help.

THE CUP OF WRATH

Part I
The Fatal Privilege

Prologue

Dietrich gave the operator his sister's number and waited. Four rings and no answer. That was strange. Christel always served her midday meal promptly at 1:30. He looked at the tall clock across the foyer—1:35. Why didn't they answer? He needed to talk with his brother-in-law immediately. Dietrich looked at the call-up notice in his hand. Hitler, in a desperation move, was reaching into government agencies—even military intelligence—for his cannon fodder.

At last the line opened and the sound of a male voice he did not recognize came over it, terse and business-like: "Dohnanyi residence."

A sharp realization lashed across Dietrich's face. The Gestapo had taken Hans and were searching the house.

He would be next.

Dietrich soundlessly replaced the receiver on its hook and turned to the stairs. Shock radiated from the pit of his stomach. He knew he should not be surprised. For a month now Admiral Canaris had been warning Dietrich and Hans of impending arrest. Heinrich Himmler hoped to get confessions and enough evidence out of them to wrest control of the Abwehr from Canaris and put military intelligence under his own Secret Police. The little admiral had tried to fend off Himmler since 1938, and had succeeded, up to now. Now, since the two failed assassination attempts, Himmler had increased his efforts, although, thank God, the resisters had been able to cover their tracks in both cases. Or had they, after all?

With that chilling thought Dietrich paused at the second floor. His parents were taking their afternoon nap. Should he tell them? No, let them rest. They would be disturbed soon enough.

As he continued up the steps his mind raced back to the heartbreaking failures of the past month—March 1943. Schlabrendorff smuggles a bomb aboard Hitler's plane. Somehow it fails to detonate. But the next day Schlabrendorff manages to retrieve it and defuse it, with no one the wiser. Then, just two weeks ago on

Heroes Memorial Day, Colonel Freiherr von Gersdorff meets Hitler in the exhibition hall here in Berlin with two bombs in his greatcoat pockets. He is to serve as Hitler's guide for the exhibition of captured war matériel. The security around Hitler has doubled in the past year. The timing is crucial, since the exhibition tour is scheduled for only thirty minutes. Gersdorff has already set the fuses and tries to interest Hitler in one thing after another, but Hitler races through the exhibition, scarcely glancing at the displays, and in three minutes is back outside. In a nearby lavatory Gersdorff defuses the bombs. Both Schlabrendorff and Gersdorff are sure that no one has suspected anything.

Or could the Gestapo have found something else? The Resistance papers at Zossen? There was enough evidence in those papers to hang them all.

In his room on the third floor, Dietrich quickly went through everything on his desk. He tried to assure himself that he had some time. Sakrow, where Hans and Christel lived, was at least a half hour away. He must be careful not to miss anything. For weeks he had been putting anything that might be incriminating into a separate folder. This he laid aside. He left the pages from the book on ethics he was writing where they lay on the desk top. They would help his claim to be merely a young Lutheran pastor doing what he could to serve the Fatherland. From a drawer he took copies of two fictitious reports, filed at the Abwehr, of earlier trips to Switzerland, trips made ostensibly as an agent of the Abwehr, but in fact made to contact the Allies on behalf of the Resistance. Now he placed them in full view. He also brought out the rough draft of a carefully crafted counterfeit letter from himself to Hans, which they recently had invented to throw the bloodhounds off the scent. The letter, predated November 6, 1940, pretended an offer by Dietrich to use his contacts with ecumenical leaders to get information for the Abwehr. In one desk drawer was a copy of an essay, "After Ten Years," which he had written as a Christmas gift for Hans von Dohnanyi, his friend Eberhard Bethge, and a few other resisters. This he hid between the rafter and the ceiling, where the roof sloped steeply above the wardrobe.

After a final check Dietrich took the incriminating folder with him and slipped quietly down the stairs. In the corner of the garden behind the bright yellow forsythia bushes he burned the dangerous papers and scattered the ashes in the dirt, then walked across the lawn between the tall pines to his elder sister Ursula Schleicher's house. Ursel would give him a good hot meal. It was uncertain when he would get another one.

At four o'clock Dietrich had just finished eating, when his father, Dr. Karl Bonhoeffer, came to the door and called Dietrich outside. "I'm afraid you have to come now," he said, his face filled with apprehension. "There are two plainclothesmen upstairs in your room, and they're asking for you."

"I'm not surprised," said Dietrich and told him of the strange voice on Christel's phone.

"Ah, then they have come for you. I was afraid of that."

The Nazis had apparently interrupted his father's consultation with a patient, for he still wore his white coat.

After the good-byes at his sister's house, which Dietrich tried to keep as light as possible, he and his father walked back across the lawn. So far none of the Allied bombs had struck the neighborhood of the Marienburger Allee; and the two houses, the Bonhoeffer house and the Schleicher house, looked almost as fresh and new as when they were built eight years before in 1935.

"They're watching from your window," his father said without looking up. "We mustn't slow our pace."

Dietrich looked sideways at his father, who moved with dignity beside him. His father's straight hair was pure white, longer than most Germans wore it these days, but carefully groomed. He was several inches shorter than Dietrich, but his erect bearing and firm stride made him seem younger than his seventy-five years.

"There's not much time," his father continued, "but I've thought of a way we might communicate. If they let you have books from us—and they will, I think—look for a pencil dot under a letter on one page and another, starting at the back." He glanced at Dietrich. "I think it will work, but we'll have to keep the markings light."

Amid rapid calculations, Dietrich answered, "Yes. It will work." It did not escape him that his father had put aside his own anxieties and gone straight to the most important consideration for a prisoner of the Nazis.

"And if you are to look for a message, I'll underline your name in the front of the book."

"Yes, of course. Thanks, Papa."

Inside the back door his mother was waiting, her face filled with suppressed anxiety. Dietrich took her hands in his. "Mama, you're not to worry. I'll be all right."

Her lips trembled.

"I don't see how they can prove anything against us," Dietrich reassured her. She looked up. "Yes, I'm afraid they got Hans, too." He quickly told her of his call to Christel and of the careful check he afterward had made of his room. "They aren't finding anything important. Really, Mama." He smiled, with as much encouragement as he could summon.

But there remained the same fear in her eyes that he had seen two weeks before, when they learned of Gersdorff's failure. Then she had said, "Go to your friends in Pomerania. There must be a fishing boat somewhere that could get you to Sweden." And he had answered, "I can't do that, Mama." She had argued that the Gestapo would not bother old people like them, but Dietrich had known better. Then Hans had spoken out of turn and said, "If they pick us up, the main thing will be to keep it in the military courts and out of the hands of the Gestapo. If they get jurisdiction, it will be a different story. None of us knows how long he can resist torture, once they start doing their worst." Careless words that had only deepened the fear in his mother's eyes.

"Well, I guess I have to go." He lowered his voice almost to a whisper and spoke rapidly. "Remember, I'm a good actor, and Hans and I have rehearsed well. Hans will take full responsibility for all our questionable activities. He's a top-notch lawyer. He can handle it, don't worry. And Admiral Canaris will corroborate all that Hans says. He'll say he ordered it as counterespionage in the interest of the Reich. I'll play the part of the simple, unworldly pastor, merely following instructions." He smiled. "It will work. I'm sure it will." With that Dietrich left them and made his way up the steps.

The door to Dietrich's room was open and leaning against the jamb stood a jackal in a gray suit, with a look on his face of one sure of his prey. At the top of the stair Dietrich stopped and looked directly at the intruder without speaking.

The man straightened up. "You are Dietrich Bonhoeffer?"

"I am."

"I am Judge Advocate Manfred Roeder." He turned to a narrow-faced man standing in the middle of the room. "My colleague here is Herr Kommissar Sonderegger of the Gestapo. I am sure you know why we are here."

"I have no idea why you are here," said Dietrich coolly. The word "Gestapo" wormed its way along his defenses.

Roeder bared his teeth in a mirthless smile. "We'll see about that soon enough."

All the while Dietrich had been trying to place the name "Roeder." Then he remembered. Roeder was the one from the legal department of the Luftwaffe, whom Hans called a "bloodhound." His recent prosecution of the Rote Kapelle, a Communist resistance group, had brought death sentences to its leaders.

Roeder nodded to the man from the Gestapo, who came forward, holding a pair of handcuffs.

"Is that necessary?" asked Dietrich. "My parents are old, and I would not like to see them frightened. If I had any thought of running away I would have done so from my sister's house."

"Argument will get you nowhere, Herr Bonhoeffer," said Sonderegger, a lighted cigarette hanging from his lips. Dietrich recognized the gravelly voice he had heard on Christel's telephone. As Sonderegger snapped the handcuffs on Dietrich's wrists, his dark, sunken eyes glittered, as though he could see a long-anticipated triumph around the corner.

Roeder pushed Dietrich toward a chair. "Sit there while we finish our business," he said.

At that the two men went back to their search of the room. Dietrich watched from the armchair and hoped they would find nothing to give them satisfaction. A drawer stood on top of the desk, and with apparent relish Roeder began examining the papers in it. He turned through them slowly and then held one of them up. After a suspicious look in Dietrich's direction, he began reading it. From where he sat Dietrich could not recognize the paper and wondered if he had overlooked something damning. Then, halfway through the page, Roeder made a sound as if he were spitting and threw it aside. "We know you've hidden something here. Be assured, we'll find it." And to Sonderegger, who was working through the books in the bookcase, he said, "Don't skip anything, Herr Kommissar."

When Sonderegger had checked through every book, he turned to the wardrobe. He felt in the clothes pockets and inside all the shoes, then looked in the hat boxes on top just beneath the rafters. Dietrich kept his eyes averted and tried to remember exactly what he had written in that essay. He knew there was nothing overt, but much could be read between the lines and Roeder was sharp enough to do it. Sonderegger poked around the rafters. There had been only one rafter with a crack large enough to slip the folded essay above it. Sonderegger put his hand on that rafter, but began knocking on it as if he thought it might be hollow. He tested the others and, when he found them to be sound, turned away.

Dietrich rested his chin in his hand and tried not to appear relieved.

After more fruitless searching Roeder bellowed his frustration. "Don't be too smug, Herr Bonhoeffer. We have plenty of ways to find out the truth and we'll use them."

It was five-thirty when Roeder allowed Dietrich to pack a small bag with toilet articles, a clean shirt, a change of underwear, and his Bible. Then the two men proceeded with him down the stairs. His parents were waiting in the foyer.

As if by mutual consent no word was spoken before the two Nazis. Dietrich looked long into his mother's face, and saw its love and encouragement trying so desperately to cover the fear and the horror underneath. She kissed him without tears, but what supreme effort that cost her he could well imagine. His father, always controlled, betrayed emotion only in his tightened jaw.

The black Mercedes, with Dietrich in the back seat, turned around. He lifted his manacled hands in a farewell wave to his parents in the doorway. Soon they were out of sight.

Roeder was at the wheel. As he circled the old Reichskanzler Platz, renamed the Adolf Hitler Platz, he drove with an arrogant disregard for other vehicles and pedestrians. At the Sophie-Charlotte Platz they turned and headed north, away from the Gestapo Headquarters. In spite of Hans's assurances, the dread of the Prinz-Albrecht-Strasse had been upon Dietrich from the moment Roeder had introduced Sonderegger. They passed the old cheese shop where, ten years before, the Nazis had destroyed Dietrich's youth club for the unemployed. Ten years? Had it been ten years? Yet when one totaled up the turbulent events of those years it seemed even longer.

When they circled the Charlottenburg Palace and crossed the Spree onto the Tegeler Weg, Dietrich knew where they were taking him—Tegel Prison, in the northwest corner of the city. A few times in passing he had seen its grim old buildings, surrounded by a high, thick wall of red brick.

They sped over the sparsely populated Jungfernheide, across the end of the old rifle range, now an airfield with camouflage netting covering Göring's fighters, and onto the Seidelstrasse. Soon the giant Borsig Iron Works appeared on the right, and a mile beyond on the left the prison.

It was dusk when they turned into the gate. Inside the outer courtyard the car stopped at the gatehouse, the solid iron door opened, they shot through the narrow passage, and behind them the door clanged shut with the finality of a death knell.

Roeder brought the car to a halt between two square buildings. An officer, who seemed to be expecting them, stepped out from the building on the left and took a paper that Roeder handed him through the car window. Immediately two burly guards hustled Dietrich from the car and into the building on the right. In a low-ceilinged room the guards proceeded to search him, while Dietrich focused his eyes straight ahead in an effort to divorce his real self from their touch. They confiscated his watch, his billfold, and the little change he had in his pocket. Then, after removing the hand-cuffs, a clerk took his fingerprints. With bored and plodding movements the clerk stood him against a black curtain, turned on a spotlight that almost blinded him, and with an ancient camera took his photograph. Then, with a grunt he asked Dietrich for the small bag.

"Why, then, was I allowed to bring it, if I cannot take it with me?" Dietrich protested.

"You'll get it back, in good time," the man answered. And to the guards: "Take him away."

"Here, you, this way," said one of them and pushed him along a narrow passage.

"What cell did they say?" said the other.

"Number six."

"Is this the last one for today?"

"God, I hope so."

They passed through a barrier of iron bars, which the guard locked behind them, and down a hall with steel doors on either side. About halfway they stopped short before one of the doors. The first man selected a key from the ring attached to his belt, unlocked the door, and pulled it open.

"In there, you damned bastard," said the other, and shoved Dietrich inside with such force that he stumbled. Before he could recover his equilibrium, the heavy door slammed shut and the key turned in the lock.

Dietrich did not know how long he stood there staring at the door in futile anger. It was a solid slab with no knob or handle. In the center at eye level was a hole two or three inches across, which narrowed to marble size on the outside. He went to it and looked through, but could see only a small portion of the wall across the brightly lit passageway. He turned around and viewed the dark-ened cell. There was no light switch in sight. High on the opposite wall a narrow slit of a window let in a cold blue light. The shadow of the bars fell across the plank bed against the wall. On the other

side stood a bench, with a low stool beside it, and a bucket, smell-
ing of urine. He stood on the bench and looked out on a small
enclosure with high walls on all sides. Another building shut off
the sky from view. The general prospect was not unlike a dungeon.

Too agitated to sit down, Dietrich walked for a long time back
and forth in the confining space. At last he sat on the bench and
leaned his head against the wall. Through his thinning hair the wall
felt cold. There was no heat in the room, and the April nights often
went down to freezing. He wished he had put on a sweater under
his coat; it had not occurred to him that there would be no heat.

Dietrich eyed the blanket on the narrow bed. It felt greasy as he
turned it back; and when he pulled it up around his shoulders, the
stench was so strong that he threw it down again. He moved into
the corner of the cotton mattress, pulled up his knees, and
wrapped his arms around them. For a long time he sat motionless.

Through the transom came muffled sounds from other prisoners nearby, shuffling feet, a muttered oath, the creaking of a plank
bed, and farther down the hall, the clank of chains. Presently a
door opened somewhere, and footsteps clumped along the passageway. They stopped at the barrier, while with a clatter of keys
and the clang of heavy metal the barred door was opened and shut
again. The footsteps advanced along the stone floor to Dietrich's
door and, without stopping, passed by. Only then was he aware of
the tension in every muscle of his body. The steps soon returned,
then moved on. It was merely the guard making his rounds. If he
reacted in such a way to that, how would he handle the real thing,
when they actually fetched him to face his interrogators?

Dietrich tried to pray. He thought he had prepared himself; deep
down he had known for a long time that it would come to this.
Other men, without a doubt, had faced such times with greater
equanimity—Martin Niemöller, for one, already six years in a
concentration camp.

Gradually, as the night wore on, the tensions in Dietrich's body
began to ease and his tortured thoughts to abate. He found comfort in the knowledge that, at least, he had not been idle in the

struggle against the Nazi regime, even in the beginning ten years ago. It had started, almost unconsciously on his part, with a talk on Berlin radio two days after Hitler's sweep to power—the first day of February 1933. He had been rather pleased with himself, he remembered, and his students had been proud and excited. His subject, "The Führer Principle," seemed propitious, although it had been planned weeks before and written several days before the change of government.

All seemed to go well that day until Dietrich came to the main point, where he warned his listeners of the leader "who makes an idol of himself and his office, and who thus mocks God." It was then that the director interrupted and told him they had been cut off the air.

Dietrich had never known for sure what happened. At first he had thought it was a technical problem, although no one at the studio thought so. Then he had begun to wonder if Goebbels, even that early, had taken control of the airways.

The cotton mattress was thin on the plank bed. He was beginning to feel tired and shifted his position, but it was too cold to stretch out. A thin chime sounded. One o'clock in the morning.

The radio talk that year had been only the beginning of a year of turmoil. It was that same month—yes, toward the end—that the Nazis had destroyed Dietrich's Youth Club for the unemployed. But before that, one night, he and the men had heard loud shouting outside and had run downstairs. He could see now the blood in the snow—*one of the men lies motionless, with blood all around his head. Dietrich thinks he is dead. The other, Roepke, one of two Communists in the club, struggles to his knees, a bloody gash down his cheek. Other club members are ranged behind him in a semicircle.*

"Nazis. Storm troopers," says Roepke. "They tried to kill us."

A block up the street Dietrich sees the SA men—five or six of them in their brown uniforms—as they pass under a street light. With his handkerchief he tries to staunch the blood on Roepke's cheek, then turns to the man in the snow. The wound on his head looks ugly—a skull fracture, no doubt of it. He lifts the man's wrist and picks up a weak pulse, then stands up, takes off his coat, and covers him with it. "We mustn't move him. You men stay here. I'll go upstairs and call my father."

In the waiting room of his father's hospital, Dietrich stays with Roepke while his father and a colleague operate on Roepke's friend.

Dietrich shivered in the cold and hugged his knees tighter to his chest. Yes, that had been the beginning. The man had survived the operation. Dietrich had always wondered whether it was the same bunch of Nazis who wrecked the Youth Club a week later. It didn't matter. A Nazi was a Nazi.

1

It was late and turning cold in the club room, but Dietrich did not want to add more coal to the stove. He only wanted to get through with the business and go home. Keeping books held no fascination for him, but it had to be done and he was the only one to do it. He totaled up the last column of figures and laid down his pencil. For the month of February, anyway, the Youth Club had come out even, give or take a couple of marks; and he could send a good report to their benefactor, Anneliese Schnurmann. Six new men had come in over the month, each with that look of hopelessness so typical of the long-term unemployed. By now that look was changing, especially today, when two of the members found jobs. That brought to thirty-eight the number of men the club had helped find work in its five-month history. It made the drudgery of bookkeeping worthwhile.

Dietrich leaned back in the old swivel chair, took off his rimless glasses, and wiped them with his handkerchief. Putting them on again, he looked about the room with its odd assortment of furniture, donated by various family members and friends. Behind him a door opened into a smaller room, furnished with two cots, where men could stay overnight when they had no place to go, which had turned out to be most of the time. Tonight no one was there. The men had all left an hour ago.

The old kitchen clock on the wall read 11:05. Dietrich rarely stayed that late. As he folded the accounts book the telephone rang.

It was his brother-in-law, Hans von Dohnanyi. "I thought you might have gone by now," Hans said. "Indeed, I rather hoped so." He paused, then spoke again in a lowered voice. "I'd suggest you vacate the place right away."

Dietrich wondered if Hans was phoning from the Justice Department.

"Don't tarry," Hans said abruptly and hung up.

If such an admonition had come a month earlier Dietrich would have laughed it off. Now he put the accounts book back in the drawer, went to the stove and closed off the damper, took his coat and hat from the row of hooks along the wall and put them on, then pulled on his overshoes. With his hand on the doorknob he paused, and turned again to the desk. From a little file box he removed a small stack of index cards with the names and addresses of the club members and put them into his coat pocket, then locked the door, pocketed the key, and walked quickly down the steps.

Outside it had stopped snowing. Dietrich thrust his hands into fur-lined gloves and walked the block and a half up the Schlossstrasse to the Sophie-Charlotte Platz. The streetcar was waiting, and he sprinted the last few feet. He swung onto the step, paid his fare, and took a seat in the middle of the almost empty car. From the corner of his eye he noticed a band of storm troopers in brown uniforms with swastika armbands crossing the plaza. Some distance down the avenue, he turned and looked again. The SA men, six or seven of them, had stopped at the street light beside the Schlossstrasse and were studying a sheet of paper one of them held in his hand. When Dietrich looked again they were turning down the Schlossstrasse toward the club. Without a second thought he rang the bell and got off at the next stop.

From a block away Dietrich could tell that the lights were on upstairs in the club across the street. Behind the yellow curtains, shadows moved back and forth in violent movements. They were there all right. He moved uncertainly up and down along the curb, never taking his eyes from the windows. Suddenly he heard the sound of shattering glass and saw something thrown from the window. Then another object fell to the snow, and another. Raw impulse would have plunged him straight across the street and up the steps. As a schoolboy he never had dodged a fight, but here there were six of them at least, and he remembered the broken skull of the week before. He looked up and down the street. No help was in sight. Half a block away stood a telephone booth.

With one eye on the club Dietrich lifted the receiver and asked for the police station.

"Police headquarters, Lieutenant Baumgärtel."

"Dietrich Bonhoeffer, here, reporting a break-in, 18 Schlossstrasse upstairs. If you hurry, you can catch the culprits."

The man asked Dietrich to repeat the address and, after a maddening delay, said he would send someone out.

"More than one, I should think," said Dietrich. "There are several men up there."

"We will take care of it," said the policeman in a tired voice and hung up.

Dietrich took his watch from his pocket. 11:30. The police should be here in five minutes, or less, he thought. He walked back down to the Black Eagle, a restaurant where he sometimes bought a hot meal for the club members. Now the restaurant was dark. Impervious to the cold, he paced back and forth in the snow, watching first the club windows and the dark figures behind them, then the head of the street. Every minute he expected the lights of a police wagon. They never appeared. Five, six, seven minutes passed.

Suddenly he heard voices across the way and stepped back into the shadow of the restaurant entrance. In a dark tangle the SA men erupted from the stairway and started up the street as if they owned the avenue. Dietrich watched, motionless, until they disappeared at the top of the street, then crossed over and bounded up the steps two at a time. The door of the club, silhouetted against the yellow light from inside, hung loose on one hinge. Beyond it he stopped still and surveyed the damage.

The Nazis had demolished the place. Books lay scattered and trampled on the floor. A pile of tumbled papers covered the table, and chairs lay disjointed round about it. The contents of the desk drawers were dumped onto the floor, and on the wall above it crudely scrawled letters spelled "Bolsheviks." They had slashed their signature on the back cushion of a mohair chair. Even the yellow curtains Dietrich's younger sister, Susi, had made hung torn and limp from broken rods.

Dietrich moved into the back room, where the disorder appeared less because the room was more sparsely furnished. Here the bedclothes lay in a heap on the floor with cotton bulging from slashes in the mattresses. The small store of extra supplies, which they had kept neatly stacked in the corner, littered the floor. He lifted a mattress pad and tried to straighten it out again on the cot.

There was no way Dietrich could fasten the door, so he propped it the best he could and left. Outside in the snow he found the books the Nazis had thrown out the window and took them with him up the deserted street. On the near-empty streetcar he paid little heed to the passage of time or to the familiar turns and twists along the way southward into the Grunewald, and he almost missed his stop. At the last minute he rang the bell for the Bismarck Platz. When the car screeched to a halt, he stepped off, pulled his hat down farther on his head, and with rapid strides walked toward the Wangenheimstrasse and the big house that had been the Bonhoeffer home since he was ten years old.

When he got there his parents were already in bed. He did not disturb them, but walked quietly down the second-floor hall to his room at the rear of the house. There seemed no point in getting ready for bed. He knew he could not sleep. Perfect stillness reigned throughout the big house, but his rage and frustration refused to quiet down. He fumbled in his pocket for a cigarette and the gleaming silver lighter his friend Franz Hildebrandt had given him for his birthday. For a time he paced the floor and inhaled the soothing tobacco. Dietrich wished he could talk over the raid with his older brother Klaus in neighboring Eichkamp. With Klaus's experience as a lawyer he might have some suggestions as to what to do. Dietrich started for the door but the clock stared him down—12:20. Even Klaus would be asleep by now. Also Hans von Dohnanyi. Then it occurred to Dietrich that it might not be a good idea to talk about the raid on the telephone. He would just have to wait it out—maybe sleep a little, if possible—and call Klaus in the morning. Anyway, his brother would want to see the club for himself.

"What did they find?" Klaus asked, as he leafed through the jumbled papers on the desk.

"Very little, I'm sure," Dietrich replied. "I took the card index with the members' names and addresses home with me last night."

"Good. How many Communists did you have here?"

"Oh, three or four probably."

Klaus's eyebrows registered mild surprise. "You mean you don't know?"

"We didn't ask that kind of question."

"Hrrmp."

Short, rotund, and fastidious as always, with coat, tie, scarf, hat, and gloves, Klaus presented a contrast with the chaos around him that was almost ludicrous. "Barbaric," he said, in an intense whisper. "Hitler's 'law and order.'"

"Some kind of complaint or redress should be possible, don't you think? We still have a court of law. Maybe Hans—"

"Hans couldn't touch it. You'd be placing him in a dangerous position."

Dietrich looked up quickly. "The danger didn't occur to me, I must say. It just seemed logical, since he has some influence in the Justice Department."

"If this raid were an isolated case, maybe so."

"You don't think it is?"

"No. I have an idea it's part of a dragnet all over the city, and since you've had Communists in here—."

"They have no proof."

"They'd find proof—or make their own. It just won't do."

"Well, you're the lawyer. I guess you're right," Dietrich conceded.

Klaus pulled on his gloves and started for the door. "I don't know what you did with that card index, but I'd suggest you burn it." He glanced around the room once more. "Come on, let's go. This place is an icehouse."

Dietrich had insisted that the raid not be mentioned that night at the Saturday Evening Musical, at least not until the music was over. This time-honored tradition in the Bonhoeffer family was an occasion when they all came together with close friends for an agreeable mix of good music, good conversation, and good food.

At five o'clock Dietrich came downstairs to the living room and stood for a moment just inside the portieres. His sister Christel von Dohnanyi was already seated at the tea table. She had learned about the raid early that morning, when she came across the street at breakfast time. Dietrich had not seen Hans, who had left even earlier for the Justice Department and apparently had not come home yet. The beams of the setting sun filtered through the great window at that end of the room, highlighting the grand piano and the three groupings of damask furniture.

Beyond the arch on the other side of the long room and up two steps, the maids, Marthe and Trude, in their starched lace caps and white aprons, were busy with preparations at the sideboard. Dietrich's mother was checking the dining table. Her reaction to the Nazi raid had been immediate. Reopen the club right away. She and Ursel and Susi would help as they had before. But Dietrich was not so sure. The Nazis were bound to find out sooner or later that the club's benefactor was Jewish; that would mean danger to Anneliese Schnurmann. It was too great a chance to take.

Dietrich sat down by Christel and asked about Hans.

"Working late again," she said, wearily. "He'll be here."

"Poor Hans."

She bridled at once. "Why 'poor Hans?'"

"Well, I wouldn't think he'd want to stay in a Hitler government."

"Who does what he wants nowadays?"

"Still, I don't think I could bear to be identified with them myself."

"Oh, for God's sake, don't be so self-righteous."

"You know if he doesn't conform, they'll eventually throw him out, and if he does conform—"

"Hans isn't like you. He doesn't care a fig what people think."

Dietrich looked at his sister's tense, unflinching face, the dark blond hair parted in the middle and pulled back loosely over her ears, the deep-set intelligent eyes turned defensive. In a softer tone he said, "What earthly good could he do in there with them?"

"He's already done you some good, hasn't he? Tipping you off about that raid?"

"Well, yes, of course. Sounds frightfully unpalatable, though."

"It is."

"To say nothing of the danger involved."

"He can take that, too."

"I'm sure he can." Dietrich stretched his long legs and leaned against the back of the sofa with his hands clasped behind his head. "Well, it would be a pity to throw over such a promising career."

Christel looked up sharply.

"Now don't get your dander up," Dietrich said quickly. "I'm not impugning his motives. I'm just stating a fact. I suppose if he has the stomach to stick it out, he might do some good. I can't imagine how—but maybe he can. I still say, 'poor Hans.'"

Christel said nothing. Presently she sat up straight and lifted her head. "Well, is Elenore Nichol coming?" she asked.

"She and her mother. Her father can't come."

Christel smiled, her eyes roguish. "We keep hoping for an announcement. One of these days."

Dietrich kept quiet. At twenty-seven years of age he could manage his own affairs. She should know better than to poke her nose in.

"Don't wait too long. You weren't cut out to be a bachelor."

At that Dietrich rose, excused himself, and walked to the piano. He ran idly through a Bach fugue, then opened the Negro spiritual he had sketched in from a record for Elenore to learn.

His mother moved to the archway and stood tall and portly in her dark blue dress, her eyes on the window. "I see the von der Lutzes are here," she said.

Dietrich watched as the chauffeur held the door of the Lutz's Mercedes and Dietrich's cousin, Count Hugo von der Lutz, and his wife, Hilde, stepped out.

"I hope Klaus will restrain himself this time," said Dietrich's mother. "I don't want a repeat of their violent argument about Hitler."

"Don't count on it, Mama," Dietrich said with a dubious smile. "Hugo can be terribly thickheaded."

An hour and a half later Dietrich stood alone at the archway, his plate in hand, and observed the group in the living room. He had enjoyed the music, but looked forward to the respite he usually took in his room after supper. He had been at the piano a good deal of the time, accompanying the songs of his mother and sisters and playing for the "Trout Quintet." His mother had sung the Brahms "Rosmarin," and the Negro spiritual had gone well.

Dietrich's grandmother, Julie Bonhoeffer, was holding court in her chair beside the gold and marble clock. At ninety-one years of age she was the undisputed queen of the family and the neighborhood. Near her chair his father, Dr. Karl Bonhoeffer, was talking with the young Jewish neurosurgeon who had operated on the Youth Club member with the broken skull. Klaus and Hugo von der Lutz were exchanging polite amenities beside the piano. Dietrich wondered how long that would last; the unctuous smile on his cousin's face was close to gloating.

After a time Klaus took one step toward Dietrich, not quite abandoning Hugo, but obviously hoping Hugo would abandon him. "Well, Dietrich," said Klaus, "what's this I hear about a possible church for you? Mama says you had to preach a trial sermon."

Dietrich stepped down beside him. "In this case, yes. There

were two candidates, you see, so the congregation votes by secret ballot."

"I expect they'll choose you."

Dietrich laughed. "I'm not counting on it at all."

"Friedrichschain, huh? I know the area. It's a slum, all right. I suppose it's decent of you to want to help the downtrodden. But the German Evangelical Church? I can think of better ways." Klaus took a sip of wine and smiled sardonically over the rim of the glass. "Don't you know the church is hopelessly fossilized? No more alive than a leaf in a lump of coal."

Hugo, his plate in his hand, moved with one quick step to Dietrich's side. "That, of course, is not at all possible," he said good-naturedly. "I'm surprised you'd say such a thing to your brother, Klaus."

Dietrich laughed. "Don't take it too seriously, Hugo. Besides, he's more than half right, you know."

"No, I'm quite serious," said Hugo, looking intently from one to the other. "I see no reason why the hour of revolution cannot also be the hour of revival for the church, if the church joins in the saving of the Fatherland." Hugo lifted his fork expansively. "The church is a unifying force, perhaps the strongest unifying force in the land. It reminds the people of their heritage as Germans."

"And that is one and the same as their heritage as Christians, I take it," said Dietrich with undisguised sarcasm.

Hugo did not seem to notice. "I don't see why not."

"No. I don't suppose you do." Dietrich handed his plate to Marthe as she passed. "Well, unity is fine. Who doesn't want it? If it is achieved honorably and justly. If it leads to peace and not war. But I see no sign—"

"War! That's really what's worrying you, isn't it? You sound like one of those damned pacifists." Always erect to the point of stiffness, Hugo rolled his six-foot, four-inch frame up on the balls of his feet. "No sense of the realities facing Germany today. Don't you know that strength is our only hope? And the only remedy for the humiliation we've undergone? Don't you think we've groveled enough? How can we expect the nations of the world to respect us if we don't respect ourselves? And demand respect of them? Demand, not beg! If Adolf Hitler can lift the German flag out of the mud, I say let him do it. Help him do it. It's damn well time!" His finger jabbed the air on each word.

Dietrich glanced at Klaus, who was studying his wine glass with intense distaste.

Hugo continued, "We're nearing a great springtime of German renewal, a unified nation, with the Bolshevik threat stopped. That is a must. And Hitler can do it."

Dietrich realized that such arguments made a pleasing harmony in the ears of most Germans.

"Dissenters crushed, no doubt?" Klaus queried with barely concealed antipathy.

"Crushed? I wouldn't say crushed. Muted—controlled."

"How will Hitler do that without violating civil liberties—free press, free speech? You're a lawyer, Hugo. Do you want to see these rights suppressed?"

"In some cases it may be necessary. Yes. We're in a state of emergency and emergency measures are called for. Like placing some restrictions on the Communist press, unless they can learn restraint, which God knows, they've never shown. I'm sick of their lies, intoxicating the rabble, inflating the worker's ego, 'til he no longer knows his place. It's like giving a child a stick of dynamite in one hand and a match in the other."

"Suppose Hitler did shut down the Communist press," Dietrich asked, "do you think he'd stop at that? Who would be next, I wonder? Whoever disagreed with him? The church, perhaps?"

"No, no. The church is vital to the health of the nation. Hitler recognizes that. He knows where the foundations of a people are laid and is anxious for the church to work with him."

"Not with him, under him."

"You see, your mind is already closed. If you read in the *Völkischer Beobachter*—"

"That's not one of the newspapers I read as a rule—"

"Well, perhaps you should," Hugo snapped. "Hitler clearly stated that he recognizes Christianity as the basis of our whole morality."

"So I heard. I also heard of his generous offer to take the church under his 'firm protection.' That has an ominous ring, to be sure. 'Firm protection.'"

"You see how you twist everything he says to fit your own notions," said Hugo. "You don't want to see any good in the man."

A hush had fallen over the room.

Hugo's voice was becoming strident. "What I see, and what you refuse to see, is the good he is already doing—setting an example that can only help the church. You must have noticed how he's encouraging his storm troopers to attend services. Sometimes whole bands of them sit together. Only last week Hilde and I saw a platoon of them sitting together in the Mary's Church."

"I wonder how many heads they bloodied the night before," said Dietrich.

A dark flush spread from Hugo's starched white collar to the roots of his ash brown hair. "Now you're being melodramatic. You've been listening to hearsay."

"Hardly, since I sat for three hours with one of the victims while the doctors patched up the skull of his friend. The SA set upon them without warning. Last night they broke into our Youth Club and ripped the place to shreds. So please don't ask me to be moved by the piety of your SA band in the Mary's Church."

Hugo had taken out a handkerchief and was wiping his right eye, which had a tendency to water. At this he stopped and looked at Dietrich in surprise. "I see. That puts a different face on it." He carefully folded his handkerchief and put it back in his pocket. "I happen to know something about the raids carried out last night. And the purpose behind them. You must have had Communists there."

Dietrich opened his mouth to speak, then closed it again. He was suddenly aware that his father had moved to his side. The Communist with the broken skull was still in his father's hospital.

"Perhaps you weren't aware of that," Hugo added, "so you must be more careful next time."

Dietrich stared at his cousin, but said nothing. With a click of his heels and a stiff bow he left the room.

2

Sitting there in the curve of the stair, Elenore looked as if she belonged to the setting that for so long had been Dietrich's own. Her ivory skin glowed against the rich dark red of her dress. She leaned her head against the bannister, her dark hair a fair match to the burnished, satiny wood.

Dietrich and Elenore talked for a time of the raid. He had told her something of it earlier in the evening, but now she wanted to know everything that happened. With one foot on the step he leaned against the paneled stairwell and gave her the details. She could not understand how such a thing could happen in Germany, she said, but her chief concern seemed to be the danger to him.

Dietrich sank down beside her on the stair. The wide foyer opened before them. "Klaus says the Church is dead," he said after a while.

"You don't believe that, do you?" she asked, her hand tucked beneath her chin.

"I don't know. Sometimes the feeling comes over me that it is too late, that the Church today is good only for sand-table exercises, especially if it prostitutes itself before Hitler to make his policies look respectable. Then it will lose its voice for years to come. If not forever."

"Jacobi agrees with you, you know."

"He does? I wasn't aware of that."

"Yes, he was talking about it the other day. He sounded very much like you."

"I'm glad to hear it. Most pastors are inclined to wait and see." He turned to her. "I'd like to talk with Jacobi."

"Come by anytime," she said. "He'll be glad to see you."

Perhaps, Dietrich thought, he could tell her about the pastorate at Friedrichschain after all. "Jacobi is good to work for, then?" he asked.

"Yes, oh yes. He has a way of making you want to do your best, without being intimidating."

"Then I'm glad you're there." He did not add that he himself found the Kaiser Wilhelm Memorial Church pretentious, although he had to acknowledge that for a young woman it must be exciting to be an assistant pastor at the hub of church life in Berlin.

"I have you to thank, you know," she said.

"How so?"

"That I studied theology in the first place. I never would have done it without your encouragement. I wouldn't have dared." She sat straighter and clasped her hands around her knees.

Dietrich thought of Friedrichshain. It was a slum indeed. If he took the parish, he would live in the rectory, which he had found in terrible disrepair. It was hard to imagine Elenore there, and it would have been unfair to suggest it, even if he were ready.

"I missed you a while ago," she said. "You were gone such a long time. Was something wrong?"

"No, no. I just went to my room for a while."

"Why? Weren't you feeling well?"

"I was all right. I simply wanted to get away by myself—too many people. Just one of my idiosyncrasies, you know." He laughed with an offhand gesture.

"I'm sorry, I just wondered—"

"Please don't think about it."

Dietrich longed to take her hand in his own and tell her all that was in his heart, let her see there the scars of his loneliness, of his deep rending struggle for faith, even—or maybe especially—of the black despairing doubts that sometimes drove him to hatred of himself and of God, and filled him with a sense of isolation. He had never been able to talk to anyone about these things. Instead, he said, "I didn't hear how your service went at the Paul Gerhard Stift. In the hospital, wasn't it?"

"Yes. It went fine, I guess," she answered. "It seems idiotic, though, that I can only preach in hospitals and schools and old folks' homes."

"Oh, that shouldn't bother you. You're doing good work there. Important work." He smiled. "Or do you wish you were a man?"

"No, silly. You're as bad as the rest. I just want to do what I know a woman can do. It's absurd when after the sermon it comes time for Communion, and I have to sit down and let someone else administer the Sacrament. Don't you think that's ridiculous?"

"I suppose so," he said, amused at her intensity. "Maybe you're trying to go too fast. Does it really make that much difference?"

"Oh, you don't understand."

"It will change with time, Elenore."

"Will it?"

"I think so."

She leaned her chin on her hand. "It will be a long time."

"At least you preach every two or three Sundays. I'm lucky if I preach once a month." He looked at her, then away. "That may change. By Easter I could have a parish of my own."

She looked up sharply. "I didn't know—" She broke off uncertainly.

"I told you I was going to look around. Remember?"

"I know. But you hadn't mentioned it in a long time. I thought you'd changed your mind."

"No, I was just waiting for an opening that would interest me."

"And you've found it?"

"It's not at all certain. Depends on what the congregation thought of me."

"Thought of you? You mean you've been there? You've preached already?"

"It was the Sunday you were away. When you went to Bethel."

"You didn't tell me." Her eyes were guarded and withdrawn.

"I wasn't sure you'd want to know."

"Why do you say that?"

"It's in Friedrichshain," he said, and watched her reaction.

"Friedrichshain?" she echoed.

"Is it so surprising?" Dietrich asked.

"I guess I thought you liked teaching so much. At least this last semester seemed to go well and then, with your work as student chaplain at the Technical High School—that's pastoral, isn't it, in a sense?"

"In a sense. But it's far too specialized, and too little." He turned aside with a slight shrug. "Well, nothing's certain. I probably shouldn't even have mentioned it. They may not elect me."

"They will, of course." She slid the silver chain of her bag slowly between her fingers. "Why would you want to go there? I'm not sure I understand."

"No, I don't suppose you do." Dietrich tried to explain but found himself skirting around the deepest reason, wary of all the traditional words, which seemed misleading and inadequate—and too "religious." At last he said, "I don't think I have the right to look for a parish that simply suits my fancy."

"I'm sure you don't. But aren't there places in this part of Berlin where you could identify more readily with the people?"

"The truth is, I want to be able to identify with these working people. You have to be willing to share their lot if you expect them to listen to what you have to say. Otherwise, with our sheltered and privileged upbringing, our shameless security—" He stopped and looked at her. "You understand?"

Elenore looked into Dietrich's eyes and then away. "Maybe."

"I can't simply leave it to someone else. If we fail here—and we've failed already, leaving the masses of the poor too long by the way—if we continue, it really is the end of our Christianity."

"Perhaps you're right," she acknowledged. "I just wish—"

He waited for her to continue, but she said no more. "What do you wish?"

"I wish men understood women a little better," she said with a rush of feeling.

"Please explain what you mean."

"I don't know how to explain." Elenore rose to her feet and pulled on her white kid gloves. "I just wish—I mean, it would be nice to hear about these things beforehand. I never have, you know." She moved down the steps to the foyer, where the guests

were beginning the ritual of overcoats and overshoes, hats and um-
brellas.

There she stopped and turned back to him. "Anyway, I don't
suppose it matters, now that it's all settled."

"It isn't all settled, you know. I told you that."

There was no more time to talk. The ongoing wave of good-
nights and good wishes engulfed them. Elenore was soon wrapped
in her black wool cape, its hood buttoned securely under her chin.

"Good-night, Dietrich."

"Good-night." He took her hand, feeling wretched and not a
little angry.

"You're preaching tomorrow, aren't you?" she asked.

"Yes. Trinity Church."

"Will President von Hindenburg be there?"

"I have no idea," he said, and realized that he had spoken sharply.
"Possibly."

"I'll be thinking of you."

Dietrich stood before the open casement at the side of his wide
bedroom window and felt the bite of the night air on his face. It
felt good. Not far away an impatient horn pierced the white stillness. And below him within its tall enclosure, the garden gleamed
in the half-moon.

After a time he closed the casement and sat down in the armchair, which knew so well every contour of his body. He reached
in the dark for the half-smoked cigar he had left earlier. Off and on
for some time he had been trying to stop smoking. He felt in his
pocket for a match. Tomorrow he would quit.

"I never have, you know." Why did Elenore have to say that, he
wondered. It was presumptuous and uncalled for. She had never
complained before. He tapped the ash from his cigar and stared
out into the night. It had been better at the beginning, he thought,
when he first began to adore her from the outer reaches of the
circle of friends and relatives in which they both moved. Even the
pain had been exquisite, devoid of all uncertainty and caution and
questions of allegiance. He was twenty then and she, seventeen.

In spite of the year in Barcelona, that busy year as assistant minister in the German-speaking congregation, the aura had held. Then came the magic spring following his return to Berlin and a particular magic evening. *They are standing under the arch of the veranda.*

"It was a long time," she says, her voice softly sighing.

"I'm glad I am back, especially now."

She turns her face up to him—clear, chaste, cool, like fine porcelain. "Did you miss me?"

"You know I missed you. I love you, Elenore." The words he has longed to say are out. He is astonished. He lifts her hand, soft and white, to his lips. Her eyes, filled with trust and adoration, do not leave his face. All thought is suspended; he knows only the promise of her lips and the curve of her slender waist as his arm encircles it. In the distance he hears the music for the dance and is glad. This is a time for music. At the shy, gentle touching of his lips to hers music and dance become one. Fantasy, mystery, and boyhood dreams are caught up in the rhythm, and awaken unexpected feelings, feelings on the verge of running away with him. Gently, reluctantly, he releases her and again takes her hand in his.

Dietrich could not remember what more they had said that night, but he remembered the happiness in her eyes. Sometime— later, perhaps—the subject of marriage arose and floated like a ship far out to sea, white and shining on the distant waves, but not yet ready for mooring. It was understood that her parents, staid, old-fashioned academics, permitted no marriage before age twenty. He could not recall any serious rebellion. There was never a hint of any other course.

It was after he returned from America in the summer of 1931 that the constraint developed between them. The cause lay partly with him—maybe even mostly—but he did not know how to change it. When she began her work under Gerhard Jacobi at the Memorial Church, their friendship had settled into an even and predictable pattern, which he, in the gathering crisis of the time, had had no inclination to alter.

With a deep sigh Dietrich turned on the light and went to his desk, where he opened up his sermon for the next day. He was glad that this first sermon since Hitler came to power would be in Trinity Church, and hoped, indeed, that old President von Hindenburg would be there, as he was sometimes. He read quickly through the sermon once again, although he had known it word for word already a week now.

In the silence he contemplated this man, Gideon, a plain reluctant warrior, "who had been brought to faith out of the midst of fears and doubts." He had wondered how that could be and had caught a glimpse of the answer as he prepared the sermon. He had long since faced up to the fact that in the beginning his real reasons for studying theology had little to do with faith. It had been more a desire to make his mark, to outstrip his brilliant older brothers. He was tired of being "little brother," of being forced to live in their shadow. Now he had come to long for a faith like Gideon's— following the Lord's command—doing the necessary, whatever the odds. Abraham—Moses—Gideon—Jesus.

Dietrich closed the sermon. It would not be popular. People did not want to hear such things: "Lay your weapons aside, I am your weapon and your thousands of weapons are not as one of mine. Let my grace be sufficient for you. My strength is powerful in weakness." He smiled when he thought what Hugo would make of that. And what would the congregation make of it—that scattering of professionals and students, bureaucrats and petty bourgeoisie? Would it change one iota the frightening course upon which Germany had embarked?

No sooner did the questions arise, like sly imps from hell, than he firmly dispelled them. To give the proclamation clearly and unmistakably—that was his part. The rest was up to God.

As it turned out, the argument over Friedrichshain had been unnecessary; when he went back to the university on Monday he found in his mailbox the notice of the election: "Of the ballots handed in, 47 votes went to Herr Sup. Patzold and 25 votes to Herr Pfr. Lic. Bonhoeffer. Herr Sup. Patzold is therefore elected."

It was not even close.

3

After they crossed the busy Königsallee and rounded the corner by their old Grunewald School, the tennis party separated. Dietrich, Klaus, and Klaus's wife, Emmi, continued up the Caspar Theyssenstrasse toward home; and Emmi's brother, Justus Delbrück, and his two friends turned toward town.

Dietrich's parents were out of town and he had invited his friend, Franz Hildebrandt, to join them for lunch. He hoped to cheer him up, since on this day the Nazis had announced a boycott of Jewish stores. Franz's Uncle Isaac had a downtown store that was likely to be affected.

Along the Wangenheimstrasse the tall, stately houses stood back a few feet from their wrought iron fences and patterned walls. At No. 14 the tennis players turned in the gate and followed the brick walk to the canopied entrance at the side of the house. Dietrich loved this house, so long from front to back, and tall—three stories, plus the basement.

Franz Hildebrandt was already there, seated in the psychiatrist's waiting room engrossed in a book. He wore his usual dark blue suit, rumpled and one size too large. Dietrich winked at Klaus and Emmi and addressed Franz with an exaggerated air. "My dear sir, how unfortunate. Weren't you informed that the doctor is away for several days?"

Franz looked up from his book with a mildly questioning air.

"No? Well, since I know a little about your case, perhaps I can help you." Dietrich went to the file cabinet and selected a file folder. "You don't mind if my brother and his wife listen in on our session? My brother is a lawyer."

"Indeed?" said Franz with a look of amused tolerance on his thin pale face. "Then please let them stay. I'll probably need a lawyer."

Dietrich opened the folder and pretended to read from it. "Now what have we here? Hm—. Your symptoms seem to be rather extensive. Color blind. Totally insensitive to the visual arts, anything visual for that matter. Can't tell a Picasso from a Rembrandt."

"Oh, but I have a good ear. I'm remarkably adept at detecting a charlatan by the tone of his voice."

"Possibly, but not at all pertinent to the case, you understand. Now, let's see, hm—yes, this is an important discrepancy. Physically out of shape. Refuses to learn tennis or other health-building sports. Keeps his head in a book all the time. So if he doesn't mend his ways he'll be over the hill by age fifty—maybe even forty."

"I'd say there are worse things than being over the hill," said Franz dryly. "One of them is being under the hill."

"You see," Dietrich said to Klaus and Emmi, "that's just an example of his irrationality. But we'll let it pass. I must add, however, that in addition to heading straight over the hill, he's already in the woods. Terribly absent-minded. At the tender age of twenty-four that is serious indeed. You'd think from all that reading he'd know something, but the truth is, he's remarkably ignorant. Really knows nothing. If you asked him when Bismarck was born, he wouldn't know it."

"First of April, 1815," Franz answered promptly.

"You see," said Dietrich, "that's another serious symptom—colossal nerve. Prevaricates without batting an eye."

"First of April, 1815," Franz repeated.

"Stubborn, too. That, of course, is to be expected with this kind. Gets a notion in his head and there it stays."

"I suggest you look it up," Franz said mildly.

"That would be a complete waste of time." He turned to Klaus and Emmi. "As you can see this is a serious—"

"Bismarck was born April 1, 1815."

"Oh well," said Dietrich, "I guess we'll have to humor him. Sometimes they get violent if you don't." He went to the bookshelf under the window, picked out the "B" volume of the encyclopedia, and flipped quickly through to the article on Bismarck. He read silently. "Bismarck, Otto, Prince von (1815–1898), German statesman and first chancellor of the German empire, was born April 1, 1815, at—"

"Aloud, please," Franz insisted.

"Luck, pure chance," said Dietrich, slamming the book shut. "That's another thing about these types. They sometimes have an absolutely uncanny sixth sense."

At that Emmi burst into laughter. "Come on, Dietrich, we've got to get cleaned up before this fabulous meal of yours. We won't be long, Franz. Wouldn't you be more comfortable in the living room?"

"No, I'll stay here a while. It seems to suit my character so well."

"Quite so," said Dietrich, and laughed as they went out into the wide foyer and up the stairs.

Dietrich stripped and began to wash up at the lavatory. He hoped to persuade Franz to join him at Gerhard Jacobi's in the afternoon. This newly formed circle of concerned pastors, calling themselves the "Young Reformers," were trying to thwart a take-over of the church by Nazi sympathizers, the so-called "German Christians." The Young Reformers needed men like Franz. Dietrich had watched with pride and some envy at the turn of the year when Franz was given a parish of his own, an accomplishment for a man of twenty-four, not yet officially ordained. Now Dietrich wanted to see Franz take his proper place among the pastors of Berlin. Franz once had told him that his parents had never heard him preach. His Jewish mother was not pleased with his conversion to Christianity; and his father, a professor of fine arts at the university, was not interested. Dietrich had not told Franz that his own father was not interested, either; but at least he had heard Dietrich preach once or twice.

The first dinner gong rang below. Dietrich quickly got into fresh clothes and went downstairs. In the hall the aroma of baked ham rose from the kitchen below. That domain, always tantalizing to Dietrich as a child, when it was off limits, had become an occasional haunt of his. Lotte, the genial Westphalian cook they had brought with them to Berlin when he was six years old, had been initiating him into some of its luscious mysteries.

The luncheon was a triumph. Even Klaus could find nothing to criticize. The liver mousse with orange sauce and the cold cucumber soup were fine, but for Dietrich what was special were the plump, tender, white asparagus spears, swimming in fresh butter, and the center cuts of ham.

"I've been reading about this boycott against the Jewish establishments," Dietrich's grandmother said, when they were seated around the table. "Have you read it, Emmi?"

"Yes. Revolting!"

"Do you really think they can keep people from buying where they want to?"

"The SA will be out in force," said Klaus bitterly, "and nothing will be done to stop them."

"It's shameful," the grandmother said. She looked small but still erect in the high-backed chair. Her lips were still firm as a girl's, but the deeply lined cheeks and brow revealed her great age. "I'm sure your dear mother is terribly distressed, Franz. And your uncle. I suppose his store will be affected, like all the rest?"

"I'm afraid so," Franz answered.

"Tell them, will you, that I apologize. That I am deeply ashamed of what the government is doing."

Franz looked up from his plate. With a trace of huskiness in his voice he said, "My dear lady, you can't help what they do. It's not your fault. But I'll tell my uncle what you said."

Dietrich and Franz stepped from the train and walked the short distance from the Zoo Station to the Memorial Church. Only when he had told Franz that Elenore would be at the meeting had he agreed to come. Dear chap—he was as guileless as rain, his faithfulness an unspoken reality between them. Also his honesty; of the outcome at Friedrichschain he had said straight out that a cold splash of adversity wouldn't hurt Dietrich that much—might even help.

Red and black swastikas surrounded the island from which the garish old church lifted up its numerous spires. Some of the swastikas, like great square kerchiefs, hung from window ledges of the buildings; others, long and narrow, dangled from standards on the rooftops.

Elenore was waiting in her office for them, bright and cheerful. As they came out the sacristy door they paused and, shading their eyes from the sun, looked westward along the wide expanse of the Kurfürstendamm. Groups of brownshirts patrolled the sidewalks in front of all the Jewish stores. They were early for the meeting, and Dietrich persuaded Elenore and a reluctant Franz to stop off at the Wittenberg Platz for coffee. They had not gone far down the busy Tauentzienstrasse when Elenore put her hand on Dietrich's arm and pointed across the street to a small clothing store where two storm troopers blocked the entry. On the window and door were painted in large letters the word *Jude*. The lights were on inside. Some of the passersby stopped and gawked, but most walked hurriedly on. No one went in. Dietrich glanced at Franz's grim face.

As they approached the Kadewe they met the same situation. He had forgotten, or maybe he had never realized that the giant department store was Jewish-owned. Here once again was *Jude*. on the windows and a sign that warned Germans not to buy from Jews: *Deutsche! Wehrt Euch! Kauft nicht bei Juden!* This time there were four SA men patrolling the wide entrance. An old lady appeared to be arguing with them.

"Dietrich, isn't that your grandmother?" Elenore whispered beside him.

He adjusted his glasses and, seeing that it was, stopped in his tracks. Immediately Franz started ahead, presumably with the thought of rescuing her.

Dietrich grabbed his arm. "We mustn't interfere. She'd be terribly insulted. Besides, they aren't going to hurt a woman her age."

"Look," said Elenore with some degree of awe, "she's going inside."

As they watched, she walked straight past the storm troopers into the store.

Dietrich's fears gave way to a fierce surge of pride, and he said, "Let's wait by the window there." They moved back to an adjacent bookstore and waited.

Twenty minutes later his grandmother's slight but marvelously erect figure emerged from the store and turned in their direction. With her smartly bonneted head held high she walked past the storm troopers as if they did not exist. In one hand she carried her embroidered shopping bag, full of purchases, and in the other her ivory-handled walking stick.

At a signal from Dietrich they all turned their backs and pretended to study the bookstore window display until she had passed, then they caught up with her.

"Meine Dame," said Franz on her left, "allow me to carry your packages."

She stopped short as if she half expected to see the storm troopers. When she recognized them, her stern face melted into a sheepish smile and finally exultant laughter.

Franz took her bag and spoke a word in her ear. They all turned around and moved again toward the Wittenberg Platz. When the SA men saw her coming once again, this time with an escort, they quickly turned the other way.

The stop at the yellow-canopied café became a celebration, with coffee and slices of Nüsstortchen all around. With a napkin tucked over her jabot, Dietrich's grandmother primly sipped her coffee. "I couldn't sit at home and let such a thing to go unchallenged," she said. "I went also to the Kaufhaus Israel and to your uncle's store, Franz."

"What did you say to those men?" Elenore asked.

"I just told them I'd always shopped there and had no plans to stop. All in all," she said, her eyes triumphant, "it was one of the most successful shopping trips I've ever had."

When they had finished their coffee, and Dietrich had called for the check, he saw Hugo and Hilde von der Lutz enter the cafe and move among the crowded tables, looking for a seat. He had not seen his cousin since their quarrel about Hitler two months before and hoped that Hugo and Hilde would not notice them. The others at the table had grown quiet. Dietrich glanced at his grandmother. Like a queen she gazed serenely at the disconcerted Lutzes, who had stopped and appeared to be debating what to do.

Hugo's breeding seemed to get the better of him and he moved toward them, with Hilde trailing reluctantly behind. He bowed over the table and took the hand the grandmother coolly proffered him, then Elenore's. Franz's distaste was so apparent as to be almost ludicrous, but he took his cue from the grandmother and rose perfunctorily at the same time as Dietrich.

The greetings over, Dietrich's grandmother said in a voice brisk, dry, and unassailably correct, "We were just leaving, so you can have our table. We were celebrating my successful shopping tour. I rarely go to so many stores, but today I felt a distinct desire to go to as many Jewish stores as possible: Kaufhaus Israel, Wertheim's, Kaufhaus des Westens"—she used the full name of the Kadewe, as if to endow it with the utmost possible dignity—"and several smaller shops." She looked from Hilde to Hugo with a defiant and reproving gleam in her eye. "I bought something at each one of them."

She hung her handbag over her arm and with the other hand pushed herself up with her cane. Franz sprang up beside her, her laden shopping bag in his hand. Dietrich and Elenore stood also.

"Now we must be going," she said. "And good day to you."

Without another word they all trooped off. At the door Dietrich looked back. Hugo had not moved from the spot and gazed after them with a baffled look in his eyes. As Dietrich opened the door he saw Hilde, tall and pale, lay a cool hand on her husband's arm and press him into the seat.

4

Ten Berlin pastors attended that first meeting of the Young Reformers. Dietrich was encouraged. They all deplored the boycott of Jewish businesses. But the main discussion was on the need for reorganization of the church, so as to present a strong, united front against the German Christians.

As long as Dietrich could remember there had been the twenty-eight regional churches—some Reformed, some Lutheran, some United—each with its own church council and superintendent.

The largest of these was the Lutheran Old Prussian Union, to which he belonged, administered only by an advisory council of the regional superintendents, with one of them serving as general superintendent. Until recently the weakness of the system had not been evident. Dietrich voted with the nine other pastors at the meeting to enlist representatives of the twenty-eight regional churches, men they knew and trusted, and with them to lay plans for a new central church government.

Before the Young Reformers could meet again, a new development took Dietrich by surprise. In a lightning move Hitler forced through a new law "for the reconstruction of the professional Civil Service," which would eliminate Jews and people of Jewish descent from its ranks. The first person Dietrich thought of was his twin sister, Sabine, in Göttingen. Her husband, Gerhard Leibholz, was recognized as one of the country's best teachers of constitutional law, but Dietrich feared that would make no difference. Gerhard's parents were Jewish. Then there were Dietrich's colleagues at the University of Berlin. Some of the best were Jewish—all to be sacked because they were "non-Aryans!" They were calling the law the "Aryan Clause." That Hitler had been able to ram it through the Reichstag showed his power more clearly than anything that had happened so far.

Franz Hildebrandt told Dietrich that he expected to be kicked out as a pastor.

"No. It won't apply in the church," said Dietrich, with more assurance than might have been warranted.

"Maybe not at first. But sooner or later—. The German Christians have already been talking about it—even before this law." He looked at Dietrich with the same grim look on his face as the day of the boycott. "Yes, I had it from Pastor Lietzer. He's thrown in his lot with them. They're saying that men of 'alien blood,' as they call it, have no place in the pulpit."

Franz looked at him with those dark, injured eyes.

At the next Young Reformers' meeting in Gerhard Jacobi's study there were twice as many pastors as before. Dietrich was confident that their reaction to this new law would be the same as his. As pastor of the Kaiser Wilhelm Memorial Church, Jacobi was the natural leader of the Young Reformers. Dietrich, seated on the floor of the crowded room, observed the skill with which this tall man of commanding mien handled the discussion. At first the talk had to do with ways to counter the influence of the German Christians. There was a report on progress toward reorganization of the church. Representatives of the regional church governments would meet in May to elect a Reichbischof of a new united German Evangelical Church, bringing the churches under one authority.

When Jacobi opened the floor again, Dietrich asked the question most pressing on his mind: "What can we do about this Aryan Clause? It seems to me the church cannot keep quiet about it."

"The church has no business meddling in the affairs of the state," said one of the pastors, Ludwig Schmidt, emphatically. "Our business is to spread the Gospel."

"And yet," said Dietrich, "when the state goes against the law of God—in this case persecuting a whole people on racial grounds—the church has a responsibility to speak out, don't you think? To remind the state of the limits of its authority."

"No, Pastor Schmidt is right. It's not the call of the Church to tell the state what to do," said Karl Sommer, a robust, blustery man, who had lost an arm in the Great War.

Dietrich could feel the blood rising in his neck and face, and forced his voice to a cooler level. "What about when the state puts pressure on us to apply this law in our own ranks. It will happen, you know. They'll try to defrock our 'non-Aryan' pastors. And we'll have to fight it. The very existence of the church stands or falls with this question."

"We've been talking about a united church, and now you're advocating a policy that will split it apart," said Sommer.

"So we should remain silent in the face of such heresies?"

Sommer's heavy brows drew together. "Heresies? Isn't that a bit of a strong word?"

"As for the Jews as a whole," Dietrich continued without answering him, "the time could come—and sooner than we think—when the Church not only will have to bind and heal those who are crushed under the wheel, but also jam up its spokes."

"Now you're getting completely out of our province."

At that point Jacobi intervened. "It is a difficult problem and whether it is expedient or not, we must speak out on it. With your permission I'll go ahead with plans for a meeting on the subject, with you, Herr Bonhoeffer, giving the introductory talk."

All murmured agreement except the two dissenting pastors, who rose to leave, saying the meeting would have to go on without them.

When Dietrich got home he found that his twin sister, Sabine, and her husband, Gert, had arrived from Göttingen with their two children. Gert's father, seriously ill with a heart condition, had taken a turn for the worse, and Gert had gone directly there; but Sabine had stayed to supervise the children's supper and get them settled for the night. Dietrich had not seen her since the Aryan Clause took effect.

"I can't believe such things are happening," she said, when they were settled in the living room with their parents, "especially at the university." She held one hand tightly with the other. Her dark brown hair waved back over her ears to a loose knot behind. When they were children Sabine had always turned to Dietrich with her hurts and problems; and he, the tall flaxen-haired Siegfried, had been her champion and protector. With their younger sister, Susi, they had been "the three little ones" in the big family. Only upon Sabine's marriage at age twenty to Gerhard Leibholz had Dietrich relinquished his special place. Now he felt helpless.

"Gert's not dismissed?" asked their mother.

"No, not yet—" She paused, as if uncertain how to tell it.

Sabine had told Dietrich earlier that Gert was in trouble with his dean. The dean had warned that his new series of lectures on "The Image of the State in the Twentieth Century" was not acceptable to the Party. They regarded the subject as a "provocation." At that time Gert had showed no signs of abandoning his plans for it.

"His first lecture was last Monday—supposed to have been, that is. He had had all kinds of threats—you can't imagine—sometimes the Nazis gang up on him in the hall, four or five abreast, arms linked, like they are going to knock him to the floor. They haven't, actually. They break apart at the last minute, then laugh and laugh."

"Doesn't the dean do something about it?" their father asked.

"No. The dean doesn't say a word. He's scared to. I never knew how many cowards there were in the world. Anyway, Monday I went with him—I do sometimes, you know. He didn't want me to go, but I went anyway. The Nazis were there, just like they said— they blocked the door so no one could get in—"

"A boycott, then."

"Yes. In that awful get-up—black boots and that awful insignia. They had scrawled a notice on the board."

"Pay no attention, Liebchen," said their mother.

"I tried not to, Mama. I thought I was prepared." Her voice broke, but after a moment she recovered herself. "I don't know what will happen. Some of the students are coming to his class, and he won't stop as long as there's a single one. I told Gert we should emigrate. I want to get away from here—away from all this madness." Tears were streaming down her cheeks.

"What does Gert say?" their father asked.

"He doesn't want us to jump into it. He's worried about what he would do. It's the language."

Dietrich looked at his mother, realizing that Sabine meant somewhere off the continent—England or America.

"He says we can manage until things get better. But things aren't going to get better. We've been thinking that for weeks now."

"I'm afraid you're right," said Dietrich. "At least, not for a long time."

There seemed to be no solution.

The next day Gert's father died. That afternoon Sabine and Gert came back to the house and asked Dietrich to conduct the funeral. He had known that this was a possibility, yet he was not prepared for it. There was a long-standing church regulation against taking funerals for unbaptized Jews. The fact that Gert Leibholz and his brothers and sisters were all baptized Lutherans made no difference, for although their father did not attend synagogue, he had never been baptized. To go against established law, even a law with which he strongly disagreed, was alien to everything that had been drilled into Dietrich. Yet to decline at this time, with Hitler's new decree striking terror and outrage in every "non-Aryan" heart, seemed doubly insensitive.

"Of course, I'll be happy to do it," he said, with some hesitation.

"Is there a problem?" Sabine asked.

"I should think not. No, surely not."

"What is it, Dietrich?"

"Oh, nothing. Some stuffy old church regulation. Probably doesn't apply here." Gerhard Leibholz, one of the gentlest of men, would be hurt to know that such a regulation existed. Annoyed with himself that he had brought up the subject, Dietrich said with unwarranted glibness, "Nothing of importance. I think I can handle it," and turned to something else.

In the evening Dietrich sought out Franz Hildebrandt in his small flat.

Franz agreed that the regulation was stupid, but could see no way around it. "It's an old law. Has nothing to do with Hitler, you know."

"That doesn't make a particle of difference."

"Couldn't you do it without your gown, just speaking as a friend?"

"No. If I can't do it as a minister, and offer the comfort of the Church to the old man's children—no, I wouldn't want to do it that way at all." Dietrich rested his elbows on the arms of the leather chair, the only comfortable seat Franz owned, and gazed through his rimless glasses at the Florentine tapestry on the opposite wall.

Franz suggested that he talk to Theodor Heckel. "He's your superior, you know, and should be the one to advise you."

"Actually, I'd rather not."

"Well, suit yourself. But I think it's the only logical thing to do. He'd probably know more than either of us about such a situation. It wouldn't do any harm to ask him."

Dietrich remained silent.

"It's not a very good time for you to go striking out on your own in something having to do with church policy."

"I'll think about it."

Dietrich put it off as long as he could. Finally, he went to Heckel, who advised against it "at this particular time," and suggested he also consult General Superintendent Stoltenhoff. The general superintendent was firm. Dietrich should not violate a church statute in such a way.

A cousin of Gerhard Leibholz' conducted the funeral in the cemetery chapel with a brief eulogy and a selection of poems by Goethe and Franz Werfel, favorites of Gert's father. Dietrich sat motionless throughout the reading and the music that followed. When the family filed out behind the casket, he kept his eyes on the seat before him. All the same, he knew the moment when Sabine passed his pew.

As they were leaving, Dietrich overheard Hans von Dohnanyi talking to Franz Hildebrandt: "If they knew my grandmother was Jewish, I'd be out on my ear tomorrow. Fortunately she's in Hungary. Even so, I have to be discreet." He laughed bitterly. "The trick will be to keep our parentage secret, Hildebrandt—if we want to stay in Germany, that is. I've worked long and hard to get where I am now. Damned if I'm going to let these brownshirted bullies rob me of it."

Dietrich looked at Christel, but she said nothing.

"This regime can't last forever," Hans continued, "and who knows what might be done from the inside that wouldn't be possible from the outside. If I can keep a level head, that is."

If anyone could keep a level head, Hans could, but what a price!

"Too bad you couldn't do the service," said Christel without warning. "I suppose Sabine and Gert understand that you couldn't go against your superiors. All I can say is, that's a stupid way to run the church."

Dietrich looked at her without answering.

She went on, "Did you hear what happened the day before the old man died?"

"No."

"He got a notice through the mail of his dismissal as an alderman of the city of Berlin. The new Aryan Clause at work."

Dietrich stopped short and turned to her. "No, I didn't know that. Surely they could have let him die in peace."

"What's more, they removed his son, Gert's brother, from his judgeship the same day. Sabine was crying when she told me about it."

"She didn't tell me," Dietrich said. At Christel's eloquent shrug he looked quickly away.

Later that night the family gathered at the Bonhoeffer house on the Wangenheimstrasse to hear Arthur Schnabel's piano recital on the radio. He was performing all thirty Beethoven sonatas in a series of seven concerts. This was the fourth.

At the end of the recital a voice came on the air with a message: "In the interest of maintaining untainted German music and German musicians, this will be the last of Herr Schnabel's recitals."

Dietrich was stunned. Schnabel was one of the great pianists of modern times. But he was Jewish. Dietrich looked at Sabine. Her eyes showed no surprise.

The final sonata had been Opus 81A in E flat, known as "Les Adieux."

5

One day in early June as Dietrich and Elenore returned from their customary walk in the Tiergarten, they stopped by the Church Federation Office on the Jebenstrasse to pick up some papers for Jacobi. Outside the door of the building two men in SA uniforms barred their way.

"Please state your name and your business," one of them demanded.

"Why do you ask?" Dietrich said. "This is the church office, is it not?" He felt the pressure of Elenore's hand on his arm.

"There's a new authority here now," said one of the SA men. "You must present your credentials for Kommissar Jäger."

Dietrich looked the man up and down, feeling that he could not allow such a thing to go unchallenged. From the corner of his eye he saw the pale look on Elenore's face. "We will go to the church," he said, taking her arm.

At the Memorial Church Gerhard Jacobi explained what had happened. In a lightning move Hitler had dismissed the employees of the new church government and dissolved all representative church bodies. In their place he had set up his own commissars.

"State commissars are also taking over the provincial offices around the country," Jacobi told them.

Elenore, still pale, asked, "When did this happen?"

"Just a few hours ago—around eleven, I think. I heard Minister Rust just now on the wireless. 'Resistance is betrayal,' he said, 'and will be rigorously suppressed.'"

"Well, that's in character," said Dietrich. "Suddenness, to knock us off balance, then the threat of treason to keep us flat on the ground."

"Well, come in. Let's see if we can talk this out and come up with some kind of strategy."

The next few days Dietrich worked tirelessly with the Young Reformers. Through their many sources nationwide they tried to assess reaction to the takeover of the church. It came back to them as a shiver of uncertainty and alarm, crackling the calm like glaze in a hot kiln. The most pressing task for Dietrich and his students was to keep the news channels open. With the Nazis controlling the press, they had only word-of-mouth and leaflets, which they printed and distributed by hand or tacked on the hundreds of kiosks around the city. They used the telephone with great care, so as not to incur the charge of treason.

The response was immediate. Dietrich had seen nothing like it since Hitler's rise to power. From all over the country protest delegations of teachers and pastors converged on the Chancellery. The Young Reformers commissioned Dietrich to draft a letter to Hitler, a "Declaration of the Ministers of Berlin," which demanded the withdrawal of the commissars and the reinstatement of the elected officials. Dietrich was circulating it among the pastors of the city, with the hope for at least one hundred signatures.

At midweek Franz showed him an order he had received from Hitler's new spiritual leaders, directing every pastor in the nation to hold services of "praise and thanksgiving" the following Sunday morning. Church altars were to be decorated with swastikas and a proclamation read from the pulpit, which stated the "deeply felt thanks of the people that the State, in addition to all its tremendous tasks, should have assumed the great load and burden of reorganizing the church."

"Do they really think I would do such a thing in my church?" Franz said bitterly.

The ousted general superintendents suggested that the churches hold services of atonement and prayer that same evening as a counteraction. When Sunday came, Dietrich went to see Franz in his flat.

"I thought I'd attend your service tonight," Dietrich said, as he sank his solid weight into the armchair, "if you would like me to."

"I've already held it. This morning, at the regular worship hour."

"What!" Laughter bubbled forth irrepressibly at such bold defiance of Hitler's new officials. "Well," Dietrich said, "you always were a stubborn one. I'll visit you in prison."

Just then Franz received a telephone call. After two or three minutes he slowly put the receiver back on the hook and said, "That was Martin Niemöller. The police have arrested Pastor Grossmann in Steglitz. It seems he had the same idea I had."

On the spot they decided to attend Martin Niemöller's atonement service that evening in the Old Dahlem Church. They arrived early, but even then almost every seat was taken. Niemöller's announcement of the arrest of Pastor Grossmann drew an audible gasp from the congregation. Such a thing was unheard of in modern Germany. Quietly, but with a firm undertone that commanded attention, Niemöller led a prayer of intercession on behalf of Grossmann and asked God's guidance for the days ahead. Then he gave a ringing call for unity against the interference of the State in church affairs. In everyday life Martin Niemöller, with his spectacles and conservative clothes, was not an imposing man; but in the pulpit he seemed in every way more impressive. Yet, according to Franz, a mere six months before he had been a supporter of Hitler.

After the service Dietrich and Franz talked with him at the side entrance of the old thirteenth-century church. Across the tree-shaded lawn, now drenched by a late afternoon thunderstorm, stood the Dahlem parsonage, where Niemöller lived with his large family. Niemöller asked when Dietrich expected to send the letter to Hitler.

"Thursday, I hope."

"How many signatures do you have?"

"About seventy."

"Seventy. Could be better."

"Oh, I expect more—after today."

"Did you notice the SA men taking notes at the back of the church?" asked Franz.

"No," Niemöller answered, "but I'm not surprised. I've seen them there before."

"I think we can expect that from now on," said Dietrich.

They said good-night and headed for home. The fog was lifting along the Königin-Luise-Strasse, and the cobblestones of the wide walkway glistened in the light of the street lamps. With Niemöller's calm, resolute countenance before him, Dietrich mused, half to himself, "It's the man who is willing to take risks who is really alive. The rest are merely figures on a stage."

The next few days Dietrich went from one pastor to another,

securing signatures for his letter to Hitler. Dietrich's superior, Theodor Heckel, asked him to come by his office at the university—he had a new proposal to discuss with him. So Dietrich took the letter with him in the hope of getting him to sign it.

After polite inquiries about Dietrich's health and that of his parents, Heckel said, "I continue to hear good things about your Genesis lectures. I don't know many professors who could draw two hundred students that early in the morning."

Heckel smiled with more intimacy than Dietrich was accustomed to. He was a considerably older man—close to forty, Dietrich imagined, although only a hint of a double chin and a few gray hairs at the temples betrayed it. His rimless glasses did not detract from his smooth, well-formed features. Their relationship had always been professionally correct but with little to spark a personal exchange, although two years earlier Heckel had served with him on the German delegation to an ecumenical conference in Cambridge, England, and had given his support when Dietrich was named a youth secretary of the council.

"It is not yet announced," said Heckel, "but I have been appointed to be Foreign Affairs Administrator for the Church. They have already asked me to fill a vacancy in London, the pastorate of two of our German-speaking churches there. I thought you might be interested. I have some literature for you that will give you more details."

The offer took Dietrich by surprise and sparked his immediate interest, though he took pains not to show it. "I appreciate the honor. I would need time to think it over."

"There's plenty of time. I'd even suggest you go over there and look the situation over. We can arrange that when the time comes."

Then Dietrich took the letter to Hitler from his briefcase and laid it on Heckel's desk, explaining its content and asking Heckel to sign it. Heckel read it over with a questioning frown, then handed it back. "My dear fellow, this document seems premature to me and rather inflammatory. It can only hurt, not help, the church's relation with the State."

"After Hitler's attempt to take the church at gunpoint?"

"How dramatic you are. Really now, we have to use a little common sense these days, accommodate ourselves to the present realities, and, when necessary, make some compromises—judicious ones, of course. We want the church to accomplish its evangelical task—I'm sure you do, too—even if we have to work in a little different framework. It's still the Lord's vineyard."

"No, we can't harvest grapes from thorns."

Heckel laughed shortly. "Ah, but you draw such grim pictures. I've noticed that in some of your sermons. No, I can't put my name to that."

So on Friday Dietrich sent it to the Chancellery with 106 names, but not Theodor Heckel's.

The following Monday, after Dietrich dismissed his Christology class, he was surprised to discover Elenore outside in the hall. "I've been waiting for you," she said eagerly. "Would you believe it, Hitler has reversed his orders."

Dietrich drew her aside into an alcove overlooking the back courtyard. "What do you mean, reversed his orders?"

"Just that. He's withdrawn his commissars and reinstated the old officials—in the Church Federation Office and everywhere. It's a miracle."

It seemed indeed unbelievable. "Where did you hear this?"

"Jacobi. He got it directly from the general superintendent himself. It's true, Dietrich, it's really true."

The facts bore her out, as the rest of the day revealed. That night in the little Bierstube near the office of the Young Reformers jubilation reigned among his inner circle of students. But amid all the raised glasses Dietrich could not escape a sense of uneasiness. He warned them that they should consider any retreat of Hitler's as purely tactical and, in all probability, temporary. That dampened their spirits not at all.

When his students turned to Dietrich to toast his leadership, "which had played a great part in the victory," he felt as if he were two selves: the one who looked on mockingly, like a magpie from a perch somewhere above and beyond, and the one who willingly gave himself over to the heady awareness of the power he held over them. When the mocking self gained the upper hand, he abruptly made ready to leave.

Outside he and Elenore walked along the tree-lined Königin-Luise-Strasse toward the car-stop.

"They're right, Dietrich, much of the credit goes to you. Jacobi said so this morning—your organization of the students, your letter to Hitler, and your persistence in garnering all those signatures, especially the letter. He thought that was brilliant."

That she did not sense his mood and desire for silence angered him. Yet, he took pleasure in Jacobi's praise. Until the streetcar came he kept casting doubt on the permanence of the victory.

Alone in his room he battled self-congratulation. Little scenes of personal triumph, when his authority or ability had won the day, skittered across his mind.

The sand is soft when he falls into it. He looks up. The bar is still in place. One-half inch higher than Ernst Abrahamsohn's jump. It flashes upon him that he has won the main track event of the school year. He tries to stand still as they place the victor's laurel wreath around his shoulders, and all the students cheer. Then he is on the way home, wearing his victor's prize, eager most of all to show it off to his older brothers. But Klaus and Walter meet him with taunts: "So, now he is the great Dietrich Bonhoeffer, huh?" they say, "not 'Little Brother' anymore, no, 'The King of the Walk.' What d'ya know about that." With deep shame Dietrich buries the wreath under dry leaves in the corner of the garden, and never brings it out again.

Could it be that such pride still held him in its coils? The thought threw him into a fit of despondency. He became intent on justifying his motives. None could be made to stand. In his heart he scorned the students and Elenore for falling so easily under his domination.

Outside his window the murky sky gave no promise of day. God seemed remote and antagonistic, if there at all. In the cold, thin silence came the striking of the clock: two o'clock—three o'clock—four o'clock. Not until the light of early dawn was Dietrich able to break out of the circle of ensnaring thoughts and fall asleep.

6

Even Dietrich was surprised at how swiftly Hitler went on the offensive again. He called for nationwide church elections on July 23, 1933, with little more than a week to prepare for it. The voters would decide between a church government headed by Hitler's man, Ludwig Müller, a little known army chaplain, or by the previously ousted Friedrich von Bodelschwingh, supported by the Young Reformers. In the allotted time the Young Reformers, with Dietrich, Franz, Niemöller, and Jacobi in the vanguard, tried to organize and draft a program that would offer persuasive alternatives to those of the German Christians. In their office in Dahlem they wrote electoral position papers and duplicated them on a mimeograph machine. No other means of publicity was open to them. Although the government had issued directives that the elections should be "impartial," they soon learned of the tactics the Nazi element was using: enrolling nonchurch people to swell the vote, impugning the patriotism of the Young Reformers and, with government backing, threatening dismissal and financial sanctions against any pastor who traitorously opposed Hitler's choice for Reichsbischof.

They hurriedly entitled their drive "Program of the Evangelical Church" and worked straight through Sunday, stopping only for morning worship services. Dietrich canceled his Christology lectures for the entire week and enlisted his students to help with poster-making, typing, and the overwhelming task of distribution. At his mother's suggestion they set up headquarters at home, where each day she served lunch in the garden.

On Monday morning Dietrich went to the Dahlem office to talk over strategy with Niemöller and Jacobi. When he got there three men in Gestapo uniforms were carrying out boxes of leaflets and other materials and loading them in a van. His two colleagues were standing on one side of the room silently watching. The long table and half the shelves were bare.

"What's going on?" asked Dietrich.

In a voice vibrating with anger, Jacobi described the Gestapo sweep. They had an injunction. The German Christians had obtained it, and they were carting off all their posters and leaflets.

Soon the shelves were empty, with only the mimeograph machine left. One of the Gestapo men picked that up, and another took the two boxes of mimeograph paper underneath. As Dietrich watched they put them in the van, closed the door, and without looking back got inside and drove away.

For a long time the three men stood mesmerized. Finally Dietrich asked, "What shall we do?"

"I don't know," said Niemöller. "What can we do?"

"They shouldn't be able to get by with it," said Jacobi.

"Why don't we go up there and protest?" said Dietrich.

"You mean to the Gestapo?"

"The headquarters, yes."

Jacobi looked at Niemöller, and Niemöller looked back at him.

"All right, I'll go with you," said Jacobi without further hesitation.

Niemöller reached into the file drawer, took out a news clipping and handed it to Jacobi. "I'd suggest you take this along. It's a copy of the government directive on the 'impartiality and freedom of the church elections.' Ask for the top man, Rudolf Diels. Underlings only waste your time. Oh, and by the way, Gerhard, wear your Iron Crosses."

Jacobi laughed. "Still the U-boat captain, aren't you?"

"Of course," said Niemöller, with a quick lift of the eyebrows.

That afternoon Fritz drove them in the Bonhoeffer Horsch to the Prinz-Albrecht-Strasse and pulled up in front of an enormous gray building that took up almost half the block. Wide stone steps led up to the heavy portal. The swastikas on either side hung limp in the still air.

With Jacobi's Iron Crosses in full view they passed the guards and moved into the wide hallway. The porter, a genial enough fellow with a round face, screwed up his small eyes and told them it would not be possible to see Herr Inspektor Diels, as he was in a conference and could not be disturbed.

"Then we'll wait," said Dietrich cheerfully.

They sat on a stone bench across from a marble stairway. After a time a large-boned woman came down the stairs in tears, followed by a guard. After she left, the porter asked the guard, "What did you do to her?"

"Damned carrion," the guard spat out. "Couldn't open her mouth and say 'Heil, Hitler.' I showed her. It'll be a cold day in hell when she sees her son again."

Dietrich looked at Jacobi. They did not say "Heil, Hitler" and had no intention of beginning today.

Two hours later they sat in the anteroom of Diels's office. There were stacks of cardboard boxes beside the secretary's desk, and the smell of fresh paint. Everywhere was the same color, medium gray.

Finally the high door across the room opened, and the assistant who had reluctantly brought them up motioned to them to enter. It was a spacious, high-ceilinged room with somber wainscoting. The sparsity of furniture heightened the focus toward the huge leather-topped desk between two tall windows. Behind it sat an officer with close-clipped hair and a sallow complexion, whom Dietrich took to be Rudolf Diels. On the wall above his head hung the inevitable portrait of Adolf Hitler. Beside Diels stood a pedestal and mounted upon it a spread eagle of wrought iron, holding a swastika in its talons. Diels made not the slightest move or sound, but continued to study some papers on his desk as if no one were there.

After a time Dietrich became aware that the man was watching them, and returned his stare. It was the first time he had encountered a Nazi official face to face. The man was younger than he had expected, perhaps in his early thirties, and immaculately groomed.

"Herr Pastor Jacobi, Herr Dr. Bonhoeffer," he said, with a cursory nod and a cold, impersonal tone, "please state your business as briefly as possible. My time is limited."

Jacobi took the newsclip from his pocket and held it out to Diels. He pointed out that the Gestapo's raid had violated the directive for impartiality in the election.

Diels waved it aside impatiently. "It is you instead who have violated impartiality."

"In what way? We certainly—"

"By the use of the title 'Evangelical Church,' as if you alone represented the church."

The charge seemed ridiculous. Dietrich pointed out that the German Christians had chosen to use another title. "Certainly a free choice. It can't be claimed that we—that our intention—"

"Your intention is not the question. The resulting impression is."

Dietrich chose his words carefully and tried to keep in mind that the object was to regain their material, not to win an argument with the head of the Gestapo. "You are aware, I'm sure, Herr Inspektor, of the extremely short notice of the election."

"No shorter for you than for your opponents."

"True," said Dietrich mildly, "but their resources for publicity are somewhat greater than ours. In all fairness—and the government claims to want fairness—if it is simply the title 'Evangelical Church' that you object to, couldn't you return our materials with the understanding—"

"I'm afraid that isn't at all possible."

"Even if we agree to remove the offending words?"

"Gentlemen, we are wasting our time, mine and yours."

"Suppose we substitute the words 'Gospel and Church,'" said Jacobi quickly. "Certainly that is inoffensive enough."

There was a flicker of uncertainty in Diels's eyes. Dietrich pressed the advantage. "Perhaps we should consult the minister of interior about this."

"Certainly not," said Diels emphatically.

So Diels guarded his authority jealously. Dietrich followed up promptly. "Actually, I doubt that the Chancellor himself would approve such action." He could not bring himself to say "Führer." "He would realize, I think, that it's certain to create an unfavorable impression with the people."

Diels glanced up sharply then down again at his desk. He turned his pencil end over end, sliding its length between his fingers. At last he said, "All right. I'll return your material. But you will both be held responsible for strict observance of the agreement. I'm warning you. Any more propaganda that is insulting to the German Christians or that carries the false slogan and you'll be subject to arrest. Both of you. We have concentration camps for just such treasonous offenders."

As they walked down the stairs, they were aware that they had pulled off a victory of sorts. That afternoon, however, they sent out a letter to all the opposition leaders to make sure they understood the terms of the agreement and the dangers of disregarding it.

On election Sunday Dietrich went first to the voting place to cast his vote for "Gospel and Church," then downtown to the Trinity Church, where he preached on the "rock against which the gates of hell shall not prevail."

The election results were announced the next day. The German Christians had won by seventy-five percent of the votes.

After the election the first meeting of the Old Prussian General Synod, the largest and most influential synod in Germany, was held in the Prussian Herrenhaus, former home of the Upper House of Parliament. From his seat beside Franz on the fifth row back Dietrich watched the proceedings with growing disgust. The staid, old chamber was meant for better things. Its rows of brown leather seats with individual writing tables formed a semicircle, elevated for open views of the rostrum below. The arrangement there, with high ceilings, polished wood panels and carvings, should have been conducive to intelligent deliberations. Instead, swastikas decorated the platform and hung from the balcony at the back of the room.

Most of the delegates to this paramilitary spectacle appeared in brown uniform; the dwindling Young Reformers made up a small minority. From the start it was clear that the German Christians were running the show. In rapid succession they elected three of their men as president and deputy moderators of the synod. They took their places at the high dais behind the speaker's rostrum. To

Martin Niemöller they delegated the harmless task of taking the minutes. With a look on his face somewhere between skepticism and unease, he moved to his seat at the left of the speaker.

Dietrich had helped formulate a motion opposing the Aryan Clause in the church, which the Young Reformers planned to put forward early in the session. With the organizational business ended, Gerhard Jacobi, who was sitting two rows in front of Dietrich and Franz, stood to make the motion. The chairman, in his storm-trooper uniform, refused him permission to speak; Jacobi was out of order, he said.

Dietrich sprang to his feet to protest, but before he could say a word the chair peremptorily cut him off and called one of the brownshirted German Christians to the podium to present for ratification new legislation, which, he unctuously intoned, would "strengthen and purify" the Church.

Dietrich sat down slowly, trembling so with rage that he dared not look at Franz beside him. Never before had he witnessed such dictatorial tactics in a church synod.

The brownshirt read the first item of the new legislation, which replaced the office of general superintendent with that of bishop—ten in all, who would be accountable to the Reichsbischof. At that point the president of the synod, from his high seat behind the speaker's rostrum, introduced the new bishops and summoned them one by one to the podium, while the German Christians cheered their approval. The last to be named was Theodor Heckel. Dietrich watched with distaste as he took his place with the others on the platform and acknowledged the cheers of the crowd.

The reading of the legislation continued with a decree that only those who were prepared to give unconditional support to the National Socialist State and who were also of Aryan descent could be ordained as ministers in the German Evangelical Church.

Karl Koch, the venerable head of the Westphalian Synod, who had been meeting with the Young Reformers, stood in his place and asked for committee work on the new legislation.

With a clap of his hand on the lectern the chairman shouted:

"Who needs committee work? It's plain the majority approve, every patriotic man with any sense at all."

The men in brown applauded and stamped their feet.

"Let's get out of here," said Franz.

"No," said Dietrich through his teeth, "we must wait for the others."

The cheering continued, and one zealous brownshirt grabbed a swastika from its stand beside the podium and waved it victoriously. When Jacobi stood again to put forward the opposition of the Young Reformers, a forest of brown shouted him down.

Instantly Dietrich and Franz stood up with him; Niemöller, too, at his place on the podium, and Karl Koch with the other Young Reformers. In a body they left the hall.

Thirty minutes later they reassembled in Jacobi's study. Franz's first words were, "I refuse to preach in any of the pulpits of this church."

Dietrich knew from Franz's tone and from the look on his pale face that the words were spoken with finality. Niemöller, Jacobi, and the others in the room seemed to recognize it too, and for a time no one said a word.

"What's needed now are widespread resignations from office," said Dietrich. "That's the only service the clergy can still render the church."

"Yes," said Franz. "The brownshirts have separated the Reich church from the church of Christ. All that's left for us is to state that fact straight out."

None of the others seemed ready to take that plunge. Finally Niemöller said, "We can understand your feelings, Bruder Hildebrandt, and fully sympathize with them, but we must not act precipitously."

"Now is the time to do it, as an immediate answer to this—this—brown synod. If we delay we seem to be concurring."

Karl Koch, older than the rest of them and highly respected throughout the Old Prussian Union, was sitting beside Jacobi's desk. When this calm, straightforward leader cast his lot with the

Young Reformers, it had been a great boost to them and had helped discount the label of "radical" that older church leaders had attached to their movement. With an elbow on the desk he fingered his white moustache. "You're talking of schism, Bruder Hildebrandt," Koch said, "and that's too grave a step to be linked merely with the Aryan Clause. For that we need a more central issue."

"What, pray, could be more central," said Dietrich. "It's a fatal privilege to remain in a church where our brothers are denied their office on racial grounds."

"But, really now, there are only eleven non-Aryan pastors in all of Prussia."

"Ten, now," said Franz. "I've resigned."

"Eleven—or ten," said Dietrich, "if there are so few, that's all the more reason to support them."

Nothing Dietrich and Franz could say brought them around. They proposed instead to wait for the National Synod in Wittenberg and meanwhile, in order to gain more widespread support, to put out a statement of protest and solidarity with the persecuted brethren. They asked Dietrich and Niemöller to write it, and adjourned at one-thirty in the morning.

The next day Niemöller promptly agreed on the forceful language Dietrich wanted in the statement. "Honest prayer is a tremendous eye-opener," Niemöller said, with the now familiar lift of his eyebrows. Their pamphlet included the assertion that the Aryan Clause was a breach of the church's Confession of Faith; anyone who assented to it excluded himself from the communion of the church. As an addendum, they called upon the German clergy to reject the Aryan Clause, to pledge themselves to a new allegiance to the Scriptures and confessions, to resist infringement of these, and to afford financial help to those affected by the new law. They sent it out as a "Pastors' Emergency League" pledge.

7

A few days later Dietrich, feeling uncertain about what his future course should be, traveled to the family's summer home at Friedrichsbrunn in the Harz mountains, where his parents and grandmother were spending a month's vacation.

When he got off the train at Thale, Dietrich decided to walk the three miles over the mountain to Friedrichsbrunn. He loved the steep wooded path, which crossed and recrossed a frothy stream as it raced down the narrow gorge. At the top the main road leveled out across a wide plateau, where a southwesterly breeze filled the air with the smell of hay and ripe apples. He picked one from a tree beside the way and munched it as he walked along.

With dusk the air had suddenly turned cool. Dietrich passed through the village with its two stores, a Gasthaus, a stone church, and several farmsteads. In the center of town he turned the corner onto the familiar road that soon became a narrow lane. At the end of it stood the old square brick house on the edge of the forest. There were candles in the windows. He knew he was expected and laughed softly to himself, remembering how, as children, they used to put candles in all the windows to welcome the parents when they came down from Berlin for weekends. His father never would hear to putting electricity in the old house.

Inside with his parents, Dietrich eagerly exchanged news, while Lotte set out a light supper for him. His grandmother had already gone to her room. His mother was as incensed as he at the goings on in the Brown Synod and fumed as she poured chocolate in his cup, "Terrible, terrible." She turned to his father. "Karl, you'll have some, too?"

"No, no more. I'll just stay here by the fire, if you don't mind."

A note of weariness in his father's voice made Dietrich look up from his plate. The fine worn face was still handsome, but there in the rocker, the firelight reflecting the silver in his hair, his father looked old for the first time. That he needed this vacation was certain. As head of the department of psychiatry at the University of Berlin, director of the psychiatric clinic at the Charité hospital, and committed to his private practice, he carried a heavy load. Dietrich looked again.

Dietrich's mother sat down on the other side of the table. Her lively blue eyes rested upon him. As always, her dark blond hair was braided and bound at the nape of her neck. They talked about the family, and Dietrich asked about Sabine and Gert. They seemed to be all right, she said. Gert was still teaching, despite all the harassment.

Dietrich set down his cup. The only sound was the rhythmic creaking of his father's rocker. "But it's been terrible for them, hasn't it? And I didn't help much, I'm afraid." The rocking stopped, and he noticed the exchange of glances between his parents.

"I'm sure Sabine understands, Dietrich," said his mother. "She wouldn't want you to feel so bad about it. Why don't you go over to see them while you're here?"

"I can't, Mama. I have to be back in Berlin day after tomorrow."

Dietrich himself brought up the question of the pastorate in London. "The truth is, I don't know what to do. I need your help." They both looked his way with full attention. "Part of the problem is with my friends in the Young Reformers. They're almost all older than I, you know, men I've looked up to for a long time, but they aren't ready for a break with this new Reich Church and its storm troopers for Jesus Christ. Sometimes I'm afraid I might be veering off the tracks, just trying to justify myself." He looked at his father. "I'd hate that, you know."

His father met his gaze from under pushed-up glasses. "I'm sure you would."

The words reassured him. Sometimes as a child Dietrich had suffered under that piercing gaze, when everything boastful or vain melted away and he felt small. He had felt like that when he was fifteen and first announced his intention to study theology. He had sensed his father's disappointment in him, his father's feeling that he was throwing away his talents. Now he wanted to be completely honest. "That's not all, though. I don't know—I don't want to be guilty of running away if I'm needed here—but the truth is, I don't know what good I can do. It's so disgusting. I just want to get away from it all." He did not add that he was almost ready to leave the church altogether.

"It might not be a bad thing," said his father. "You don't need to flail yourself too much with questions about your motives. It could be helpful to see things from the outside for a time. I don't think your influence would be lost, only brought to bear in a different way. No one else is quite in the position you are, with your ecumenical connections. Isn't that true?" His brown eyes, so often skeptical, were now warm and concerned.

Surprised and deeply moved, Dietrich did not speak.

"Who better than you could keep the ecumenical people informed of the real situation in Germany. They're certainly going to get a distorted view otherwise. Then, besides that, I think it's valuable to save oneself up for the right moment."

Dietrich looked up quickly. "Yes, I've thought of that, too. What we're going through now is only the preliminary skirmish. The real struggle lies ahead. Of course the National Synod in Wittenberg next week will ratify everything the Brown Synod did."

"Surely something can be done about that?" said his mother. For her there was no such thing as an insoluble problem.

"We've written a leaflet protesting the whole thing, but I doubt it will do much good." He reached in his bag and took out a copy of the pledge that he and Niemöller had composed and handed it to her.

She read it and passed it to his father. "Good, very good. Are you and Franz going?"

"To Wittenberg? I suppose not. We aren't delegates. None of the Young Reformers was elected delegate."

"Why should that stop you? Why don't you go and take your leaflets with you?"

"We'd be intruders, you know."

"Good. Be intruders. You might nail a copy up on the door, like Luther, and on the trees and the like. Had you thought of that?"

"I'm thinking of it now," he said with a broad grin.

"Would you like to take the car?" his father asked. "I could send Fritz along to drive, if you wish."

"That would be splendid." Dietrich could hear the click of the shutter, capturing this moment of time and printing it on some hidden fold of his brain, to remember in a disheartening hour. "Thanks, Papa. Franz will go along with it, I'm sure."

"What about Elenore?" his mother suggested. "Isn't she also caught up in all of this? She might like to go."

"I hadn't thought of it but, yes, she might."

When Dietrich went up to his room he found that Lotte had already lit the lamp. A cool mountain breeze swept in from the low-arched windows, and nearby he heard the mournful call of an owl. Then all was still again; no man-made sounds, only the forest breathing its rhythmic creature medley.

He thought of Sabine and Gert in Göttingen, fifty miles or so on the other side of the mountains. Straightway there came to his mind the picture of Gert's face when he told him he could not preach the funeral. He rubbed his fingers over his eyes to wipe away the oppressive vision.

Finally he carried the lamp to the battered old desk in the corner, scrounged through the drawers for a clean sheet of paper, and began a letter to them. Once the preliminaries were over he wrote rapidly and compulsively, without a break:

> I must tell you that I've been tormented for a long time by the thought that I didn't do as you asked me last April, simply as a matter of course. To tell the truth, I can't think what made me act the way I did. How could I have been so terribly uneasy about it at the time? It must have seemed equally incomprehensible to you, and yet you said nothing. But it preys on my mind horribly now because it is the kind of thing that can never be made good. So all I can do tonight is simply beg you to forgive my weakness then. I know now for certain that I ought to have behaved differently.

When he had finished and sealed the envelope, he blew out the lamp. A lone star, unperturbed and steady, gave off its meager light over the darkened countryside. He watched it from his bed until he fell into a fast, unbroken sleep.

The castle church in Wittenberg was crowded. Dietrich, Elenore, and Franz found seats in the balcony that edged the chancel on three sides. Through the stained-glass windows behind them the afternoon sun beamed iridescent light on all the scene below. On the floor at the right stood Martin Luther's tomb of rosy marble, and against it lay a wreath of greenery. Near the tomb the pulpit steps curved upward beside a stately column. Perched in the pulpit, a news photographer aimed his humpbacked camera down at the chancel area. There swastikas flanked the altar, and above the triptych hung the new purple and white banner of the German Evangelical Church. Its rich folds incorporated on one ground the Cross of Christ and the Nazi swastika.

There was an expectant hush as the crowd awaited the entrance of the new Reichsbischof. Precisely on the hour the heralds' trumpets pierced the imprisoned air. Chords from the organ, full, exultant, and to an exact beat reverberated to the vaulted ceiling. The congregation stood as Ludwig Müller entered the sanctuary and proceeded down the center aisle. The ten bishops followed in his train, with Theodor Heckel third in line. Cameras clicked on all sides. Hossenfelder, the head of the German Christians, met Müller near the altar, bowed to him, and called out triumphantly, "I greet thee, my Reichbischof." Hossenfelder led him up the steps, where he placed the new seal of office around his neck and the staff of authority in his hand.

During the lunch break the intruders had nailed up about half of their flyers, with Dietrich nailing the first one on the door of the castle church. In the interim that followed the ceremony they were out again. It was a brisk September day. Red and yellow leaves scattered before a strong breeze. Dietrich and Elenore crossed the square with arms full of leaflets and paused at the steps of Luther's statue. The great man stood at ease beneath his elegant, airy cupola, with an open Bible in his hand. A few yards to the right was the companion statue of Melanchthon.

"I wonder what Luther's advice would be at this point," said Dietrich.

"About what?" asked Elenore.

"Whether or not to stay around and watch this rudderless ship break up on the rocks."

"You mean you've decided to go to London," she said evenly, as if stating a fact she had known a long time.

"Yes, I think so."

If there was alarm, her upturned face masked it well. Dietrich continued, "I've thought about it a long time and have come to the conclusion it's the best thing. For right now, anyway."

"How long do you think you'll stay?"

"I'd be expected to stay at least a year."

"That's a long time." She sighed inaudibly and looked away.

He hastened to add, "I'll be coming back fairly often, I expect. It will be hard to keep my finger out of this stew."

She looked at him but said nothing. Then her eyes moved past him to someone approaching, and he heard a voice at his elbow.

"I heard about these leaflets, but I didn't know you were at the bottom of it." It was Theodor Heckel. He bowed to Elenore and murmured a greeting.

"Are you surprised?" Dietrich asked, rudely shifted from one arena to another. "Perhaps you'd like to read it." He held one out to Heckel.

With reluctance Heckel took it and glanced over it. "I'm surprised you'd put your signature to something so extreme," he declared, "but then, you've always been one to exaggerate."

Dietrich looked around for Elenore, but she had moved aside and stood looking up at the monument. To Heckel he said, "Yes, and two thousand others have joined me in this exaggeration. We've formed a Pastors' Emergency League. This is our pledge."

"Pastors' Emergency—. That sounds terribly dramatic and, of course, ridiculous." Heckel handed the leaflet back to Dietrich.

"Hardly, in view of the consequences of the 'Brown' Synod."

"You need not call it that."

"That's what it is. Now we have a 'Brown' Church."

Heckel brushed this aside. "You know, you've disappointed me, Bonhoeffer. I had hoped you'd be a good representative for us in London."

"I never had any intention of representing the German Christian cause over there. You should know that. Or to give up speaking for the ecumenical movement. If that's what you want, you should prohibit my departure altogether."

"I've said nothing to that effect," Heckel protested, with a trace of alarm in his voice.

Dietrich guessed that the man did not want to make an issue of it. Maybe Heckel was afraid the congregations in London might break away from the mother church, if their new young minister were prevented from coming. When Dietrich visited them a few weeks back, he had sensed that they were independent enough to do just that.

"And if I go," Dietrich added, "I want this understanding written down for the record. I'd rather forego the post altogether than give rise to any uncertainties about my point of view—or my intentions."

"All right, all right. But in the matter of this manifesto, couldn't you simply state that you've changed your mind because of obligations within the church?"

"Surely you know I won't do that."

Heckel turned on him a skeptical glare, as if he could not imagine such foolishness. "Well, as long as there's no collaboration with foreign propaganda. You know those British journalists put the worst possible face on everything."

Dietrich made no sign of assent.

After Heckel left, Dietrich turned to Elenore. "I don't understand such people. What does he take me for, anyway?"

"He just doesn't know you very well," she said. "Well, we'd better move on if we're going to get these leaflets up." She began walking slowly across the square.

Dietrich followed her and for a time neither of them spoke. The London decision was apparently on her mind and he felt duty bound to speak again. He was aware that he was skirting around the real question. No word of marriage had passed between them since his return from America two years ago. In his mind marriage had become something to be desired at some future point, but not yet. "You understand, of course, why I have to go?" he said.

She did not answer.

He tried to be reasonable. "Right now, don't you see, there are so many uncertainties, and the picture is changing every day. One has to be free to move as the calls change. I would like to know that you understand."

"Maybe I do. I'm not sure." Elenore's glance was restive and faintly challenging. "I thought—. Always before you've wanted to be in the thick of the fight."

"The fight is over. For the time being, anyway."

"Still, I can't see you going off and sitting under a juniper tree."

"I have no intention of sitting under a juniper tree."

Elenore's eyes scanned Dietrich's face with penetrating scrutiny. "Perhaps not, but—." She seemed to want to say more, then to think better of it.

Dietrich waited for another word, a word to allay his growing dissatisfaction with himself.

Instead she held up one of the flyers and said lightly, "We have a job to do, remember? Let's get on with it. Time's running out."

With all the preparations made for Dietrich's departure, the Saturday Musical became something of a going-away party, with toasts and parting gifts. The serious talk was of Hitler's decision that day to withdraw Germany from the League of Nations, a move that the Bonhoeffers and many of their guests found dismaying. Dietrich noticed his mother's subdued mood and knew what she was thinking. This move of Hitler's—coupled with his recent ranting about equality of status among the nations, revision of the 1919 boundaries, and a call for Lebensraum, seemed to bring the danger of war closer.

As everyone was preparing to leave, Elenore met Dietrich in the foyer with her present, a small leather datebook, with Luther's head embossed on the cover. "I hope he'll give you good advice," she said with an enigmatic smile.

For Elenore, Dietrich had ordered from New York a songbook of Negro spirituals. She seemed genuinely delighted and leafing through it asked, "Which ones are your favorites?"

"I don't know. I like them all. Just pick out the ones that appeal to you, and sometimes when I'm back over here you can sing them for me."

That seemed to please her. When she gave him her hand in good-bye, the reserve was gone. "I hope this will be a good time for you, Dietrich."

They were standing a little apart from the others, beside the stair. Something more was called for, some word or promise, yet Dietrich knew instinctively that leave-taking was not a time for promises. She turned toward the door, and he saw that her parents were waiting.

"Coming," she said to them. To Dietrich she flashed a bright smile. With a crisp "Auf wiedersehen" she was gone.

8

During his time in London, Dietrich often felt torn between his duties as pastor and his deep concerns for the church in Germany. He was grateful for his two small congregations and especially for the opportunity to preach—nothing in the ministry compared in importance—and gave himself conscientiously to confirmation classes, counseling, sick calls, and administrative duties. For living quarters the church provided him with two and a half upstairs rooms in an ungainly old Victorian house, perched like a bird of passage on the brow of Manor Mount Hill.

Dietrich's mother served as an information link between him and his friends in Berlin. By telephone and post she told him of the new Reichsbischof's repressive measures: the dismissals and arrests of pastors, the forced incorporation of the Evangelical Youth into the Hitler Youth, the repeated attempts to apply the Aryan Clause in the church, and the "muzzling decree" that forbade discussion of these problems on church property.

Dietrich organized the eight other German pastors in England, and jointly they protested by telegram and letter each repressive action. Two or three times a month he made the channel-crossing or flew over for one meeting or another. He wondered why he had ever thought the English sojourn would be a time of refuge. Instead, he felt he was straddling half a continent, with one foot in London and one foot in Berlin. But it was clear that Dietrich in London and the Pastors' Emergency League in Berlin had succeeded in slowing down some of the more extreme actions of the Reichsbischof.

As Dietrich's father had suggested, the ecumenical connections in England turned out to be helpful to the cause. In his position as youth secretary Dietrich had come to know the president of the Ecumenical Council, George Bell, bishop of Chichester. Now Bell welcomed Dietrich to London and showed an immediate interest in the repressions in the German Church.

In late November Bell invited Dietrich to the bishop's palace in Chichester. On the day appointed, after an hour's train ride due south through the Sussex downs, Dietrich arrived in the quiet cathedral town. The bishop met the train in his chauffeur-driven car, and on the way to the palace they toured the church, an edifice that held its place among England's great cathedrals. The conversation moved back and forth between the beauties of the church and the latest happenings in Germany, where there had been more arrests of pastors. They came through the vaulted nave and stood outside on the walkway, looking up at the cathedral's graceful spire.

"A magnificent church," Dietrich said.

"I'm much endeared to it by now," said the bishop. "I don't think I'll ever want to leave it."

They had learned earlier that they shared the same birthday, February 4, Bell being twenty-three years Dietrich's senior. The idea of being fifty had always seemed appalling to Dietrich, yet, standing there in the warm sun, Bell did not seem so venerable. Although not a tall man, he was nevertheless trim from head to toe, with none of the usual middle-age thickening. His face still retained a boyish look, and Dietrich was struck again by the unusually bright blue of his eyes, with their direct, forthright look. The impression was one of strength and gentleness combined, of culture unmixed with any degree of hauteur.

When they came to the palace drive, Bell stopped. A young boy nine or ten years of age was leaning against the high, red-brick wall, his head down and his book satchel drooping from limp hands.

"What's this, Robbie," Bell said, as he went over to him. "Has something happened that you aren't in school? It's terribly late, you know."

"Yes, sir, I know," the boy said in a low voice. He lifted his red-rimmed eyes to the bishop. "I don't want to go."

"There must be a reason for that." Bell leaned forward and the child whispered in his ear.

After a while the boy's face brightened and he stood up straight.

"Now, do you think you can run along to school?" asked Bell.

"Yes, sir, I think so."

Bell's eyes, filled with concern, followed the boy down the street. "Poor boy," he said. "Terrible home conditions—father drinking a lot. Very sad case. The child was late for school again and was afraid. The schoolmaster is rather intolerant. I'll have to speak to him."

"You have children, my lord Bishop?" said Dietrich, as they walked on.

"No. We were never so blessed." A regretful smile flitted across his face, and behind his reserve Dietrich sensed that this was the tragedy of his life. "These schoolboys are my children," the bishop added.

The subject turned to India. For years Dietrich had dreamed of studying with Mahatma Gandhi in India. Two years earlier Gandhi had visited Bell at Chichester, and Dietrich tried to imagine the wiry little man in his native attire, walking here among these trees. He told the bishop of his dream. Bell thought it might be arranged and offered to write and inquire about the possibility, a prospect so exciting that Dietrich could only mumble his thanks. But soon he was firing one question after another and learned more of this faraway hero than he had thought possible.

At evening prayers in the palace's narrow, frescoed chapel Bell asked God's blessing on Dietrich's family in Germany and on the church there. There on his knees Dietrich felt warmed and comforted. He had often longed for a "spiritual father." In Chichester he began to sense the possibility.

The months following strengthened the bond between Dietrich and the bishop. Bell showed a willingness to speak out in the name of the churches of the world against the repressions in the German Church. He wrote letters of protest to Reichsbischof Müller and to President von Hindenburg, which also were published in *The Times* of London.

In early March a call came from Heckel ordering Dietrich to return to Berlin at once. "I'm afraid it's urgent," he said. "I must ask you to come by air."

Dietrich landed at Tempelhof that afternoon and took the underground to the Zoo Station. From there it was a short walk up the Jebenstrasse to the Church Federation offices. Heckel's office smelled of sweet pipe tobacco. An antique bronze lamp cast light on the perfectly ordered desk. Dietrich thought of the tumbled papers and open books on his own desk and wondered how much work Heckel got done.

After a perfunctory handshake Dietrich eyed his superior across the desk until the other turned away his glance, cleared his throat, and motioned to a leather chair at the side. "Please sit down." He rested his elbows on the polished wood and looked at Dietrich over intertwining fingers. "I suppose you've guessed I didn't order you here on routine business," he began.

"I didn't think so, no."

Heckel paused and cleared his throat once more. "To begin with, let me say that your activities in London have not gone unnoticed."

Dietrich returned his gaze, but said nothing.

"It appears you have fallen under foreign influence—unwittingly, perhaps." He paused as if he hoped Dietrich would deny that. "Well, unfortunately, the Reichsbischof has the idea you are using your ecumenical contacts to undermine the reputation of the German Evangelical Church."

"I hadn't noticed that it needed my help."

"Now why did you have to say that?"

Dietrich smiled.

"I suppose your contacts with the bishop of Chichester have been purely routine."

"I've seen Bishop Bell a number of times, yes, on matters having to do with the ecumenical movement—"

"And the German Church disputes?"

"It would have been unnatural, don't you think, never to have mentioned the church struggle."

"And Bell's letters to Bishop Müller and President von Hindenburg? Do you deny you had a hand in them?"

"I saw them, yes. You forget they were written to express legitimate concerns of the ecumenical movement."

"Not in the eyes of this office, as you should know by now. Please bear in mind that not only as a pastor are you responsible to us but also in your ecumenical position."

"I was elected as youth secretary by the Ecumenical Council, not the German Church."

"Ah, yes. But you were elected because you represent this church. And in view of your continued opposition, and the evidence that you've been giving false information to reporters of *The Times*—"

"I don't know what you mean." Dietrich made an effort to keep his voice cool. "The *Times* reporters have their own sources in Berlin. Altogether excellent reporters, I must say, whose information seems to be correct. Unfortunately I haven't had the pleasure of meeting any of them."

Heckel's face took on a pained expression. "I don't know why you make it so difficult for me. I'm speaking in your own interest, you know. I don't want to see anything happen to you."

"Just what do you think might happen to me?"

"If you continue abusing your freedom, you're going to be seen as working against the State. That would be a pity for a person of your youth and talents."

"Why don't you say it plainly? You're accusing me of treason."

"I'm not accusing you, but the Reichsbischof and other high officials are going to see it that way, unless you clarify your actions satisfactorily. The foreign press is presenting the view that the controversy within the church is a struggle against the State. I can't have someone from this office disseminating such propaganda."

Dietrich said nothing.

Heckel sank back in his chair. "It was a mistake to let you go in the first place."

"You knew precisely my position before I ever left. I very carefully put it in writing and just happen to have brought along—"

"Never mind. I know what you wrote."

"So if you want me out of that church you'll have to come to London and drag me out yourself."

The shock and dismay on Heckel's face were almost laughable.

Dietrich leaned back again. "There's no way you can prove any of these charges."

"We don't need proof," Heckel said with a snort. "The results are evidence enough." He looked at Dietrich as if at a loss as to what to do with him. "Let me remind you that we have the power to withdraw your passport," he said finally. Dietrich's face must have shown his consternation, for Heckel added hurriedly, "But I'm not saying we will. We simply want you to see that the good of the church is served when you remain a good soldier in the field."

Dietrich sat motionless as the cloying tone rolled over him.

"Now, as to the ecumenical conference at Fanö in August," Heckel continued, "I see you have been asked to speak."

"Yes, twice. A lecture and a sermon."

"That was Bell's doing, I suppose. Well, I don't want you going up there to Denmark spreading around all kinds of false impres-

sions about our church. It will not help if we bring down the Führer's ire upon us. Oh, I know. You do not agree with all the Nazi
ideology. Neither do I. But we need to show solidarity before all
those foreigners."

"Are they foreigners or are they Christian brothers?"

"Well, at least we should present a united front." Heckel's voice
fell into an aggrieved whine. "You might try seeing things from
my point of view."

"Oh, I do," said Dietrich, aware that his own voice was heavy
with sarcasm. The man was now answerable to the State, and its
minions were putting the screws on him.

Heckel eyed him questioningly for a time, then opened his desk
drawer and withdrew a paper. "There is, I'm glad to say, a simple
solution that will solve the matter for both of us. I hope you'll have
the good sense to cooperate. You need merely to sign this statement here," he said, as he turned the paper around and slid it toward him, "agreeing to refrain from any ecumenical activity not
authorized by this office. That's all." He smiled encouragingly, like
a father trying to persuade his child to take a dose of bad-tasting
medicine. "I don't see why we can't confer amicably on these—"

"I can't do that, of course."

Heckel's smile faded. He stood up, the paper in his hand. In the
same instant Dietrich also rose from his seat.

"At least take it with you and think it over. You can write me
your answer."

Dietrich hesitated fractionally, and Heckel quickly added,
"There's no need to make a hasty decision. You can send your answer from London."

Dietrich thought a minute, as instinct battled caution. "All
right," he replied reluctantly. "I don't see what could change my
mind, but I'll take it along." He folded the paper and put it in his
pocket.

Heckel smiled. "Good. Good. It's merely a matter of conferring
with me about these things. Surely we can work together. We always have in the past. Let me add, about Fanö. We would expect

you to make a fair selection of our youth to represent the German Church in the youth conference."

"I will naturally choose young people who look upon the youth of other countries as Christian brothers."

Heckel's face went rigid. "I suppose you intend to stand on your authority as youth secretary."

"Yes, I do."

"Well, all right. Have your little fling. But don't carry it too far." At the door he put his hand on Dietrich's arm. "Please believe me, Bonhoeffer, I'm thinking of your own good. I always have. Surely you've made your point in all this. I repeat, don't carry it too far. I'd hate to see you come to a bad end."

Feeling stifled and soiled and angry with himself, Dietrich stepped out onto the Jebenstrasse and breathed deeply of the fresh air. He wondered why he had not stuck fast to his first refusal. On the street he stopped, halfway ready to go back again. Then he walked slowly on, barely dodging a passerby. After a time he comforted himself with the thought that it would be better to have his answer written down in clear, unmistakable terms. Assured beyond doubt of his course, he lifted his head and walked faster.

From London Dietrich sent the statement back, unsigned, by the next post. As it turned out, that was his last encounter with Theodor Heckel as his superior, for in May there came news from Franz of the long hoped-for secession of the Free Confessing Synod from the Reich Church. Now it became the Confessing Church. Dietrich liked the name "Confessing" because it stressed the Confession of Faith in Jesus Christ as the one Lord, a direct rebuttal to Nazi claims of Hitler's divine mission.

Dietrich was unable to attend the synod in Barmen, where this formal declaration was made, but he took consolation in the fact that indirectly he had made a contribution to it. At Ascensiontide Bishop Bell, in his position as president of the Ecumenical Council, had sent out a pastoral letter to church leaders around the world laying out in no uncertain terms the essential grievances against the Reich Church, which were, Bell said, "without precedent in the history of the Church and were incompatible with the Christian principle." Dietrich felt sure that this show of ecumenical support gave courage to his Confessing friends as they made their decision to declare against the "false doctrine" of the "Brown Church" and cut themselves off from it.

Then, one day at the end of June, Dietrich awoke to the astonishing news that there had been some kind of massacre in Germany. The head of the SA, Ernst Röhm, the dictator's longtime crony, had been shot in cold blood, apparently on orders from Hitler. The estimate of others killed in the roundup was near seventy. News accounts in England were sketchy and contradictory, and Dietrich could learn nothing from Germany. His mother and Franz made only the most guarded references to it on the telephone. "The extent remains to be seen," his mother said.

Some time earlier Dietrich had invited Franz to come to London for his vacation, and he accepted, but they had not set a date. Now, feeling more isolated than at any time since he had come to England, and clamoring at every pore for reliable news from Germany, he called Franz and urged him to come within the month.

Two weeks later Dietrich stood at the tall window of his living room and tried to absorb all that Franz had told him. Nobody knew exactly how many had been killed, he had said, maybe as many as two hundred. As he talked Franz sat on the sofa and rested his arm on the unopened suitcase beside him.

Dietrich paced back and forth, his hands behind his back, then stopped in front of Franz. "How much of this do the people know?"

"They've heard a good deal, in various forms, rumors mostly. But Goebbels has managed to turn every fact to suit his version of the whole thing—that the Führer's bold action saved the country from bloody revolution, led by Bolshevist elements. Hitler made a semblance of a defense before the Reichstag. Those he couldn't convince he tried to frighten into submission. He said that from now on anyone who raises his hand to strike the State will 'reap certain death.' I think those were his words."

Their eyes met and held for a moment. "And our new Confessing Church? What was the reaction there?" Dietrich asked.

Franz sighed. "Not too good. There were plenty of sermons and prayers thanking the Führer for saving the nation from dire peril."

Dietrich looked out the window and over the sea of chimney pots to the Kentish landscape beyond. "'Unless you repent, you will all likewise perish.' We'll have to teach them that, won't we? We can no longer be spectators."

"I didn't expect any less than that from you, but I'm especially glad to hear it," Franz said. "I brought along a message for you, Dietrich. A rather important one, I think."

Dietrich came out of his reverie and looked at Franz.

"It's from the new Council of Brethren of the new Confessing Church," Franz said. "They want you as director of one of the seminaries we're setting up. Small schools, you know, four or five scattered around the country, the course to run five months or so."

The possibilities of such a venture quickened Dietrich's interest immediately. To be able to teach young pastors in a close-knit community setting, where practical expression of his thinking on discipleship and the Sermon on the Mount was a real possibility. But, of course he needed time, lots of time to think about it. Besides, with Bishop Bell's help he had just received an invitation from Mahatma Gandhi to join his ashram in India sometime in the next few months. "When do they expect to begin?" Dietrich asked.

"It depends. The first of the year, maybe. All the arrangements have to be made, locations found, and all that."

"The truth is, I have other plans."

"Not plans that can't be changed, I hope." Franz's eyes widened in surprise. "You're the man for this, Dietrich, I'm sure of it."

They stood silently facing each other, then Franz took a turn around the room, stopping again behind the sofa. With a familiar tone of dogged reasonableness he began again. "I suppose there are plenty of objections you could raise, like not wanting to give up your pastorate. But then, in such a small seminary you'd have to be almost everything to your ordinands, including pastor."

Dietrich listened without comment.

"But maybe it's still important to you to stay in London, near the ecumenical people."

"I was thinking about my India plans." He told him of Gandhi's invitation.

"Oh, I didn't know. I thought it was just an idea—a dream. You're always making plans of some kind."

"No. It's definite."

Franz turned and faced him squarely. "And you think that should take precedence over something as vital as this?"

"I didn't say that, but it's very important to me. I want to learn Gandhi's methods of solving conflict without violence. It is something I've wanted for ages, and now, all of a sudden, it's there."

"I had no idea it had gone so far." Franz sat down again on the sofa, his head in his hands. Presently he looked up. "Dietrich, don't make a mistake about this. Don't do something you'd regret the rest of your life. This seminary is crucial, isn't it? What else have we been agonizing over all these months? Here's where the future of the Confessing Church lies."

"I'll have to think about it."

As they walked back home after lunch Franz said to Dietrich, "About the seminary—they weren't entirely unanimous, you know."

"Who wasn't?"

"The new Council of Brethren of the Confessing Church. When they discussed you for the position."

"Oh? One could hardly expect complete approval, I suppose." Dietrich said more lightly than he felt. "What was the objection?"

"Not sufficiently discreet," Franz said with a glimmer in his eye.

"Huh!" A trifle stung, Dietrich changed the subject to the upcoming Ecumenical Conference at Fanö, Denmark. Franz had told him earlier that neither Koch nor Niemöller was coming to the meeting. "You realize, don't you, that if they aren't coming, I'll be the only one there to stand in the breach. Frankly, I think that's a mistake."

"Maybe so."

"They should be there," Dietrich said. "Heckel will sweep in with full force, flanked by all sorts of big guns."

"Dietrich, it's not timidity. In the wake of all that's happened since the Röhm massacre, and with the new high treason law, they felt it was just too risky. You know—to speak out against the Reich Church in the full glare of the international press. They don't want to give Hitler any excuse to outlaw our Confessing Church in its infancy. You'll have to be cautious, too."

"I will." Dietrich turned the change in his pocket over and over. "Not discreet enough, eh?" he said presently. "That's what they said?"

"Something like that."

"I must say I resent that. I'm always discreet."

The next day Franz returned to Germany. As they waited for the train at Victoria Station, he asked, "What does Elenore think of this India scheme?"

A little taken aback, Dietrich said, "To tell the truth, I haven't told her very much about it."

Franz looked over at him. "What's happened, Dietrich? There was a time when you talked everything over with her."

"Now I'm in London. Remember?" Dietrich leaned back on the bench. "Since it's Monday, the boat at Harwich probably won't be too crowded."

"That's good," said Franz absently. "I wouldn't like to see her hurt, Dietrich."

"I have no intention of hurting her. You should know that."

"I don't think you do. But sometimes intentions are not enough."

Dietrich was annoyed but said nothing.

"But then, if you take the seminary—"

"I haven't decided yet." He did not miss the implication.

"Well, I hope you can decide soon. Koch would like an answer."

The train pulled in, and Dietrich went aboard with Franz and saw him to his seat. Outside again, he waved good-bye as the train backed out.

9

At the first plenary session of the Ecumenical Conference on the island of Fanö, Dietrich sat with his students at one of the long tables. The large airy hall, used normally as the hotel dining room, had a wall of windows facing the sea. Theodor Heckel was at the podium speaking.

"The Third Reich represents the corporate will of the people. People and State constitute one single thing in Germany," Heckel asserted, an almost exact repetition of what he had already said two or three times in the last hour. "Rather than absolutism, as some imply, the State intends to sustain the divine order. Under the Third Reich the church has the unique responsibility and the proud duty to proclaim the message of positive Christianity."

Earlier one delegate after another had stood in his place and questioned Heckel in what had begun to sound like "The Case Against the State Church of Germany." It was plain that they viewed recent happenings there in the light of the letter Bishop Bell had sent out at Ascensiontide.

When his speech ended, Heckel asked that no other Germans be allowed to attend the meetings except the official delegation. Some of Dietrich's German friends from London had joined him there as visitors. Obviously Heckel's request was aimed at them.

Bishop Bell took his place at the podium and answered, "In view of the—of the unprecedented nature of the request and because it is, in the judgment of the chair, contrary to the ecumenical spirit, it must be denied."

Bell's flushed faced and slight stammer, which Dietrich had noticed sometimes before, revealed the degree of his disapproval. He was thankful that in this year 1934, the English bishop was president of the Ecumenical Council. He remembered what Bell had said months before when he wrote the letters to Müller and Hindenburg: "Not only is our neighbor's wall ablaze, but, in a more subtle and not less dangerous way, our own wall is ablaze, too."

Now, where it counted most, before the whole world, Bell was fighting the fire.

After the meeting Bell stopped Dietrich in the hall. "So many of the delegates want to hear what you have to tell that we need to arrange for them to see you privately. Perhaps in your room, if that's agreeable."

"Certainly."

"Could we start tonight?"

"That's fine with me."

The weary countenance broadened into a smile. "Good. Leiper and Homrighausen from America are already waiting for my call. The Czechs would also like to see you tonight, and Karlstrom from Sweden. We'll need their support to get the kind of resolution we want."

"Yes," said Dietrich, smiling. "I'll do what I can."

Not a night that week was Dietrich in bed before two. The delegates came one after another with their questions about what was happening inside Germany. In these private meetings Dietrich held back nothing. And they listened eagerly.

On the last day came Dietrich's sermon at the opening worship service. The service began with the "Gloria Patri" sung in unison. One song, one Lord. Every hymn in the hymnal, issued for the first Stockholm Conference in 1925, was printed in three languages. Following the singing, the Lord's Prayer was spoken by each in his native tongue. Dietrich walked to the plain maple pulpit at the side of the platform. For a brief moment before he spoke he surveyed the group, the most prestigious he had ever addressed. Some of the members of the youth delegation were sitting in the windows. That surprised him. None of the other morning services had been crowded.

The sermon was in English. He had chosen Psalm 85:6 as his text. "I will hear what God the Lord will speak: for he will speak peace unto his people, and to his saints."

As Dietrich spoke, all apprehension left him. "There shall be peace because of the Church of Jesus Christ, which lives at one and the same time in all peoples, yet beyond all boundaries, whether national, political, social, or racial. These brothers in Christ cannot take up arms against Christ himself—yet this is what they do if they take up arms against one another. Even in anguish and distress of conscience there is for them no escape from the commandment of Christ that there shall be peace.

"How does peace come about? Through a system of political treaties? Through the investment of international capital in different countries? Through the big banks, through money? Through universal, peaceful rearmament in order to guarantee peace?

"Through none of these, for the single reason that in all of them peace is confused with safety. There is no way to peace along the way of safety. For peace must be dared. It is the great venture. It can never be made safe. Peace is the opposite of security. To demand guarantees is to mistrust, and this mistrust in turn brings forth war. Battles are won, not with weapons, but with God. They are won where the way leads to the cross. Which of us can say he knows what it might mean for the world if one nation should meet the aggressor, not with weapons in hand, but praying defenseless, and for that very reason protected by a bulwark never failing. Who will call us to peace so that the world will hear, will have to hear; so that all peoples may rejoice because the Church of Christ in the name of Christ has taken the weapons from the hands of their sons, forbidden war, and proclaimed the peace of Christ against the raging world?

The hour is late. The world is choked with weapons, and dreadful is the distrust that looks out of all men's eyes. The trumpets of war may blow tomorrow. What are we waiting for? Do we want to become involved in this guilt as never before? No, we want to give the world a whole word, not a half word—a courageous word, a Christian word. We pray that this word may be given us today. Who knows if we shall see each other again another year."

That afternoon in the plenary session the resolution that Dietrich had worked for all week long passed overwhelmingly. It was clear and uncompromising in its reproach of the repressive measures of the German State Church and in its support of the Confessing Church. It amounted to censure of the Nazi regime, in spite of Heckel's cajoling and suave assurances.

With the last session ended, Dietrich made his way to the hotel where he was to meet his students for the swim meet he had been promising them. He was early and sank gratefully into a comfortable chair on the mezzanine. As he half dozed his thoughts ranged back over the events of the week and his part in it all. Yes, the sermon had gone well. The whole week had gone well. Dietrich was too tired to suppress the feelings of satisfaction that welled up as drowsiness overtook him.

The voices of his students in the hall dragged him awake. There was laughter. Then another voice. A smiling voice, unmistakably Heckel's.

"So, you're swimming this afternoon? You feel you must wash away your sins, after your resolution against the church?"

They came into view around the palm beside Dietrich's chair. Dietrich stood up and Heckel caught sight of him.

"Ah, Bonhoeffer, so it's you, lying in wait," he said in a tone at once jocular and supercilious.

"Quite so," said Dietrich, coldly.

"Well now, you shouldn't be angry, with the day you've had."

The turn of the encounter clearly shocked Dietrich's students and they sidled away, down the steps into the lobby, where they waited near the door.

Heckel went on speaking. "With Bell on your side you got what you wanted from the council, and now you have all these young people bowing down at your feet. I should think you would be highly gratified, while I, I've had Berlin breathing down my neck. I'm the one who should be upset but you see I am not." He smiled and with a turn of his perfectly manicured fingers continued, "I don't even begrudge the acclaim for your sermon this morning, though, of course—but never mind—. Now, don't you think we should shake hands like honorable opponents after a hard-fought game?"

"Let's not pretend this is a game, if you please."

An angry cloud mottled the bishop's face. "You've made no effort to understand what I'm trying to do, or how difficult—"

"Of course. You're attempting to serve two masters and you have run into problems. Did you not expect that?"

"Holding the church together means nothing to you!"

Serving the Lord of the church means everything to me, Dietrich thought. But the words froze on his lips. They were not for the ears of this man.

Heckel looked at him as if he expected a rebuttal, but Dietrich merely returned his stare. With a bow and a curt nod, Dietrich moved past him and down the steps. He was still trembling when he joined the group at the door.

The wind had risen when Dietrich emerged from his hotel late that night. High on his left, tenuous clouds skimmed across the moon, but as he turned the corner of the building and faced the sea, he saw a storm brewing on the western horizon. He decided, nonetheless, to risk the rain; sleep was out of the question.

As he walked he kept hearing the seductive voices: "You have to realize that a great deal of the credit is due this young man." "The kind of courage we all need." "Yes, you shook us up all right." "It was magnificent. You dared to throw down the gauntlet." That last had come from the young Swedish student who had joined them for the swim meet. As they relaxed in the sand, he had said, "You quite simply threw the gauntlet at our feet and dared us to pick it up." He had gone on to say, "If I may ask, Sir—you hinted strongly in your sermon that you believe Hitler is headed for war. If war does come, then what will you do?"

Dietrich had been silent for a time. He had known it was the inescapable question. As he let the white sand sift through his fingers, he had quietly replied, "I pray God would give me the strength not to take up arms."

A little later, when he told the students of the possiblility of his heading a Confessing Church seminary, they all had become suddenly wide awake. How eager they had been. Ready to line up for it immediately.

Heckel's words intruded sharply into Dietrich's thoughts—"All these young people bowing down at your feet."

"Despicable!" Dietrich cried aloud and stumbled over the rocks at the edge of an inlet. The sound of the word died away and left a cold, echoless silence. Without thinking, he turned and followed the stream inland. As he walked a familiar vision from his childhood suddenly reared itself up before him as if it had happened that day. He saw himself a boy of sixteen in his Greek class. *The schoolmaster asks what he wants to study. Breathlessly, he answers, "Theology." His head swims as he finds himself the center of attention. He is intoxicated with a dream of himself: tall and blond and solemnly robed on the soaring pulpit high above the people, herald of his knowledge and his ideals. But in the silence he notices the looks from his fellow students— bored, curious, mistrustful, silently mocking. The stillness of the room is leaden. The overhead light, suspended from the ceiling just before him, is too big for its sickly green shade. How he hates it and wants it turned off.*

Dietrich shook off the vision and stopped, looking right and left, neither knowing nor caring where he was. A bitter anger engulfed him. He felt that all his powers had forsaken him—the powers of body and mind and will, of which he thought he was master, had oozed away silently like water from a broken cistern.

A salty gust from the sea whipped keenly about him. He buttoned the top button of his sweater. Heaviness weighed down his legs, yet he trudged on, his hands in his pockets, his eyes on the road ahead. Presently there floated on his memory the words "My grace is sufficient for you; for my power is made perfect in weakness." He listened and spoke the words softly.

Up ahead a small light swam before his eyes. Then another. Soon he could make out the dim form of a village, its church steeple faintly etched against the scudding clouds. It must be Sonderby, at the south end of the island. He had not realized he had come so far.

Past a few outlying cottages Dietrich came to the little church. He found a gate in the surrounding wall and opened it. The churchyard inside was quiet, protected by the wall from the wind and the roaring of the sea. He walked slowly among the graves.

Briefly the moon broke free from the clouds and shed its pallid light on a gravestone beside him. On the marble block a carved dove poised motionless with upspread wings. Dietrich touched the dove with his hand. It was cold. On a low wall opposite the stone he sat down to rest. Slowly a measure of tranquility stole over him.

Presently he rose, followed the walkway around to the side of the church and paused in the shadow of the vestry door. It was a simple entrance, adorned only with a plain iron cross at the peak of the arch. His plans for India intruded sharply into his thoughts. He was more convinced than ever of the greatness of Gandhi and of the value of what he could learn from him. Now, with the realization of this dream within his grasp, there came the seminary.

Dietrich wondered how he could handle a situation in which inevitably he must be set up as an example for twenty or more young pastors-to-be. But he knew he was a good teacher and that he had insights these young men needed.

He felt a drop of rain and looked up. The heavy clouds had moved directly overhead. He stepped away from the arch and turned again to face it. The iron cross stood upright in the dim light, constant and immovable in the gathering storm.

It was four miles back to the hotels. He stuck to the road, for the tide was in. In the distance came the sound of fierce waves lashing the dunes. The rain, light at first, grew heavier. Soon he was drenched. It did not matter. As he walked Dietrich began to see more clearly the way ahead for him. By the time he reached his hotel the fetters had fallen away, and he knew he would take the post at the seminary. The risks of that course, which this night had shown him with such clarity, he would have to entrust to the care of God.

Part II
A Voice for the Voiceless

10

The rickety old bus swerved in the sand as it turned a curve and lumbered up over a rise. Then suddenly the clustered buildings of the Zingst Conference Center spread out before them; and beyond, over the rolling dunes, were the serene waters of the Baltic. Eberhard cheered with the others that the long journey from Berlin was ended. The seminary had opened three days earlier, on April 26. They were late because of a mix-up in the Brethren Council. When Eberhard had left the Reich Church seminary in Wittenberg the previous October, he never imagined it would be almost the middle of 1935 before he was settled in a new Confessing Church school.

The bus turned into a narrow drive that led to the main building and came to a jarring halt. The four men piled out and unloaded their luggage, an odd assortment of suitcases and boxes tied with rope.

As the bus backed away, the candidates for ordination looked around them. The place seemed deserted. Two plank steps led up to a double door at the front of the timber-framed building. Above it, set in the steeply sloping roof, a dormer looked out on the sea. With some uncertainty Eberhard lifted his heavy luggage and climbed the steps. His cousin, Gerhard Vibrans, and the other two followed. A dour-faced matron of middle age met them at the door.

"You must be the ordinands from Saxony," she said without a smile.

"Yes, we are," Gerhard answered heartily.

At least they were expected.

The woman looked them up and down without enthusiasm. "You might as well come in," she said with a tolerant sigh. A tall, angular woman, with faded blond hair pulled tightly into a bun at the back of her neck, she pulled the door wider and stood against it. "You'll just have to leave your luggage here in the hall," she said. "I don't know where he's going to put you."

Without a word they deposited their bags along the wall.

"I hope you've had your supper," she added. "The dining room's closed for the day."

"Well—" Gerhard began.

"Oh yes, thank you," said Eberhard quickly, without looking at his cousin. He glanced at Beckmann and Dell, whose faces had become rather long. There was an awkward silence.

"They're all down by the beach," the woman said. "I suppose Herr Dr. Bonhoeffer will want to know you're here." She pointed toward the left. "The path is there, through the dunes."

"Yes. Thank you. Thank you very much," said Eberhard, feeling less cheery than he sounded. The others mumbled their thanks and followed him down the steps.

They walked in single file among the scrubby pines that dotted the dunes. As they neared the water there came sounds of laughter and shouting from the left. The path widened, and when they stepped out onto the beach they found a lively game of dodge ball in progress.

For a while Eberhard and his companions watched, unnoticed by the seminarians. But after a time one of the ordinands walked over to them. "You're our new men from Saxony, no? Albrecht Schönherr, here." He smiled with easy assurance and gave each hand a confident shake as they told their names. "We've been expecting you all afternoon. Welcome to Zingst. The game is almost over. I think—"

Schönherr led them closer and they sat down in the sand a little behind the others. Beyond the players the waters of the Baltic glistened red in the setting sun. When the game ended, the "dead" men rose from the sand, laughing and joking as they brushed themselves off. A tall blond retrieved his rimless glasses from a fellow teammate and turned toward them.

"Ah, our Saxons have arrived," he said warmly as he approached.

Schönherr introduced them. "Our director, Herr Dr. Bonhoeffer."

"'Bruder' Bonhoeffer," the director corrected him, with a smile. He shook each hand; Dell and Beckmann, then Gerhard. Last he turned to Eberhard. It was a strong, vibrant handshake, and the lively blue eyes were alight with welcome.

"Eberhard Bethge," Eberhard said, and returned the friendly pressure of the hand.

"Eberhard Bethge," Bonhoeffer repeated. "Bruder Bethge, good to have you with us."

"Bruder" seemed strange, although Eberhard knew that the old-fashioned appellation was taking on new meaning within the Confessing Church. On the playing field he had taken Bonhoeffer for one of the ordinands and now, at close range, he was even more surprised that one so youthful could be the director of the seminary. Bonhoeffer was well over six feet tall, Eberhard judged, and solidly built, with a strong, muscular neck and thinning blond hair.

The director introduced them to each of the other twenty or so ordinands and to his assistant, the inspector of studies, Bruder Willi Rott. "Now we can begin our work in earnest—and our play," he added laughing. "There must be a balance, you know."

To that Eberhard was glad to agree.

"And how was your journey?" Bonhoeffer inquired. "You must be hungry after that long train ride."

"Well, we ate something on the train—" Eberhard began and stopped, aware of Gerhard's distress signals.

"Oh, but that must have been ages ago! You couldn't have had anything on that little local train from Stralsund. We can't let you go hungry your first night at Zingst. That's unthinkable. I'm sure Frau Struwe can scare up something in a hurry." A trace of skepticism must have crossed Eberhard's face, because Bonhoeffer looked at him sharply and added, "Ah, you've met her already. Hmm. She's a trifle unbending, I'm afraid. As our housekeeper she has her hands full." Bonhoeffer's eyes lit up with laughter. "Come along, we'll get you something to eat."

When they reached the house Bonhoeffer took the four of them upstairs to his room, where he gave each one a mimeographed copy of the daily schedule. The room had a minimum of furniture and some boxes stacked in one corner. Only a shelf of books and a tapestry of Christ over the rough-hewn desk relieved its severity— that, and the view of the Baltic from the dormer window.

Bonhoeffer went over the schedule with them, beginning with the suggested half-hour's silence upon arising. "The first word of the morning belongs to God," he said.

Eberhard glimpsed a questioning look in Gerhard's eyes, but immediately turned his attention back to Bonhoeffer, who showed them a text of Scripture he had penciled in at the bottom of the page.

"This is for the meditation period following breakfast," Bonhoeffer explained. "These verses were agreed upon the first day by all the ordinands, and the same text is to be used each day of the week." He said nothing about how they were to go about meditating, but his smile conveyed assurance of their willingness and ability to do this.

Eberhard had no such assurance and wondered what they were getting into.

Then Bonhoeffer said in a matter-of-fact tone, "Now, Bruder Maechler will show you to your quarters."

Winfried Maechler, a wiry young man with a sunburned look, led the way to the cabins. These were two-story buildings, thatched with marsh grasses, not only the overhanging roof, but the sides as well. The entourage struggled with the luggage up shaky steps to a covered deck, supported on spindly legs.

"Welcome to your castle," said Maechler, as he opened the plank door and moved inside with Eberhard's heavy suitcase. "Not quite the comforts of Wittenberg, but maybe it'll do for a while."

Eberhard and Gerhard were to share the room with Fritz Onnasch, Maechler himself, and Ernst Thom, a pudgy fellow, who struggled over the threshold with Gerhard's largest bag. Walking with a limp, Onnasch came last with one of Eberhard's boxes. Maechler had lodged the other two men in the cabin next door. The large, open-beamed room was spartan indeed, with youth-hostel bunks under the slanting roof, a couple of benches along the wall, and packing cases for seats and tables.

"Bonhoeffer was right when he said you'd find it different here. I hope not too different," said Maechler with a twinkle in his eyes, as he deposited Eberhard's luggage beside the bunks and stood up again.

"It won't bother us," Eberhard said, "we're not used to finery."

"I meant the ordering of the day. It's rather strict."

"I'll say," said Ernst Thom. "You'll think you're in a monastery instead of a Lutheran seminary. He'll probably realize before long that we aren't interested in this monkish stuff and drop it."

"I wouldn't count on it," said Maechler.

Eberhard was puzzled. "He didn't seem that kind of fellow."

"What kind?"

"Pious, or so."

"Oh, he's not the pious sort. Not at all."

"Some of us studied with him at the University of Berlin. We were s—s—sort of in his inner circle, I guess you'd say," said Maechler. "You won't find him easy. I hope you like to dig."

"Not especially," said Eberhard, and laughed.

In the dining room Eberhard and his friends finished the simple meal as other seminarians began to assemble around the large U-shaped table. Bonhoeffer entered and took his place at the head of the table. Frau Struwe, who until then had not put in an appearance, followed him and sat on his right. She did not look once in the direction of the Saxonians.

Bonhoeffer stood up, and the murmur of conversation gradually subsided. "Now that we are all here," he said, "all twenty-six of us, we are very happy to welcome our four Saxonians to the common table."

There was a round of applause.

"Let me say, this table is the most important piece of furniture in the house. We eat here, we hold classes here, and we worship here. So we hope you will soon feel very much at home around it and quickly become a vital part of our brotherhood." With that he sat down.

The service began. Three of the ordinands read from the Psalms, the Old Testament, and the Gospels—long readings, they seemed to Eberhard, who caught himself more than once drifting into a doze. The hymns were sung in unison. There was no musical instrument, but one of the students gave the pitch and led the group. As the service progressed Eberhard detected varying degrees of tolerance on the faces of the ordinands, from mild interest to resigned acceptance of this unusual practice. Only a few seemed heartily responsive to the serious intent of the service.

The serious intent was clear with Bonhoeffer. He listened and participated with close attention, and near the end he led a communal prayer. The firm timbre of his voice, with its tinge of huskiness, carried no trace of unctuous piety. It was a simple prayer of thanks and of intercession for each of them and their life together as brothers. He prayed by name for the leaders of the Confessing Church and especially for the three pastors who had been interned in the Dachau concentration camp a few weeks earlier. He prayed for their enemies. And with unfeigned simplicity he confessed the sins most common to theologians and pastors, pride and self-righteousness in particular, and asked forgiveness for these. Eberhard felt the deep sincerity of the man; but the prayer was becoming long and he was glad when it ended.

After they were dismissed Eberhard walked with the others through the cool, clear night back toward their cabin.

"Well, what did you think of that?" Ernst Thom asked. "Remember now, it's not once, but twice a day—morning and night."

"Yes, so I understand," Eberhard said.

"Don't you think it's a bit much?"

"Perhaps. It's too soon to say, really. A bit long, maybe."

"A bit? Humph!"

Eberhard laughed. At this point he was inclined to agree. But then, he would wait and see what tomorrow would bring.

11

Eberhard struggled with the half-hour meditation after break-fast. He sat on his bunk and leaned against the wall, reading the verses over two or three times, trying diligently to hold his mind to what was written there. Through the window across the room the bright sun strode across the dunes. With an effort he dragged his eyes back to the text and tried to dwell on it one sentence at a time.

But by the time the three hours of classes ended Eberhard knew he was into something new and fresh. In his lecture on "Disciple-ship" Bonhoeffer introduced the twin stories of Jesus' call to Levi, the tax-collector, and to Simon Peter, to leave their posts, their means of livelihood, and become his disciples. He concluded with the surprising statement, "It was necessary for Peter and Levi to plunge into absolute insecurity in order to learn to believe," and added, "Only he who believes is obedient, and only he who is obedient believes. It is quite unbiblical to hold the first proposition without the second."

In the end Bonhoeffer attacked the Protestant practice of "pour-ing forth unending streams of grace, when the call to follow Jesus in true obedience is hardly ever heard. What happened to all those warnings of Luther's against preaching the gospel in such a manner as to make men rest secure in their ungodly living? Luther knew this was an offer of cheap grace. It could only leave men bewil-dered and deceived, mercilessly extinguishing the smoking wick."

"You think Luther would say now the opposite of what he said then?" asked Maechler.

Eberhard was surprised at his daring.

Bonhoeffer smiled. "Perhaps. But if he did he would still be say-ing the same, vital thing. At one time faith for him meant leaving the cloister. It might come to mean reopening the cloister; it might even mean taking a stand against the State, which, as you know, is taboo for the Lutheran Church."

No one said anything. This was a startling idea, one which Eberhard had not considered before.

Bonhoeffer continued, "Like, for instance, taking a stand for all the Jews, not just our baptized Jewish brothers. One thing for sure, it is a living faith he is talking about and a living Word of God and living obedience. He would not try to pin these down and flatten them into rigidity, like butterflies under glass."

In the afternoon there was an hour of track on the beach, in which everyone participated, including Bonhoeffer. Eberhard was in his element and was pleased that he reached the finals in each contest.

"A proper end to this workout would be a dip in the Baltic," said Bonhoeffer, "if anyone has the fortitude to join me!" He proceeded to unbutton his shirt.

By this time Eberhard was halfway to the water and did not notice that none of the others were joining them. He dove into the icy waves. When he resurfaced with involuntary shouts and gasps, he looked around for Bonhoeffer. The director was already swimming calmly out to sea.

"Come on," Bonhoeffer yelled. "You have to keep moving."

Eberhard caught up and they swam briskly side by side out about a hundred meters, then circled several times. "They mustn't think we're in a hurry to get out," Bonhoeffer said.

"Certainly not," Eberhard answered.

Presently, as if by silent consent, they swam in and arrived together on the beach, to the accompaniment of envious applause by the other ordinands. Once again dry and dressed, Eberhard and Bonhoeffer walked side by side back to the house. Schönherr and the other Berliners followed with the rest of the ordinands, a circumstance of which Eberhard was marginally, if not a little triumphantly, aware.

On the first of May a late blizzard swept in over the sea from Finland and blanketed the dunes with snow. In the evening Eberhard joined the seminarians in the common room to hear a radio address by Hitler, which had been touted in the newspapers as "major and concerning the glorious future of Germany."

In the speech Hitler formally announced a policy he had already initiated six weeks earlier. He proclaimed Germany's resurgence as a military power and decreed nationwide conscription to build the ranks of the armed services. In addition he announced openly the establishment of a German Air Force, which Göring had been secretly forming since 1933 under the guise of civil aviation. The faces of the other students reflected excitement and elation, that at last the shackles of the Treaty of Versailles were broken. Eberhard too could not restrain feelings of national pride.

"Watch Bonhoeffer," Maechler whispered beside him.

The director sat motionless, his eyes fixed on the floor in front of him, as Hitler's hoarse, impassioned voice cried, "Now by this bold and fearless move, Germany pulls out by the roots the ignominy of Versailles." The crowd at Tempelhof roared its approval.

At the end of the speech the ordinands erupted with excited questions.

"How soon could we be called, do you suppose?"

"I'd say it's best not to wait to be drafted."

"Right! Most of us could get commissions, I bet, if we volunteer."

"How do you think you'd look in uniform, Eberhard," Beckmann asked.

Eberhard looked at him but only laughed.

Bonhoeffer was saying nothing. The Berlin students also were quiet. Gradually the enthusiastic clamorings subsided into an uncertain hush.

"Have you ever thought that for a Christian there is the possibility of conscientious objection?" Bonhoeffer asked quietly.

The ordinands eyed one another as if they were not quite sure they had heard correctly. Eberhard was shocked. Maechler threw him a sly look from under his eyebrows that said, "I told you."

"You can't be serious, Herr Doktor," Ernst Thom protested vigorously.

"I am serious."

"But you have to admit that in this one stroke the nation's honor has been restored."

"It depends on what you call honor."

"It means holding up our head among the nations and refusing to submit to such an unfair treaty. Besides, pacifism is really shirking one's duty."

There was a murmur of assent around the circle.

"You think that is the extent of Hitler's aim, Bruder Thom, refuting the Versailles Treaty?" Bonhoeffer queried mildly. "I would like to believe that."

He got up and put another log on the smoldering fire, then, turning his back to the newly crackling blaze, faced them all. "Has it occurred to you that it requires more courage to be a conscientious objector and bear the consequences, than to submit passively to military service?"

The director went on. "Couldn't you agree that one could simply take the Sermon on the Mount seriously? That it could be an option for a Christian to do as Jesus said?" He received only blank stares. "Why don't you read it again carefully and think about it. Read it with a willingness to take Jesus at his word."

As the ordinands made their way toward the door and their various quarters, they lapsed into a more reflective mood. In the foyer Eberhard heard his name called. It was Bonhoeffer.

"You forgot your sweater, Bruder Bethge."

"Thanks. I would have remembered it as soon as I stepped outside."

"Yes, it's terribly cold, I'm afraid. Will you freeze in that cabin?"

"No, I'll be fine. I'm used to sleeping in unheated rooms. In Kade there's no such thing as central heat."

"You've lived there very long?"

"Most of my life. My father was the village pastor." Eberhard did not want to detain him, but the genuine interest in Bonhoeffer's eyes encouraged him to go on. "He died when I was a boy—fourteen."

"He must have been a fine man for you to want to follow in his footsteps." He inquired about Eberhard's mother and drew from him an account of her struggle for the children's education.

"It wasn't too bad," said Eberhard. "We worked hard, but I don't think that hurt us!"

Bonhoeffer smiled and said good-night at the door.

The chill of the night went unnoticed as Eberhard walked thoughtfully back to his cabin. The more he knew of his teacher the more he wanted to know. Every day brought surprises. But that this aristocratic and learned man showed a sincere liking for him was the biggest surprise of all.

Twice since the opening of the seminary Präses Koch had sent Dietrich on missions for the Confessing Church. This time Dietrich had gone to Paris to brief Bishop Bell and other ecumenical leaders and to seek their help in fending off the growing Nazi persecution of the church. As was always the case, Dietrich left Bell with gratitude for his concern and willingness to help.

When he stopped overnight in Berlin, he found a different set of problems. Rüdiger Schleicher, married to Dietrich's eldest sister, Ursel, was suddenly faced with the choice of either joining the Nazi Party or giving up his position as a jurist in the Air Ministry. Göring had ordered it specifically, so there was no way out.

Dietrich, Rüdiger, and Christel had gathered in the dining room, where Ursel had offered to count the laundry for their mother. Dietrich rarely saw Ursel idle. In her mid-thirties and the mother of four, she was still one of the most beautiful women Dietrich knew—tall and slender, with dark eyes, smooth skin, and thick brown hair, which she wore in braids wound over her ears. All but Rüdiger sat around the table; he paced back and forth before the double window, his almost completely bald head gleaming. His limp from a wound received in the Great War seemed more pronounced than ever. He had told Dietrich some time back that he would not have another operation; that piece of shrapnel would just have to stay there.

"I don't want to join the Party, no matter what the reason," said Rüdiger.

"Then don't," said Dietrich.

"Klaus and Hans are insisting. We argued half the night last night."

"And I got a headache," said Ursel.

"I don't know why they're insisting," said Dietrich, "it's your life."

"That's what I told them," said Ursel, without a skip in her laundry count.

Anxiety clouded Rüdiger's normally cheerful face. "They say it could be a crucial source of information someday, 'when the beams start cracking.'"

It was already a good source, Dietrich thought, the best the family had for inside information.

Rüdiger continued, "I'm no good at deception—if it came to that—if I tried to make up something in some situation, nobody would believe me—so I don't know how much help I'd be. But I want to do the right thing and if I'm really needed—"

"Don't do it if you don't want to," said Dietrich. "They shouldn't insist on such a thing." The very idea offended him.

"I have to disagree," said Christel, who had kept quiet until then. "They're right because it's so important—or could be anyway. Besides, it's just his name in a book. Nobody has to know it. He doesn't have to wear an armband or anything."

"It's the principle—" said Dietrich.

"What principle? Is some abstract principle more important than ridding the country of this evil regime?"

Dietrich looked at the others and back to Christel. "Nobody argues with that, but how could it involve us?"

"It could. Someday."

Dietrich said no more against it, and Rüdiger left soon afterward to go to the Party membership office. He took his eleven-year-old son, Hans-Walter, with him and walked to the carline. Despite his lameness, he never used a car from the Air Ministry, even for such semiofficial business.

Sabine had come up from Göttingen with the children to meet Dietrich in Berlin. Later that afternoon as he and his three sisters talked in the garden, Sabine told them that Gert had decided not to go to England, at least, not any time soon. He didn't want to rush into it.

"Does he think things are going to get any better?" Christel asked. "You'd better go while you can. Concentration camps are for real."

"I know that, Christel. You don't have to tell me." Lines of doubt and anxiety marked her usually smooth features, and she sighed deeply. "But even to contemplate leaving Germany—"

"Well, you'd better contemplate it, whether you want to or not."

For a time no one said anything, then Christel asked Dietrich about the seminary. "Mama says you're going to look at another location."

"That's right. Near Stettin. We have to vacate the conference center by the middle of June."

"Is Elenore going this time?"

"No." There was silence. He became aware that they were all looking at him. "Why?"

"Nothing, I just assumed you'd be taking her," Christel said.

"Why should you assume that?"

"Oh, Dietrich, don't be so dense! Of course we assumed it, since you took her before."

He supposed she meant in March, when Elenore had joined the delegation to look at possible seminary locations in the Mark Brandenburg.

Christel's eyes lit up teasingly. "What we really want to know is when we can start looking forward to the betrothal party."

With expectant eyes Ursel and Sabine surveyed him.

"I think you have jumped to conclusions," he answered coolly.

"I don't know what other conclusion you would expect," Christel continued. "Why else would you take her if not to have her appraisal of the place she'd be living?"

He opened his mouth to speak, but closed it again when he realized he had no adequate answer. He scrambled to his feet. "You really don't know what you're talking about. Not at all. Please excuse me." With a stiff bow he turned and without looking back made straight for the house.

Dietrich walked slowly upstairs and down the long hall to his room. With a groan he threw himself into his armchair and stared before him, his chin resting on his hand. *He sees Elenore's half-averted glance as they inspect an apartment in one of the large houses. The agent says, "Ideal for the seminary director, don't you think, with the view of the grounds on three sides."*

Dietrich tells the man it is too large for one person.

Later he and Elenore are left alone for a time in the train compartment, and Elenore says in an oddly constrained voice, "You seem to have the plans for your seminary pretty well laid out."

"I hope so. But I don't know. Sometimes I have misgivings." Then he tells her something of the tormenting doubts he had had that night on the beach at Fanö. She listens with a look of puzzled surprise. When he tells her it was not the first time for such a tussle with demons, she asks him if he has talked with his father about it.

"No. Oh, no. I wouldn't trouble him with anything so stupid."

"It isn't stupid, Dietrich. Your father wouldn't think it stupid."

Not another word is said about the seminary.

Half an hour later, on the way downstairs with his grandmother, Dietrich met Hans-Walter, hurrying up the steps two at a time, with his little sister, Renate, close behind.

"Well, where are you two going in such a rush?" Dietrich asked.

"Grandmama promised we could listen to our program on her radio. It's time right now."

"All right, but just a minute. You went with your father to the Party membership office?"

"Yes, just got back. It took forever."

"Why?"

"Oh, every time we got to the entrance of the building, he'd say 'let's walk around the block first.' We did that three times." His voice crackled in his remembered frustration.

"But you did go in?"

"Yes. The last time. The door was locked. They'd closed for the day. But they let us in. I waited in the hall. That part didn't take long."

Renate tugged at Hans-Walter's arm as if to hurry him along.

"Well, go along, you two, and listen to your program."

Neither Dietrich nor his grandmother spoke as they continued slowly down the steps. He knew that she, too, had misgivings that their "Parsifal," as they sometimes called Rüdiger, should have been brought to such a pass.

12

Paula Bonhoeffer sometimes felt closer to her son-in-law, Hans von Dohnanyi, than to Christel; he would open up and tell her things more readily than her daughter. That went back to when he was a lonely teenager, staying with the Delbrücks down the street during the divorce of his parents. It had taken all Paula's skills to befriend the proud, sensitive lad. It was during the year after her son Walter's death at the front. Paula shrank, as always, from the memory of those months at Frau Schöne's house across the street, when she was stricken with grief and unable to leave her bed. She had been back with the family only a short time when this boy appeared—so lonely and hurt—and she had reached out to him. Later she had come to see that she had been as much the beneficiary as Hans.

And Christel—just fifteen at the time—with Walter's death had lost her childhood. It had taken Paula a long time to realize that; first because in her own devastation she was not there to see, and also because Christel had kept it inside herself. From earliest childhood her older brother had been her idol. She never played with dolls, but with Walter's collection of frogs and turtles and butterflies and white mice.

When Hans's father, Ernst von Dohnanyi, the well-known pianist and composer, returned to Hungary, Hans's mother had found a modest house in the neighborhood; and Hans had become a permanent member of the circle of Bonhoeffer and Delbrück young people. Soon he and Christel, who was two years younger, were walking to school together. He came everyday to fix her bicycle, then found other excuses for seeing her. They became inseparable. Karl had insisted that they wait to marry until Hans had finished at the university and was firmly established in a good job. Christel argued that Hans was the most brilliant man she knew and was certain to do well. But Karl stuck to his guns.

In the first years of their marriage they had little money, although Christel's unswerving faith in Hans never faltered. When, in 1929, Hans was appointed personal information officer to the minister of justice, Christel's belief in him seemed justified. After Hitler's takeover, when Franz Gürtner became justice minister, Hans had remained, he said, because the ministry of justice still maintained a certain degree of freedom. So far, no one had brought pressure on him to join the Nazi Party or any of its organizations. Now, after ten years of marriage and three children, the remarkable attachment still held, apparently as strong as ever. Sometimes Paula would see a look between them so intimate and warm that she felt she was intruding.

Hans often dropped in to talk with her in her little sitting room on the second floor; and on that afternoon, when the rest of the family was relaxing in the garden with Dietrich and Sabine, he appeared at her door. She put down her pen, for she had been trying to catch up on her correspondence, and turned to him, motioning to a chair.

He had on a pair of knickers, a new fad she did not care for; but since he was slender, they were not so bad, she supposed. Often he came with some ironic tale, but today his narrow face was serious. Without preliminaries he began to tell her about a new law that was in the works. Hitler wanted to strip the Jews of their German citizenship, rule out their right to vote and to protection under the law—Hitler especially wanted that, he said—and to outlaw marriage between Jews and Aryans. The laws were to take effect in the fall after the party rally in Nuremberg.

Paula was too outraged to say anything and Hans continued, "Gürtner told me that he and some others in the Justice Department have been trying to temper it down, but without much success."

"Hugo von der Lutz doesn't have anything to do with it, does he?" she asked.

"Sorry, Mama, he's the one who first told me about it. Matter of fact, he's working on the draft, along with some others."

Paula smoothed the folds of her blue linen dress. She raised her head, reluctant to ask the question in her mind. "What did he have to say? What does he think of it?"

"He thinks by and large it's a good thing. It will regulate the treatment of Jews, he says. Eliminate excesses."

"I must say I thought he had more sense."

"You might as well give up on him, Mama."

Paula shook her head, unable to feel anger—only a great sadness. Hugo had always been one of her favorite nephews. "I hope you reminded him of the effect it would have on Gert."

"I did. He said he had nothing against Gert, but he had to look to the greater good for Germany."

She was unwilling to accept defeat. "I may try to talk with him."

Hans looked at her as if he thought she would be wasting her time, but he said nothing. She wondered about his own position, with his grandmother in Hungary being Jewish, but he assured her that no one in the Justice Department knew that, not even Hugo. Paula was not so sure. It was generally known in the family; and Hugo's wife, Hilde, in her zeal for Hitler and the Nazi cause, might have picked it up somehow.

That evening, with all the family gathered in the living room, Hans broke his news. Paula could not believe the German people would go along with such a law, but the others disagreed.

"The German people were looking for a scapegoat in 1933 and Hitler knew it," said Rüdiger. "He gave them the one he wanted them to have."

"Not everyone, Rüdiger. You don't usually generalize." Paula sat up straight in her chair. "At any rate we can't sit and fold our hands. We have to do something."

"Bravo!" said Emmi. Her eyes shone with approval. She glanced at Klaus as if to say: Here's your example. Take heed.

Up to now Paula had found some consolation in the willingness of the Confessing Church to take a stand against Hitler. Now she declared on the spot her intention to join Pastor's Niemöller's congregation and give it her full support. She glanced at her husband, sitting alone by the etagere. At one time his look would have been one of tolerant amusement; now there was ungrudging accord, although that did not mean he would join her.

Although his eyes were smiling, Dietrich made no comment, but after a while he warned that the Confessing Church itself was vulnerable. Hitler's people were trying to find its soft underbelly with new laws that could split it open. Many good Lutherans would be unwilling to go against state legislation; obedience to the State was too much drummed into them. "As for my young brethren at the seminary," he said, "the probability of a clash with State authorities will just whet their appetites. They even look on the primitive conditions at Zingst as a privilege."

"Primitive?" Paula echoed. "I thought you were fairly comfortable. That's what you wrote."

"We're fine, really and truly," said Dietrich laughing.

Later that evening, with the implications of the new laws still swirling in his head, Dietrich saw Hans beckoning him to one side. "Come with me across the street," Hans said in a low voice. "I have something to show you."

On the other side of the narrow street the Schöne house cast its dark moon-shadow over the cobblestones. They still called it the Schöne house, although Hans and Christel had been living there for two years since old Frau Schöne died. The maid let them in the front door. They climbed the stairs and moved quietly down the hall, past sleeping children's rooms to a secluded, far corner of the house, where Hans had set up his study. He took a key from his pocket and opened the file drawer in his desk. From the back he withdrew an index card box and set it down, then brought out four manila folders and laid them beside the box.

"Sit down, Dietrich," he said, and pulled a chair over for him. "I have something here I think will interest you." He opened the first folder and turned half of the documents over face down. "That's a closed case." Then he picked up the remaining papers. "Now this is a case that is not yet opened, and probably won't be, unless Hitler is overthrown, or unless he decides someday that he wants to get rid of Göring, which doesn't seem likely." Hans turned slowly through the papers. "This is documentation of several counts of bribery. This one here shows a transfer of 3,000,000 marks by Göring to a bank in Zurich. That was just after the criminal proceedings against Schmidt, the tobacco magnate, were dropped. Remember that?"

"Yes. I remember rumors of a bribe."

"Well, here's proof of it. A transcript of a telephone conversation between Göring and Schmidt, arranging the deal."

"You mean Hitler tapped Göring's phone?"

"Oh, yes. No one's immune. Not even Göring." He opened the next folder and turned to the back. "This one documents the assassination of Chancellor Dollfuss last summer in Vienna. It was carried out by the Austrian SS, but Hitler got a report of the whole operation. You remember how all the while he disclaimed involvement?"

Dietrich took the papers and read them over hurriedly. There was a detailed account of how the Nazis secured the Austrian Army uniforms for the thirty men who broke into the Chancellery. They shot Dollfuss point-blank, at a range of two feet. "Hans, where did you get this stuff?" he asked.

"From the justice minister. Most of it comes to him from Hitler, who trusts him as much as he trusts anyone. Gürtner was Hitler's advocate and protector years ago in Munich, around the time of the Beer Hall putsch. I have orders to keep it under wraps." Hans laughed grimly. "I'll keep it under wraps, but not exactly for Hitler's advantage." Dietrich's shock must have shown on his face because Hans went on to assure him: "Gürtner turns it all over to me, without exception. No one else sees it."

"Why you, of all people? Doesn't he know where you stand?"

"I think he guesses. We don't talk about it."

Dietrich silently tried to assimilate the import of this revelation. "Does Hitler know you have this material?"

"No."

"How do you know?"

"I believe Gürtner," Hans said simply. "He's disenchanted with Hitler. Like many others he was fooled by his ability to get things done. Now he finds himself propelled into the unhappy position of gravedigger of German law."

"And with this he's trying to make amends?"

"Something like that. He's said nothing overt, of course. He's afraid to. He is especially afraid of Himmler; certain he is out to get him, and I don't doubt it. Gürtner tried a few months back to intervene with Hitler and abolish the concentration camps or, at least, get some degree of control over them. Irrefutable evidence had come to him of the torture of inmates by a Gestapo official. Gürtner sent the evidence to Hitler, with a recommendation that the official be prosecuted. Hitler ordered it dropped. That gave Gürtner chilling second thoughts. Himmler has hated him ever since."

"What is Hugo's position in all this?"

"He knows nothing about these chronicles, of course. He thinks I'm dedicated to the Third Reich." He raised an eyebrow resignedly. "That means I have to put up with Hugo's company far more than I would like." Dietrich said nothing, and Hans continued with a more defensive tone: "He's part of my protective system. He has Hitler's ear. That could be useful in that nest of vipers."

"Why are you telling me this?"

"I don't know." He looked straight into Dietrich's eyes. "Because you will tell me what you think. Without a lot of histrionics. And you'll keep it to yourself."

It was plain that Hans had chosen the path he would follow. He knew where it might lead and the dangers involved. And now he wanted Dietrich's approval. With dismay Dietrich sensed his own involvement with this disclosure. He had no desire to be drawn into something so distasteful and dangerous. "I'm surprised you would keep all this here," he said, noncommittally.

"I don't keep it here. I only brought these few folders home to show Christel—and you."

"She knows it, then?"

"Of course. I don't keep anything from Christel." He looked up. "Not because she insists on knowing, but we've always shared everything." He smiled a crooked smile. "Your sister is a wonderful woman."

Dietrich was astonished. Hans had never, in all their long acquaintance, spoken so personally to him.

Hans closed the folder. "There's more, much more in my files at the office, detailed evidence against Nazis, usually high officials—everything from murder in the concentration camps to currency smuggling by the Party bosses, and accounts of homosexuality among the SA and Hitler Youth leadership. I call it the 'Chronicle of Scandals.'" He opened the index card box and flipped through it. "It's all cross-filed here. Each name is listed on a separate card, you see, with position, address, and so forth. On the back of the card in one of the corners I have a number. It corresponds to the name on the folder where it may be found. You see, you wouldn't notice it."

"No." Dietrich could see the tiny, light marking there and could barely make out the number. "You keep the numbers and the matching names in your head, I suppose."

Hans smiled. "I have a record of them underneath my drinking cup in the office. Looks like a coaster but it unfolds and inside it's all there. You'd be surprised how much you can write in so small a space."

Dietrich shivered involuntarily. "Sounds terribly dangerous."

"Not if I'm careful. It only becomes dangerous when I use it against Hitler."

"But you plan to do that."

"When the time is ripe. It will have to be used in conjunction with an overthrow of the regime."

Dietrich did not ask the question that came immediately to his mind, but Hans seemed to sense it. "If there's a conspiracy on the horizon, I haven't found it yet. But it will form itself eventually. Then this material might be useful to convince a wavering general, or anyone else who is ready to listen. Meanwhile I'll keep adding to it."

Dietrich turned the signet ring over and over on his finger. "I don't think you can simply let this material lie dormant indefinitely. That would make you an accomplice."

"Yes, I know."

"I'd rather tell you to forget it, but I think you're right. You have to be prepared to use it. Just be careful!"

Hans said nothing, but the tense lines in his face relaxed as he carefully replaced the folders and the box in his desk.

The next day, after a fitful sleep, Dietrich left early for the trip with Superintendent Niesel to the little village of Finkenwalde near Stettin. He hoped to arrive back at Zingst by nightfall with news of a permanent location for the seminary.

13

The best thing about the house at Finkenwalde was that it was large. This was important to Dietrich. He had hopes that the seminary might become a center of activity for the Confessing Church in western Pomerania, where retreats and conferences could be held from time to time; and in the long run, a haven where former students and others who needed a place to lay their heads could come and find a warm welcome.

The old dwelling was situated on a gentle rise some distance above a wide, meandering arm of the Oder Estuary. On the first floor the three main rooms were large and high ceilinged, with rows of double windows. All agreed that the center room, with its wide brick fireplace, should serve as the common room; on either side, the refectory and a lecture room. Up the stairs from the entry hall were many small rooms, with low ceilings and half-sized windows. Dietrich and Rott set these aside as study rooms, and one of the first priorities was to have them outfitted with tables, chairs, and shelves for books. At either end of the long hall and down a few steps were two larger rooms, each of which could accommodate as many as ten beds for the ordinands. For himself Dietrich took a small one-and-a-half room apartment over the garage, with a view of the slope down to the water. Willi Rott chose a larger room above the kitchen.

Lectures went on as usual in the mornings in the near-empty rooms. In the afternoons they scrubbed floors, painted the stained and peeling walls, washed windows, repaired broken panes, mended the roof and the cracked plaster on the ceilings, and overhauled the plumbing. Outside they struggled to rescue the garden and the house from strangling weeds and shrubs, which almost covered the windows. Dietrich set aside one corner of the garden for vegetables and put a group of men to work, spading and planting. There was lots of singing and shouting and laughing and arguing about how this or that should be done. In the breaks they played table tennis. Dietrich rarely allowed himself to be beaten, although Eberhard Bethge sometimes got the best of him.

The congregations of western Pomerania astonished Dietrich with their outpouring of support. Wagons, loaded with beds, chairs, tables, dishes, and a great variety of food, arrived almost daily. All this pleased Frau Struwe, the housekeeper, who had deplored the rough camp furnishings at Zingst. Eight churches pledged to furnish one study room each. Some of the wealthy landowners sent more substantial furniture: leather and damask armchairs, worn but still comfortable. One kindly old Junker countess patiently made cotton covers for all the chairs.

Dietrich brought his grand piano from Berlin, and a second one was loaned by one of the ordinands. His books formed the core of the library, which expanded slowly with gifts from interested patrons. It was a pleasure to see the ordinands' response to his gramophone records, especially the Negro spirituals, a new sound for them. Among his possessions in Berlin he unearthed two almost life-size prints of the Dürer Apostles. It was the unanimous decision of the students that the paintings, with their brilliant reds and greens, should hang on the wall behind the dining table, at Dietrich's back. He charged them with wanting something more interesting to look at than their teacher, with Peter and John on his left and Paul and Mark on his right.

In midsummer, when the seminary work was firmly established and flourishing, Dietrich began to make plans for the establishment of a small community of brothers who would stay on at the end of the term and live and work together as Christian pastors on a more or less permanent basis. He would call it the Brethren House. The need justified it—a group of unfettered pastors who could put themselves at the service of the Confessing Church in areas where the church was hard pressed. To do this, the seminary would provide a common home and the support of brotherly fellowship.

But when the image of Elenore drifted into his thoughts, there came a rub. The Brethren House ran straight up against the prospect of marriage. Dietrich saw her only a few times during that summer, once when he made a quick trip to Berlin for an ecumenical committee meeting. While he was there he walked with his parents, and his sister Ursel Schleicher and her family over to the Marienburger Allee, in neighboring Charlottenburg, to see the progress on the two new houses that the elder Bonhoeffers and the Schleichers were building side by side. He invited Franz and Elenore to accompany them.

Dietrich's father had been planning for several years to move out of the big house on the Wangenheimstrasse to a smaller home, built to their own design. Dietrich had already seen the large lot, located in a little cluster of streets on the northern rim of the Grunewald Forest. It faced not directly onto the street, but on a short, uninhabited lane that ran at right angles to the street. There was enough land for two houses, and it had not taken his parents long to persuade Ursel and Rüdiger to buy half of it and build a house

next door. The houses faced north, which gave the gardens at the
rear a warm, southern exposure.

Not much happened to make that short outing memorable. It
was more the feel and texture of those brief hours. Ursel's children
raced excitedly over their new and as yet unaccustomed territory,
up and down unfinished stairways, shouting to one another from
dangerous perches.

Inside the new house Dietrich's mother pointed out the advan-
tages of the central foyer, with its access to all other parts of the
house, like a Roman atrium without the open sky, she laughed
regretfully. On the right were the stairs up and down, the kitchen,
the dining room, and—at the back—the living room, which
looked out on the garden. On the left, his father explored with
them his new waiting room and counseling room, which ran the
whole length of that side of the house. On the second floor they
saw the bedrooms and the suite for their grandmother, with a door
to a sunny balcony across the rear.

There were astonished looks when Dietrich gave his long-
awaited decision as to which room would be his.

"The attic? Really, Dietrich. That crow's nest?" his mother
protested. "That is simply for the overflow, when everyone's
home."

But he was firm in his decision. He liked the privacy. And he
wanted the west room. "Besides," he said, as he drew the children
over to the wide window, "from here I can keep an eye on you and
see what you're up to down there in your garden."

Dietrich made no attempt that crowded afternoon to see Elenore
alone. After he and Franz put her on the streetcar at the Bismarck
Platz, Dietrich began to question Franz about church matters.
Franz's answers were brief and abstracted.

After a time, Franz threw him a speculative glance, then finally
said, "Is something wrong between you and Elenore?"

"What do you mean, wrong?"

"I just don't understand what's going on. Or what's not going
on. I'm just surprised. I expected—"

Dietrich looked at him. "I don't think it's something we need to discuss."

"Why not?"

"Am I obliged to give a reason?"

"There's only one reason you wouldn't want to discuss it," Franz countered obstinately, "and that's if you've changed your mind about her. And I can't believe that."

Dietrich looked away. Somewhere along the way his habit of confiding to Franz his feelings about Elenore had tapered off. Finally he said with a moderating smile, "I can't give you answers when I don't know them myself."

Franz looked skeptical and, slowing his pace, walked on for a time in silence.

"There's something else I have to take into consideration," Dietrich said half to himself, then straightway told Franz of his plans for the Brethren House.

Franz, who had little sympathy with anything more "monkish" than the seminary as it was already, was plainly shocked. "I just think you've lost your senses."

"Yes, I suppose you would think that," Dietrich said without anger. "Look, Franz, I'm not trying to lead the church back to the cloister in the Catholic sense, believe me. There are many distinctions. No vows of celibacy. No vows of permanency. No abbot wielding power."

Franz smiled sardonically at that.

"I believe in the uniting power of common prayer," Dietrich said simply.

"So do I."

"The emphasis here will be on helping, supporting, admonishing one another, learning how to be true followers of Christ."

"Sounds rather Utopian to me," Franz commented, with a marked lack of enthusiasm. Then he added, "Where does Elenore fit into all of this?"

"I don't know," Dietrich answered lamely.

"No, I don't think you do. I just wonder. I saw how she looked at you today, when you weren't looking."

"How?"

"Like you don't deserve, I can tell you that."

Dietrich glanced at his face, but there was no levity there. "It seems you have a habit of reading more into some things than is really there."

"Oh, for God's sake, Dietrich."

Dietrich looked up and for a moment their eyes held, then he looked down. "It's always been as much a childhood friendship as anything else. She's been like part of the family, you know, even if she is only a distant cousin: always at the same parties, the same dancing classes, the same picnics, musical evenings, her grandmother's house just across the street—all that. It was just natural for us to become friends."

"I don't know who you're trying to fool. I suppose you're going to say you haven't spoken marriage to her at all."

Dietrich hesitated. The tall iron bars of the gate were warm in his hand from the heat of the afternoon sun. "That was a long time ago, on the tide of a youthful crush. Since then so much has happened. You know how it's been." He looked at Franz's open and unguarded face. "You realize I haven't seen very much of her lately."

"I know that very well. And I'm just wondering what she's been thinking. And feeling."

"Nothing very different from me, I should think. She likes her work, talks about it a lot."

"No. Very different from you. You're fooling yourself, Dietrich." Then Franz excused himself, saying he would not come in this time after all. Dietrich watched, his hand on the iron gate, as Franz retreated and realized that his attempts to justify himself had collapsed like a house of straw.

14

In honeyed tones the newspaper article projected the State as the good intermediary on behalf of the muddled, quarreling churchmen. The ordinands crowded around Dietrich in the common room as he read it. For weeks they had been hearing rumors that the State was planning to shut down the new Confessing Church government and its Councils of Brethren. It now appeared that Hitler was darkening the waters instead. He had created a new Ministry of Church Affairs to do the darkening for him and named a lawyer, Hanns Kerrl, as its head. His scheme was to lure the Confessing Church by offers of "plausible and reasonable" alternatives that could bring about "pacification." In the article Kerrl announced formation of a committee that would be made up of leaders from both the Confessing Church and the Reich Church. This Reich Church Committee, as it would be called, and the provincial committees to follow, would serve as an umbrella government, under which "all factions of the church could participate." This would provide a "guarantee" that the Confessing Church's vital interests would be looked after. And William Zoellner, a respected Lutheran theologian, would be its head. A skillful move indeed.

The three former University of Berlin students—Schönherr, Kanitz, and Maechler—recognized the dangers, but most of the others were swayed by Kerrl's arguments. Ernst Thom knew Zoellner personally and could not believe he would be a party to anything basically wrong. Fritz Onnasch noted the emphasis on fair representation by the Confessing Church. "We'd be on equal footing with the Reich Church, isn't that true?"

"Yes," said Thom. "Wouldn't that be worth a try? Should we just throw it out, without even considering it?"

Dietrich lowered the newspaper and looked around at the other ordinands. Their eyes were on him as they waited for his answer.

"The Reich Church and the Confessing Church would both be under Zoellner's committees, that's true," he said. "But remember, Zoellner takes orders from Kerrl. And Kerrl takes orders from Hitler. There's no way we can get under that blanket without snuggling up to Hitler."

Not another word was said in favor of the committees.

Kerrl's flashing mirror had thrown the sun straight into the eyes of many church leaders. The seminarians, however, followed Dietrich's lead unswervingly. But one day in the midst of an intense discussion on ways to withstand the committees he saw in their faces an idolizing look. Only a few seemed to retain their independence of mind. It seemed to Dietrich a pitiable show of weakness that they would so belittle themselves because of his power to dominate their thinking.

For the first time since Dietrich had taken the seminary appointment, the black demons descended upon him. In despair he went about his tasks automatically and for two days forced himself to make the necessary motions and speak the necessary words.

After that the bouts of depression came at increasingly frequent intervals. He wondered what was the matter with him; and on his next trip home, after some research among his father's psychology books, he gave the malaise a name: *accidie tristitia*—the first for his weariness of spirit when he failed to be the Christian he had set himself to be, and the second for the melancholy that followed. After that he wondered if naming the evil would make it go away.

For some time, even before the seminary opened, Dietrich had been thinking about private confession as a voluntary practice the brothers might consider. One day in the discipleship class he spent most of the time explaining the meaning and elements of confession, and suggested that anyone who wished might seek private confession to one of the other brothers or to him. Most of their faces expressed surprised embarrassment, even resentment, that he was stepping over the bounds of normal Protestant practice. But some of them showed a degree of curiosity. One man asked how to go about it. Dietrich did not give specific rules beyond the need for prayer at the beginning and again at the conclusion. "As for the confession itself," he said, "isn't it simply to say where you think you have hurt God's will, God's presence, in your conduct, in your heart, in your thinking? Where you have not loved Christ? As to the manner in which it is carried out, I think that is something that you can work out for yourselves. You can find the way together.

Martin Luther never lived without oral confession, you know. I would like for us to find it again, to learn it together, one brother to another."

Gradually one or another of the ordinands came to Dietrich for confession, and he heard echoes of some such movement among the brothers themselves, although it was not discussed in a personal way. He knew he should not expect them to do something he would not do himself; but when it came down to the moment of speaking to one of the brothers about it, he found himself putting it off. He felt an intense inner resistance, a veil of woven ice, which he could not break through. He knew he would have to do it, and he would—soon.

One of the sturdier spirits among the ordinands was the young man from Saxony, Eberhard Bethge. Bethge, who appeared to be light-hearted and free-spirited, but not an exceptional scholar, surprised Dietrich in his first sermon before the homiletics class. The assigned text was Isaiah 53:5: "But he was wounded for our transgressions, he was bruised for our iniquities: the chastisement of our peace was upon him; and with his stripes we are healed." Bethge's thoughts showed deeper and clearer insights than Dietrich had heretofore noticed.

Equally interesting was Bethge's musicianship, and sometime earlier Dietrich had made him assistant choral director. On the day of Bethge's sermon Dietrich met him on the stairs and stopped to ask about some music plans. Then, with the Brethren House in mind, he casually inquired, "I suppose you already have plans for when you finish here."

"Well, yes, I do, in fact," Bethge replied with a modest smile. "If it works out, of course. My superintendent in Saxony says he has a church in mind for me. Then I'm hoping—to get married—" There was a slight hesitation. "That's the plan. If I have a church, of course."

Dietrich asked no prying questions.

One morning a week or so later, during the class on discipleship, Dietrich noticed that Bethge seemed extraordinarily preoccupied.

Bethge leaned on the table with his hand cupped over his mouth and during the whole hour scarcely looked up. Once Dietrich asked him a direct question, to which he answered, somewhat startled, "I'm sorry, I'm afraid I didn't understand the question."

Dietrich remembered noticing his absence from the common room the evening before and wondered what the problem was. After the midday meal he called Bethge's cousin, Gerhard Vibrans, aside and drew from him the answer. Bethge's fiancée had thrown him over for someone else. He was terribly cut up about it—couldn't believe it, and all that.

A short time later from his window Dietrich saw Bethge walking along the dirt road that curved southwestward where the beech forest arced out on to the crest of the hill. Dietrich waited about ten minutes then walked out in the same direction, following a footpath in and out among the trees at the edge of the forest. On a ridge in the open field he found Bethge—seated on a crumbling, semicircular rock wall, part of an ancient fortification.

Bethge looked up and saw him coming.

"Would I be intruding if I stopped for a while?" Dietrich asked, as he drew near the wall.

"No, not at all," Bethge answered. "Please sit down."

"A pleasant view," Dietrich observed, as he took a seat.

"Yes."

"Your cousin told me about your fiancée."

Bethge looked up but said nothing.

"I hope you don't mind."

"No. No. I don't mind."

"I'm terribly sorry."

"I guess she had a right to change her mind," said Bethge in a low voice. He leaned his arms on his knees, his broad shoulders hunched forward. "I don't know. I just didn't see any of the warning signals, I suppose, if there were any."

"You haven't seen her since April. Isn't that right?"

"That's not very long. Just four months, or so. I don't see how she could have changed in that short time." Slowly Bethge sank down again. "It's like your whole future's been lopped off with a meat axe, and there you are, standing at the edge of nothing. I simply hadn't envisioned such a thing. Stupidity, that's all."

"I'd hardly call it that. Naiveté, maybe. But that's not so bad."

Bethge turned to Dietrich, his face open and defenseless. "Her name is Rosalinde. There was no reason not to trust her—no reason." His eyes beseeched an answer; he seemed willing to accept any judgment, however cruel.

"No, I'm sure not," said Dietrich. "And you wouldn't have looked for it. There are some people who give of themselves without counting the cost. The stupid ones are those who never dare to trust."

Bethge seemed to give tentative scrutiny to that idea, to see if it was in any way acceptable as a balm for his wounded self-esteem. "Maybe," he said, and left it there. "I suppose Gerhard told you she found someone else. I'm afraid I got used to the idea that I was the one she preferred," he added with a one-sided smile.

Dietrich was glad to see a spark of humor, even dark humor, glimmering through the pain. "Could it be that she decided she just didn't want to be a pastor's wife after all? Perhaps the drawbacks outweighed everything else. And they are considerable, you know. Especially for some women."

"She knew that from the beginning."

"Maybe she wasn't realistic about it in the beginning. Too much charmed away. That's possible, I think," Dietrich added matter-of-factly, to play down the implied compliment.

Bethge said nothing, but the tautness around his eyes seemed to slacken and there was a hint of a wry smile on his lips. They talked of music for a time, then walked together back to the house.

Five months under Bonhoeffer's tutelage had awakened Eberhard Bethge's interest in many things, but especially in the Jews. He had shared the director's outrage over the passage of the new anti-Jewish laws ten days earlier at Nuremberg. Even so, Eberhard had been surprised that Bonhoeffer considered it a matter of such

urgency as to bring all of the ordinands to this meeting of the Old
Prussian Confessing Synod at Steglitz-Berlin. The day before,
Bonhoeffer had summoned them all and explained the situation.
He had learned that a committee of the synod had drafted a reso-
lution that seemed to condone the Nuremberg laws. He could not
let such a thing go unchallenged, he said.

Nine of the ordinands, including Eberhard, were being housed
at the Bonhoeffer home on the Wangenheimstrasse. With its rich
and ordered life, the fine old villa contrasted sharply with the
simple village parsonage of Eberhard's childhood years; and there
was not the slightest hint of superiority in the attitude of the Bonhoeffers. Quite the contrary. During the evening Frau Bonhoeffer
took time to speak personally with each one of the ordinands. The
father said little but listened attentively to the conversation.

Everywhere were signs of an affluence Eberhard was unaccustomed to: Persian rugs, parquet floors, original paintings on the
walls, and elegant but comfortable furniture. He and Fritz Onnasch had a room to themselves and the other seven fared as well.
He would have liked to explore the whole house; there was no
telling how many rooms there were. The servants, in their white
caps and aprons, accomplished everything so smoothly that there
was not the least hint that he and the others were causing any
trouble. Bonhoeffer himself seemed especially pleased to have
them there.

The next morning in Steglitz the first session dealt with matters
unrelated to the Jews. But during lunch Bonhoeffer and Karl
Koch, president of the synod, joined the table where Fritz Onnasch and Eberhard were eating. After the introductions, Bonhoeffer and Koch began talking about the problems facing the
synod.

Bonhoeffer asked Koch one or two tame questions about the
goings-on of the morning session. Then in a dry and restrained
voice Bonhoeffer said, "I understand that a resolution is proposed
on the Aryan Clause that has some people rather alarmed."

The president looked up, as though not quite sure what to expect but with an idea it would be troublesome. "What have you sniffed out now, Dietrich?"

"I'm wondering about one clause, the one that concedes to the State the right to legislative settlement of the Jewish question."

"Oh, that. Yes, yes, that drew some fire in the committee, but it passed."

"That disappoints me, I must say. I expected better of my Old Prussian brethren."

Koch shot him a look of sharp surprise. "It's nothing to make such a fuss about, is it? Just a minor clause."

"Is it minor to have the church condoning persecution?"

"Certainly not, if that's what it is."

"Of course, that's what it is. You're handing it to them on a platter."

"I'll concede it might look that way," Koch said slowly, seeming as he spoke to catch a glimmering of what it meant. "But, you understand, I can't overrule the majority. They feel such matters are out of our domain."

"Particularly at this time," Bonhoeffer said with unmistakable irony.

"Yes," he sighed, "that business of the Nuremberg laws puts us in a bind."

"They want us in a bind."

"Yes, yes. Look, Dietrich, the church intends to deal with that problem soon. We've talked about it. But this is a ticklish time for a confrontation with the State. Actually, the very validity of the church is at stake."

Bonhoeffer looked down at his plate, but Eberhard caught the glint in his eye. "But then, in a situation where millions of people are threatened in their very existence, we have to ask, don't we, What is the church's true validity? I have to believe it lies in the willingness to risk everything—even legal status—to speak up for those who cannot speak up for themselves."

"I'm sure that is the intention eventually. It's just a question of timing."

"I don't see how the timing could be more urgent."

The president said nothing but studiously drank his tea.

Bonhoeffer continued, "The time is crying out for it, actually. The real impact of the Nuremberg laws is just beginning to be felt. What happens to the church's credibility, if it condones these laws?"

Koch looked sharply at Bonhoeffer, then appeared to study the point. "Well—perhaps I can call the committee together again and see what can be done. But I think that's as far as we dare to go at this time."

Bonhoeffer ran his finger slowly around the rim of his cup. "It would take courage, wouldn't it—it would be breaking new ground—for the church to become—clearly and openly—a voice for the voiceless. Yes, that would be daring." There was a touch of sadness in his tone, as if he realized that this was too much to expect. He turned and looked directly at Koch. "Can we afford not to do it, though? It is standing with Christ that will save the church. Can we deny that he stands with the persecuted?"

Koch was silent for a moment. "Ah, it's too bad you can't speak to the synod. You're terribly persuasive. Well, we'll do what we can."

The resolution passed that afternoon, minus the clause favorable to the Nuremberg laws, but nothing was said against the State for promulgating them in the first place. The synod referred that unpleasant discussion to the Reich Council of Brethren for a recommendation at the "earliest opportunity."

As they sped toward Stettin on the train that evening, Bonhoeffer asked grimly how long that "earliest opportunity" would be in coming. Presently, across from Eberhard, he fell asleep with his sweater folded under his head. In the days since their encounter on the hill Eberhard had found his appreciation of Bonhoeffer increasing, but did not allow this interest to give way to curious questions. For, although Bonhoeffer kept himself open to any of the brothers in real trouble, there was a certain aloofness about him. It was not easy to infringe uninvited upon his privacy. Still Eberhard had never stood in complete awe of his teacher. And now, in spite of the differences in their backgrounds and Eberhard's own shyness, he had begun to feel the beginning of a bond between them.

People were lining up in the corridor with their baggage for the stop at Eberswalde. Soon the train glided into the high-roofed station and came to a silent, joltless halt. The scramble of passengers off and on the train proceeded amid shouts and whistles. A column of SS forces, in their new black uniforms, marched to a halt outside their window and waited to board the train. It was a scene that was becoming ever more frequent.

It was about a week later that Bonhoeffer called Eberhard aside and, without any preliminaries, asked him if he would come to his room after the midday meal and hear his confession. The request was so unexpected, and Eberhard himself so unprepared to deal with it, that for a moment he said nothing at all. Bonhoeffer's partially shuttered countenance failed to conceal a look of earnest entreaty. Eberhard heard himself answer in the affirmative. Then, at an acknowledging nod from Bonhoeffer, he moved on to the table and sat down beside Gerhard.

When the meal was over and everyone, including Bonhoeffer, had gone, Eberhard left the table and turned slowly to the stairs.

"Yes. Come in, Bruder Bethge." From habit Dietrich looked the young student in the eye, but only briefly. Clearing his throat, he indicated a chair beside the desk. "Won't you sit down."

"Thank you," said Bethge, and took a seat.

Dietrich sat in his own chair. He turned it toward Bethge and they faced each other, a few feet between them. Neither spoke for a time. Then Dietrich, feeling constrained and uncomfortable, asked, "You have been doing this already?"

"No. No, I haven't," Bethge said with an apologetic smile.

Dietrich was a little surprised. He had imagined that Bethge was one of those who would have tried to follow his suggestion. Bethge seemed at a loss and apprehensive. "I think we must first pray," said Dietrich.

Bethge bowed his head and Dietrich did so, too. There was a long silence.

"If you, as confessor, could perhaps lead?" Dietrich said.

Then Bethge, in a voice almost inaudible, began to pray. "Be with us, Lord—grant us your presence and your strength. Help us to know that we are in the presence of the Confessor Christ—who is listening, whose grace is being offered us—just now—." In the heavy silence he whispered, "Amen."

Dietrich looked up for only the briefest moment, then down quickly again to his hands. He knew that now he must speak. But he could not. The thought of uncovering his deep inner feelings—his sins, yes, no less—to this other man was a humiliation altogether unbearable. Besides, such a thing went against his upbringing. One kept silent, so as not to burden the other.

Still, in his heart Dietrich desperately wanted to become a true follower of Christ. He longed for forgiveness—forgiveness that could free him and make this kind of discipleship possible. He believed also—he wanted to believe—that "God breaks gates of brass and bars of iron."

Dietrich looked up once more into Bethge's face. The younger man's eyes held recognition and a gentle, selfless proffering of the spirit. Dietrich drew a long, slow breath. He abandoned the last stronghold of pride, and with a single thrust swept aside the barrier and stepped into the abyss.

In between the freighted silences the words came slowly and in forced tones, as had all the others the teacher had spoken. Bonhoeffer was close by, almost touching distance, and scarcely lifted his head as he spoke. In the beginning, when Eberhard first sensed that Bonhoeffer was in difficulties, he was alarmed, and felt woefully unprepared for the situation. But when the extent of Bonhoeffer's distress became clear to him, Eberhard's own alarm began to subside. He wanted only in that moment to be there for the other man; to let him know somehow that he wanted to help, however helpless and inarticulate he himself might feel.

As the painful, hesitant words came out Eberhard's surprise increased. Relentlessly specific, Bonhoeffer gave himself no quarter.

After a time—how long, Eberhard did not know—Bonhoeffer

ceased speaking, his head still bowed, his shoulders drooped. Eberhard thought he should then ask, "Is that all you wanted to say?"

"Yes," Bonhoeffer said softly. There was a long pause.

Eberhard knew only the words of forgiveness that the pastor spoke in the general confession in the church. "I ask you to believe that I am here in the name of Christ and I have the—that I am— commissioned—to say you are forgiven. So I, in the name of Christ, forgive your sins." Eberhard knew also that a prayer must follow.

When he looked up from the prayer, Bonhoeffer's eyes, calm and clear, were resting upon him. Neither spoke but they shook hands. It was a handshake of the brother, of acceptance, of communion— of liberation. Eberhard turned and walked to the door. He looked back once to the man standing there—quiet and at peace. Then he went out and closed the door softly behind him.

15

One Monday afternoon at the beginning of Advent the evening paper announced a new government ruling, the "Fifth Decree for the Implementation of the Law for the Safeguarding of the Church." Dietrich read it with increasing apprehension. Although it did not propose to shut down the Confessing Church by force, the effect was almost the same. It made all its administrative activities, including the running of its seminaries, illegal; there could be no conferment of offices, no examinations or ordinations. The word spread rapidly among the men; and when they came together after supper to discuss it, Dietrich was met by many troubled faces around the circle.

He deliberately kept his voice cool as he spoke to them. First he went over point by point the directives and obvious designs of the decree, then tried to give a realistic appraisal of the situation. "Now we are truly illegal. With this decree the State confirms it.

The consequences are quite clear, I think. All the powers of the press and everything that shapes public opinion will now attack the Confessing Church, the sole remaining 'disturber of the peace.'"

No one spoke. With sober faces they waited for him to continue.

"The prospects for your future were none too good before. Now there can be no guarantees at all that when you've completed your work here you will find employment. Hardly any of you can expect to be given an ordinary living with a house and garden.

"There are some Confessing superintendents who still aren't afraid to take the heat, thank God. One of them might take you on as an assistant. But there'd be no prospect for advancement. You could be called to one of the newly formed emergency congregations, but now they'll be dependent on free-will offerings. I want you to understand that each of you is free to decide whether you will go or stay. I can't say how the Councils of Brethren are going to reply to this decree, but I don't believe they will knuckle under. They will certainly need the cooperation of all of us. There'll be no let-up in this struggle anytime soon, I'm sure of that. As for myself, I'll go on with the work as long as there remains one ordione ordinand, and I will see to it that all who stay are fully provided for."

The response surprised him. The ordinands crowded around him with pledges that they would stay with the seminary and would yield to nothing but force.

Later, when the others had gone up to their rooms, Dietrich said to Eberhard, "Their tactics are extremely clever. First, the olive branch of the church committees, then these harsh, crippling measures, which will make the olive branch seem ever more attractive. As it says in 1 Peter: 'The time has come for the judgment to begin; it is beginning with God's own household.' The lightning strikes the high trees first."

Eberhard smiled, but said nothing.

"Pray for me, Eberhard. I need it very much. And pray for the church. We must not cease to pray for the church."

One evening about the middle of December Dietrich received a call from Berlin that his grandmother was gravely ill. Some weeks earlier his parents had settled into the new house on the Marienburger Allee, the grandmother in the new suite his father had built for her. She had insisted on walking to the post office, his mother said. It was a cold, damp day and she had contracted pneumonia. Dietrich left immediately in the little Opel that belonged to one of the ordinands, and arrived at the new house at 1 A.M.

He found his father at her bedside in her new apartment.

"How goes it, Papa?"

"Ah, my dear boy, I'm so glad you're here," his father said softly, weariness spinning out the words. His reticence rarely allowed him to speak in such an intimate tone.

His father rose and walked with him to the door, out of earshot of the grandmother. "The fever has not broken. It's been steady at 103.6 degrees for several hours. If she can make it through the night, I think she will begin to get better."

"Let me stay with her, Papa, and you get some rest."

His father looked up uncertainly.

"Please. I'll call you if there is any change."

"Yes. Thank you, Dietrich. Thank you."

Dietrich did not leave her side the remainder of the night. Her fever broke the next morning, and she began to take a little nourishment. Dietrich stayed over another day for his lecture at the University of Berlin. He had taken a class there once a week to keep his options open in the unlikely event that a change of policy would occur, but also to have regular access to political information directly from the family.

That afternoon when Dietrich came home he found Elenore beside his grandmother's bed. She touched her finger to her lips, and he saw his grandmother was sleeping. He hesitated for a moment, just inside the door. Elenore belonged there, he knew. There had always been a warm friendship between them. Dietrich tried to remember when he had written Elenore last and realized that he had received no letter from her recently either. He had seen her only once since the visit to the new houses in the summer.

He tip-toed across the floor and stood on the Persian rug by the bed. "How is she," he whispered.

"Better, I think. She talked to me a little."

"Good." He felt the awkward pause. "And you. How are you?"

"Very well, thank you."

"It was good of you to come."

"Not at all. I had to come." She looked at the grandmother. "She is a very dear and great lady."

"Yes."

Elenore said nothing.

"I hope your parents are doing well."

"Yes, thank you."

There was a stirring on the pillow and his grandmother opened her eyes. She saw Dietrich and moved her hand feebly on the comforter. He took it in his own.

"Ah, Dietrich, you're back," she said, with some difficulty.

"Yes, Grandmama."

She turned her head slowly toward Elenore. "Still here?" She smiled and looked back to Dietrich, then to Elenore again. "I'm very tired. I'm sorry. Go along and talk, my dears. I'll only sleep."

Dietrich let go her hand and watched as her eyes drooped shut again. He turned to Elenore. "Perhaps you'd like to come onto the balcony? It would be pleasant there."

It was an exceptionally mild December afternoon. The latest snow was almost gone, and icicles at the eaves were melting with a rhythmic drip on the wooden floor. A few doomed red leaves clung to the branches of the oak beside his father's new sunroom-office. Dietrich and Elenore stood at the rail. Neither of them spoke.

He tried to find his voice and said, at last, "I'm sorry not to have written." He made no attempt to explain. There was no valid excuse. "I hope your work has been going well."

"Quite well, thank you."

"I didn't see you at Steglitz."

"No. I wasn't there."

She offered no explanation and Dietrich asked none.

"How is Jacobi? What does he think of this new decree?"

"The same as you, I'm sure. Koch and some of the others are talking of negotiating with Zoellner."

"Negotiating?"

"They don't call it that, but it amounts to the same thing."

"You mean Koch could go over to the committees?"

"I don't know. Maybe he thinks he could bring some kind of influence to bear in the new situation."

"That's stupid, of course. If you board a wrong train, it's no use running along the corridor in the opposite direction."

"Let's don't jump to conclusions. He hasn't done it yet."

"There are dark days ahead, I'm afraid," Dietrich said gloomily.

"Yes."

He was aware that the conversation had fallen into the usual pattern. Slowly this awareness burned through all other considerations. The silence became oppressive. He knew what it was he needed to say but did not know how to say it. The drift apart had been gradual and unpremeditated, the ties between them stretched increasingly thin by long separations. It might be, he reasoned, that for her, too, the thought of marriage had waned, and a final break would not be a matter of great disappointment.

"I have never wanted to cause you pain, Elenore," he said at last, "and if I have, I pray you'll forgive me."

She said nothing, her face alert, as if she expected something more.

"I'm not much good for you, anyway, I'm afraid. I'd be nothing but a burden around your neck, you know. I'm a burden to myself. I told you that last spring. Remember?"

"No, I don't think you said exactly that."

"Maybe not exactly, but—"

"But I should have understood it that way? As a forewarning?"

"It was just simply true."

"What am I supposed to say, Dietrich? It's been a pleasure knowing you? All these years?" Tears started to her eyes.

Dietrich was not prepared for his sudden sense of remorse. He wanted to take her hands in his and say it wasn't so, he didn't mean it—anything to smooth away the pain from her face. Instead he said, "I would be grateful if we could go on being friends."

"You really don't understand at all, do you?" She brushed her eyes impatiently with her fingertips and without looking at him said, "I must say good-bye to your grandmother."

"Forgive me, Elenore."

She looked at him steadily now as if to show him that her insubordinate feelings were once more reined in. "Good-bye, Dietrich." Then she turned and without looking back walked through the door.

Dietrich stood by the rail for a long time, unaware of the creeping chill in the air as the sun sank behind the trees. Then he returned to his grandmother's room and sat down beside the bed. She opened her eyes.

"I wasn't asleep," she said slowly. "I was hoping you'd come back. I wanted to talk to you while I still have the strength."

"You'll soon be better, Grandmama." The words fell empty on his ears.

"No, it's time to die. *Jetzt leg' i' mi' halt hin.*" She spoke in the old Schwäbisch dialect, "Now I can't hold out any longer. The time comes when it's better to die. It is not meant to go on and on." She picked at the bed covers with her fingers. "I was never able to be sure in my mind about many things—the divinity of Jesus—I don't know what it means—the Incarnation. It's difficult for me—" Her troubled eyes rested upon him.

She was of the so-called "liberal time," when everything was called into question. Some of it, he knew, was healthy questioning. At fifteen years of age he had cut his teeth on it during long walks in the Grunewald with Adolf Harnack. His grandmother had been disillusioned with the German Church in those days and rarely attended Sunday services. But her heart was set unwaveringly on what was right in all her dealings, and on the rights of others. She could not bear to see these violated.

"I know it's difficult, Grandmama. It's difficult for most people. Perhaps we can speak of the Incarnate One, instead of the ever so perplexing Incarnation."

She thought about this, her eyes fixed upon him.

He said, gently, "I believe God will reveal in his own time what we do not now understand. Yet even now we can know that in the Incarnate One the whole human race recovers the dignity of the image of God. Isn't that true? Now any attack on even the least of men is an attack upon Him."

"Yes." Her eyes did not leave his face.

"Of this much I am sure. He is the one who knows your heart. He holds it safely in His hands. And He forgives your sins. Remember in Psalm 103 where it says, 'His love lasts from all eternity and forever.'"

No word more was said. No words were needed. He looked into her eyes. Understanding—communion—flowed between them.

"Yes," she said, after a time. Then, quoting, "'and let us always until death commend ourselves to thy care and faithfulness.' Sing it to me, Dietrich, 'Make an end, O Lord—'"

He held her hand in his and sang softly. "Mach End, O Herr, mach Ende / mit aller unsrer Not; / stark unsre Fuss und Hande / und lass bis in den Tod / Uns allzeit deiner Pflege / und Treu empfohlen sein, / So gehen unsre Wege / gewiss zum Himmel ein." ("Make an end, O Lord, make an end to all our distress; strengthen our feet and hands and let us always until death commend ourselves to thy care and faithfulness, so to go our way with assurance into thy Heaven.")

As night fell she slept, her breathing even, her face peaceful.

It was near midnight when Dietrich arrived at Finkenwalde. As he drove into the garage, he saw a light in his upstairs window and wondered what that meant. He doubted if anyone would wait up so late if there were not a problem of some kind.

The door was ajar and when he pushed it open one of the ordinands, Gunther Weiss, was standing beside the desk, one hand on the back of the chair, and on his intelligent face a smile, apologetic and apprehensive.

"Ah, Bruder Weiss, I'm afraid I'm rather late. And you have been waiting for me? I hope nothing is wrong."

"No, not really. I just wanted to talk with you. I just thought I'd wait until you came back. I don't want to trouble you."

Dietrich saw that the young man was indeed perturbed. "No trouble. Please sit down."

Weiss was silent for a time and kept his eyes on the floor. His carefully groomed hair, dark and shiny, had begun to recede above each temple. "I've been thinking a lot these past few weeks, Bruder Bonhoeffer, trying to figure out what I should do." His voice faltered, and he pressed his hands together.

Dietrich said nothing, but listened attentively.

"I've tried to look at the thing from all sides, and I just can't see that much wrong with the idea of working with the church committees."

He looked up at Dietrich with a trace of defiance, all the more surprising because it seemed out of keeping with his nature. From all Dietrich had learned of him in the six weeks since the new course began, he seemed a thoughtful fellow, and one of the most responsible of the new brethren. Pietistic, perhaps, but not to extremes.

"I'm sorry, but it just seems to me the logical and sensible answer to a lot of problems," Weiss said.

"Indeed?" Dietrich asked. The thought of one of his own students defecting to the enemy had not occurred to him, not since they had vowed so fervently to stand by him, Fifth Decree or no. "How have you arrived at this conclusion?" he asked with a calmness he did not feel.

"Well, in the first place, I don't think all the wrangling is getting us anywhere at all. It's all so negative and circumscribed. The way I understand it now, the committees don't propose to be the one church government, but the cooperative effort of both governments—all church governments, in fact. I hadn't understood that before," he added in an aggrieved tone.

"That isn't possible, Bruder Weiss. I don't know where you got

your information, but it's mistaken. Whatever they call themselves, the church committees are intended in the final analysis to
replace all other church governments, including that of the Confessing Church. They may not be showing that card right away
but they will soon enough, and by then it will be too late. Remember, they have the whole Nazi regime at their back."

Bruder Weiss said nothing. It was something he obviously preferred not to think about.

Dietrich continued, "The church committees have their calling
from the Nazi state. We dare not forget that." The young man's
eyes shifted to the side and down. "Only Jesus Christ calls his
Church. How could we lead His Church with the wrong calling?"

In the deep silence the clock in the downstairs hall chimed the
half-hour—half past twelve. Dietrich searched the ordinand's face
for a sign that his words were engendering a positive response. But
the eyes remained cool, resistant circles and the jaw, rigid. "Yes,
we are circumscribed," Dietrich said. "We are negative, if that's
what it takes in this time and place. We cannot compromise and
remain in the truth of God."

"I don't know about that," said Weiss. "I just want a chance to
preach the Gospel to people, ordinary people who don't understand all these fine points, who are going to be left without any
preaching of the Gospel at all, if the Confessing Church keeps on
trying to go it alone." He looked up, his eyes flashing defiance. "I
don't think it's unreasonable to ask for some degree of security so I
can do this."

"I can understand that. God knows, we all long for a peaceful
ministry."

"Zoellner is working in a spirit of good will to heal the breach.
He's offering a free decision of conscience and peace in the church."

"Does it matter what he offers, if it is offered under the auspices
of the Hitler regime?" Dietrich moved forward slightly and said
gently, "Bruder Weiss, do you really want to sell the promise for a
mess of pottage?"

"But you don't have to give up your belief in the tenets of the

Confessing Church. You shouldn't have to give up being in the Confessing Church at all."

"Not from their point of view, of course not."

"Not from any point of view, begging your pardon. To my way of thinking any such demand is just unevangelical legalism. I'm sorry sir, but that's the way I feel about it."

"I see." They were going in circles. Dietrich began to feel that Weiss had come to him with his mind already made up—shut, locked, and sealed. He got up and walked to the window. The night was black dark—no star in sight. He turned to Weiss and said, "May I ask who told you all this?"

Weiss paused, a little taken aback. "Superintendent von Scheven."

"So he wants you to come under his Pomeranian church committee?"

"Yes."

"What did he say about your staying on here if you do that?"

"He said that would be impossible."

"That doesn't sound very much like a real intention to cooperate or make peace, does it?"

Weiss had no answer to that.

Dietrich said, "Did you know that they are establishing their own seminary just across the Oder from here at Kuckenmuhle?"

"Yes, he told me that."

"Clearly for the purpose of torpedoing ours, you know," Dietrich said, and sat down once more at the desk. He glanced at Weiss's pale, unyielding face and wondered what had gone wrong—where he had failed the man. "We're a seminary of the Confessing Church, Bruder Weiss, and subject to the direction of the Councils of Brethren. If anyone refuses his confidence and obedience to his leadership, he cannot remain in our seminary." Dietrich looked into his face. "But I hope you will reconsider." He stood up. "Let's talk no more tonight, but simply pray about it."

For a long time after Bruder Weiss left, Dietrich stood by the window and looked out into the dark night. When he got into bed he could not sleep. He heard the clock strike all the small hours and finally dropped off sometime after five A.M.

In the days that followed, the members of the Brethren House and some of the seminarians talked long and earnestly with Bruder Weiss. But in the end nothing did any good. So Bruder Weiss left. It was a dark day in Finkenwalde.

16

The next week Dietrich found his grandmother a little better. She was taking more nourishment and for short periods of time was able to sit in a chair. She had made up her mind, she said, to hold out until Christmas Eve and sit in the living room with all the family for one last time.

That afternoon, as Dietrich left the little restaurant near the Luther Bridge, where he often had lunch after his lecture at the university, his cousin Hugo hailed him in the street. When he learned that Dietrich was walking to the Zoo Station, he suggested they walk together.

Hugo was his charming old self, as if no differences had ever separated them. They talked of Dietrich's grandmother, whom Hugo called "that formidable little old lady"; of the lecture that he had just attended on "Land Reform," which had been "beastly boring" ("You're lucky you don't have to be subjected to such bureaucratic tedium"); and of Dietrich's seminary, which Hugo's mother had told him about. He was surprised that Dietrich could be content with that and hoped he could still find some time to write. Hugo had always expected Dietrich would do great things in the academic world, and then could proudly say, "my cousin, the famous theologian."

Dietrich laughed. "Once I may have entertained such ideas, too, but no more. They've doused the light in the university. It's fallen from a house of learning to an indoctrination center."

"To some extent, perhaps. But that's not the important thing right now."

Dietrich knew an argument on that subject would get nowhere and explained instead his reasons for taking the seminary. As boys Dietrich and Hugo had often talked theology and spoken with awe of their great-grandfather, the theologian Karl August von Hase. To them he was a hero. The king of Württemberg had imprisoned him in a dungeon for his beliefs.

Hugo was five years Dietrich's senior and toward the end of the Great War had entered the ranks of the already beaten German Army. His father, General von der Lutz, had served from the beginning. When the war ended, Hugo was seventeen, and the humiliating defeat and unjust peace treaty that followed seemed to have seared his patriotic soul. Dietrich remembered his passionate cries of outrage when the victorious allies heaped upon Germany the entire blame for the war and exacted ruinous reparations. Hugo had strongly defended Hitler's swift dismantling of the patched-up Weimar Republic. "Now we'll see some action," he had said. "That's what we need, somebody who can get things done." His admiration for successful power politics had exempted the leader from ethical yardsticks. Dietrich and his brother Klaus had argued valiantly with Hugo but had failed to shake these convictions.

Now, after the Nazi regime's overt attacks on the church, Dietrich felt compelled to speak again. He voiced his oneness with the Barmen Declaration and expressed his concern for the steadfastness of the church in the face of persecution. "The church must stand as a watchman and speak to the need of the times, no matter what it costs," he said. "In such circumstances it was quite impossible for me to refuse the seminary."

"I have no doubt of your sincerity, Dietrich. Who could doubt that? You speak of persecution, but who is causing the problem anyway? Surely it's this Confessing element, this breakaway faction, which is disrupting the unity of the church."

"It is not 'breakaway' and it is not a 'faction.' It's the Reich Church that has broken away from Christ."

"Now, there you're mistaken. There've been some extremists. Yes, I admit it. I don't like them either, but let's look on the bright side. Much good is being done, you know. People are going to church again with genuine enthusiasm. You ought to be glad of that instead of splitting hairs."

As his cousin talked Dietrich noticed a commotion beside the Queen Louisa monument. Two SA men faced a slight, well-dressed man seated on a bench.

One of them said, "Can't you read, Jewboy?"

The man lowered his newspaper in alarm.

"I said, can't you read?" the Nazi repeated, and pointed to the sign on the bench, which read "Jews Forbidden."

The man rose, folded his paper under his arm, and stepped sideways around the end of the bench, his wary eyes never leaving the SA men.

"Looks like we'll have to teach him, Kurt," the storm trooper said, his hand on his billy club.

With three quick steps Dietrich passed the storm troopers, addressing the hapless victim as he went, "Ah, Johannes, have I kept you waiting? I'm terribly sorry. I was held up at the university." He winked at the startled Jew, put his hand on his shoulder, and steered him to the path, where Hugo waited in obvious amazement. In a voice loud enough to be heard by the storm troopers, Dietrich said, "I'd like you to meet my cousin, Herr Councilor von der Lutz, of the Justice Department." He tried to reassure the frightened man with a look, then turned to Hugo. "My friend, Herr Johannes Ertzberger." Without a backward glance, Dietrich nudged them forward. Hugo, three inches taller than Dietrich, towered above the man walking between them.

"We'd better hurry or we'll be late for the matinee," said Dietrich, and continued in the same vein until they were out of earshot of the SA men. Hugo, whose face had become a battlefield of conflicting emotions, moved with them automatically.

Dietrich introduced himself to the man and told him he was a pastor in the Confessing Church.

The Jew gave a name, which Dietrich did not catch, and said, with tears in his eyes, "Thank you. Thank you very much. Those men—there's no telling—."

"Never mind, just try to be careful after this."

Hugo said nothing at all. At the footbridge near the Zoo Station the man, with a bow and repeated thanks, took leave of them. When he had disappeared through the gate, Hugo turned to Dietrich and said, "Next time you indulge in this kind of impulsive heroics, please leave me out of it."

"For God's sake, Hugo, don't be a fool! You saw that bully reach for his club."

"I saw nothing of the kind."

"Then you weren't looking. They could have killed the poor man."

"How you exaggerate. But then, you've always had a lively imagination."

A shock of anger rocked Dietrich's entire frame. "I'm afraid you're deliberately closing your eyes to plain facts."

"Not at all. There are extremists, yes. I've said so. And I dislike that as much as you. But on the whole—. Listen, Dietrich, I'm seeing things accomplished that I've been yearning for for years, for years. A new Germany is emerging. Of that I'm proud and grateful. You should be too."

"I suppose you're proud of the Nuremberg laws?"

"They're not perfect, I'll be the first to admit. You understand, we tried to eliminate some of the more extreme measures."

"Why couldn't you then?"

"The Chancellory kept sending our drafts back. There were certain guidelines."

"You mean you had no real autonomy."

"No, I said there were guidelines. Please be reasonable. I believe there was a need for something like this. Maybe not quite so stringent. But most people agree that the Jews had too much influence. They were running things. In the arts, in business, in publishing. People were tired of it. These laws were meant to correct that state of affairs."

"By putting the law on the side of bigotry and hate."

"You see, we can't talk without getting into an argument. Look, Dietrich, it's the Fatherland I care about. If the side effects here and there are sometimes—distasteful—well, so be it. It's not my place to criticize or interfere or let these minor episodes upset me."

"What are these minor episodes, as you call them, leading to? When the government backs the criminal, what will that do to Germany? To all that is good and decent? If you care about the Fatherland, think about that."

Hugo stared at him. "I can see we have nothing further to say to one another," he said. "Good-day." With a click of his heels he turned and strode through the gate out onto the busy street.

Dietrich watched him go and remembered something Christel had said earlier: "Folly is a moral, not an intellectual defect. Hitler counts on people's folly." So far, they were proving him right.

Dietrich's grandmother, her face pale as parchment, was propped on pillows to aid her shallow breathing. A little after midnight she had lapsed into unconsciousness. But she had known Dietrich when he arrived earlier, and had greeted him with a faint, flickering smile as he took her hand. She had been sinking fast since Christmas, when Dietrich had carried her down the stairs to sit with the family around the tree.

Dietrich's father, his stethoscope dangling from his neck, sat beside her, holding her hand. He had scarcely left his place the whole night through, steadfastly ignoring fatigue. Dietrich wondered what memories of her crowded his mind, memories that went back more than twice as many years as his own. It came to him more forcefully than ever before how much he owed his father, how despite his deep reserve he had communicated to him so much of what he now held to be valid.

Now the breathing changed, becoming only short, light gasps. Each gasp followed more slowly upon the other until it seemed that one would be the last. There was no other sound in the room. Dietrich exchanged a glance with his father across the bed, and with his mother, standing behind him, her hands on his shoulders. Then came one more light breath; after it, no other. So lightly, so easily her suffering ended.

Three days later they buried her, and Dietrich gave the funeral address. He took his text from Psalm 90, a Psalm that was read at home each New Year's Eve. "Thou art our refuge, O Lord, age after age." In the course of his remarks he spoke of her great grief over the suffering of the Jews in Germany, and in that moment his eyes met Hugo's, who sat three rows back.

Afterward in the crowd he came face-to-face with Hugo. Dietrich was struck by the incongruity of the two lives: his grandmother and his cousin. In deference to the occasion and to his mother, who was standing nearby, he put out his hand in greeting. Hugo stared at it a moment. His cold, indignant eyes moved to Dietrich's face. Then, without shaking the proffered hand and without a word, he turned and walked away.

In the trees at the edge of the crowd Dietrich caught a glimpse of Elenore with a young man he had not met. He was surprised that instead of relief, he felt a twinge of regret.

Back in Finkenwalde the next day Dietrich wrote her a long letter. He tried to explain clearly and sensibly the reasons for the gradual divergence of their two paths. He did not put on paper all the tangled motives. They were beyond his own understanding and mixed with remorse. For the first time he told her openly the course his spiritual odyssey had taken. And he wished her well. In his heart, too, he wished her well.

That January of 1936 there were many compromises and defections by Confessing Church leaders and pastors. The most devastating setback came when August Marahrens, the national chairman of the provisional government of the Confessing Church, announced his readiness to cooperate with the Reich Church Committee. But after that the wobbling compass began pointing in the right direction once again. The Old Prussian Council of Brethren was asking for a proclamation from the pulpits, which would refuse cooperation with the church committees.

Dietrich was asked to speak at a number of meetings in Pomerania, where with all his powers he encouraged pastors to read the proclamation in their churches. At a meeting in Stettin the whole seminary joined him. But the group that took the opposing view resorted in the end to accusations of "power-grabbing" and "demonic fanaticism." There were some embarrassing outbursts from the Finkenwaldans. An extemporaneous speech by one of his ordinands, Winfried Krause, disturbed Dietrich with its lack of moderation.

Afterward he talked with his students and others on the wide steps before the church. One of the Stettin pastors, Dr. Friedrich Schauer, said that Satan was speaking through such utterances as Krause's.

In the face of that Dietrich could not remain silent. "I must say that seems a singularly uncharitable verdict."

"And it was singularly uncharitable for your young firebrand to label Marahrens a traitor to the church."

"He said that Marahrens had betrayed the church, yes. I would say that Marahrens could not possibly have betrayed the Confessing Church, since he clearly never belonged to it."

Dr. Schauer looked profoundly shocked. He was a good man— a devoted, honorable, hardworking pastor, and a Confessing Church stalwart.

Dietrich softened his voice. "He was never really one of us, you know, Dr. Schauer, and should never have been head of our church government."

"With that I cannot agree," Dr. Schauer said stiffly and turned and walked away.

The look in the eyes of his students proclaimed Dietrich their champion. Dismayed, he turned quickly from them and walked alone back into the church.

The next Sunday in Finkenwalde's emergency chapel Dietrich preached the sermon and read out the proclamation of the Council of Brethren, which ended with these words: "We have to make it quite clear to ourselves that we shall not arbitrarily abandon the claims of the Confessing Church, even if this should lead us along a fresh path of suffering."

Afterward the Finkenwalde congregation, which had been meeting together since the previous September, formally constituted itself as a Confessing congregation and elected a parish

Council of Brethren. Some of the parishioners came from as far away as Stettin, including an aristocratic old Junker lady, Frau Ruth von Kleist-Retzow, a wealthy landowner who arrived each Sunday on the train with her grandchildren. In the churchyard after the service the parishioners lined up to sign the red commitment card of the Confessing Church. At the edge of the crowd there was one young man whom Dietrich had not seen before. He observed him more than once making notations in a small book he held in the palm of his hand.

As he glimpsed once more in the faces of his ordinands the look of total allegiance toward him, cool disdain slowly spread its poison through his veins.

Dietrich said little during the noonday meal. He ate his stew and potatoes without relish. The tone all up and down the U-shaped table was high-pitched and charged with excitement, a proud excitement, tinged with the awareness of danger. Soon Dietrich found himself wanting desperately to get away—off by himself.

In his room he fared little better. He tried to read, but the speeches of the play ran together and he kept starting over. Finally, in disgust, he threw the book aside and went to the window. Gray clouds, like saturated blankets hanging from four corners, dripped a fine freezing rain. There was no movement anywhere. He turned and put on his overcoat, overshoes, and a wool cap. As he walked again downstairs he was dimly aware of Eberhard passing him on the way up. He gave no sign of recognition, but like one deaf and mute, headed out the front door into the cold drizzle.

From his place at the supper table Eberhard watched Dietrich, whose preoccupation he had noticed from the beginning of the meal. He had seen the withdrawn look on his face when he went out earlier in the afternoon; and seeing it still, he began to wonder what was the matter.

The intervening months since Dietrich had asked him to be his confessor had cemented a friendship that daily became stronger. At Dietrich's invitation Eberhard had joined the House of Brethren, along with Kanitz, Schönherr, Maechler, and others, seven in all with Bonhoeffer. There had been a lighthearted ceremony with a toast in good Mosel wine, when Bonhoeffer made the shift in address from the formal "Sie" to the familiar "du." From then on first names were used among them, including the director himself.

Some members of the House of Brethren pastored small Confessing congregations in the area or assisted hard-pressed pastors. Others worked with students at the nearby university in Greifswald. Eberhard assisted in the seminary with correspondence, accounting, a tutorial, and was available for service in any Confessing Church emergency. At midday, while the seminarians had singing instruction, the brethren met for discussion and prayer in Dietrich's room.

Several times during those months Eberhard had noticed Dietrich going off by himself for no apparent reason and remaining unapproachable for several days. This time, when he discovered that Dietrich had left the table, Eberhard excused himself. He needed in any case to borrow Dietrich's copy of the Bernanos for a Bible study the next day, so with that as an excuse, he knocked on Dietrich's door.

Dietrich was standing by the window. "Yes, of course," he said, without moving. "You'll find it there." He pointed to its place in the bookshelf.

Eberhard found the book and stood for a moment looking across the room at his mentor and friend. "What's wrong, Dietrich?"

Dietrich looked up quickly. His eyes, taken off guard, betrayed the beleaguered spirit within. "Nothing. I'm all right."

"Sorry. I just wondered. You seemed disturbed about something. I thought maybe—," Eberhard broke off lamely. He turned the book over in his hand.

Dietrich made no response.

"I guess I'll be going then." Eberhard turned toward the door and took hold of the knob.

"No, Eberhard, don't go," Dietrich said, his voice strained and weary. "Come and sit down a minute."

They each came to the desk and Eberhard took the side chair. For a long time Dietrich said nothing but sat motionless, his elbows on the writing table and his hands clasped before his face. Finally, without turning his head, he said, "Jeremiah was right. 'The heart is a defiant and despairing thing.'"

Eberhard did not know the significance of the allusion, but the hopelessness in Dietrich's voice told him that something was seriously amiss.

After a long pause Dietrich continued, "It falls so easily back into old ruts. A man thinks, sometimes, that he is at last pulling free. Maybe even winning the struggle. Then—" He broke off and looked directly at Eberhard. "It isn't fair to subject you to all this—to expect you to understand—."

"I might. I could try."

Dietrich turned to him a look of conjecture, then his eyes moved to the Spanish tapestry, the head of Christ, above the desk. "It is unutterably hard to be a follower of Jesus Christ. A man grows weary. Worse than that, he often catches himself turning his calling, or letting it be turned, to his own glory. I find that despicable. Despicable," he repeated.

"Sometimes people are too hard on themselves," said Eberhard. "They think their actions and responses are worse than they really are." He wanted to get at the heart of the matter, but was afraid to say what he was thinking. He began again, "I know there are times when it's hard to find a reason to be grateful."

"Grateful? Must a man be grateful for a nature that makes him do and say and think things he despises in himself?"

"I don't know. I don't know about that. But for the ability to see the truth clearly, yes, I believe so. For that, yes. It's a gift not many people have."

"Such a gift can be more a curse than a blessing."

"I don't think you really mean that. I don't think you would despise what God has given."

Dietrich looked at him despairingly as if that were a thought he had tried to hold on to before, without success.

Feeling his way along, Eberhard continued, "It seems to me unavoidable to see the truth in one area without also seeing it in another, even where you'd rather not."

Dietrich said nothing but turned away with an almost inaudible groan.

"Without it you couldn't lead."

"Who wants to lead? And place himself in such jeopardy, with that kind of power? What man, if he is a Christian, wants to have other men follow him blindly, unquestioningly?" Dietrich got up, moved to the window and stood there motionless, looking out. His broad shoulders slumped. Without turning around, he said, "And what of such a leader? When he knows within himself that he is not what he seems—that he is not fit to lead—and mistaken to think he should try."

Eberhard was deeply shocked, for the first time aware that the self-condemnation he had heard in the confessional ran so deep. He had not understood it then and did not understand it now, but he saw that for Dietrich it was painfully real. He realized all at once the peril of the situation—the peril for everyone else, as well as for Dietrich. The seminary was in the gravest danger from all sides. Only because of belief in this man's leadership did it hold together at all. Bonhoeffer was so sure, his decisions so clear-cut; and because of that the men were sure. Maybe it was a kind of "blind" following, and Eberhard began to glimpse dimly why that disturbed Dietrich. For himself, Eberhard could not see the harm in it. Such leadership was desperately needed.

Eberhard dared not think what would happen if Dietrich were no longer able to relate to them, to lead them. As he spoke again, he weighed his words carefully. "Do you think God would give you such a gift if he didn't also give you the ability to use it—and overcome whatever it is that hinders you?"

Dietrich turned around sharply. "Then why am I not allowed to see that? Is it asking too much? In this moment I can't see it. I can't see it at all. In fact, quite the opposite."

The bitterness, restrained though it was, took Eberhard by surprise. It was so out of character with the man he thought he knew.

He did not know how to answer. Finally he said softly, "Maybe you should try to find what it is that keeps you from seeing it."

Dietrich stopped still and said with simplicity, "If you think you know, I wish you'd tell me."

"I can't tell you. How could I possibly know?"

"Tell me, Eberhard."

"I can only tell you some things it might be, that's all," said Eberhard. He felt himself pushed into a corner and knew he could not escape.

"Then tell me that," said Dietrich. He came back to the desk and sat down again.

"It may be," Eberhard began haltingly, "that—in certain moments or so—a person comes to the point where he's just not listening to the Word of God, but demanding a sign from him instead—his own special sign, maybe—I don't know. Kinda putting God to the test? We're all guilty of that sometimes, I think."

Dietrich sat perfectly still before him. He did not take his eyes from the pen in his hand, and he did not speak.

Eberhard continued, "Sometimes we want to take only what is due us—in a kind of pride, I guess, not wanting to accept a gift. And that is sin."

Dietrich glanced up quickly.

His boldness, instead of checking him, strangely spurred Eberhard on. "We prefer—I don't know—earned punishment, maybe, to unearned kindness."

A rueful smile played around Dietrich's mouth, and Eberhard felt he had somehow come near the mark. He said, with a light twist, "We'd rather go under in our own strength, than live out of grace."

Now Dietrich smiled fully, and the tension loosened in his face. But he did not speak, and Eberhard added, "We're only responsible for our gifts, you know. You said that once, I remember."

Dietrich looked at him questioningly.

"I remember it made a deep impression on me. You spoke of Goethe and Napoleon and said they would have to answer for how they used their great gifts—not primarily for their weaknesses.

'God knows what we've been given and will judge us accordingly,' you said."

"Yes, I think I did say that. I'd forgotten."

"Which means he takes into account your weaknesses—your nature, which you say makes you do things you hate. Isn't that so?"

"Maybe," Dietrich said thoughtfully. "Yes, I believe so." Silently he turned the pen between his fingers. After a long time he looked up, his eyes calmer once more. "I'll need to think about what you've said. You have probably come closer to the truth than you know."

Eberhard smiled and said nothing. He picked up the Bernanos from the desk where he had laid it and stood up.

"Thank you, Eberhard," said Dietrich rising. "Thank you for staying by me."

17

Eberhard sat by the fire with the other seminarians and listened to Dietrich's stories of his travels in the United States. He relaxed, pleased that the celebration of Dietrich's thirtieth birthday had gone well. He and the students had spent days preparing for it. Early that morning, before the wake-up trumpet, they had gathered in the hall outside Dietrich's door and sung the songs of greeting. The cook had prepared a sumptuous meal for the party this evening, and every ordinand had written a special tribute, some funny, some serious. Now they were smiling expectantly as Dietrich's story reached its climax.

"I was half asleep," Dietrich said, "but I kept hearing a deep, snuffling sound very near, almost in my ear, and could feel the weight of something big and warm and alive pressing against me through the tent. I jumped up, shook Lassere awake, and in the dim light of dawn we cautiously slipped outside and around the tent. It was a pig lying there. Apparently I had snuggled up all night to a big old sow."

The seminarians broke into loud guffaws.

"We had set up camp in a hog pasture. Somewhere in the middle of America—Missouri, I think it was."

When the laughter died down one of the students asked dubiously, "And you went this whole journey to Mexico with a Frenchman?"

"Yes. Jean Lassere. From northern France. There are Frenchmen who are Christians, too, you know," Dietrich said with a smile. "Well, you've probably heard enough for tonight."

Eberhard, his imagination inflamed with the thought of traveling in the United States, joined the others in a clamor for more. But one student, Werner Koch, a brash young blond, who seemed to revel in keeping one step ahead of the game, suggested that Dietrich take the seminary on a trip to Sweden. Koch had it all figured out. He was aware, he said, of Bonhoeffer's ecumenical connections in that country and was sure the church leaders there would be interested in hosting a seminary tour from the persecuted church in Nazi Germany.

"It would be interesting, of course," Dietrich said.

The other ordinands perked up.

"But quite impossible," he added quickly. "Not enough time to make the arrangements and get the trip in before the end of the term."

Teetering on the edge of hope, the ordinands had an answer for every obstacle and promised to help in all possible ways. Eberhard backed them up at every turn.

"You realize, of course," Dietrich said, "the government would allow us to take only ten Reichmarks each out of the country. We would be wholly dependent on the hospitality of the Swedish Church."

"But wouldn't it be worth it to them?" Koch asked.

Dietrich scrutinized Koch's affable face. "Perhaps." He stretched out his long legs and pressed his forefinger against his lips. Eberhard watched for signs of acquiescence. Then Dietrich sat up straight. "Well, I thought one was supposed to get wiser with age," he said with a rueful smile, "but never mind. I'll call Birger Forell at the Swedish embassy tomorrow and sound him out."

An excited cheer broke out from the men.

Two weeks later at nine-thirty in the evening Eberhard, with Dietrich and the Finkenwaldans, crossed the quay from the train. The large white steamer, *Odin*, rode at anchor in ghostly silence. Across the river the lights of Stettin gleamed dimly through the misty rain. The ship was due to set sail at ten. Inside the office they relinquished their passports to be checked, and waited in the anteroom for their names to be called. A quarter-hour passed. Two plainclothesmen entered from a door beside the cashier's window and walked toward them. The taller of the two, a man with a long head and a narrow, high-cheeked face, stopped before the group and called out Dietrich's name.

Dietrich, who was sitting next to Eberhard, stood up.

"You are Pastor Dietrich Bonhoeffer?"

"Yes."

"And these men?"

"Students."

"Students?"

"Seminary students. Ordinands."

"I see." A light sneer crossed the man's classically Aryan features. He exchanged a glance with his square-jawed companion. "You, of course, cannot go to Sweden," he said to Dietrich. The corners of his mouth twisted in condescension. He turned his lapel. On the underside the insignia of the Gestapo was clearly visible. Eberhard's anxiety rose several notches.

Dietrich looked from one officer to the other and spoke in a voice cool and reasonable. "Gentlemen, you might find it advisable to get clearance from your superiors in Berlin, because we are invited by his eminence, the archbishop of Sweden. The brother of the king also is informed of our visit. If you prevent us, there's likely to be an unfavorable reaction in the newspapers abroad."

The two men exchanged hesitant glances.

"If you wish to avoid a blunder, I suggest you think it over."

The tall man stared at Dietrich as if he wished his glance could make him disappear, then turned abruptly and walked back into the office, followed silently by the other. After twenty minutes the Gestapo returned, gave back their passports, and announced that they could travel.

Eberhard had never been to Sweden, and every one of the next ten days was an adventure for him. The Swedes received them warmly everywhere and treated them as honored guests. There were numerous meetings with students, pastors, and leaders of the Swedish Church, who listened eagerly to Dietrich's message on the church in Germany and on discipleship. The archbishop gave them an official reception at his palace in Uppsala and assured them that the Swedish Church remembered in constant prayer the struggling and suffering churches in Germany, and would continue to pray for them. Crown Prince Oscar Bernadotte, brother of the king, met them at an evening reception given by the Swedish YMCA. Another brother of the king, Prince Eugen, took them on a tour through the private art gallery in his castle. Their visit received full daily coverage in the Swedish press, with many pictures in the newspapers.

Eberhard was the first to hear on the hotel radio that Hitler, in a breach of the Locarno Treaty, had marched troops across the bridges into the Rhineland and reoccupied the demilitarized zone. Eberhard's first reaction was a surge of pride. The Rhineland belonged to Germany by rights. But Dietrich's response was restrained. He snapped on the radio and for the next three days listened to every news report. It had not occurred to Eberhard to wonder what the Allied Powers would do about it.

By the time they arrived back on German soil it was clear that Hitler had won the dare. France and England, with great reasonableness, counseled moderation and the avoidance of further conflict. In the open-seated car of the local train from Stettin to Finkenwalde, Eberhard joined in the nationalistic exultation of the ordinands.

"He pulled it off."

"He simply snubbed his nose at all of them."

"And it worked. It worked."

"Yes. You can't argue with that, can you?"

"He must have known it would work, don't you think?"

"Yes. You'll have to hand it to him. He's smart. Really smart, sometimes."

"The Rhineland back, my God, it's marvelous. No self-respecting German can object to that."

Eberhard looked at Dietrich, who was sitting a little apart. Up to now Dietrich had not commented, but now he said, "Nobody can object to the aim of the return of the Rhineland to German sovereignty. But, of course, Hitler broke a treaty to do it, a treaty he specifically recognized only a few months ago."

The ordinands looked at him silently, with varying degrees of resentment on their faces at this intrusion into their jubilation.

"I think we have to ask ourselves a question," Dietrich continued, "If he broke one treaty with such spectacular success, won't that embolden him to break another, and then another? Where will it end?"

No one ventured to join him.

"Well, just think about it after while, when you get down off your cloud."

Eberhard's feelings were so mixed up that the rest of the way home he avoided Dietrich's eye. A few days later on a walk through the beech forest behind the seminary Eberhard and Dietrich came out on a bluff overlooking a newly built airfield, where Göring's fighters were drilling.

As they stood and watched the planes land and take off, Dietrich said, "The Rhineland was just a practice run. Someone should tell that to the British."

The falling away of Confessing Church people was threatening the financial status of the seminary. One day Dietrich and Eberhard were going over the accounts. As they worked, the mail arrived. For Dietrich there was a copy of a letter from Heckel to the provincial church committee in Stettin about the trip to Sweden. The last paragraph said: "The incident has brought Lic. Bonhoeffer very much into the public eye. Since he may incur the reproach of being a pacifist and an enemy of the state, it might well be advisable to take steps to ensure that he will no longer train German theologians."

Dietrich looked up and was relieved to find that Eberhard was engrossed in a letter of his own and did not notice anything. With some trepidation Dietrich picked up the next letter, which was from Klaus, with a newspaper clipping and a note: "It seems you are being noticed—in some of the wrong places. I hope you'll be careful."

The clipping was from the SS newspaper *Durchbruch,* and it took exception to a study of King David that Dietrich had published some time earlier. The writer called it "such disgusting praise of the adulterer David, which clearly offends against the moral sense and feeling of the German race."

"Is something wrong?" Eberhard asked.

"Nothing much. Just that 'King David' drew some fire from the SS. That's to be expected, I suppose."

Eberhard looked up with a trace of alarm. "What do they say?"

Dietrich handed the article to Eberhard and watched as he read it. The last paragraph he read aloud. " 'One questions whether it is fitting to engage in that kind of Bible work with such a brotherhood of vicars. There is much that is harmful in such teaching, which has the audacity, even now in the year 1936, to represent the world-enemy Judah as the "eternal people," the "true nobility," the "people of God." ' " Eberhard put the clipping down. "Could that mean serious trouble?"

"I have no way of knowing."

"They might shut down the seminary."

"They might. But let's hope not." Dietrich picked up the ledger sheet again. "Now what else do we have on the plus side?"

"Well, 225 eggs came in this morning."

"225?" Dietrich said laughing. "Did you count them?"

"No. I took their word," Eberhard answered with half a smile. "Kanitz's church sent a cartload of apples and sausages, bacon—

two sides of bacon—eggs, butter, and a great sack of flour. Then we got seven more pledges today, some for 1 RM a month, some for 2 RM."

Besides that, Frau Ruth von Kleist-Retzow had promised to raise some substantial gifts from other Junkers. Dietrich leaned back in his chair. "I think we're going to make it, Eberhard. I'm very thankful." He crumpled the SS clipping and the letter from Heckel and threw them in the wastebasket.

Not long afterward, Dietrich became involved in a new venture on the part of the church—a memorandum to be addressed directly to Adolf Hitler. Since the disappointing Steglitz Synod the previous fall, he had waited for some such protest from the Confessing Church against the evils of the Nazi system. Franz was working on the memorandum with the Brethren Council and asked Dietrich's help on some of the fine tuning. At the end of the second seminary course they went together to Friedrichsbrunn for a few days work on it.

During the mornings they concentrated on the memorandum to Hitler and in the afternoons they reveled in the mountain springtime. Twice, on the wooded trails around Friedrichsbrunn, their pleasure was marred when they encountered groups of young hikers—not the free-singing hikers of old, but uniformed members of the Hitler Youth singing Nazi songs.

Neither of them spoke of Elenore, although Dietrich was sure that Franz had heard, as he had, that she was getting married in the fall. By common consent, they had let that subject slip into the irredeemable past.

Franz had never seen the old tenth-century Stiftskirche in nearby Quedlinburg, and Dietrich suggested that they drive over while they were there. He had long been drawn to this old church, which lifted up its mossy stones from the craggy plateau on which it was rooted.

The narrow street wound between ancient timbered houses. The way was steep and the uncut stones rough to the feet. Around the curve of the wall the gatehouse came into view. The iron portcullis was closed down.

"What is wrong, for heaven's sake? These old churches are always open in the daytime," Dietrich said.

At the gate they rang the bell and waited. No one came. In frustration Dietrich looked at Franz and rang again. The gray walls stood silent and reproachful. He rang the third time.

They heard the clatter of boots on the rough stones before they saw the SS man turn the curve. As he bore down upon them, his broad countenance glowering, he demanded, "Why do you keep ringing? Can't you see the gate is closed? This place is no longer open to the public."

Dietrich stared at the man on the other side of the grille. From the corner of his eye he glimpsed the slight but urgent warning movement of Franz's hand.

"Perhaps you will tell us why it is closed," said Dietrich.

"For the Reichführer's purposes," the man said without explanation.

Dietrich wondered what Himmler wanted with that old church. He was aware that Franz frantically wished to leave, yet he did not move.

The Nazi stood tall, one hand on his holstered hip. "Now, get going! I have no time for such as you. Or do you want to be arrested for loitering?"

Dietrich held his cool gaze on the man a moment longer before he turned and, erect and straight-kneed, walked unhurriedly down the hill.

In a little Bierstube near the train station they drank Patzenhofer beer at the counter, Franz pale and silent, Dietrich still trembling with anger.

Presently the proprietor reentered from the back room.

"Excellent beer," Dietrich said to him.

"The best around," the man said with a merry flash of his blue eyes. "That's because of the good Harz water." He wiped the counter with a clean white cloth.

"I brought my friend here to show him the old Dom, but it's closed," Dietrich said.

The man stopped his cleaning and moved nearer. His eyes

quickly scanned the room. Only one bedraggled old woman sat in
the far corner. He continued to clean slowly and looked up at them
from under bushy eyebrows. "Himmler's taken it over," he said
softly.

"Indeed? Whatever for?"

"For his SS."

"I wasn't aware they went to church."

The man laughed, a short derisive laugh. "They make their own
church. That's what Himmler's doing with the Dom. He's taken a
fancy to it, with its old Germanic symbols above the columns—
birds and snakes and all that. He's looking for Thor and Wodin."

Dietrich glanced at Franz's pale, silent face.

The man continued, "He's taken away all the Christian symbols,
the crucifix and all that. Brings his young SS men here for special
ceremonies. Cult worship, that's what it is."

"What kind of ceremonies?" Dietrich asked.

"Weddings. Dedications. And something with the little children. Something like baptism. They bring their babies. I've seen
them." He looked up at them with solemn eyes. "Going up that
street, full dress uniform, women dressed up fancy, carrying their
children. I hear they have some kind of solemn service, with the
babies lying there before the altar—a picture of Hitler overhead—
dedicate them to the Führer or some such thing. They give each
one a miniature sword at the end."

In the hope of salvaging something positive out of the trip, Dietrich and Franz looked up the Confessing congregation in Quedlinburg. They learned that the night before the young pastor had
been attacked and badly beaten by a group of SA men. The pastor
had no close relatives, so Dietrich made arrangements to take him
to Finkenwalde and care for him until he recovered. Then, with
Bishop Bell's help, he would get him to England. The young pastor's name was Wilhelm Süssbach and, like Franz, his mother was
Jewish.

An official of the Confessing Church delivered the memorandum to Hitler in person at the Reich Chancellery on the fourth of

June 1936. Dietrich was especially pleased with its strong protest against the concentration camps and the activities of the state secret police. Most of all, he welcomed its condemnation of the Nazi Party's anti-Semitism, which, it said, encouraged the people of Germany to hate the Jews.

The memo directed its final blast at Hitler himself. "His views are made, in a more and more extreme manner, the norm not only of political decisions but also of morality and justice in our people, and he himself is invested with the religious status of the people's priest, indeed of the mediator between God and people." It ended: "What we have said in this address to the Führer, the stewardship of our office compelled us to say. The church stands in the hand of her Lord."

The days lengthened into weeks, and no answer of any kind came. Dietrich was especially concerned for Franz's safety, although his signature was not on the memorandum. An announcement from the Chancellery at that time increased his unease. Hitler was consolidating all the police forces of the nation under Heinrich Himmler, the archenemy of the church. Almost simultaneously Dietrich received official notification from the university of his dismissal as a lecturer. There was no explanation.

At the end of the sixth week Franz called with news that someone had leaked the memorandum to the foreign press. As soon as classes were ended Dietrich drove the one hundred miles to Berlin at top speed and went straight to Franz's flat. There Franz brought him up to date. The full text of the memo had appeared in both the *Baseler Nachrichten* and the *Times* of London. No one had any idea who had done it. Only a few people had access—the five who actually signed it, one or two secretaries, and Friedrich Weissler, the legal advisor. The two secretaries had sworn their innocence. Weissler, who was of Jewish parentage, said no, he didn't do it.

Admonishing Franz to lie low, Dietrich set out for Jacobi's office to see what he could learn. There he found his former university student, Ernst Tillich, with Jacobi, in what appeared to be a serious conversation. Dietrich offered to leave, but they both wanted him to stay, especially Tillich. From his strained face Dietrich imagined the student to be in some kind of trouble. He remembered the boy's fiery, impetuous nature.

After they were all seated, Jacobi turned to Tillich. "Perhaps you'd like to tell Pastor Bonhoeffer what you've told me."

Tillich looked at Dietrich as if trying to gauge the degree of tolerance he might hope for from him. "You see, I'm the one who leaked the memo."

In his astonishment Dietrich said nothing.

"You see," said Tillich, "we were told that the church planned to publish it after six weeks. We waited six weeks and nothing came out."

"So you just took it upon yourself—" said Jacobi. "Didn't it occur to you that this might put the church in a dangerous position?"

"But they said the church was going to publish it anyway."

"Not in the foreign press."

"How else? If you'll excuse me, Sir, they couldn't hope to get it in the German newspapers."

"There are other ways. Pulpit proclamation, pamphlets."

"We got the feeling they were backing down."

Dietrich smiled to himself, much inclined to agree.

"Who is 'we'?" Jacobi asked.

"Friedrich Weissler and Werner Koch."

Dietrich was surprised again. Koch had just graduated from Finkenwalde.

Jacobi continued, "You were working together, the three of you?"

"But they didn't leak the memo. I'm the one who did that. You see, I copied the whole thing myself—word for word—one night."

"You took that decision upon yourself," said Jacobi, his voice heavy with sarcasm. "I see. Who all got it, Herr Tillich?"

"Reuters, UPI—"

"I assume you got it from Dr. Weissler."

"Weissler gave it to me, but—"

"He told Superintendent Albertz he didn't do it."

"I know, I know. He didn't know any better. I lied to him. You see, when he asked me if I copied out the whole thing, I told him no, because he looked so worried—terribly worried. You know, he's Jewish and he's really scared."

"He has every reason to be," said Jacobi. "The Gestapo is in the office of the Reich Brethren Council right now, searching the files."

Tillich, looking very young and vulnerable with his blond hair drooping onto his forehead, glanced at Dietrich and back to Jacobi.

"What will they find?" Jacobi asked.

"He keeps it in his file. Second drawer from the top. I've seen him put it there." Tillich was silent for a time, his head down. Then he looked up and said, "What will they do to him?"

"Maybe nothing, yet. They'll find several other copies in those offices. They'll have no way of knowing for sure that it was Weissler who gave it out. Not at first."

"Oh my God," Tillich groaned. He turned to Dietrich. "Herr Dr. Bonhoeffer, I didn't realize—I mean—Weissler agreed the people should know about it. I just thought that since I was the one copying it—" He picked up his hat from the desk. "I think I'd better turn myself in."

Dietrich said, "I'm afraid that wouldn't help matters, Bruder Tillich."

"No," said Jacobi. "That would be foolhardy. They would know you got it from somewhere. And they would find out—from you. That wouldn't be too pleasant, you know. What you should do is disappear from sight for a while. Hire out as a shepherd in Bavaria or somewhere. And, please, say nothing to anyone of your conversation here."

When Tillich was gone Jacobi brooded silently in his chair, his long curved pipe in his mouth. "They'll get him eventually," he said after a while. "All three of them. I've heard that Hitler is absolutely livid."

"It's Weissler I'm most worried about. They'll show him no mercy."

"Yes. It's a pity. These rash kids."

"Well, since it's done, what will the church do now about the

memo? Will there be a proclamation from the pulpit? And a pamphlet, I hope?"

"That's to be decided."

"We'll have to do it, won't we? To let the world know we really
did write that memo? We really meant it?"

"Yes. I suppose we will."

"I hope so."

It turned out that the church had not completely lost its voice. It
did, in fact, order a modified version of the memorandum to be
read out from the pulpits, and the church printed and distributed
one million copies to the people.

Three months later news came to Finkenwalde that the Gestapo
had caught up with Ernst Tillich and Friedrich Weissler. A month
after that they picked up Werner Koch. The seminary immediately
added the three prisoners to their intercessory prayer list. Early in
1937 the Gestapo transferred all three to Sachsenhausen concentration camp north of Berlin. Word leaked out that the Nazis had
separated Weissler from the others and subjected him to such torture and maltreatment that he died six days later.

18

Every month of the new year brought another slash of the
sword against the church Dietrich loved. By June of 1937 it became
impossible to serve it without breaking the law. There were prohibitions against "subversive" proclamations from the pulpit,
against intercessions, against collections, even against the use of
duplicating machines. Dietrich got around the prohibition against
circular letters by writing "Personal Letter" at the top of each copy
and signing each one in his own hand. Elsewhere, from all accounts, church activity slowed to a crawl. But for some pastors
and leaders, like Martin Niemöller, all the prohibitions were a
spur. Dietrich's mother reported that Niemöller's bold, fiery sermons and intercessory prayers continued, despite the fact that a

number of times the police summoned him to Alexanderplatz for interrogation and stern warnings to stop his "seditious" preaching. Sometimes they locked him up for two or three nights, but he preached on, she said, and the people still thronged to hear him. Often he preached as many as four times in one Sunday to accommodate the crowds. Other pastors took heart and followed his example.

And the arrests began. The intercessory prayer lists began to lengthen. In the circular letter Dietrich asked former Finkenwaldans to remember without fail to pray daily for each other and for the imprisoned brothers. He gave names and places of imprisonment.

The defiance continued, and in midsummer the Gestapo arrested Niesel, Jacobi, and two other leaders and brought them before a summary court. Dietrich went immediately to Berlin, where he attended one of four intercessory services for the arrested leaders. Niemöller preached and there were so many people, he had to give two successive services.

Afterward Dietrich and Franz went to a secret meeting in the back room of the Café Estelle in the Nollendorf Platz. At the entrance one of the young Confessing pastors was keeping a watch for the Gestapo. He directed them to a back room, where Niemöller, Asmussen, and Albertz were sitting at a table counting the collections from the four evening services.

Niemöller looked up. "Well, Franz, it's time you were here. This is your job."

They finished counting the money and divided it into three equal amounts. Niemöller pushed one pile with a money bag along the table to Franz. "Please count it again before we record it and put it in the safe." Asmussen and Albertz each took a part and tagged it.

Dietrich looked at Franz questioningly.

"We've taken to separating it so it won't be all in the one safe in Niemöller's office."

"Safe? I've never seen a safe there."

"No, I guess you haven't. It's in the wall behind a picture."

"Oh, I see. Behind a picture." He almost laughed. The idea was as incongruous as if they had taken to bowling in the church aisles.

The trial of Niesel and Jacobi and the others was set for July 2. Since its outcome could affect the seminary and all theological education in the Confessing Church, Dietrich decided to go back to Berlin that day and talk things over with Niemöller. He took Eberhard with him. In the hope of seeing Niemöller before the trial, they arrived at the Dahlem parsonage at eight-thirty in the morning.

Surprisingly, Franz met them at the door. From the look on his face Dietrich knew that something had happened.

"The Gestapo just left with Martin. Five minutes ago. You barely missed them."

"Frau Niemöller?"

"She's upstairs with the children. The two littlest ones are rather frightened, I think."

"How is she?"

"Not too alarmed. He's been summoned before, you know. But not quite like this, I must say. The faces of those two men were rather grim. They let him pack a bag—supervised it piece by piece. They wouldn't allow him to take any books or papers."

At that moment Frau Niemöller came down the curving steps, with one hand on the bannister. In the other arm she held the youngest child, Martin. The six-year-old Jan followed close behind. He held to the fold of his mother's skirt, his eyes red with weeping.

Dietrich greeted Frau Niemöller and expressed regret at what had happened. Then he knelt down on the level of the child. "Well, now Jan, tell me what has happened."

"Bad men. Took away my Papa. I don't like those bad men."

"No, of course not. But perhaps they will let him come back soon."

The child looked at him solemnly, but said nothing. Franz, who was the same as an uncle to these children, took the youngest from his mother.

Frau Niemöller did not know where they had taken her husband; they had said only that they were acting on express orders from Hitler himself.

Just then Lisa, the eldest, who had gone ahead into the living room, ran back. "They're here again, Mama! Out there. Big black cars. Lots of them."

Frau Niemöller turned quickly, took the little one from Franz's arms and said, "They've come back for you, Franz. All of you, quickly, get out the back way. Hurry! Hurry!"

"But what of you?" Dietrich asked.

"They're not after me. Not at all. Don't worry. Just go—hurry!"

As they turned away, Dietrich heard her say to the children, "Upstairs now—quickly. Stay with Elfriede."

Franz led them through the hall and across the dining room to a small sun porch. As they reached the outside door a thick-set man in a dark suit rounded the corner of the house and met them at the steps. Two other rough-faced bruisers followed close behind.

"You were going somewhere, gentlemen?" the thick-set man said. "No need for such haste. I'll have to ask you to turn back inside." He produced from his pocket a small metal disk on a chain and flashed it toward them with a curt flip of the wrist. It was stamped "Geheim Staatspolizei."

They all turned silently back through the door.

In the foyer they found that three or four other men had arrived through the front door. Frau Niemöller stood straight and impassive on the bottom step of the stairway.

Their captor appeared to be the foreman. His subordinates called him Herr Lieutenant Holz. He immediately stationed one man at the front door and another at the back, then ordered the others to search the detainees. "Thoroughly, please." To Frau Niemöller he said, "You will please show me your husband's study."

She led him silently to the door beneath the curve of the stair.

One of the men turned to Dietrich, ordered him to lay out everything he had on the table, then proceeded to search him. As he retied his shoes Dietrich glanced at Franz, who cast him a baleful look from under drawn brows while he slowly put his possessions back in his pockets. Dietrich tried to reason that the Gestapo had no way of knowing that Franz was Jewish. Beside the hall table, Eberhard looked sideways at him with a glint of suppressed excitement in his eyes. No word was spoken.

The foreman came to the door of the study and motioned them inside, where he ordered straight chairs positioned for them along the inside wall. Frau Niemöller already sat near a window, which faced the church. Holz assigned his men to various areas of the study. They hung their coats on the rack by the door and proceeded to search through everything in the room.

Dietrich had noticed before how neat Niemöller's desk top was, with papers and carefully penned sermons stacked in perfect order. Not exactly what one would expect from the fiery prophet. Now two of the men emptied one drawer at a time onto the desk top and sifted painstakingly through every paper, pamphlet, and notebook. Those at the bookshelves leafed through everything, a page at a time.

Meanwhile, beginning with Eberhard, Holz took each man's particulars in short terse questions: name, address, parents, grandparents, race, religion, occupation. Dietrich was concerned for Franz, but the man asked him no unusual questions and appeared to have no suspicions about his ancestry.

Thirty or forty-five minutes passed in silence. From outside the open window came the normal street noises; from inside the shuffling of paper and the thin squeak of rubber soles on the polished floor. Several times the phone rang and Holz answered it in clipped tones, stating only that Pastor Niemöller was not at home.

Late in the morning there came a flurry at the front entrance, and a tall black-uniformed officer strode into the room with an air of brusque authority. The men stopped their work and stood at attention, while the foreman spoke with the officer, whom he addressed as Herr Colonel von Scheven. He led him to a picture on the right of the door, which he removed from the wall, disclosing a small safe.

"Ach so," smiled Colonel von Scheven. He turned around to

Dietrich and the others. "And now, Herr Pastor Hildebrandt," he purred, "which of you is Pastor Hildebrandt?"

"I am Pastor Hildebrandt," said Franz.

"Ah, yes. You will be good enough to open it for us, I believe."

Franz made no move, and Dietrich whispered to him under his breath, "Go on, you fool, open it."

Whereupon Franz went straight to the safe, flicked the combination a number of times, and the door opened. Without a glance at the officer, he returned to his seat.

Von Scheven removed three medium-sized money bags from the safe. He opened each one, filtered through it with his fingers, then with a chuckle drew it tight again and put it in his briefcase. "So, you see what comes of your illegal collections. Too bad."

After von Scheven left, Dietrich whispered to Franz, "How much?"

"Thirty-thousand. Someone has betrayed us," he said from the side of his mouth. "They went straight to it. Did you see them?"

"Yes. Any ideas?"

"I don't know. The new sexton, maybe. Hasn't been here long. I didn't trust him; he wouldn't look me straight in the eye."

After a while Holz took one of the men and started out the door. Springing up, Frau Niemöller asked, "Where are you going?"

"Does it concern you where I'm going, Frau Niemöller?"

Frau Niemöller stared fixedly at the man without speaking.

"I am merely going to check the rest of the house. If you have nothing to hide, you have nothing to fear."

"I'll come with you."

"No. You will stay exactly where you are."

Frau Niemöller licked her lips and glanced across the room toward Dietrich, Franz, and Eberhard. Entreaty crept into her voice even though she was obviously fighting to keep it out. "You will let me, I'm sure, go upstairs to my children. There can be no problem with that."

"It is necessary for you to remain here. No harm will come to your children."

"I am the one to assure them of that, if you please."

The authority with which she spoke had its effect. Holz hesitated, and in that moment Frau Niemöller walked to the door as if there were no further question. The foreman shrugged and followed her out.

In the afternoon the detainees were allowed to stand up for a while. Through the front window Dietrich saw his parents' car moving slowly down the avenue, his mother's anxious face pressed against the glass. Without a word he ambled over to a table near the window. The men of the Gestapo appeared to take no notice. He picked up a magazine and stood idly perusing its pages. Soon the car returned. He hoped his mother would see that he was safe.

About three-thirty the whole thing ended as quickly as it began. The search complete, Holz told them they were free to go. Outside they crossed the wide boulevard and turned back toward the house. From the center upstairs window, with her children around her, Frau Niemöller waved to them. Half a block down the street they ducked into a Gasthaus and watched until the men of the Gestapo got into their black cars and drove away.

Only after they had checked again with Frau Niemöller, to assure themselves that she and the children were all right and to offer all possible help to her, did they turn again homeward.

Only Paula Bonhoeffer and two or three elders knew that this was to be Franz's last Sunday in the Dahlem Church. No announcement could be made because plainsclothesmen from the Gestapo were always present. Franz had preached on three Sundays in Niemöller's place and had read the intercession lists and taken the illegal offerings as usual. After Niemöller's arrest, Paula and also Dietrich had urged Franz to leave the country. Franz had written Julius Rieger in London about helping him settle in England, and received an affirmative reply, but had been postponing a final decision. He could not leave the church work in its dark hour, he said, nor could he leave his aging parents. The dangers to his Jewish mother increased every day, but emigration seemed impossible for them; his father, who was old and frail, was unable to endure such an upheaval. Finally, he had capitulated and planned to leave after the morning service.

The church was packed and there were chairs in the aisles. Paula had come early to get a seat near the front and had brought along her grandchildren, Renate and Hans-Walter Schleicher, to say good-bye to Franz. He had been "Uncle Franz" to them since they were small children and for the past several months had been giving them confirmation instruction.

After the sermon Franz descended from the pulpit and read the names on the intercession list. The number of those in prison had grown now into the hundreds, so that in the reading the names had to be combined by districts—"fifty from East Prussia, thirty-seven from Saxony." The last name he read was Martin Niemöller.

After the prayer Paula noticed a number of damp eyes around her; even some of the men took out their handkerchiefs. The reverent defiance continued with the taking of the collection, which was brought to the front and, after a prayer of thanksgiving, placed on the altar table.

During the benediction she heard footsteps moving rapidly down the side aisle. When she lifted her head, two men in black uniforms moved in on Franz and took his arms. Simultaneously two others entered from the sacristy and went straight to the altar table. One held a bag while the other emptied the offerings into it. Then, without a word to anyone, or even a glance in the direction of the congregation, the four of them marched Franz out the side door.

It all happened so fast. It was not the arrest that was so surprising; she knew that Franz, like all Confessing pastors, had been living with that expectation for some time. It was the arrogance of it, before the whole assembly, as if their feelings could not matter.

"Look, Grandmama," said Renate, "where are they taking Uncle Franz?"

"They've arrested him," said Hans-Walter, "just like Pastor Niemöller."

Around them the resentful murmur swelled into angry cries. They moved out of their pew and were swept along by the people, out the sacristy door and around to the gate in the high rock wall surrounding the church and parsonage. Outside they lined up with the others along the sidewalk.

Franz was seated in the back seat of a long Mercedes, with one of the Gestapo on either side. The driver slammed the door and tried to start the car. With a snarl the motor turned over several times, then stopped. Again a second time, the motor whined and stopped. After five or six tries one of the men got out and raised the hood. He poked around at the machinery, while the congregation watched in silence. Nothing seemed to work.

Paula and the children were standing near the car. Franz saw them and smiled with perverse satisfaction.

Finally the blackshirts took Franz out of the car and marched him off down the sidewalk. At the Königin Luise Strasse they turned right, in the opposite direction from the avenue where he lived. Obviously he had not seen fit to correct them but, slender and erect in his long black gown, walked straight ahead.

Paula and the children, with the enraged parishioners, formed a long queue and followed a short distance behind. For a block they walked in silence in the August heat. Paula could not restrain a smile at the spectacle they were making.

After three blocks the Gestapo seemed to realize something was wrong and stopped. They pulled out a map and consulted it.

"Arnim Allee, that's where you live? 126 Arnim?" she heard the officer ask impatiently.

"That is correct," Franz answered.

One of the others pointed to the map. "Here it is. The other way. We've come the wrong way."

The officer's face turned a deep red. Paula fully expected him to strike Franz. Instead he glowered at the congregation ranged behind him, whipped out a small notebook from his pocket, and jotted something down in it.

With that the SS men turned around and, with their prisoner in tow, retraced their steps until they came to the Arnim Allee and Franz's building. The congregation again brought up the rear. Before going inside Franz turned and waved to them.

After the experience on the day of Niemöller's arrest, Paula expected it to be a long wait. The members of the congregation stood about in clusters and tried to console one another. Paula wondered how many of the congregation knew of Franz's Jewish ancestry. Very few, she was sure. But the Gestapo would know. Or they would find out.

A green police van drove up and parked at the curb in front of Franz's door. In less than an hour the door opened and Franz and his captors came out again. At the curb he waved to them once more, then entered the back of the van, followed by two of the men. The door closed and the van carried him away.

The first priority was to get Franz transferred out of the Gestapo's hands. Rüdiger knew of a Dr. Carl Langbehn, an anti-Nazi lawyer, who was personally acquainted with Himmler. It was agreed that he should do what he could through that channel, while the others worked more indirectly through their own connections. Dietrich came home in answer to Paula's hurried call, but they all agreed that under no circumstances should he try to visit Franz.

The next week the Dahlem congregation announced a service of intercession for Niemöller and Franz. When Paula arrived that evening, she found the square in front of the church cordoned off by the police so that no one could enter the building from any side. Angry parishioners ranged up and down the line. Far across on the other side, more church members had gathered behind another line in front of the parsonage. Soon they joined forces, and the crowd grew until it filled the avenue. Someone began the hymn *Ein feste Burg ist unser Gott*, and immediately everyone joined in.

The police on the other side of the rope, eight or ten strong, demanded that they disperse. No one paid attention. Without a break in the singing, the whole congregation, with Paula in the middle, began to march along the Königin Luise Strasse. All the

suffering the Dahlem Church had endured over the weeks coa-
lesced into an iron solidarity. Paula sang with the others, full of
defiant joy. They had gone about two blocks when the up-and-
down wail of police sirens rose above the singing. The crowd came
to a halt as other sirens sounded to their rear.

There was no panic or resistance when the police began the arrests. It suddenly came to Paula how worried Karl would be, and
she was sorry. He would agree—she knew he would agree—that
it was worth it. Four loaded vans drove away on one side and three
on the other. Immediately others whirled in and stopped. More
people were hustled aboard, but still a sizable crowd remained.
After three more rounds, the vans did not return. A collective sigh
rose from those who were left, then silently they began to disperse. Paula went to the car, where the chauffeur waited.

It was three more weeks before the efforts on Franz's behalf suc-
ceeded. That same day Hans whisked him to the Swiss border.
Only when he returned with news that Franz was safely over, did
Paula breathe easy again.

19

"Somebody at Justice is trying to get Hans."

"What do you mean, Christel?" Dietrich asked.

"Just that. Somebody wants his scalp. They're digging into his
ancestry."

"Why?"

"Jealousy. He runs rings round all of them. And Gürtner favors
him too much. They can't stand that."

"I see. How does he know about this?"

"Oh, he has some friends. A few. The inquiries are coming out
of Roland Freisler's office."

Hans had told Dietrich something of Freisler. He was a Nazi
fanatic, who headed a Party clique in the Justice Department and
had taken it upon himself to purge the ministry of "unreliable"

elements. He held it against Hans that he was not a Nazi and had not joined the League of National Socialist German Jurists.

Christel shivered involuntarily. "That man is evil. His face shows it. It's as if he makes no effort to hide it. I don't think he does." She shivered again. "I hope you never have to meet him."

"Here, let me warm up your coffee." Dietrich filled her cup. "What will Hans do?"

"What can he do? Wait. Wait it out."

"And Freisler is after proof that Hans's grandmother is Jewish? I wouldn't think that too difficult."

"No. Although he'll have to go all the way to Hungary to get it. He'll do it, though. Hans is trying to figure out a way he can warn his father over there." She held her cup to her lips without drinking. "I don't know how much danger he is in, but I don't underestimate the vindictiveness of men like Roland Freisler. He'd delight to make Hans out as the serpent in the fruit basket. Hans thinks he can outmaneuver him. You know Hans. I wish he wouldn't try to play chess with the devil."

Dietrich ate the last of his roll and jelly in silence. "Have you thought of talking this over with the rest of the family?"

"No, I wanted to wait until you were home."

"Mama has excellent ideas, you know."

"Yes. But I don't want to frighten her."

"She'd be less frightened if she were not in the dark."

Christel looked up quickly.

"She's bound to know something is wrong, you know."

She drew a deep breath and let it out slowly. "Maybe so."

The next week Hans, on business in Stettin, paid a surprise visit to Dietrich in Finkenwalde. Dietrich took him out in the rowboat he had bought for the seminary. As they rowed among the reeds, Hans told him that Hugo had offered to help. "He says he can convince Hitler to see me. He's confident he'll give me a 'dispensation' that will put a stop to Freisler's machinations. I'm to bring along photographs of my blond little offspring as added proof that they couldn't be Jewish."

Dietrich said nothing. His immediate reaction was one of revulsion, and he was sure it showed on his face.

"I have to fight this thing. Otherwise I'll be forced to leave Germany."

Dietrich knew that was true. The harshest treatment was reserved for non-Aryan "deceivers" in the government.

"I don't want to stand by and let these criminals defeat me like that! I want to be in a position to defeat them—someday. That's what I really want. Just that!" His oar cut sharply into the water and the skiff shot forward. They rowed silently for a time. "If I play this game cooly, now. Hugo, of course, has no idea—"

"I must say, I simply couldn't bear such a pretense," said Dietrich.

"You can bear more than you think, when you have to."

"Maybe so."

"If I left, the keeping of the chronicle would have to be abandoned. Quite a bit has come in since you saw it. Some things so vile you'd hardly believe it. I'll have to show you sometime."

Dietrich was not anxious to see it, but he knew it was important—his duty, even—to receive such exclusive information.

"Anyone seriously trying to topple Hitler is going to need that kind of clear documented evidence."

"I quite agree."

"When that time comes, it will be necessary to have the right people on the inside."

It was not hard to imagine what the future might hold for such a course. In comparison, the church struggle seemed simple—black and white—where, as with the memo to Hitler, a man could stand up, say "no," and take the consequences. Dietrich had no inclination to take the leap from one to the other.

On the surface the three days since their arrival in Göttingen for the between-semester holiday had been pleasant and relaxing. It had always been a pleasure to stay in Sabine's house, where wealth and good taste combined with warm hospitality; and Dietrich had looked forward especially to introducing Eberhard to them. In the evenings, after the children were in bed, they thrashed out the problem of the future for the Leibholz family. Half the time Sabine and Gert seemed to accept the inevitability of emigration. Then the thought of life in a strange land and separation from family seemed to overwhelm them, and they said, "We'll wait a little while longer." Gert had not taught for more than a year, but they were financially secure, with a trustworthy banker who was still a friend.

Late one evening Dietrich spent an hour alone in the garden, and when he turned inside, the full moon was already high in the sky. Gert and Eberhard were in the dining room poring over a map of England on the table.

Suddenly Sabine burst into the room from Gert's darkened study, where she had been sitting by the front window. "Two men are coming up the walk. They're SA. Gert, you have to get away." She began to push him toward the kitchen. "Right now! Hurry! Through the orchard!"

Just then the doorbell rang.

"You go with him, Sabine," said Dietrich. "I'll answer the door."

She turned back. "The children."

"I'll take care of them. Go on." To Eberhard he said, "You stay here with the maps, just perfectly natural." The dining room opened onto the foyer, with the line of sight directly to the front door.

Dietrich turned on the light and, feeling not at all natural himself, opened the door. The brownshirts stood there, one with a notepad in his hand.

They gave the Hitler salute, then the one with the notepad asked, "Herr Libowitz?"

It was enough like Leibholz to frighten him, but Dietrich said calmly, "I am Dietrich Bonhoeffer."

The storm trooper consulted his notes. "You are not Mordecai Libowitz?"

"I am not."

"But he lives here."

"No, you must have the wrong address."

The man looked back toward the street. "What street is this?"

"The Herzberger Landstrasse."

"Well, we seem to have turned down the wrong street. Please excuse us." With another Hitler salute, the two men turned and went away.

From the darkened study Dietrich and Eberhard watched them drive away, then Dietrich sent Eberhard to the orchard for Sabine and Gert while he tried to call Mordecai Libowitz. He found the name in the phone book, but when he called there was no answer. Perhaps the unknown man had fled already. Dietrich would never know.

Two days later a little after eleven a call came from Finkenwalde. It was Frau Struwe, the housekeeper at the seminary.

"Bruder Bonhoeffer, is that you?"

"Yes, Frau Struwe. What is it?"

"Two men were here from the Gestapo. I wouldn't have let them in, but they had a paper. It was signed by Himmler, Bruder Bonhoeffer. I wouldn't have let them in, except for that."

"What did they want?"

"They've shut us down. They said we can't go on anymore. They had this paper—I wouldn't have let them in—." She was crying.

Frau Struwe never cried, not in the two years she had been with them.

She went on with intermittent sobs. "They said the seminary was a forbidden undertaking. They were closing us down. Right now."

"I see. Frau Struwe, you mustn't cry. It can't be helped. They took nothing?"

"No. They didn't take anything. I didn't let them past the hall."

"That's good. You did exactly right." It was hard to think. "I'm not sure how soon we can get there. We'll have to stop in Berlin and see the Brethren Council. Do you think you could stay on a few more days?"

"Of course. Where else could I go? This is my home."

"Yes, certainly. I'm glad you can look after things. Thank you, Frau Struwe. Thank you."

They arrived at the Heerstrasse Station in Berlin at five that afternoon and had to shove their way through crowds and barricades and innumerable swastikas to get up the steps to the street. The preparations were for the imminent arrival of Mussolini on a state visit. The entire Soldauer Platz, where the streets that led to Marienburger Allee came together, was cordoned off. There was a band on one side, surrounded by flags of both countries. The excited, laughing, flag-waving crowds waited for their Führer to arrive and accompany Mussolini on a parade down the Kaiserdamm.

In disgust bordering on physical illness, Dietrich made his way with Eberhard around the outer perimeters of the mob to the Teufelseestrasse and the back way home.

Dietrich's mother heard the news in shocked silence. For once she had no suggestions of what to do. On the train he and Eberhard had turned over every conceivable possibility, but had come to no conclusions.

The cold anger, which had been building since Frau Struwe's call, suddenly exploded. "We simply can't give in to this. Something will have to be done."

"What, Dietrich? You can't fight the Gestapo."

"No, Mama. But we'll have to go on some way. Somewhere else. Underground, probably."

"That would be dangerous."

"Yes. I guess it would. We'll have to do it nonetheless, if that's the only way."

"Will the Brethren Council go along with something like that? You can't do it alone."

"They'll have to. They'll just have to."

With mixed feelings Paula had greeted the Brethren Council's decision to let Dietrich go the underground route. They had tried through various means to bring about a review of the closure order. Nothing worked. Instead, the other four Confessing Church seminaries met the same fate, one after another. After two months Dietrich and Bethge now had found a way to set up a facade behind which the seminary could operate.

Dietrich made it sound quite simple. One hundred miles up the Baltic coast from Stettin were two adjacent administrative districts where the deans and their pastors were willing to help them. Each student would register with the police as working with one of the pastors in the district as a Vikar, or "learning minister," a perfectly normal procedure. The superintendent in each district had agreed to house the students. One of them, Superintendent Onnasch, was the father of Dietrich's new inspector of studies, Fritz Onnasch. Superintendent Onnasch offered his large vicarage in Köslin to house up to ten ordinands, including classroom space. His wife agreed to supervise the meals, for which the Brethren Council would provide the money.

Twenty-five miles farther east at Schlawe, Superintendent Eduard Block agreed to a similar arrangement. He found an unused forester's house for them near a small village called Sigurdshof. There was no electricity, but Dietrich was sure Frau Struwe could manage. His main concern was to get his radio hooked up to a battery so he could hear the news on the BBC. "It's the first thing needed to guarantee one's independence," he said.

As to the classes, he would make Eberhard a faculty member at Sigurdshof and Fritz Onnasch at Köslin. Dietrich would divide his time between the two locations each week. He was going to buy a motorcycle. "I'll just strap my book satchel and my toilet case on the back," he said, "and away I'll go."

Paula had encouraged them at every point, although secretly the whole prospect of an underground operation intensified the alarm that she felt at the closing of Finkenwalde. She had trouble sleeping. In dreams she saw Dietrich alone in a bare cell, like those she had glimpsed in Plötsensee prison when she visited Franz with his mother. Paula could see the suffering on his face, but he could not see her. She could not even make him hear her. Her pain and distress would then reach such intensity that she would wake up, grateful and relieved that it was just a dream, but deeply shaken.

A few days before Dietrich and Eberhard were to leave for Pomerania word came that Fritz Onnasch had been arrested in his church.

Dressed for bed that night, but not the least inclined to sleep, Paula leaned against the jamb of the balcony door and stared into the darkening night. She was vaguely aware of the building of a late fall thunderstorm. Lightning darted, but there was no sound of thunder yet. She shivered in the cool breeze and drew her robe more closely about her, but did not close the door.

"Is it going to storm?" Karl asked as he sat down on the little sofa to take off his shoes.

A rush of wind sent the filmy curtains billowing into the room. "Yes, I think so. It's heading this way." Still she did not move.

"Don't you think you should come inside and close the doors, Paula?" Karl asked as he buttoned his nightshirt.

She pulled the doors together and turned the latch. The curtains sank silently back into place on either side of her.

"You mustn't take all these arrests so much to heart, my dear. Onnasch will be out again soon, most likely."

"I don't know. Look at Niemöller."

"Niemöller's a special case, I think."

"Maybe so." Paula came to the sofa and slowly sat down. "Dietrich doesn't seem to realize—. He talks like there's nothing to worry about."

"With the set-up they're planning, he thinks they'll go unnoticed."

"I don't see how. There are too many of them. And Dietrich riding back and forth on a motorcycle. What could be more obvious?"

"Do you want his work to continue?"

"You know I do."

"Then there's not much we can do about it, is there?"

She looked at him. His left brow was lifted in the familiar way, but the eyes smiled indulgently. "Maybe tomorrow things will look better."

Karl was right. The next day they heard that Onnasch had been released from the prison in Stettin. But within a week Hans brought the most disquieting news yet. At a meeting with the top brass Hitler had laid out his war plans. Every generation needed its own war, he said, and he would take care that this one got its own. He wanted to begin with Czechoslovakia.

20

At the turn of 1938 Wilhelm Niesel, superintendent of the five Confessing seminaries, called the seminary leaders to Berlin for a conference, the first such gathering since Dietrich began the new work in Further Pomerania. With him was Fritz Onnasch, who was doing a splendid job with the Köslin half of the seminary. A half-hour into the meeting the doors of the parish house burst open and a whole column of uniformed Gestapo rushed in. They quickly surrounded the small circle of thirty or so brothers.

The officer in charge clicked his heels and rapped out, "Heil Hitler! You are under arrest in the name of the Führer."

Niesel stood to protest. "Gentlemen, you have made a mistake—"

"Save your explanations for the magistrate, if you please," the officer said. He took their names, then ordered his men, "Proceed!" With drawn guns they pushed the pastors, silent and subdued, outside in the bitter January cold to the dark green police wagons ranged along the curb.

Inside the darkened Grune Minna one of the secret policemen sat on either side of the door, with its small barred window. The van was cold. And their overcoats still hung in the Gemeindehaus in Dahlem. After fifteen minutes the wagon screeched to a halt in front of the police headquarters on the Alexanderplatz. The doors opened, and the officers motioned them out.

The secret police herded Dietrich, Fritz, and the others through an arched door at street level into a narrow passageway, which led past numbered doors toward the inner reaches of the building. Fritz, his limp more pronounced than usual, walked between two Gestapo men just ahead of Dietrich.

The passageway opened into a concrete courtyard, surrounded by three floors of heavily barred windows. Up a flight of steps and inside again, they passed through an iron gate, which was locked behind them, and into a hall lined with wooden benches. There they were told to wait until their names were called.

On the left wall hung a poster in black and white, with a montage of Jewish faces, each with a dubious smile. In the center were the words "When Jews Smile" in bold, yellow letters; and along the bottom a boxed inscription: "The Jews are born criminals. They cannot smile openly and above board. They only twist their mouths into a diabolical smirk." Below the poster hung a lavatory, painted green.

Against the other wall sat a forlorn family—mother, father, and daughter. They appeared to be Jewish. The girl, about eleven, clung to her father's hand and glanced curiously at the pastors.

The mother's urgent whisper carried on the forbidding air, "You're sure you have the receipt?"

"Yes," the father replied. "I told you."

"I don't know that it'll make any difference. They're out to take our store."

The father looked around quickly, alarmed. "Hush, Anna."

"What difference does it make what we say or who hears us. It's all the same."

"Hush, I said."

She shrugged eloquently and fell silent.

Time dragged on.

Finally, Dietrich heard his name and went to the desk. The clerk wrote down his particulars in a deliberate, copybook handwriting, dipping his pen in the black inkwell at every line. Then the adjutant motioned Dietrich to follow him. The large anteroom on the other side of the door held two desks, behind which young, fresh-faced secretaries typed determinedly without looking up. Behind them were three smaller offices. The adjutant led Dietrich into the office on the left, announced his name, and closed the door.

The official behind the desk was a heavy-set man with close-cropped bristly hair sprouting from a slick scalp. He looked up when Dietrich entered. "Please sit down, Pastor Bonhoeffer. It is Pastor Bonhoeffer? Dietrich Bonhoeffer?"

"Yes."

The man offered Dietrich a cigarette, which he declined. With a shrug he consulted a folder before him, its contents beyond Dietrich's view. "You are a seminary director for the so-called Confessing Church?" he asked in a thick voice.

"I was a seminary director."

"And where was that?"

"Finkenwalde, near Stettin."

"Now you say you are an assistant pastor. That is correct?"

"Yes."

"In Schlawe. Schlawe?"

"Pomerania."

"Never heard of it."

Dietrich said nothing.

"Assistant pastor." The thick lips turned in a skeptical sneer. "Something of a comedown, no, Herr Dr. Bonhoeffer?"

"I do not consider it a comedown."

"Ah, now, you don't expect me to believe that, do you? A man who's published several books. One this past November."

Dietrich wondered how *The Cost of Discipleship* could have interested the Gestapo enough for them to record its publication.

"You have been to Sweden."

"Some time ago. Almost two years."

"With your whole seminary."

"Upon invitation of His Eminence, the Archbischof of Sweden, yes."

"And from under his wing you felt safe to publish slurs against the German Reich."

"We made no slurs against Germany. We may have spoken of some of the differences of viewpoint within the German Church. That was hardly news."

"We've been looking into that. And into your article praising the world enemy, Jewry." The man looked up sharply. He clearly expected some sign of alarm.

Dietrich forced himself to look his inquisitor in the eye.

"How many students were attending your lecture?"

"What lecture?"

"Please, Pastor Bonhoeffer, no games. We know you were holding a secret seminary lecture back there."

So that was it. They thought the Dahlem meeting was a clandestine seminary class. Relief flooded through Dietrich. He had begun to fear that they were on to the new seminary arrangement. He quickly mustered a cool, impersonal tone. "Your surmise is entirely mistaken. That was a gathering of pastors to discuss important church questions."

"Pastors? No students?"

"No students. None at all." He was tempted to add "as I'm sure you're learning" but caught himself in time. "Such a meeting as that is not forbidden. There was certainly no attempt at secrecy, as the location makes plain."

"We're looking into that," the official said with a disdainful flick of his cigarette. "It may not be illegal at present."

With that he closed his file and made a motion with his chin to the adjutant, who took Dietrich out again through the anteroom and through a different door into a second waiting room. There Fritz Onnasch, Wilhelm Niesel, and a number of other pastors waited.

Dietrich sat down by Fritz and they compared notes. "They've made a mistake and won't admit it," Dietrich whispered. "So now they're trying to wring something out of the affair."

Four hours had passed since they first arrived. The bench was hard and the wall unaccommodating to Dietrich's back. He was fiercely hungry. They sat in the drab room for two more hours. Finally the adjutant called Dietrich and Fritz together and took them into a large office, where a higher official sat under a portrait of Heinrich Himmler. Without a word he handed them back their passes. Dietrich's was stamped "Restricted from Berlin."

"What does this mean?" Dietrich asked.

"Exactly what it says," the Nazi said coolly. "You will not be permitted to reenter Berlin."

"But we have done nothing illegal," Fritz protested.

"That is for us to decide."

A sense of overpowering rage had the effect of constricting Dietrich's throat.

The Nazi leaned back in his chair with folded arms. "I assure you, your activities do not interest us in the least," he said with a bland smile, "as long as you refrain from unlawful and disruptive practices. Our first duty is to guard and protect the German people. For that reason we find it necessary to limit your movements." He pressed his fingertips together before his face. His oily voice caressed the words. "It would be a great pity, Herr Assistant Pastor Bonhoeffer, if the government also found it necessary to curtail your privilege to speak in public."

From there two of the Gestapo men took them directly to the Stettiner Station and put them on the next train for Stettin, with transfer to Köslin.

A few miles out of Berlin, as the shock began to wear off, Dietrich turned to Fritz. "What if they start checking in Köslin and Sigurdshof?"

"I've thought of that. But I don't know how we can warn them."

"We'll have to try to call from Stettin."

"Won't they be watching us?"

"Maybe. We'll have to try anyway."

At Stettin they had one half hour. For five minutes they walked casually around the station, then moved down the street a block and into a little Bierstube. There was no sign that they were being tailed. Dietrich had Fritz stay in the Stube while he went to the phone booth on the next corner. To his relief Superintendent Onnasch answered the phone.

"Yes, Bruder Onnasch. Just thought I'd let you know. Fritz and I are a little late. Detained, you know, rather unexpectedly." He paused and cleared his throat. "Some acquaintances of ours might be dropping by your place, if they haven't been there already."

"No." There was guarded hesitation. "No one's been here."

"They may come yet." He paused to let that sink in.

Then in Bruder Onnasch's best tongue-in-cheek tone, "Should we plan on supper for them?"

"Wouldn't be a bad idea. Well, just thought you'd want some advance notice. And could you let Eberhard know too?"

When they got to Köslin there was no sign of the Gestapo. After Dietrich's call the ordinands had taken all the seminary-related material from the shelves and drawers and hidden it in the pantry among the flour and sausages, and in the old carriage house out back. For the rest of that week seminary operations remained limited. They still kept papers and books out of sight and met for curtailed classes in a different location each day. By the first of the next week, when nothing had happened, they fell back into their usual pattern.

Being cut off from Berlin and the family, with its flow of reliable news, became more oppressive to Dietrich every day. He was afraid to use the telephone for anything except the most mundane matters. The same with the post. The ten o'clock BBC news became sacrosanct. Sometimes he was able to get the *Times* of London in Köslin. Whenever possible he sent messages to Berlin by courier, but there were very few reliable people traveling that way. Occasionally he heard from Franz in England, who was helping Bishop Bell in the work with the refugees. Franz's English was getting better, and he sounded reasonably cheerful.

Weeks passed. The BBC reported rumors of problems between Hitler and the military, but there was no confirmation and no way to find out anything. Relief finally came when, through his father's intervention, the Gestapo lifted the ban to some degree; Dietrich could come to Berlin to visit the family, but was still prohibited from meeting with church leaders in the city. On his first trip back he learned the facts of the military situation from his parents. The commander-in-chief of the Army, Colonel General von Fritsch, had been accused of homosexuality and forced to step aside. The charge was a fabrication, Dietrich's father said. It was clear that Hitler was trying to get rid of Fritsch because he opposed his war plans. Hans von Dohnanyi and Colonel Hans Oster of the Military Intelligence Service, the Abwehr, were trying to uncover evidence of a plot against Fritsch by the Gestapo.

The next afternoon, which was Sunday, Dietrich spent an hour with Hans in his study and learned that Hans and Oster were making headway.

"We have new information from top sources in the Gestapo," said Hans.

"How, pray, could you get information from them?" Dietrich asked.

"From Arthur Nebe, director of the Reich Criminal Police Office in the Alexanderplatz. He has routine access to the front offices of Himmler and Heydrich. Much can be picked up from loose-tongued adjutants in an antechamber."

Dietrich said nothing. He was thinking of the grim walls of the police headquarters, where he had so recently spent seven intensely unpleasant hours. "Why would somebody like Arthur Nebe want to help you?" Dietrich could almost taste the foulness in his mouth.

"He isn't too happy with the regime himself, especially the Gestapo and the SD."

"But he still works for them, doesn't he?"

"Well, yes."

Dietrich got up and walked to the window. Outside in Hans's small garden his two sons, Christoph and Klaus, aged nine and ten, were playing lustily in the new-fallen snow.

Hans's words, crisp and incisive as a surgeon's scalpel, sliced the air. "If we waited for clinically pure sources we'd never learn anything. Nebe's in a position to *know*. The only man available to us who is."

Dietrich kept his eyes on the children. "I'm aware of that. Still—"

"Somebody has to take on the shady business, Dietrich, if we're going to try to stop Hitler."

Dietrich turned and faced Hans. "Has this developed already into a full-scale attempt at that?"

"Not yet. But we're working on it. We've waited in vain for the people who could have done something to make a move. Now—"

"Yes, of course," Dietrich walked back and forth in front of the window in a conscious effort to shake off his aversions. "But if you're talking about a coup d'etat, I'd like to know something of the means and methods."

"It hasn't quite come to that point. The urgent thing now is to keep the Army out of the Gestapo's hands. When the time comes for a full-scale move against Hitler, it will have to be a military one."

"That's a little surprising, the way you've always scorned the military."

"Yes," Hans said with a wry smile. "I'll have to admit I've more or less looked down on soldiers as a class—too narrow in their concepts of honor and patriotism. But Colonel Oster is different. I'd like you to meet him. He has a burning hatred of Hitler. He's been working for years inside the Abwehr—and out—to build up support for a move against the regime."

Hans continued with the surprising assertion that everything they learned went first to Admiral Wilhelm Canaris, the head of the Abwehr, who was backing them up, then to General Ludwig Beck, the Army chief of staff.

"How does he feel about all this Fritsch business?" Dietrich asked.

"Beck? He's shocked at such a dastardly plot. When Hitler offered him Fritsch's post, he refused it out of hand."

It was more than a month before Dietrich learned the outcome of the Fritsch trial. Hans and Colonel Oster supplied evidence to prove that the whole thing was a lie. The Gestapo's witness became so deeply entangled in a web of lies that he gave up and admitted his story was false. There was nothing Göring, as judge of the court, could do but acquit Fritsch. But Hitler did not restore the general to his command. In a graceless gesture he appointed him to the colonelcy of his old cavalry regiment.

21

In April Dietrich and Eberhard embarked on a walking tour of Thuringia. It was Holy Week. They let the early springtime forest bestow its benediction and left the trail only for food and lodging. In the villages they encountered the jubilant air of celebration for the Austrian Anschluss. There were swastikas everywhere, even on some of the church steeples. Once, they saw people lined up at the polling place to vote endorsement of the annexation of Austria. A poster hung beside the door: Hitler on horseback, suited in full armor and holding aloft the Nazi flag. Underneath was the title "The Standard Bearer."

The trail wound through the mountains in the vicinity of Wartburg Castle, a place dear to Dietrich, where Luther had translated the Bible in the sixteenth century. Darkness was falling when they noticed a youth hostel tucked under the side of the mountain. A dusting of spring snow had already whitened the hillside. They were tired and cold, and decided to stop and rest before continuing the three or so miles to Eisenach. Inside they found a troop of Hitler Youth seated in a semicircle on the floor. Their leader and a smaller group of boys stood facing them.

The speech-chorus began to proclaim in perfect unison: "Your name, my Führer, is the happiness of youth, your name, my Führer, is for us everlasting life."

Then the uniformed leader spoke, "Now the youth of our sister Austria are one with us. They have come home to the Reich. Thank God, Adolf Hitler has created a communion of German will and German thought. This plebiscite today is for us not an election, for us it is a German prayer of thanksgiving and this prayer says: Yes, *mein Führer*."

The boys seated on the floor raised their arms in the Hitler salute and repeated: "Yes, *mein Führer*. Yes, *mein Führer*. Yes, *mein Führer*."

The speech-chorus spoke again, "He who serves Adolf Hitler, the Führer, serves Germany, and whoever serves Germany, serves God."

"Let's go," said Dietrich, and turned half-blindly back to the door.

They walked in silence down to the trail again and soon re-entered the cavernous tunnel through the firs. Eventually, they emerged onto a bend open to the valley below.

"I think there's a lookout here with a good view of the castle," said Dietrich. "It should be nice by moonlight."

Around the next curve they scaled the highest rock and a startling spectacle greeted them. Across the deep valley lay the Wartburg like a long wedging ark, anchored so long on the mountain top that it had become one with it. The cross on the tower keep, usually lit up for Holy Week, was gone. In its place there hung from the parapet a floodlit swastika, as wide as the keep itself.

Without a word Dietrich turned his back on the scene and walked stiffly down the trail.

They had left the car in Eisenach; and instead of visiting the castle the next morning as planned, they drove to Kade, where Dietrich dropped Eberhard off for a visit with his mother, and then continued on to Berlin. One afternoon, in answer to a call from Hans, Dietrich walked over to their house on the neighboring Kurlander Allee. Something interesting was going on involving Colonel Oster, and Hans wanted Dietrich to be there and to meet him.

Dietrich sank down on the sofa beside Christel and stretched his feet onto the battered leather ottoman. The morning paper had slid to the floor, along with several books at the end of the sofa. Of all his sisters Christel was the least inclined toward housekeeping.

Comfort and utility were what counted for her; tidiness, less so. She liked old, well-worn furniture. Expensive new possessions were nothing but a care, she said.

"It's good you're early," said Hans, "so we can brief you a little." Usually cool, Hans seemed now unable to sit down and kept moving around the room as he talked. Oster was trying to enlist some of the generals for an action against the Gestapo, he said. Today he was with General Erwin von Witzleben.

"I'm not sure where I'd fit into such discussions—or plans," said Dietrich. "Would Oster want me here?"

"He knows you are coming."

Before Dietrich could recover from his surprise, Hans Oster entered the room. A slender man with a jaunty step, he acknowledged Hans's greeting, bent low over Christel's hand, then turned to Dietrich with an open smile. Offering him a firm handshake, he said in a rich Saxonian accent, "Dohnanyi told me you were coming, Pastor Bonhoeffer. Excellent, really excellent." The smile was genuine enough, although he wore the careless, almost cynical air of a cinema actor—with his handsome features, high-arched brows, bow tie, and tweed jacket. He appeared to be in his late forties.

Oster told Dietrich that his father was also a pastor and no doubt had wanted him to follow in his footsteps, but he was far too much a worldling to do that. He asked questions about the seminary. Assuming that he asked out of politeness, Dietrich gave only a brief sketch of the work. But as they sat down Oster pressed for more details with one question after another. He listened attentively to Dietrich's answers, seemingly unaware of Hans's impatience.

"It is a good work, I'm sure. Something to be thankful for. But you are a young man and there's conscription ahead. What will you do, Pastor Bonhoeffer, when that time comes for you?"

"I don't know. It is coming soon. Next year. That's the year of call-up for men of my age—1906. I'll have to decide." Dietrich looked directly into Colonel Oster's eyes. "I cannot serve in Hitler's army."

"Then something will have to be done. If you need help—and you will, I'm afraid—call on me. I might be able to do something." Oster lit a cigarette, placed it in an ivory holder between his long slender fingers, and turned to Hans, "I have good news."

"Witzleben?" Hans asked.

"Yes. He says we can count on him and on his troops. We will strike at the root. Clear out the whole shop in the Prinz-Albrecht-Strasse and occupy it. Arrest Himmler and Heydrich and all their henchmen. Witzleben is ready to undertake it. We'll break open their files and show the people what they've been up to. Not only against Fritsch, but the whole sorry chronicle."

Dietrich was skeptical. It did not seem possible to limit such an action to the area of the Prinz-Albrecht-Strasse. Hans agreed, but Oster believed that with swift action it would work. Admiral Canaris would go along with them—to a point. He was eager to be rid of Himmler and Heydrich; they wanted to take Military Intelligence away from him. But he was not ready to back an all-out overthrow of Hitler. To Dietrich any halfway measure seemed bound to fail, but he held his peace.

Then Oster himself said, "But it's not the ultimate answer. We have to get rid of Hitler before Germany can ever be whole and decent again. He is the central scourge."

The openness in his manner emboldened Dietrich to ask, "Do you have a plan for that, Herr Colonel?"

"Yes, I have a plan—in my head. Have had for months. I'm ready any time to commit it to paper, when I have the backing I need from the generals." He hooked his arm over the back of his chair and shook his head. "Ah, but these generals are so afraid. They're always full of excuses. They were too afraid even to come to the aid of their beleaguered commander in chief. Poor Fritsch. My God!"

"And then there's the oath—" said Dietrich.

"Yes, that damned oath. Hitler knew what he was doing when he required that oath of the military after Hindenburg's death. With it he bound them to his person, knowing full well their Prussian sense of honor would hold them." Oster seemed to be swept on by an intense wave of feeling that overflowed the bounds he had set for himself. "What is honor, anyway? What is true patriotism? Am I the one who is wrong, Pastor Bonhoeffer?" A genuine plea escaped the curbing intent in the voice. "I, and Dohnanyi here, and a few others seem to be in a terrible minority. A great many people deplore the state of affairs. Only a few are willing to do something about it—whatever it takes."

"You are not wrong," said Dietrich, surprised at the dispassion-ate calm of his own voice. "As to the means—'whatever it takes,' as you say—I don't think I know enough to judge there. But you are not wrong. When a mad driver is careening down the street, destroying everybody right and left, someone has to wrest the wheel from his hand."

"We have to do it. That's certain. Whatever it takes."

Dietrich came away convinced that Oster would stick to his word.

At the end of May, Dietrich made a dash for Berlin for a quick overnight stay. His parents and the Dohnanyis had made plans for an evening at the opera and when Dietrich arrived they quickly arranged a reservation for him also. Dietrich was not an opera en-thusiast. Too often the performance fell short of its promise as an art form. The habitual overacting and artificial posturing of the singers offended and distracted him. Half the time he listened to the music with his eyes closed. But this was "Fidelio," and the leading singers were passable actors. So he looked forward to an enjoyable evening.

By six-forty-five they were in their seats on the first ring of the balcony, just the right distance away for the best view and the full-est sound. The Staatsoper maintained the grandeur of imperial days: a ceiling of intricate carving and gold leaf; a proscenium arch sustained by golden columns; a velvet curtain of forest green, with the same velvet crowning the royal boxes; a two-tiered crystal chandelier overhead, with light from hundreds of bulbs. Yet even here the swastika claimed its place on either side of the stage.

The pre-performance sounds of rustling movement, murmuring voices, and tuning instruments filled the room. Dietrich watched with interest and some distaste as the elite of Berlin—an unseemly intermingling of the old elite and the new Nazi "elite"—moved in leisurely fashion to their places. There was a generous sprinkling of people from the upper echelons of the military. Hans pointed out Admiral Canaris as he entered a box below them. He was a slender man of surprisingly short stature, with almost white hair. His rounded shoulders drooped slightly as he sat down beside a younger woman, whom Hans identified as his daughter. On the other side of the house Dietrich recognized General Ludwig Beck, Army chief of staff, alone in one of the boxes. As the lights dimmed, Colonel Hans Oster and his family took seats near them on the same ring.

When they left the hall at intermission, they met Colonel Oster in the lobby. Hans introduced him to the parents.

The colonel bowed low over the hand of Dietrich's mother and said warmly, "My pleasure, gnädige Frau, Herr Professor. I hope you're finding the opera enjoyable?"

"Entirely so, Colonel Oster," said Dietrich's mother. "I am quite captivated by the Leonore. The whole act moved with much spirit, don't you think? Even Dietrich liked it. And he's hard to please."

Oster was also a devotee of the opera and the rapport between the two of them blossomed instantaneously. Dietrich expected their exchange to last the entire intermission, but soon Oster turned back to Dietrich and Hans and suggested they step outside for a moment. Oster's eyes transmitted an extra emphasis that was unmistakable.

Outside, where the walkways crisscrossed between beds of roses, the three of them made their way past strolling operagoers to a spot at the end of the walk, where the crowd thinned out.

Oster scouted past the bush in the corner and around to the street side. No one else was near. "General Beck is coming over to us," he said. "He's made up his mind that Hitler has to be stopped one way or another."

"So you've finally convinced him," Hans said.

"Hitler has finally convinced him. I've only seen to it that he got every tidbit of information needed."

"What brought him around?"

"The threat of war. Though that's just the final straw. Beck says we must go all out—bring Hitler down—no halfway measures."

A group of strollers approached them, so they walked around the corner and stopped in the alcove before a marble sculpture. Dietrich glanced across the Unter den Linden to the university. In the harsh glare of the street light the Humboldt Brothers sat immobile in their marble chairs on either side of the gate.

Oster continued, speaking rapidly, "Hitler came back from the Berghof yesterday morning and called the Wehrmacht heads to the Chancellory. Beck was among them. The Führer announced to them that it was his 'unalterable will that Czechoslovakia be wiped off the map.' They must be ready to attack by October 1, at the latest."

It struck Dietrich immediately that he could be subject to call-up sooner than the next year, as scheduled. In the same moment he thought of Sabine and Gert. If war came and the borders were closed, they would not be able to get out.

"Beck believes the British and the French will intervene?" Hans was asking.

"He's certain of it. So is everyone else. Except Hitler and Ribbentrop. And Keitel, who is capable only of parroting Hitler."

"And the other generals?" Hans asked.

"They're in a tailspin. An absolute tailspin. They know full well that Germany's in no position to embark on a world war." Oster's voice rose with excitement. "It's our chance, Dohnanyi. We may never have a better one."

Dietrich looked around apprehensively and saw an officer approaching behind Oster, a woman on his arm. Without dropping a beat, he said to Oster, "Yes, their best rower has an injured shoulder I understand. So we might just win. It should be quite a race."

Oster's eyes slid sideways as the couple passed. The officer's red-and-black armband was clearly visible in the street light. "Yes,

quite a race," he said. "I'd like it better if you were helmsman."
Oster moved up beside the monument, turned his back to it, and
watched the couple amble on down the sidewalk. In a low voice he
said, "Thanks, Pastor Bonhoeffer. I'll race with your crew anytime." He shifted his feet and leaned against the marble. "You
understand, it wasn't all so sudden with Beck. He's been deeply
disturbed for a long time. It took the Fritsch affair, I guess, to open
his eyes completely. If the generals will not pressure Hitler to halt
his war plans, he'll be ready for a Putsch. He has asked me to begin
work immediately on detailed contingency plans. I'd like you to
help me, Dohnanyi."

"Gladly," said Hans.

"I don't expect Hitler to back down."

They got back inside just as the first warning lights were flashing
and people were beginning to return to their seats. Halfway across
the lobby they met Admiral Canaris. Oster introduced him to
Dietrich, saying under his breath, "Pastor Bonhoeffer is on our
side, Herr Admiral."

For all his snow-white hair and bushy white eyebrows, Canaris
did not appear to be an old man. The admiral looked both right
and left, then said softly, "So you're also an initiate to these con-
spirings, Pastor Bonhoeffer? I, myself, am an observer. Oster proposes. I listen. The opposite is supposed to be true, I believe. But
never mind," he added, a trace of merriment kindling his pale blue
eyes. "If he strays too far off course, I pull in the rein." He turned
to Oster and said quietly, "General Beck is here, I believe. Just
across the way from me. Would you be so kind as to arrange a
meeting with him after the opera. At my house, please. And you
be there too."

"Yes, sir," said Oster, and nodding to Dietrich and Hans, he
moved across the lobby to the door on the far right.

Admiral Canaris bowed to them and with a distinctly unmilitary
gait walked to the door on the left, where his daughter was waiting. As Dietrich watched, he concluded that the head of the Abwehr did not cut a very impressive figure in his rumpled dark blue
uniform with the baggy pants.

"Don't let the admiral fool you," said Hans, at his elbow. "He doesn't look much, but he's as sharp as they come."

In late July all members of Paula's family came to Berlin for the festivities at the Charité, when Karl made his farewell speech to his colleagues. He had been due to retire two years earlier in 1936, but had been asked to stay on until now. He had done so willingly, partly because his position there made it possible for him to help a number of patients who were in danger. To save them from sterilization and possibly even euthanasia he had invented fictitious names for their diseases. Sometimes he hid them from the authorities by admitting them to his hospital under assumed names. In the past several months, knowing of his upcoming retirement, he had managed with the help of sympathetic friends to transfer those who were still there to safer havens. Karl's successor was to be a Professor Max de Crinis, a prominent member of the SS.

Over the years Paula had observed the growing esteem in which Karl was held by people inside and outside the medical profession, but as she watched from her seat in the auditorium, the outpouring of honor and affection far exceeded her expectations. To see Karl's happy face was the best of all. He looked young again. She remembered those days of their courtship in Breslau. At first she had not been greatly impressed by the young psychiatrist. She was a lively and outgoing girl of nineteen; he, small of stature and no taller than she, was soft-spoken and a man of few words. Although she had soon learned that when he said something, it was worth listening to. She had liked his face. He was handsome and, more than that, there was something there she trusted. As she looked back now, she was thankful for the slow-paced academic society in which her family had moved. At another time and in another place she might have missed the most important decision of her life.

When the farewells were over and the family members were leaving, they passed a new, larger-than-life bust of Adolf Hitler in the vestibule. When they were safely out of earshot of the crowd, Karl explained: "When de Crinis found out I had no portrait of his

Führer in the hospital he was horrified. The other day that bust appeared. A mere portrait wasn't good enough."

At the cars she heard Hans ask Dietrich if he could go by their house for a while. "Something has come up," he said without elaborating.

Paula waited up for Dietrich, and when he came she poured him a cup of chocolate and they sat down at the kitchen table.

"What's wrong, Dietrich?"

He looked at her as if he were not sure how much he could tell.

"They've learned which end of the rope Hans really pulled in the Fritsch case," he said.

"How much have they learned?"

"A good deal, I'm afraid. They've been snooping for some time. His desk has been rifled more than once, he said. Very carefully, of course."

"The 'Chronicles'?"

"No. They didn't know to look for that. He'll have to leave Justice."

"Won't Gürtner stand up for him?" asked Paula.

"No chance. This is coming from the Chancellery—from Bormann. Gürtner is terrified. He showed the letter to Hans. No direct accusations about the Fritsch case, but the complaint that Hans was much too close to Gürtner for one who is not a Party member. Nothing was said of his ancestry, though."

"What will Hans do?"

"They're thinking of Leipzig. Karl-Friedrich might help him find something there."

For a long time she said nothing. Finally, without looking up, she said, "So I'm losing them too."

When Dietrich reminded her that they would still be in Germany, she smiled wistfully. Leipzig still seemed a long way away.

"By the way, Colonel Oster would like to come and see Papa as soon as it's convenient."

"Whatever for?"

"Hans didn't say. But I think we can guess."

"It's General Beck's view that Hitler must be taken alive," said Colonel Oster, "so that his crimes and his insanity can be made clear to the entire people. The hope and intent, of course, is to prevent the birth of any new 'stab in the back' legend after his arrest."

Paula looked at Karl across the room. He was listening intently and showed no sign that he had guessed the colonel's mission.

"Dohnanyi will prepare the trial, using his secret 'Chronicles' as irrefutable evidence, for which we are all grateful indeed. Beck prizes it highly. He was dumbfounded when he learned the extent of it. For the insanity declaration," Oster added, with a straightforward look at Karl, "we need the most credible and highly qualified panel of psychiatrists available, with you, sir, as its chairman."

Karl glanced across at Paula, then down at his hand as his finger traced the brocade on the arm of the chair. "May I ask, Colonel Oster, at what point in the proceeding would this declaration of insanity be required?"

"That would depend to some extent on how much time you would need."

Karl looked up quickly. "Then you want observed data and not merely—"

"We are not asking you to violate your professional integrity, Herr Professor. Still, in this case, time will be of the essence."

Paula saw the relief in Karl's face, though no one else would have noticed it. Karl looked again at Oster and said, "There is certainly abundant evidence of megalomania in much that Hitler has said and done. I have no doubt in my mind that he is psychopathic. But no authoritative diagnosis could be rendered without medical examination and consultation with the patient himself."

"That will be possible after the arrest. He'll be held at an undisclosed location, pending trial. But you understand, in those first few days it will be crucial to get accurate information to the people as quickly as possible."

Hans asked, "How much could you depend on extant medical history?"

"Quite a bit, if it were available," said Karl.

"I believe it may be. A copy, to be sure. Gürtner has one in his possession."

Hans sat carelessly drooped in his chair, one foot resting on the ottoman. Paula never ceased to be amazed at the way he could come up with hard evidence, where others could do no more than guess.

The colonel left the selection of the panel up to Karl. They needed to be ready to strike by the last of September, Hitler's date for attack on Czechoslovakia. They talked out the details of the plan, and the colonel spoke of the difficulties in persuading the British to take a tougher line with Hitler. They had already re-buffed one emissary. "First bring us Hitler's head," they had said, "then we will talk."

"Hitler assumes they won't intervene," said Karl.

"Right," said Oster. "Ribbentrop's been shouting that loud enough to be heard across the Channel." The colonel reached a long slender hand for the ashtray on the table.

"You don't believe it, do you?" Karl asked.

Oster stopped dead still. "That they won't intervene?" His voice tightened down on the words, squeezing them out, short and clipped. "No, I don't believe it. I don't let myself believe it." He laughed abruptly. "Whoever, in any other country, has actually wished for a hostile move against his own nation, or at least the show of it. What a position this maniac has put us in."

How terribly true, Paula thought, aware of the danger to all those she loved. Now even Karl. She had tried to think only of what had to be done in the present; but now, here was Hans in the thick of it, the Nazis already breathing down his neck, and Sabine and Gert—she halfway decided she should go to Göttingen herself and help speed things up. With Dietrich facing call-up, separation from all of them was now a strong possibility. If war came it could be for years. Even forever—. With an inward shudder she turned her attention to what Oster was saying.

General Beck had resigned as chief of the Army general staff, Oster said. The timing was bad—he would have been in a stronger position for the Resistance if he had stayed put—but Oster could understand his reasons for leaving. Beck had agonized for years, he said, over the evils of this regime. With a stab of bitterness Paula wondered what had possessed the man to wait so long to do anything about it.

When Oster was gone she said nothing to Karl about her feelings. She would cast no shadows on the course he had chosen. Whatever her fears she knew it was the right course.

22

One evening in early September at the close of the term at Finkenwalde, Dietrich received an urgent call from Sabine. "We have finally made the decision we've been talking about," she said. "Do you think you could possibly come to Göttingen?" Her voice sounded strained.

"We'll be there tomorrow night," he said.

Dietrich and Eberhard helped them pack late into the night and drove the two cars with them partway to the Swiss border the next day. At Giessen the time came to part. For one brief moment Dietrich held his sister close to his heart. To Gert, he gave a firm handshake.

"See you soon," he said, as they drove away.

Brave words.

They waved until the shiny, almost-new Ford disappeared far down the road and around a curve. As prearranged, Dietrich and Eberhard returned to Göttingen to guard the Leibholz house until Dietrich's Aunt Elizabeth could come from Breslau in three weeks and take over. That night they waited anxiously for Sabine's call from Basel; it came at ten past eleven. Sabine and Gert were safe. No problems at the border.

"Thank God," Dietrich whispered, as he hung up the phone.

While Dietrich and Eberhard were in Göttingen the Nazi Party Rally met in Nuremberg. Dietrich tried to ignore Hitler's orgy of zeal, with its hypnotic power over the masses. Yet, as they sifted through the news for some scrap of truth, there was no way to escape it.

Dietrich and Eberhard listened to part of Göring's threatening speech on Saturday. "This miserable pygmy race of Czechs, devoid of all culture, is oppressing a civilized minority, and behind all this is Moscow and the eternal mask of the Jew devil." At the end of the harangue, Göring challenged any country on earth to a fight against Germany's superior war machine.

The next day the *Times* carried pictures of Jews crowding the Prague railway stations and airport in frantic attempts to get out of Czechoslovakia.

After the rally it became almost an obsession with Dietrich to know what was going on with Oster's group in Berlin. He dared not use the telephone for fear some stray word might endanger the plans. Then late one night came a startling bulletin on the BBC—Chamberlain proposed to come at once to Germany to see Hitler "with the view of trying to find a peaceful solution."

"They're backing down," said Dietrich. "England is backing down. If Hitler gets what he wants without a fight, not one general will lift a hand against him."

At first, during that week it seemed that Chamberlain had given in to all of Hitler's demands; but after a second meeting, the talks broke off and Chamberlain returned to England empty-handed. Suddenly the entire picture reversed again.

"We're going to Berlin," announced Dietrich.

They left the next morning. It was the last Saturday of September. Requisitioned cars and lorries, moving south and west, jammed the roads. At almost every railroad crossing they had to stop for long trains to pass carrying troops and tanks. Finally they got off the main road and headed up through the country in the hope of avoiding the Army traffic. South of Schönebeck they came upon a barricade across the road. Two soldiers, dressed in battle fatigues, directed them onto a side road. There was no explanation. From a little rise a mile or so farther on, they saw low-flying planes in the distance near the road they had left. Eberhard stopped the car, and they got out and watched as a formation of Stukas flew in from the north. The first plane pealed off and turned into a steep dive, shrieking like a vulture.

"What is that unearthly sound?" Dietrich asked.

"Sirens on the undercarriage," said Eberhard, "for psychological effect."

The plane leveled off over the road and dropped its bombs.

"They're not real bombs. It's just an exercise," Eberhard said.

"I don't know how you know." For Dietrich it looked and sounded real enough. Far too real. And too efficient. In sober silence he climbed back in the car and they moved on again.

At home in the Marienburger Allee Dietrich's father told them that the turnaround of events had centered all thought on plans for a coup d'etat. He and his colleagues had met several times on the question of Hitler's sanity, with remarkable unanimity on how they should proceed. His father's involvement had brought to Dietrich a sense of an unspoken bond between them that made them comrades in a new and subtle way. Hans still had his office in the Justice Department, though ostensibly he was in the process of moving to Leipzig. He had been meeting with Resistance leaders far into every night.

That evening Hans, Klaus, Dietrich, and Eberhard gathered around Hans's dining table. As always, Hans kept a cool exterior. Klaus made no effort to hide his excitement as he and Hans brought Dietrich and Eberhard up to date.

The plan was set. Hans and Oster had checked it out backward and forward. General Witzleben would go to the Chancellery with an escort of thirty young officers, plus workers and anti-Hitler students, sixty in all. Admiral Canaris had supplied them with a floor plan of the Chancellery and with weapons from the Abwehr. The entire group had been training intensively for a month.

Count Wolf von Helldorf, the Berlin police vice-president and a Resistance sympathizer, would see to it that the great double doors behind the sentry at the Chancellery would be open. Immediately upon entry the raiding party would seek out Hitler, and Witzleben would demand that he resign. No one believed he would comply, in which case they would have to arrest him.

At the same time units of the Third Army Corps, aided by a panzer division from Potsdam, would occupy Berlin and crush the anticipated resistance from the SS. They would take over all major government buildings, including radio stations and newspaper offices, and arrest the Nazi leaders. Simultaneously they would make proclamations to the people on the radio. Lieutenant General Erich Hoeppner's First Light Armored Division would bar Hitler's personal SS units at Grafenwöhr from entry into Berlin. Other army groups throughout the country were poised to take over major SS strongholds. Until all was secured the word to the people would be that the move was aimed primarily at the SS and that the Führer was being held in protective custody.

Dietrich looked at the map that Hans had spread out on the table and listened intently, alert for any possible flaw or weakness in the plan.

"The strike must be swift," said Hans. "Paralyzing."

Dietrich agreed. His eyes met Eberhard's across the table, which communicated the same tingling sense of risk that Dietrich felt.

Klaus had one main worry. Hans, too, though he said less about it. That was the role of General Franz Halder, who as Beck's deputy had succeeded him as chief of staff of the Army. There was no doubt about Halder's antagonism to Hitler and his desire to see Hitler and his regime eliminated, but he seemed plagued with a variety of inhibitions. Halder had doubts about the other generals. Most of them, he said, believed Hitler was merely preparing a colossal bluff, not war. Also, Halder was afraid of the people's attachment to Hitler. If there was civil war, Halder, as chief of staff, would be held responsible. So he insisted on reserving to himself the signal to march against the Chancellery. He would, after all, be the first to know when Hitler gave the order to attack Czechoslovakia. He assured them that he would have at least forty-eight hours notice.

The next two days the family members tended to congregate at Dietrich's parents' house or next door at Schleichers. One or another of them stayed by the radio most of the time, though there was little hard news, mostly martial music.

On Monday evening Hitler harangued a howling mob of his followers in the Sportspalast. Dietrich forced himself to listen with the others. Shrieking like a madman, the chancellor of Germany hurled gross insults at the president of Czechoslovakia. Hitler insisted that he would have the Sudetenland "in any case" by October 1, but kept his head enough to throw a scrap to Chamberlain—thanking him for his efforts for peace and reiterating that this was "his last territorial claim."

The next morning Christel came while Dietrich and Eberhard were at breakfast. She told them that Chamberlain had sent another letter to Hitler the night before by special envoy. "He's trying to persuade Hitler to be reasonable and accept their gift of the Sudetenland, only, please, accept it peacefully. The whole thing may turn on Hitler's reply. Anyway—." Her voice trailed off and she turned her tired eyes to Dietrich. "Hans didn't come home until very late last night and was gone again by six this morning. He's afraid to be away from his office for a minute and won't be home today 'til he finds out something one way or another. He thought you might drop by his office late this afternoon. Then you can let us know what's happening—that is, if nothing breaks before then."

The sun had set and the chill of fall was rapidly settling in when Dietrich boarded the city train. In the uncrowded car not one of the somber-faced passengers spoke above a whisper. Dietrich got off at the Potsdamer Bahnhof and walked up to the Leipzigerstrasse and the wide intersection at the hub of the government district. There was no traffic on the Wilhelmstrasse. Rows of swastikas hung all the way up to the Linden. A contingent of police was rerouting all cars south and west past the Air Ministry, which signaled another of the innumerable parades that Dietrich disliked so much. With luck he would miss it if he waited in the tearoom of the Kaiserhof Hotel. Since he was early he crossed the tree-lined park to the stately, white hotel.

Across the wide plaza stood the old Chancellery; and along the

Vossstrasse, boarded off from through traffic, Hitler's extravagant new Chancellery building neared completion. Dietrich turned into the tearoom. The sign over the door read, "The German's greeting is 'Heil Hitler.'"

When he came out of the hotel it was dusk and the street lights were on. Coming onto the Zietenplatz he discovered that the parade was still in progress. Columns of troops goose-stepped heavily past the Chancellery, their steel helmets clamped low on their foreheads, their eyes straight ahead. Behind them rumbled tanks and cannon and baggage trucks in single file. Surprisingly the wide square was nearly empty, with only two hundred or so people clustered here and there in cold, resentful silence. Most pedestrians continued along the sidewalks, their eyes averted from the marchers, doggedly rejecting all reminders of war.

Dietrich too had no wish to be a spectator; but at the corner of the Wilhelmstrasse he slowed his pace, his eyes irresistibly drawn to the balcony of the Chancellery and the figure standing there high above the square. Dietrich had never seen Adolf Hitler before. He had in fact carefully avoided it. Now he paused momentarily and watched the self-styled Führer of the German people as he stood, frozen and grim-faced, his hands in the pockets of his brown tunic. At a respectful distance behind Hitler stood two officers. Their gold embroidery gleamed in the yellow light from inside the building. Dietrich recognized Admiral Erich Raeder and the new commander in chief of the Army, Colonel General Walther von Brauchitsch.

No one in the square raised a hand in the Hitler salute. The chancellor's anger communicated itself to the people below in an almost tangible wave. Then, just as Dietrich started around the corner, Hitler turned stiffly and went inside. White-gloved SS men closed the doors behind him. He had left his motorized division to pass on unreviewed.

A young workman in mortar-spattered coveralls pulled his cap tighter on his head and muttered, "If that don't mean war, I'm badly fooled."

His neighbor, older and dressed in the uniform of a streetcar conductor, nodded in agreement. "And we're the suckers," he whispered, then looked around quickly at Dietrich, fearful of his own boldness.

Dietrich smiled encouragingly and lifted his hat to them before turning again to go.

All the way up the Wilhelmstrasse that same mood prevailed among the spectators and others, who hurried on to their trams and subways with sober, tight-lipped faces.

Hans was not in his office, but had left word for Dietrich to wait for him. The secretary covered her typewriter and left the room with an enigmatic smile. Unable to sit still, Dietrich walked into Hans's private office, which faced on the street. Everything there was in perfect order. The only sign of moving was a stack of boxes beside the file cabinet. He went to the window and saw that the parade was still going on. As he watched, the last of the tanks turned the corner from the Unter den Linden and passed down the street directly below. Diagonally across the street stood the gaudy yellow palace, which housed Ribbentrop's Foreign Ministry. Two globes, twined around with ugly, yellow snakes, crowned the pillars on either side of the gate.

Just then Hans came through the pillars and stopped at the curb, where he waited for the end of the parade before crossing the street. A moment later he entered the office. "Sorry to keep you waiting. Hitler's show backfired, don't you think?"

"Resoundingly," said Dietrich, and told how it had been in front of the Chancellery.

"Too rushed, I guess. They didn't have time to turn out the party faithful."

Hans had sought news of Hitler's reply to Chamberlain from the Resistance people in the Foreign Ministry. It had not come up yet from the Chancellery for transmission to England. Everything depended on that reply.

"If it's a rejection," said Hans, "I'll have to get a copy to Oster as soon as possible. Maybe when the foot-draggers see it on paper, it will convince them." Dietrich and Hans moved side chairs to the small table by the window, where they could keep an eye on the

Foreign Ministry. By then the lights were on in all the upstairs offices. In a suppressed whisper Hans added, "I hope it works. My God, I hope it works." Suddenly alert, he looked at Dietrich quizzically and asked in a different voice, still almost a whisper, "How long have you been here?"

"Ten or fifteen minutes, maybe."

Hans nodded and put his finger to his lips. He hunched down and looked under the table and the chairs, then gently ran his fingers under the edge all around. Crossing to his desk, he did the same thing, then picked up the telephone and examined the mouthpiece and the connection.

"It's all right," Hans said, as he came back to the table. "Oster's taught me a few tricks. I try to be careful." He took his handkerchief from his pocket and wiped his hands; then he sat down and leaned on the window sill, his eyes fixed on the offices across the street. "I've been over the details fifty times, at least, looking for weak spots. There are not any in the plan, I don't think—but the people, I'm not so sure. So much depends on just one or two. Not Witzleben and his young men. They're top notch. Ready to walk right into the lion's den." He kneaded his chin nervously between thumb and forefinger. "Soon we'll know whether we have a chance for a decent Germany once more. You realize, of course, there's almost certain to be some shooting. Hitler's not likely to submit like a lamb."

"I realize that."

"He could even get shot," Hans said with a faintly ambiguous smile.

Dietrich wondered briefly if Hans knew more than he was saying; but he did not ask. He did not want to know.

Then Hans turned an open, questioning countenance to Dietrich, more open than was customary in his brother-in-law. "That passage in the New Testament—'All who take the sword will perish by the sword—' do you think that applies in a situation like this?"

Dietrich was silent. It was a question he had not expected. He had known all along that his own knowledge of what was going

on and his willingness to keep quiet about it made him an accomplice, no different from Hans or Oster. Dietrich had thought a
great deal about the moral implications of the whole undertaking,
but had not arrived at any hard and fast conclusions. In the terms
in which Hans had put it, there were no easy answers. Against his
wish Dietrich found himself saying, "That word is true for us too,
I'm afraid. We can't escape it."

"Can a man stay innocent, then, simply by letting things be?"

"No. That's complicity. In this case, anyway."

Hans seemed relieved. "Yes. I would say so."

"But we're not let off the hook so lightly. There's no clear answer."

"Well, there should be," Hans said with crisp logic.

"It's not that easy. It's never easy, even here. As I see it, there's
guilt either way."

Without a moment's hesitation Hans shot back, "Then we have
to decide where the greater guilt lies, don't we?"

"Yes, we have to decide." Dietrich thought of Sabine and Gert
and their friends who had been driven from their homes; of the
Jewish family he had seen in the police headquarters; of Süssbach,
so badly beaten it had taken weeks for him to recover; and all the
evils to which Hans's "Chronicles" attested. And there was more,
far more, of which they knew nothing.

Hans said, "I can't see that I'm the one who incurs guilt when I
do something about all these crimes, while others turn their heads
the other way or refuse outright."

"Oh, they're guilty, of course. But as for us, when we resort
to—"

"The only means left us? You yourself said to Oster, 'we have to
wrest the wheel from the hand of this madman.'"

"Yes. I didn't say to shoot the madman."

Hans stood up and looked out across the rooftops to the trees in
the Tiergarten beyond. "If that were the only chance of getting rid
of this regime, what would you say?"

"But it's not the only chance. At least I hope not," Dietrich said,
knowing in his heart that it most likely was.

Hans leaned his hand on the table, his narrow face urgent and insistent. "But if it were?"

"It wouldn't release us from that word in Matthew. We can't get around it. At least, I don't see how." Dietrich looked into his brother-in-law's tense face. He wanted to say something that would help, but there was nothing. Finally he said, "But I believe such a time as this requires the extraordinary—men who are willing to make hard choices and take upon themselves the responsibility for those choices—and the guilt, if need be." He looked for a response, but Hans had turned his head away.

The telephone rang, and Hans went quickly to answer it. The exchange was brief and ended with Hans's words, "So sorry she isn't well. Please let me know what the doctor says. I'll wait here." He put down the phone and looked up. "That was the Foreign Ministry. It's a rejection. They'll call again as soon as the reply is translated and sent over the wires. Then they'll try to get a copy for us. If Halder—and maybe Brauchitsch—actually see it in print, that should be the proof they need. Maybe then they'll be ready to get this thing going."

Dietrich took his hat from the hat rack. "I'll go along, then."

"Yes. Tell Christel I might not get home 'til late. But not to worry." Hans's weary face showed hope and anxiety at odds with one another. "Tomorrow may be the day."

Tomorrow brought an unexpected turn. In mid-afternoon, after a tense time with no word from Hans and an absence of news on the radio, Hans and Christel finally arrived. Hans, haggard from loss of sleep, sank into a chair. "It's all off, postponed, at least for today. Chamberlain's coming back to Germany—and Daladier— and Mussolini. They meet with Hitler tomorrow for further talks. In Munich. If Hitler gets what he wants without a fight, that'll be it. No general will back us."

First there was stunned silence. Then hope slowly faded from everyone's eyes, not only for the immediate plan but for the future of Europe.

With bitter resignation Hans began to tell what had happened. That morning Witzleben had taken the copy of Hitler's answer straight to Halder in the Bendlerstrasse. Halder seemed to be convinced. They went over all the plans—how much time Witzleben needed—everything. Then Halder wrote out the executive order to set the coup in motion.

But Halder wanted to check it out first with the commander in chief. He was sure that when Brauchitsch saw Hitler's letter he would go along with them. To have the commander in chief with them would guarantee their success.

"Brauchitsch wasn't sure," said Hans. "He wanted to see for himself. So he went to the Chancellery. That was about 11:30. A little later we heard from the Foreign Ministry that Mussolini had called with the proposal from England that they all meet together and try to reach a compromise. Hitler agreed to it—in obvious relief, they said, because he didn't want war with England. And that's it."

All the next day they waited, but the tension was gone. Hitler would get his way. The radio carried nothing but reports from Munich, which built up the Führer as a great statesman, whose initiatives were saving Europe from war.

Emmi was pregnant with her third child and that evening, because the time for her confinement was at hand, the family gathered at her house to wait for the expected communiqué from Munich. Klaus and Hans were still downtown. As long as there was any possibility of a breakdown in the negotiations, the coup was not abandoned.

In the living room Emmi, Rüdiger, young Hans-Walter, and Dietrich were in the middle of a quartet, when Emmi stopped short and put down her violin. "I'm afraid I'll have to leave you," she said matter-of-factly. "There's some insistence here. Please go on with the music."

The music continued, interrupted by periodic checks of the radio. After two hours the communiqué came over the air with much fanfare. The agreement in Munich gave Hitler essentially everything he had asked for. His soldiers would begin marching into Czechoslovakia on October 1, two days away. The only concession was that he would do it in stages over a period of ten days instead of all at once, as he had demanded.

For a long time nobody said anything. Then Rüdiger said, "We shouldn't be terribly surprised, should we? I can understand why the British are afraid. For years they've watched Göring's bombers devastate Spanish cities and towns. They know that for the first time in a thousand years their own island is vulnerable to firepower."

"Your pardon, Rüdiger," said Dietrich. "I think the British people were ready to take the risk. It was their leaders who were afraid. And Hitler knew it."

At that moment Dietrich's mother appeared in the door, smiling broadly. "It's a boy. And all's well."

It was another hour before Klaus got home, so shaken by the outcome in Munich that at first he did not grasp the announcement that he had a new son. Finally his mother steered him toward the stairs.

Later Dietrich went up to see the new baby, tiny and wizened, and asleep on Emmi's arm. They had named him Walter.

"He picked a bad day to come into this world," said Emmi.

"But he's the reason we have to keep trying," said Dietrich. "He's the one who really matters."

Emmi smiled and looked over at Klaus, who stood by the radiator with his hands in his pockets.

Klaus looked at the floor and said, "It would have worked. I know it would have worked. If they just hadn't waited so long." He turned and came slowly to the bed. "What is it that has a little head, a big mouth, long red legs, and stands with his feet in the swamp?"

Emmi looked at Dietrich and back to Klaus. "A stork?"

"No," said Klaus bitterly, "a German general."

The baby awoke and began to cry.

23

In the seclusion of Sigurdshof, Dietrich had not heard of the pogroms until the day after they happened; and what information he had came from old Otto, the dairyman, back from his Thursday trip to Köslin to deliver butter and eggs. During the night someone had set fire to the synagogue in Köslin, and it had burned to the ground.

"The SA stood out front in the street 'n wouldn't let nobody put it out, not the fire brigade nor nobody," Otto had said, "and they broke the windows in Saloman's store 'n just tore the place up—drug all his goods out in the street and smashed 'em all up. Then they got him 'n his two boys and shoved 'em in a truck 'n took 'em off. Barefooted, too. Weren't time to put their shoes on, cold as it was. Where they took 'em, nobody knows." The old man shook his head. "Bad business, I tell you, bad business."

When Dietrich reached Köslin that evening, he had found the synagogue a heap of smoldering stones. The brownshirts were still guarding the area. The newspaper had shown with lurid pictures the same thing all over the country—synagogues and residences burned, shops destroyed, and Jewish "offenders" arrested. Goebbels claimed that the rampages against the Jews were a spontaneous outburst of anger from the "boiling soul of the people."

Since Dietrich could not get away on Thursday, he had sent Eberhard to Göttingen to check on Sabine's house. Eberhard had returned the next day with the report that the house was safe. On the night of the pogrom, however, the Nazis had come to the house and awakened Dietrich's Aunt Elizabeth, looking for Gert. On Gert's desk they had seen the picture of Sabine, wearing her pearls and asked: Where is the Jewess? Where are her pearls? Dietrich's aunt had told them they were on a walking tour in the Harz mountains. With Eberhard's assurance that his aunt was all right, Dietrich had taken the car and raced to Berlin.

There his father gave his account of what happened. "If someone had told me what I saw in Berlin that day, I would not have believed him. The synagogues were on fire all over the city. I saw two of them myself from the station at Savigny Platz—the great dome on the Fasanenstrasse was hidden in clouds of smoke; and the other way, in Wilmersdorf, I saw that one too, all aflame. I think they destroyed every Jewish store in the city. From the Memorial Church I could see broken glass in all directions; the Kurfürstendamm was a virtual sea of glass and merchandise strewn on the street.

"Then something happened at the Charité—an encounter with the kind of mentality that's behind these deeds. The elevator operator—I didn't remember him, so he must have come after I left—was gloating about what had happened. Gloating! He dared to say to me, 'They had it coming. What a pity you weren't there to join in, Herr Doktor. You really missed something.' I've never had so strong an urge to throttle a man. Instead, I said, 'Quite the contrary. Only animals behave in such a way.'"

His smile was one of bitter satisfaction, but Dietrich thought how people like that elevator operator took seriously the new People's Reporting Service initiated by Heydrich, which encouraged the German people to spy on one another.

His father looked at him. "Yes, he may report me, but it was worth it."

That afternoon Dietrich drove downtown with Rüdiger and saw the devastation with his own eyes. Six hours later he had heard and seen enough and, heartsick, began the long drive in the darkness back to Pomerania. He arrived at Sigurdshof at three o'clock in the morning and slipped quietly into his room for a few hours' sleep before the morning service.

That night in his Bible he underlined the words in Psalm 74, "They burned all the meeting places of God in the land," and wrote in the margin the date, 9 November 1938.

Once, during the long discussions that followed, one of the students spoke of the curse that had haunted the Jews ever since the crucifixion of Jesus.

Dietrich looked up sharply from his place at the table. "That is in no way a possible interpretation of what has happened here. Not at all. This was a case of sheer violence, without excuse. To construe it as a punishment—as the fulfillment of a curse—no. That is not possible."

The men around the table—seven of them now—seemed taken aback at the passion with which Dietrich spoke. In front of them he usually kept a rein on his feelings. Now he wanted them to know how strongly he felt and continued, "The Church has been doing that for too long already. Down through the centuries. No, if synagogues are set on fire today, churches will burn tomorrow." Then he referred them to Zechariah 2:8, where the prophet said of Israel, "He who touches you touches the apple of his eye." And to Romans 11, when Paul repudiated the idea that God had rejected his people Israel.

The days passed and Dietrich waited in vain for a proclamation from the church denouncing the pogroms. But the church had lost its voice. The Brethren Councils were still cringing in fear since the SS blast that had followed their call a month earlier to a prayer for peace. The accusation of treason hung over them like the voice of doom. And they kept silent.

Dietrich repeated to his ordinands a phrase he had coined at Finkenwalde at the time of the Nuremberg Laws: "He who will not speak out for the Jews has no right to sing Gregorian chants."

Soon after the New Year, notice arrived that Dietrich would have to register with the "Military Register Record," a prelude to call-up for those on the list for 1939. It was unavoidable. The act of filling out the registration form brought him straight up against the decision he soon would have to make—whether or not he would allow himself to be drafted into Hitler's Army.

Immediately Dietrich set about renewing contacts with people he knew who might help him when the time came. He wrote to Julius Rieger in London and to Reinhold Niebuhr in New York, the latter being one of his professors at Union Seminary with whom he had stayed in touch in recent years on behalf of Jewish refugees.

The attitude of some of the church leaders complicated the

problem. The Brethren Council was reluctant to grant Dietrich a leave of absence. For one thing, they said, there was a shortage of teachers, especially teachers of his caliber, and it would be difficult to find a replacement. On the other hand, they did not want him to plead conscientious objection.

"I suppose you've heard what's happening to Hermann Stöhr?" said Superintendent Albertz, on the day when Dietrich met at the church offices to talk with them about his future.

"A little, yes. I heard he was in trouble with the authorities."

"The Gestapo picked him up," said Albertz. "Yesterday."

That prophetic shot took Dietrich off guard. Dr. Stöhr, a pacifist, had recently declared himself a conscientious objector. Dietrich had known him since the Finkenwalde days. Dr. Stöhr's office as secretary of the German Fellowship of Reconciliation was in Stettin. "Then we must try to help him."

"We will, of course. But there's not much we can do," Albertz added quickly.

"I have some contacts—" Dietrich began.

"He'll not give in. Not an inch. And you know what the outcome will be," Albertz said with a direct look at Dietrich.

Dietrich knew well what the outcome would be, and the subtle pressure he sensed in the superintendent's words annoyed him.

"I'm not sure such a sacrifice will do any good in the circumstances," said Hans Böhm, the council member in charge of ecumenical affairs.

The others around the table echoed Böhm's sentiments—it was a waste, a terrible waste.

Albertz sighed. "I'm rather glad Stöhr isn't closely affiliated with us. Just at this time, anyway. Maybe I shouldn't admit it, but it's true."

"You think it would hurt the church that much?" Dietrich asked Albertz.

"I think so, Dietrich."

Dietrich looked at Albertz and at the other troubled faces, with their speculative looks. They all knew Dietrich's stand on the subject and they were afraid. All of them were afraid, even Albertz and Böhm, who had shown the most courage heretofore. Now they ducked their heads and looked here and there around the room, but not at Dietrich.

"To swear an oath to Hitler—that's almost the worst thing of all," said Dietrich.

"I agree," said Albertz.

"I don't see how I can do it."

They all looked at him. It was apparent that they felt the same way, but dared not say so for fear of encouraging him.

"In America I might be some help to the Confessing Church—an ecumenical link to our friends over there," Dietrich suggested. "They really don't know what's going on here."

The church leaders obviously had not considered that possibility, and after some discussion agreed that the idea held promise.

"I would only be gone for a year, you know," said Dietrich.

In the end they gave their consent, but that did not allay Dietrich's doubts, which he conveyed to Eberhard as soon as he returned to Sigurdshof.

Eberhard said he should go. "There might be a call out there waiting for you somewhere."

"Maybe." Dietrich sat at his little writing desk and leaned his forehead on his hand. He had been round and round for days with all the reasons for going and those for staying. At this point he had no idea what his real motives were.

Eberhard continued, "And you may just have to go out there before you can hear it clearly."

That made sense. Here in the midst of the battle Dietrich could hear only the clash of steel on steel and the wearying din of discordant voices; and of late the swords had become rusty and the voices muffled. The future in Germany held little promise of a time for undisturbed work in theology; now he realized how deep that longing was within him. He had already begun to think, in the few spare moments he could salvage here and there, of a work on Christian ethics.

"The world needs your theological gifts, Dietrich. So maybe

you should go where they won't be squelched, where you can develop them freely."

Dietrich smiled, amazed once again at how closely their thoughts paralleled. Still, he wondered about Eberhard's words—were they the truth or simply concern for Dietrich's safety.

"Why don't you go on with the arrangements, anyway, so you'll be ahead of the game?" Eberhard suggested.

"Yes, I can do that, I suppose." Dietrich mulled that over for a time and then turned to Eberhard. "And what about you?"

"Well, that's some way off. We don't have to worry about that right now."

"It could be before the year's out, couldn't it? What if I'm across the ocean somewhere when this comes up for you? That wouldn't do, you know. I'd either have to come back or get you out, one or the other. I couldn't leave you here to face that situation alone."

Modest but fleeting surprise sent Eberhard's brows upward in the familiar way. It was the closest Dietrich had ever come to expressing the deep and ever-strengthening bond between them—a bond in some ways closer than blood brothers. He added brusquely, "So that's that!"

Eberhard laughed, a free and easy laugh, and said nothing.

Dietrich thought of Hans and Oster and Klaus, and the chances they had taken and would take again. They had suffered a defeat, but they would try again, he had no doubt. This time it would be even more dangerous. If Dietrich stayed in Germany he would be drawn more deeply into the conspiracy. That was inevitable. He could not hide behind his status as a pastor, keeping his own hands righteously clean, while his family and friends risked their lives.

"If I stay here and somehow get around the call-up—" Dietrich began.

"But you won't get around it."

Dietrich slumped back in his chair. "I know."

In mid-April, after positive response from Niebuhr in New York, Dietrich went to Schlawe and applied for permission to go to the United States for a year. Instead, after a month into the new term, he received a summons to report for call-up in one week. Dietrich's only hope now was intervention by his father. He wrote him that same day, Monday, and carried the letter to the post himself. If his father did not succeed by the end of the week, Dietrich would have to make a final decision. Would he allow himself to be posted to an Army unit or would he appear before a court martial as a conscientious objector?

The days dragged by. On Wednesday Dietrich went to the post himself. There was nothing. He did not dare use the telephone to talk with his father. On Thursday he forced himself to wait until the mail was brought, as usual, by one of the seminarians. No word from Schlawe or from his father. Friday Eberhard brought the letter from Schlawe to Dietrich's desk and stood watching over his shoulder. With trembling fingers Dietrich opened it. The letter stated that the order to report was withdrawn and he was granted permission to go to the United States for one year.

The relief was so great that Eberhard and Dietrich both broke out laughing.

There was also a letter from Dietrich's father, which made no mention of recruitment, but informed him that his elder brother, Karl-Friedrich, was going to the United States too, for a series of lectures in Chicago and that maybe they could go together on the *Bremen*. To save time Dietrich could fly to England and catch the ship there. To do so, he would have to leave Berlin on June 2.

That was less than a week away. It meant he would have to leave the seminary without a replacement.

Eberhard was smiling. "You're not to worry. We'll be fine. They will get somebody very soon, I'm sure."

Dietrich tried to believe that, but his anxiety would not go away.

24

Dietrich stood at the wide bay window of the Prophet's Chamber and looked out on the Union Seminary quadrangle. He had forgotten how lovely the quadrangle was—beautifully kept and enclosed on all sides by the gray stone walls of the seminary. Directly across from him rose the spire of the chapel. Behind it he glimpsed the much taller and altogether grander spire of Riverside Church across the street.

Dietrich had forgotten much, but it all came back quickly, even the oil and leather smell of the house. Earlier as he toured the building he had seen only a few familiar faces, mostly faculty. Union was not the same place without the students he had known. He himself was a different person from the censorious youth who had walked these halls nine years before. He had given his teachers a hard time then, with his criticism of their unbiblical theology. But he had been right, of course. In his exploring he had come across Emmanuel, the steward in Hastings Hall, whose warm brown face kindled happily at the sight of him. In 1930 Emmanuel had taught Dietrich to operate the seminary switchboard.

"Who'd a thought you'd tackle such a job," Emmanuel said, with a deep-throated, musical laugh. "Another language 'n all. I tell you, that took nerve."

"But, of course," Dietrich replied laughing, "I needed the money." In those days Dietrich was saving every penny for India. Emmanuel had also introduced him to Harlem, where for six months of that year he had taught a Sunday school class in the Abyssinian Baptist Church.

Dietrich walked around the bed and the latticed divider to the other end of the long room. It was a comfortable layout, this Prophet's Chamber. He should feel honored, he supposed, to be occupying it. The window, a matching bay with a window seat, overlooked Broadway. There was no breeze on that side of the building either, just waves of hot air from the pavement below. Dietrich stared at the buildings across the street and yearned for Sigurdshof. He wanted to know how they were there, whether they were still safe, whether they had a replacement for him yet. He doubted it, and he knew that the added responsibility must be putting a heavy burden on Eberhard. He asked himself again, as he had on the ship, if he had left behind him the place where God was—where God was for him. "If any man serve me, let him follow me; and where I am, there shall my servant be also."

The situation in New York was not what he expected. He would teach one summer school course at Union; but his main job, according to Henry Leiper, who had met him at the boat, would be pastoral work with German refugees in the city. A puzzling business. There had been no word of such an arrangement in the letters and cables to Dietrich in Germany. He was afraid that such open activity would endanger his chances of going back after the year was up. If I take this post, he asked himself, would it change me? Would I be tempted to stay here, in security, if war came? Dietrich did not know the answer. But he knew he could not stay in the United States without an income. He had asked Leiper for time to think it over.

He looked at his watch. He was to meet President Henry Coffin at four o'clock that afternoon and travel with him to his country house in Connecticut for a few days. Dietrich would have preferred to stay at the seminary and have time to get a feel of the familiar, perhaps shake off this terrible sense of uncertainty. But he could not insult his host.

Dietrich sipped the cool drink that Mrs. Coffin had brought and with fascination watched the fireflies. There seemed to be thousands of them, like candleflames on the night air. The house was in the mountains, and the garden where they sat was cool and surrounded by lush vegetation. Dr. Coffin was as Dietrich remembered him: a handsome gentleman of great culture and learning, and a hardworking administrator, who confessed how much he treasured these stolen days in the hills. Under Coffin's friendly questioning, Dietrich related in detail the plight of the church in Germany and his concern for the brethren there. That night he went to bed feeling a little better.

Breakfast was served on the veranda the next morning. The entire family knelt for devotions, and in a short prayer Dr. Coffin asked God's blessing on the brothers in Germany. As they rose, Dietrich busied himself with his napkin and bit his lip in a prolonged effort to keep it from trembling.

The next day the Coffins took Dietrich for a drive through mountains very much like the Harz, but the villages had a different look. In the evening there was a party, twenty-five or so people—pastors and teachers with their wives—smiling strangers, who made small talk and exchanged pleasantries about matters of little importance to Dietrich. They seemed to skirt questions about the issues at stake in Europe.

Thursday the Coffins and Dietrich visited a cultivated lady, higher up in the mountains. They sat for an hour and chatted about music education in New York, summer camps for children, and the plans for a new parkway along the Hudson. It was all Dietrich could do to sit still on the rich pink damask. He thought how well he could have made use of that hour in Germany and longed to take the first ship home.

That night, alone at last in his room, a great weight of self-reproach bore down and almost smothered Dietrich. Why was he in the United States? Nearly two weeks had passed without any word from Germany. Here he was, three thousand miles away, knowing nothing of what was happening there. Mechanically he undressed and got ready for bed. In the Losungen, which Eberhard had given him as he left from Tempelhof, he turned to the reading for the day, Lamentations 3:26: "It is an excellent thing that a man should be patient and place his hope in the help of the Lord."

When the Coffins and Dietrich returned to New York, Dietrich went straight to the seminary post office. Nothing from Germany. Only a card from Karl-Friedrich, who was finding Chicago an exciting city. After supper he walked aimlessly down Broadway. From a grill in the sidewalk rose the clean smell of the steam presser. At one of the fresh food markets he bought some Georgia peaches. Presently he arrived at Times Square, where the clock read eight o'clock. He had been walking for an hour without realizing he had come so far into the concrete canyon. He turned into the Newsreel Theater and in the narrow, darkened room watched as the newsman narrated the rapidly changing pictures on the screen.

"The war of nerves continues in Europe. Germany, with two million men under arms, adds daily to its forces along Poland's borders. Polish authorities in Danzig say the Nazis are smuggling SS men and ammunition into the Free City every day. What will the next step be? Will it ignite the conflagration Europe fears?" Hitler's smiling, self-satisfied face looked out from the screen. He was boarding his private plane for Berchtesgaden.

As Dietrich came out of the theater he overheard a remark some-one made behind him, "Damned Germans. We'll have to fight them yet. They're all alike—can't seem to learn their lesson." For an instant Dietrich wanted to turn and answer. But the crowd spilled quickly around him, and the voice was lost in the babble.

As he turned the corner and headed down the subway steps at Forty-second Street, Dietrich could smell burning hot dogs. In the crowded, rocking, subway car he held tightly to the strap and wondered if the remark he had heard as he left the theater reflected the general feeling about Germans. He might as well face that possibility; with war it would get worse. As the car moved on, he scarcely noticed the stops. Suddenly the subway car braked and almost threw him off balance. The Eighty-sixth Street sign slid into view on the white-tiled wall. A tangle of people pushed their way off, and at last Dietrich could sit down.

If war appeared inevitable, what would he do? How could he stay alone outside of Germany? If he went back before the year was up, how could he get around the call-up? Would the authorities pass the word on to the recruiting office in Schlawe? It seemed probable. Even if they did not, Dietrich would still have the problem of keeping out of sight. In the deep woods behind Sigurdshof was a log hut, which the hunters used on occasion. But the Gestapo had dogs. He would have to decide what to do before long. His meager funds were dwindling fast; and his stocks, which had doubled in value since 1930, he wanted to save for Sabine and Gert.

That night he tossed in bed for two hours before going to sleep.

On Sunday he went to a Presbyterian church a few blocks from Union. The sanctuary was simple and unpretentious, with the pews intimately arranged around a central pulpit. Above the choir were the words, "We preach Christ and Him Crucified." He prayed with fellow Christians and listened to a kind of prophetic preaching that had been up to now unknown to him in the United States. Only the music was poor—a moldy cellarful of piety and bad theology. Dietrich wondered why the preacher would put up with it and considered speaking to him about it, but quickly thought better of it. As he left the church some of his loneliness fell away.

From post to post Dietrich waited in vain for a letter from Eberhard. He could not understand it and tried not to be angry, but he wanted some leading for the decision he had to make. Sometimes he walked over to Riverside Park, where he sat on a bench and looked out across the Hudson River. But these waters had no power to calm his spirit; he saw instead Sigurdshof—and Berlin—and wondered. Every day he went to the Newsreel Theater. One day the face on the screen was Josef Goebbels. "You need have no anxiety for the fate of your city," he shouted wildly to Nazis at the conclusion of Danzig's German Culture Week. "We are behind you one hundred percent. Your Danzig will return to the Reich."

There was nothing in the rest of the news to offset that alarming proclamation, and Dietrich left. A thunderstorm had cooled the air. He decided against the subway and walked home along Central Park. Back in his room he tried to concentrate on the lectures he was to give at the seminary in August. It was no use. Finally he took a clean sheet of paper and wrote to Paul Lehmann at Elmhurst College, hinting that he might need work in the fall—if he stayed. Lehmann had been one of his closest friends at Union nine years before and had already indicated a willingness to help.

As the days passed the news got worse, and war seemed ever nearer. The British and French stepped up their warnings to Hitler, saying that they meant business this time. Hitler did not seem to believe a word of it. *Time* magazine published a disturbing account of a purported speech—leaked out through the Reichswehr—that

Hitler had made to his "War Council." Leaked through Admiral Canaris, Dietrich wondered? "The die is cast," Hitler was quoted as saying. "We cannot retreat now. Our backs are against the wall. I hold that Germany, Italy, and Japan are in a position today to conquer all their enemies combined. The hour, therefore, has sounded to take the supreme risk."

The next day was Dietrich's meeting with Leiper—the time of decision. That night Dietrich read by chance the Apostle Paul's petition to Timothy: "Do your best to come before winter." Timothy was to share the suffering of the apostle and not be ashamed. "Come before winter"—otherwise it might be too late. That thought was with Dietrich every waking hour and all the next morning. He felt like a soldier who had come home on leave and, in spite of everything, longed to be back at the front again. Yes, with his brothers. That was where he belonged. "Come before winter."

From his place by the rail Dietrich could hear the water below slapping against the sides of the *Bremen.* Shouts and scurrying on the dockyard signified the imminent departure of the ship. Across this busy scene and halfway up the block, Paul Lehmann waited under the street light, where Dietrich had left him. Paul had wanted to come aboard, but with so many Gestapo agents around, Dietrich could not risk drawing attention to himself.

"Too bad," he said to Karl-Friedrich, who was returning to Germany at the same time as Dietrich. "I would like to have introduced Paul to you."

"Yes," said his brother, "if he came all the way from Illinois just to see you, I'd like to have met him."

"Paul wanted me to stay. He had lined up speaking engagements for me all over the Midwest and tried awfully hard to persuade me, but it was too late. I had already made my decision." Dietrich spoke in an undertone. A little farther down the rail there stood an enigmatic figure with a lighted cigarette in his hand.

"I just wonder if you shouldn't have listened," said his brother. "I hope you aren't making a mistake." Leaning against the rail,

Karl-Friedrich looked skinnier than usual in his dark, ill-fitting suit.

"No more than you," said Dietrich.

"I have a family."

"So do I, after a fashion."

"What did this Paul Lehmann say?" Karl-Friedrich inquired.

"Among other things, that the world will need an authoritative interpreter of the church struggle."

"That's true, isn't it?"

"Oh, there'll be plenty of those. Paul's main argument was my theological task—what he saw as my theological task."

"I think he is right, Dietrich. Isn't what you have to say more important than what you might do in the conflict at home?"

"No. If I stayed here and war came, I'd have nothing to say. I would have compromised my witness. Don't you agree?"

"Oh, I don't think so."

"Yes. Not only that, I would have no right to take part in the reconstruction of Christian life after the war. You and I know what the alternatives will be for Christians in Germany—either willing the defeat of the Fatherland so Christian civilization can survive, or willing victory and the destruction of our civilization. I know which one I must choose. But I cannot make that choice in the safety of America."

"Well, I hope there's someplace in Pomerania where you can hide," said Karl-Friedrich.

"I'll think about that when I get there."

"You'd better start thinking about it now."

Later that night in the cabin Dietrich read the passage for the day: "It is good for me that I was afflicted, the better to learn thy statutes" (Psalm 119:71). It was one of his favorite verses from his favorite psalm.

Part III
Into the Tempest

25

"You know the endless attempts I have made for a peaceful clarification and understanding of the problem of Austria and later of
the problem of the Sudetenland, Bohemia, and Moravia. It was all
in vain—"

The voice of the dictator was defensive. Dietrich wondered if
this master deceiver could possibly be feeling some doubt in his
ability to lie his way out of this one.

Hitler continued. "My proposals to Poland have been refused.
For two whole days I sat with my government and waited to see
whether it was convenient for the Polish government to send a
plenipotentiary or not." His voice took on a pained righteousness.
"I am wrongly judged if my love of peace and my patience are
mistaken for weakness or even cowardice."

The faces of the other family members showed their contempt.
Dietrich glanced at his mother. Shame slid over the set anger on
her face. He also felt shame that most of his countrymen, in their
eagerness to justify themselves and their Fatherland, would believe
this lie.

The announcement they expected finally came. "This night, for
the first time Polish regular soldiers fired on our own territory.
Since 5:45 A.M. we have been returning the fire, and from now on
bombs will be met with bombs." And then the declaration: "I am
from now on just the first soldier of the German Reich. I have once
more put on that coat that was most sacred and dear to me. I will
not take it off again until victory is secured, or I will not survive
the outcome."

No one spoke. They were left in a vacuum. The silence evoked
for Dietrich another silence from the distant past. . . *The coffin of
his brother Walter rests on its bier in the living room; at its head, a Dresden
urn on a stand holds white roses. The child standing by the portieres sees
only the still gray face of his brother. Just two weeks before the family had
sent Walter off to the front.*

His mother's face is deathly pale beneath the black mourning veil, as they follow the horse-drawn hearse. In the chapel beside Sabine, Dietrich sings loud and clear, the way his mother had always liked them to, the verses of the hymn "Jerusalem thou city built on high, would to God I were in thee." As Walter's comrades bear his coffin to the grave the trumpeters are playing the hymn "What God has done, that is well done." Hymns his mother had selected.

Now that same stricken look fell across his mother's face. She sat with one hand tightly clasping the fingers of the other and stared down at the floor. When she looked up, her eyes met Dietrich's as if she knew they were held by the same vision. Apologetically she stood up and walked out of the room.

After a few minutes Dietrich's father left also. Later Dietrich saw his parents standing together on the terrace. His father's protecting arm encircled her, a rarely shown outward sign of the deep affection between them.

On Sunday Britain and France declared war on Germany. Dietrich, who was at Klaus's house, immediately jumped on his bicycle and raced home to be with his parents. Nothing at all happened. No siren, no bombs, nothing. Dietrich told his mother that the war could not last long. The entry of France and Britain would certainly bring about the final catastrophe for Hitler, and soon.

All she said was, "I hope you are right."

A few days before Hitler's assault on Poland, Dietrich and Eberhard, with the help of the students, had boarded up the windows of the seminary and gone their separate ways. None too soon. By now the whole area would be overrun by German forces en route to Poland. The papers and the radio boasted as wave upon wave of dive-bombers assaulted Polish towns and cities. One after another they fell. Dietrich shuddered when he remembered the shrieking Stukas he had seen in Saxony. Tanks rolled mercilessly over Poland's antiquated defenses. There was no rain and the unpaved Polish roads stayed hard and smooth. People called it "Hitler weather."

A month before, Admiral Canaris had called Hans to a post in the Abwehr. So for the time being he and Christel and their three children were living with the parents. One evening when it came near time for supper, the family members began to assemble and sat about the living room in quiet conversation. Dietrich sat with Renate at the piano while she played; and Christoph, Christel's youngest, sang one song after another in his true, clear boy soprano.

There was a knock at the door. Marthe announced Herr Leitzinger.

"Herr Leitzinger?" Dietrich's mother asked in mild surprise.

"Who's that?" asked Dietrich.

"The greengrocer across on the Preussen Allee." She turned to Marthe. "What would he be doing here?"

"He's the new block warden, gnädige Frau," said Marthe.

"It's rather late," she began. Annoyance flitted over her face, then she seemed to realize the futility of any protest. "Well, show him in."

The block warden stood before them. Starched and polished in brown uniform and boots, with a pillbox hat straight on his head, and his thumb hooked in a wide leather belt, he clicked his heels and raised his right arm in the rigid salute.

"Heil Hitler!" was his staccato greeting.

No one spoke or made a move.

Herr Leitzinger opened his notebook and took a pencil from his breast pocket. "You have the black material for your windows, as ordered?"

"Certainly, Herr Leitzinger," said Dietrich's mother.

"May I see it, please."

Dietrich's mother turned to Marthe. "Fetch it, please, Marthe."

Silence. Herr Leitzinger shifted from one foot to another, looked again at his notebook, and pointed with his pencil to a notation there. "I did not see the flag displayed outside your door. Perhaps you did not understand the order?" he asked with a hopeful smile.

"It was, of course, an oversight," said Dietrich's mother.

"An oversight, yes, to be sure." Leitzinger surveyed the calm, unsmiling faces around the room.

"Perhaps I should instruct Marthe to leave the black muslin and put out the flag?" she said, with a perfectly straight face.

At that moment Marthe returned with the black muslin.

"Ach!" Herr Leitzinger pursed his lips and made a smacking sound. "It is permissible, I think, to proceed first with the windows." Again the pucker and cogitating smack. "Yes, I think so. Now, if I may, I will demonstrate exactly how you are to cover them."

Dietrich's mother rose from her chair. "Thanks very much. I believe we are quite capable of following the instructions in the newspaper."

"But it is necessary for me to demonstrate exactly, gnädige Frau."

She indicated that Marthe should receive his instruction and sat down again.

Dietrich nodded to the children to start their music again. Christoph began to sing, but could barely hold the pitch for snickering.

One day when the newspapers were displaying the improbable picture of Russian and German soldiers shaking hands at the line of demarcation, Dietrich met Hans downtown for lunch. Afterward his brother-in-law took Dietrich to the Abwehr Headquarters on the Tirpitz Ufer to show him his new office.

On the second floor, where a balcony overlooked the lobby, they came to a folding metal grille. At the turn of Hans's key the grille slid open. They entered a long, well-lit corridor, which echoed with bustling footsteps and varied accents. On a side hall near the far end of the corridor they came to Hans's office.

In the anteroom Hans introduced Dietrich to his secretary, a plump little woman who gave a cheery nod and returned immediately to her clacking typewriter.

The inner office could not be called luxurious by Department of Justice standards. Hans's desk, with two worn armchairs facing it on either side, stood near the window, which overlooked a courtyard. Within arms length and at a right angle to the desk, a heavy steel file cabinet flanked a table, which held papers, books, and a shortwave radio. A map of Germany and a smaller one of Berlin covered half the wall above the table. In a corner beside the door that led directly into Oster's adjoining office sat a green safe with embossed scrolls.

While Dietrich looked around the room with unconcealed curiosity, Hans took their hats and hung them inside the gray metal clothes locker. Already he had told Dietrich something of the Abwehr and the way Canaris—with the help of handpicked subordinates—had built up an espionage system, which had earned him a reputation in Europe as "Herr Spymaster." Although he had managed to fill vacancies and increase personnel with men of anti-Nazi leanings, there remained many National Socialist sympathizers and some out-and-out Nazis. This forced the corps of resisters around Oster to exercise a measure of caution, although Oster himself seemed to find that difficult.

Canaris' major problem lay outside his own Abwehr. Heinrich Himmler had long coveted the little admiral's control over military intelligence; but Canaris, with many shrewd moves, had shielded the Abwehr from Himmler's interference. Two years before Canaris had pressed for and attained an agreement called "The Ten Commandments," which defined the areas of operation of the two agencies and set up rules for noninterference. The Abwehr alone was to inquire into military matters, while all political investigation fell to the Gestapo on Prinz-Albrecht-Strasse. But always, when it came to the crunch, Canaris refused to allow the Gestapo to dictate where the fine line between the two would be drawn. According to Hans, the agreement was a major victory for Admiral Canaris; but Himmler—and especially Reinhard Heydrich, the head of the SD—never stopped sniping. The wily admiral seemed to take pleasure in outmaneuvering the enemy and for this reason maintained contact with Heydrich, who had been a navy comrade in former years.

Hans took his major's uniform from the clothes locker and showed it to Dietrich. "Thank God, I have to wear it only on formal occasions," he said.

It was hard to imagine Hans in a military uniform, but in his new position it was necessary. Hans headed the policy section of Oster's Central Division and at the same time served as a kind of private secretary to Admiral Canaris, especially in matters having to do with the Resistance. As such, he was always present at the morning briefings in the admiral's office and had access to all information that came into the Abwehr.

Hans turned to the steel file cabinet and showed Dietrich his system for hiding the now greatly expanded "Chronicles of Scandals." The folders of the chronicles had false headings and were interspersed with those of the regular files. They were coded for location according to the preceding file folder. He selected a folder and pulled it out. "You might like to see the latest one—the Gleiwitz business."

Hans already had told the family about the charade on the morning of the attack on Poland, when the "Polish soldiers"—who, according to Hitler, attacked first at Gleiwitz and other places inside the German border—had been in fact German SS men and prison inmates, dressed in Polish uniforms.

"It's all here," said Hans, spreading out the papers on his desk. "This is a copy of the order to Naujocks for the whole operation. This one to the Gestapo's Müller, to supply the prisoners. And to the Gestapo doctor to give the fatal injections. All signed by Heydrich, you see."

As Dietrich read them chills crept up his spine.

"And then the letter to Goebbels requesting news photographers," Hans continued.

Dietrich remembered the pictures of the dead "Polish soldiers" that appeared in the papers that day.

"This last one, Canaris himself gave me," said Hans, handing the paper to Dietrich.

It was an order to Canaris to deliver 150 Polish uniforms and small arms to Heydrich. No explanation. The order was signed by Adolf Hitler.

Dietrich looked at Hans. Conflicting questions raced through his mind. Hans said nothing as he stacked the papers together again and put the folder back in its place.

Just then Admiral Canaris appeared in the doorway. Dietrich was not greatly surprised. Hans had told him that the admiral, a restless man who did not like to stay in one place for very long, often strolled the halls and dropped in unannounced.

The admiral remembered Dietrich, which surprised and pleased him. As they sat down again, Canaris said softly, "Dohnanyi tells me you went to the United States and then came back. I don't understand it. You're an intelligent man. Why would you come back here?"

Dietrich smiled and murmured, "Sometimes one does what one cannot help but do, even if it seems foolish. Is that not true, Herr Admiral?"

Canaris' penetrating blue eyes surveyed him from under bushy white brows. At last he said, "You are right, yes."

Nothing more was said about it, but Dietrich felt a resonance between himself and the little admiral.

Canaris seemed frail and distinctly un-Prussian in his rumpled blue tunic, with the Iron Cross, First Class, pinned not quite straight. He took a pillbox from his pocket, extracted a pill, and put it into his mouth; then, leaning back in the armchair, he said, "I need your help, Dohnanyi. Last night I had one of my cat-and-mouse talks with Heydrich."

"And you were the cat?" said Hans.

"I hope so. One never knows with him. Last night he seemed not to suspect it. He was quite frank, and what he said horrified me. He was fulminating against the Army for its lack of vigor in handling the Polish population. The courts-martial, with two or three hundred executions a day, are too slow and circumspect for him." The initial sarcasm in his voice gave way to such aversion that it seemed to sap his energy. With a sigh and a dark look he continued. "He wants to proceed without trials. He said to me with a perfectly straight face: 'The little people we shall spare, but there has to be a housecleaning of the nobility, priests, and Jews.' He would arrange it with the Army, he said, after the entry into Warsaw."

Canaris stood up and walked around to the back of his chair. "I went to Keitel this morning and warned him that the world would hold the Wehrmacht responsible, if such deeds took place under its eyes. He said that it was the Führer's decision and that the Wehrmacht would just have to tolerate it. After all, he said, the SS will be carrying it out, not the Army. That seemed to him an excuse." His hand jerked on the back of the chair and some of his words came out with a lisp. "I asked if he was going to let the Gestapo usurp the Army's prerogative. He could do nothing, he said. Lackey!" Canaris stood for a long time staring into space. "Ah, but this madman makes lackeys of us all."

Dietrich glanced at Hans.

Canaris saw his look and lowered his eyes. The shame of the 150 Polish uniforms pulsed in the air. In a subdued voice the admiral began to speak again. "I was for Hitler, you know, in the beginning. I applauded his firmness, particularly with the Bolsheviks. God knows we needed that—and still do." He turned his eyes to Dietrich, as if soliciting his opinion.

"Firmness is one thing, Herr Admiral, gangsterism quite another," Dietrich said.

The admiral sighed. "That's it, of course. This war will destroy us all and, with atrocities like these, the soul of Germany. Our country is in the hands of a maniac. He intends to attack in the West before winter. He told us that yesterday in the Chancellery. From one side of his mouth he will talk peace, while from the other side he plans attack. He has to have all or nothing, he said. All or nothing. What would you do, Pastor Bonhoeffer, if you were in my place?"

"I'd do everything in my power to stop it."

"The war?"

"All of it."

"Yes." Canaris came around and sat down again. "I sent Tippelskirch to General Halder. He already knew about the atrocities and agrees that the Army's leaders will have to intervene vigorously." Then with a skeptical inclination of his head, he added, "The trouble is, Halder invariably listens to everything, then produces threadbare excuses for doing nothing." Canaris turned to Hans.

"I've ordered all Abwehr agents in Poland to keep me informed of any such measures. I'm going to Poland myself tomorrow and am taking Oster with me. Now, what I want you to do, Dohnanyi, is to get proof for me of what's going on, everything you can get—reports, pictures, even film if possible." His voice was once more quiet and controlled. The lisp was gone. "Everything, if you please."

"Yes, Herr Admiral."

"That's the only way we can stop it. The generals of the Army have to know what's being done in Germany's name. When you've finished, I want you to go the rounds with me to show them the evidence."

One night, before he started the rounds with the admiral, Hans brought home some of the reports and pictures to show the family. They confirmed Dietrich's worst fears, showing scenes of such criminal destruction and misery, including mass executions, that Dietrich would have doubted them without the proof. In one picture he identified three priests in a group lined against a wall before an SS firing squad.

With dread and horror in her eyes, Dietrich's mother spoke for them all. "The wrath of God will fall on Germany. And we will have to drain that cup to the dregs."

The Poles surrendered before the month was out. No attack had come from the British and French in the West. That night Rüdiger brought home word that Hitler's western offensive would strike, not against the strongly fortified Maginot Line, but around through the neutral Low Countries.

The effect of this announcement in the family was amazement, horror, and an instant spark of hope: amazement, at the foolhardiness of a mechanized offensive in the mud and slime of early winter; horror, at the monstrous notion of violating the neutrality of the Low Countries; and hope, that these considerations might reignite the Resistance and, at last, spur the generals to action.

At the end of that black September, with the Polish campaign ended and Pomerania no longer a theater of war, Dietrich sent for

Eberhard to come back to Berlin. Together they discussed with the Brethren Council the possibility of reopening the seminary at Sigurdshof. Surprisingly, there were eight ordinands still free for seminary training. As Dietrich and Eberhard were packing to return to work, the postman brought a simple card addressed to Dietrich. It was edged by hand with black ink. In the center were the words "Theodor Maass, fallen, September 3, 1939, Poland." Underneath were the names of Theodor's parents and brothers and sisters and the words from the Gospel of John: "He has passed from death to life." In silence Dietrich handed the card to Eberhard. Maass had been Eberhard's fellow ordinand in the first course of the seminary.

Dietrich lifted from the corner of his desk pad a list he had made of his former seminarians in the forefront of the fighting. Anxious that the link should not be broken and that they might receive as much support as possible, he had written them at their fieldpost numbers at the front. Some of them had answered. But this little black-edged card was the first tragic reality.

"I don't think I can bear to stay here much longer," Dietrich said.

Eberhard looked up questioningly.

"Here or anywhere in safety—doing nothing—while they are out there in such danger and suffering. What are we going to do about it?"

"What can we do?"

"I don't know. I simply have the feeling—the compulsion almost—that I must be there with them," Dietrich said.

"You mean you want to join—"

Dietrich shook his head. "No, no. No, I can't carry a gun in this war. But I might go as a chaplain." He looked up. "Would you be interested in joining?"

"Certainly."

The next day Dietrich and Eberhard applied to the Army chaplaincy. They were told not to expect an answer for at least a month.

In mid-October Hans came back from his western tour with Canaris, disgusted, he said, with the "flabby generals" and their same old excuses: their men would not obey them; the soldier's responsibility does not lie in the political arena; they were bound more than ever now, in wartime, by their oath to Hitler. All the generals agreed on one thing: an offensive in the West would fail.

Soon after his return, Hans came to Dietrich with a unexpected request: "Oster would like to see you before you leave. If you don't have other plans, he wants to come by here tonight."

"Do you know what he wants?"

Hans's look was noncommittal. "I'm not sure, but I think it's important."

"Well, yes, of course, tell him to come."

26

"There's no going back for me!" Oster's words poured out with such a rush of feeling that they were almost indistinguishable. "I've determined to do it. It'd be much simpler, of course, to take a pistol and shoot someone down, or to run into a machine gun burst, than what I'm going to do!"

Dietrich looked at Hans, whose face gave no clue as to what was coming.

Oster stood facing them. The blackout material over Dietrich's window formed a backdrop that accentuated Oster's sharp pale features, and the dim light from the lamp on the desk lengthened his shadow along the floor and up the far wall to the ceiling. "The situation is hopeless, gentlemen." Oster continued. "It's becoming more so every day. We're stymied. The generals have resigned themselves to this western offensive. Today Canaris went to General Halder and found him on the verge of nervous collapse. Halder is caught between Hitler's hot breath and the force of what he knows he should do. Brauchitsch, too. He hitches his collar a notch higher and says, 'I am a soldier. It's my duty to obey.' They're both completely unmanned. Hitler demands attack. He has ignored all arguments and set the date for November 12. Halder knows a coup is the only answer, but he can't bring himself to make a move without the commander in chief. But Brauchitsch will do nothing. His constant refrain is, 'If we revolt, we will be smashed from the rear by the English.' So there we are."

Oster threw up his arms in despair and sat down in the armchair they had left for him. "I've come to the conclusion that I must do what I can to ensure the failure of this offensive—the decisive failure—since we can't seem to stop it. Enough to halt Hitler in his tracks and prevent what happened in Poland. What I saw there—God knows, I wish I hadn't seen it—I can't sleep nights. We can expect more of the same in the West if Hitler chalks up another of his miracle victories. We must not underestimate this sleepwalker under a lucky star. He may prove right about striking now while Britain is still unprepared."

Oster turned to Dietrich with the look of a man about to enter a burning building. "People won't understand, but I have to do it. The Dutch military attaché here in Berlin is a close friend of mine. I'm planning to tell him the date of the offensive." Oster's sharp look seemed to gage Dietrich's reaction, but he pressed on without waiting for a response. "People will say I'm a traitor, but I regard myself a better German than all those who trot along behind Hitler. Yes, they'll call me traitor. The generals follow their Führer's orders and send millions to their deaths 'doing their duty,' and so are honorable. I'm ready to risk everything to save human life—the country, really, in the end—and I'm the traitor."

"You're not a traitor, Herr Colonel," Dietrich said quietly.

Oster lowered his eyes. When he spoke again, the passion was drained from his voice. "I cannot talk to Canaris about this. He is incapable of drawing the line between high treason and treason against country."

"This is not treason against country. I know that." Dietrich looked at Hans, who offered no help, but returned only a look of expectancy. Dietrich turned again to Oster. "When a madman is violating all that a government, under God, owes its people—"

"You're saying I should go ahead?"

"I can't say that. You must decide that on your own. But to me—to me it seems a just course. In this abnormal situation there's no really good way out. It's not a situation you created, you know."

"I helped create it. We all did, isn't that true?"

Dietrich thought to himself that if the church leaders had half Oster's courage to face the truth, their actions would tell a different story.

They talked on, and Oster seemed more at ease. Presently, he spoke of his childhood and his father. "He was not a great preacher, but he was honest. I wonder what he would say now." Oster sighed deeply and shook his head. "I did many things that disappointed him—got away from the Church, for one thing. I'm sorry to say so, but I came to find it—terribly innocuous." He seemed to be trying, with his half-apologetic smile, to recover his usual light, negligent style, but finding it impossible. "I will confess though, the only fear I have is of the anger of God."

"I wish more people felt that," said Dietrich.

After Hans and Oster left, Dietrich sat for a long time pondering the interview. The thought that kept coming back to him was of church people who were more afraid of Hitler than of God. It occurred to him that this man who, in his own words, had "gotten away from the Church," could be, in reality, closer to Christ than those who professed him as Lord. Yet the deepest pain was the realization that the Church, by its own guilt, had given such offense that men like Oster were prevented from accepting its message.

A little later he told Eberhard what Oster was planning to do.

"But I have a cousin in that army!" Eberhard's words tumbled out in a voice filled with horror and perplexity. He stood with his hands in his back pockets, his elbows bristling out on each side.

"So do I, two of them, one with Bock and one with Rundstedt."

"What are we talking about, Dietrich?"

"We're talking about what generally passes for treason."

Eberhard turned away, and Dietrich watched him as he walked around the room. He stopped at the bookcase and stared at the book titles. "I guess I just don't understand it." For a time Eberhard said nothing more, then turned and faced Dietrich again, his voice sharp and insistent. "Is such a thing really necessary? Isn't it just going too far, after all?"

Dietrich knew that the action Oster contemplated was against Eberhard's upbringing. It was against his own; so much so that he was still marveling at the calm, dispassionate answers he had given the tormented colonel. Now he felt unsure exactly how to answer Eberhard. "The truth is, I don't know," Dietrich confessed. "I suppose we have to think again of where, above all, our allegiance lies."

Eberhard was silent. He did not move from where he stood.

"That has to be the foundation of our thinking, doesn't it?" Dietrich asked.

"I never thought it would come to a conflict between allegiance to Christ and allegiance to country. Hitler is one thing. But the country?"

"It hasn't come to that."

"It sounds like it."

"No, Eberhard, it's not that. I believe Colonel Oster is as true a patriot as you'll find anywhere."

"That's hard to see. I suppose he's thinking only of overthrowing Hitler, but surely there's some better way of doing it, without endangering hundreds, maybe thousands, of men."

Dietrich told him of Oster's experience in Poland and Oster's conviction that the Nazis planned the same kind of aggression, with the accompanying bestialities, in the Low Countries and France. "At this point the range of options is severely limited. This action seems to be the only thing that might work."

"He'll be disgraced, if it ever comes out," Eberhard said.

"He knows that."

"You told him to go ahead?"

"No. He's doing this on his own," Dietrich answered.

"Yet you approve?"

"If it is necessary. For Oster, at any rate, it comes down to that." Eberhard seemed about to speak, and Dietrich quickly added, "As for us, there will be no more easy answers. The time will come—

maybe it's already here—when every available alternative will seem equally intolerable. We'll end up trying to decide between what is bad and what is worse. But if we do nothing, we're sure to go under. That would make us the most hypocritical of pharisees. At least we don't have to make these decisions alone, and that's worth a great deal. Perhaps something new will emerge from all this that we can't see in the existing alternatives. In any case, we can be confident that we are in the hands of One who can turn even our mistakes to good account."

Paula awoke, and before she opened her eyes, one thought—today is the day—electrified every nerve. It was still pitch dark outside—cold November dark—and Karl was still asleep beside her. They had gone to bed late. As he had most nights recently, Hans had come in around eleven, and Paula and Karl had remained downstairs with him and Christel, discussing the final plans. Everything was set to go, unless Hitler changed his mind about the offensive. Hans had completed his work on the proclamations, which General Beck and Carl Goerdeler, chosen to be the new president and chancellor respectively, were to read to the people immediately following the coup. Karl had alerted his panel of psychiatrists once more. Paula thought of Dietrich in Sigurdshof, relieved that he was in a safer place.

Soon Paula heard Hans and Christel stirring in their room across the hall. After a few minutes their soft footsteps passed her room. She got up quietly and opened the door. The two of them stood in the dim light at the top of the stair, Hans below, his intense face turned upward, and Christel leaning over to him, her hand on his shoulder. Paula could not hear their words, but saw the tender look between them, the gentle kiss, the clasped hands as he backed away and turned to go. Christel stood without moving until the front door closed behind him, then lifted both hands to her face and held them there. Paula longed to take her daughter in her arms as she had when she was a little girl. Instead, she stepped back and quietly closed the door.

The hours of the day crept slowly by. Hans was to take up his station at Zossen, the new underground army headquarters fifteen miles south of Berlin. Oster was to remain at the Tirpitz Ufer and monitor all information channels.

In the middle of the afternoon, when they least expected it, Hans came home. Something was wrong, but he said nothing until they had maneuvered the children next door. Then the story tumbled out. The coup was off. Halder had been about to give the orders, when Brauchitsch, who knew nothing of the coup plans, decided to make one final attempt to persuade Hitler to abandon the offensive. Halder had accompanied Brauchitsch to the Chancellery, and had come back in a panic and ordered everything burned. Halder expected the Gestapo to arrive at any minute and start making arrests. Hitler somehow had got wind of their plans. All the evidence had to be destroyed.

Hans opened his briefcase. "I managed to snatch my proclamations from the flames and get out of there." A jumble of scorched papers slid onto the table.

"The Gestapo?" Paula asked.

"I saw no sign of them."

In a few days it became clear that it was a false alarm; Hitler had known nothing, but in his rage at Brauchitsch's attempt to dissuade him, had thrown out some rabid phrase that Halder misinterpreted. The plans were in shambles. Soon afterward Hitler postponed the offensive because of weather. On Saturday Dietrich came from Pomerania, and the family together told him the whole story.

"Halder has begun to recover," said Hans. "If someone would just shoot Hitler for him, everything would be fine."

"Why doesn't he do it himself?" asked Emmi.

"He doesn't have it in him. He admitted as much the other day. He said, with tears in his eyes, that he had tried but could not bring himself to do it. He'd been carrying a pistol in his pocket for weeks—every time he went to the Chancellery—hoping he could get the nerve to shoot Hitler."

Klaus waved his hand impatiently. "At least half the opposition people I know are in favor of it."

"You mean assassination is being considered as a serious option?" asked Dietrich.

"Why not?" said Emmi.

"Not by Beck or Canaris," said Hans. "They're firmly opposed to it."

"Why?" Emmi insisted. "What are their reasons, I wonder?"

"Religious, mainly. That was Halder's reason. He said that as a Christian he couldn't bring himself to shoot an unarmed man."

"It would solve a lot of problems," said Hans.

"Would it not also create some?" Dietrich asked. "Anyway, I thought that was to be contemplated only as a last resort."

Emmi turned her rapid fire directly on him. "You Church people are a funny lot. You don't want to kill him, but if someone else did, you'd be glad. Isn't that so?"

Dietrich said nothing.

"What's the difference? Why not kill this devil? Why should it be a problem to kill this devil? If I could get near him, I'd do it."

From Emmi's determined look Paula was sure she would.

Before she went to bed, Paula climbed the stairs to Dietrich's room. His smile seemed more welcoming than usual, and more tender. He gave her his armchair and sat facing her.

"You probably know what's on my mind," Paula said. "I can't bear to hear Emmi talk that way. And she shouldn't have said those things to you."

"But she's right, you know. I've thought of nothing else the past hour. Just because I'm a Christian doesn't mean I can hold back from this thing—evil as it is—if it has to be done."

"But it is intolerable."

"Yes, it's intolerable. I told Eberhard the other day that the time would come when every alternative would seem equally intolerable."

Paula said nothing. She knew already—had known for some time—that it would come to this in the end. "It's hard to face. I don't want to face it."

"I know you don't, Mama. Neither do I. But I'm afraid that before this is over we'll have to walk through all kinds of slime. We can bear it. If we're doing what has to be done. If we do it in the name of God's creation. You've taught us that, you and Papa—to do what we do in the name of life." A warm look of encouragement came into his eyes. "And we're in it together as a family. That's something to be thankful for." He smiled, as though the credit for that belonged to her, and she was comforted.

Before she left, Paula and Dietrich invented a simple code, so that Dietrich would not be devoid of information in Sigurdshof.

"It's two miles to the nearest phone," he said. "If it keeps on snowing I might have to resort to snowshoes. But I'll try to make it once a week."

Dietrich got home only once that terrible winter, during a January thaw. The rest of the time he was snowbound in Sigurdshof—he had been right about the snowshoes. In March he came home again. While he was there word came that the Gestapo had shut down the seminary again, this time for good. In the slush and snow he and Eberhard returned to Sigurdshof and moved their belongings to Berlin. Not long afterward Hitler launched an attack on Scandinavia. The war was in full swing again.

In early April Dietrich listened with the rest of the family as German radio proclaimed that the Wehrmacht had occupied Danish and Norwegian soil "in order to protect those countries from the Allies, and will defend their true neutrality until the end of the war. And so an honored part of Europe has been saved from certain downfall."

Thus did success spread its carpet for the "sleepwalker under the lucky star," and snatched the rug from under the feet of the resisters.

27

On June 19, 1940, France signed an armistice with Hitler. Eberhard and Dietrich heard the news in East Prussia, where they were two weeks into a teaching and preaching circuit for the Confessing

Church, a temporary job while they both looked for something permanent. After the initial shock, Dietrich's comment was, "We're going to have to make some adjustments in our thinking. We've underestimated Hitler—that's plain. And overestimated our ability to bring him down. Now it's going to take much longer and be much harder than we imagined."

On the church circuits they were finding a great need for their services. The government did not give Confessing Church pastors the same exemptions as the others and drafted them into the service indiscriminately. Eberhard and Dietrich often found parishes where elders were leading the services and pastors' wives were handling all the religious instruction in the absence of their husbands. Surprisingly these churches were fuller than those in the Reich proper.

At Blöstau, where they were to hold a weekend conference of Confessing students, Dietrich was concerned when he learned that the pastors in the district had circulated handbills to announce the conference. Despite the breach of the law, everything seemed to go well on Saturday.

On Sunday morning Dietrich preached and afterward, when the regular parishioners had left, Eberhard sat with him talking to several of the students. The doors and windows of the church had been left open to let in the summer breeze. Suddenly a shadow fell across the room. Led by a Gestapo officer, a large contingent of police blocked the light from the front portal as they advanced down the aisle.

The officer, who was a head taller than the other policemen, spoke in clipped tones as he looked around the small sanctuary. "Where are the others?"

"There are no others," Dietrich said.

"The other theological students in your course."

"We are all here. There are no others."

The officer seemed unwilling to believe him and signalled his men to search the building. As the officer waited he strode up and down before the altar, his whip under his arm. Eberhard stole a glance at Dietrich, who was sitting at an angle from him on the first pew of the transept—his face emotionless, but his teeth clinched.

The policemen returned with a negative report. The officer worked his mouth in frustration and said to Dietrich, "Stand up."

Dietrich got slowly to his feet. Eberhard stood also and the four or five students with them.

"These are students?" the officer demanded.

"From the university, yes, except my colleague, Pastor Bethge."

"You met here yesterday also, did you not?"

"Yes."

"You must disperse," said the officer. "Such meetings are prohibited."

"How's that? This is merely a small, student conference, as you can see."

"There's an order. End of June. Part-time meetings of Christian youth prohibited."

"We never heard of it. Was it published?" Dietrich asked.

"That doesn't matter. It's an order."

"May we see it, please?"

Eberhard tried to catch Dietrich's eye, in the hope that he would say no more, but Dietrich did not seem to notice.

"That is not necessary," said the officer. "You must leave. But first we will need some information."

Eberhard had expected arrest or at least interrogation, and was relieved when the police took down only personal particulars and let them go.

At first Dietrich seemed inclined to dismiss the incident as just another harassment of the Confessing Church. "I'm sorry they got your name down," he said to Eberhard, after the others had left. "That won't help, I'm afraid, when it comes to your call-up. We'll have to try to head that off. I've already been thinking of it, but now it's even more urgent."

As so many times before, Eberhard was surprised to find Dietrich ahead of him in his calculations. Only later did Dietrich express some concern that the order might have been motivated against him from higher up. Eberhard felt once more the anxiety of that day the previous August, when Dietrich returned so unexpectedly from the United States. Dietrich had explained his reasons for coming back, and knowing Dietrich's sensitive conscience, Eberhard had understood some of it. Then quite calmly, as if he were saying nothing out of the ordinary, Dietrich had added, "I know what I have chosen." Eberhard had never questioned him about it again.

Now Dietrich decided to continue with the tour regardless of the Gestapo. Their next stop was Eydtkuhnen on the Lithuanian border. There the atmosphere was markedly different from the towns farther west. While the rest of Germany had watched fascinated as the mighty Wehrmacht hung the swastika on the Eiffel Tower, these East Prussians had been feeling the cold chill of the Soviet Army on their necks. Almost simultaneously with the great victory in Paris, Russian soldiers had begun to occupy Lithuania.

Now, just a few weeks later, Eberhard was preaching at a small church at the edge of this border town. After the service he noticed that very few people lingered about for the usual exchange of news and conversation. The tone was subdued and the glances apprehensive as they spoke at the door and left straightway for their homes. In the afternoon one of the elders walked with Eberhard along a shaded lane to a spot overlooking a low-lying meadow. On the rise beyond, dozens of soldiers in red-trimmed brown uniforms worked furiously at what appeared to be a gun emplacement.

"Russians," said the elder.

All up and down the slight ridge as far as Eberhard could see, fortifications of various kinds were going up.

In the evening he told Dietrich, and they went back the next morning so Dietrich could see for himself.

"Extremely interesting," Dietrich mused.

By the middle of the morning Dietrich had decided they should cancel the rest of the circuit trip and return to Berlin. "We need to talk to Hans," he said.

The farther west they rode the lighter the mood of the people. After Stettin they began to notice wooden arches thrown up across the road at the western edge of each village. Evergreens and bouquets of flowers twined about them, hiding the crude construction. Once, they stopped and looked back to read the legend across the top: "Vierraden greets its triumphal heroes." Dietrich looked at Eberhard and said not a word.

They had read in the morning paper of a victory march to be held in Berlin, celebrating the demobilization of a whole division of Berlin infantry back home from France. When they reached the city, Dietrich said he would take the wheel. He wanted to get home and, if humanly possible, steer clear of the mobs. Instead he took a wrong turn and they found themselves blocked off from every exit.

"Well," said Eberhard, "we might as well walk over and see the thing for ourselves."

"That's just what you wanted, isn't it?" Dietrich fumed.

"I've never seen a division demobilized."

With a skeptical grunt Dietrich got out of the car.

The buildings on the Unter den Linden were awash with great red and white banners. Throngs of people lined the street, laughing and weeping for sheer joy at the prospect of the end of the hated and dreaded war. Little children broke through the police lines and handed bouquets of flowers to the soldiers, while confetti rained from the buildings above. Entering through the Brandenburg Gate, the battle-scarred infantrymen goose-stepped past the triumphal reviewing stands erected on either side of the Pariser Platz. Goebbels received and returned their salute, along with a general, whom Eberhard thought he recognized as Dietrich's uncle, Paul von Hase, the commandant of Berlin. Eberhard turned to Dietrich to confirm it, but he was staring studiously ahead, as if determined to disregard the fact. Eberhard said nothing.

The surging hope was infectious, and Eberhard could not help but catch it. One sobering look from Dietrich tempered his elation.

The spirit of the triumphal scene did not carry over to the Bonhoeffer household. Eberhard remained silent as the cool, reasoned talk washed over him like ice water. Even if the British were willing to talk peace, which none of the Bonhoeffer family believed, what would it do but increase Hitler's power and make Germany even more a prison? On the other hand, if Churchill stood his ground and was able by some miracle to fend off attack, it would mean a long, long war.

"It looks like we're in for a bad time," said Dietrich's mother.

Renate, who had come over with her parents after supper, was sitting beside her grandmother. The children did not usually join in the evening discussions, but Eberhard realized suddenly that in the six months or so since he had seen her, Renate had been growing up fast. He thought she must be near fifteen, although she still had her pigtails. Renate had listened in silence to all the talk, but now she said in an agitated voice, "Will they keep on killing people like Gustav's sister?"

"Let's pray not, my dear," said Frau Bonhoeffer.

"Who is Gustav?" asked Dietrich.

"A friend of mine in school," Renate answered.

"And what happened to his sister?"

"Well, *she* wasn't killed, but it's a wonder. She's retarded, you see—in an institution. Lots of people, even children, are being killed in those places. They are, really!" Her eyes, filled with horror, turned to Eberhard.

"Yes, I've heard about it," Eberhard said.

For months there had been rumors of the systematic killing of the retarded and others considered a drag on the society. A few weeks earlier Eberhard had helped Dietrich with a scheme to save epileptic patients at Bethel and Lobethal. Dietrich had brought his father into it, and there had been tedious work drawing up the necessary papers for Dr. Bonhoeffer to sign—papers that provided the directors of these institutions with authoritative medical grounds for refusing to hand over their helpless inmates to the Nazis.

Renate continued, "Her parents had been hearing all these rumors so they decided to bring her home. Well, a few days after they got home with her—not long, but I don't know exactly— they got a letter of condolence, an official-looking letter—Gustav showed it to me—telling them of the death of their daughter. It was sudden, it said, a heart attack or something. The Nazis had made some kind of stupid mistake, you see. But what about the others? Gustav says there are lots of others, where there's no mistake."

"He's right," said Dietrich. "There are lots of others."

"But that's awful."

The look on Renate's young face struck Eberhard with particular poignancy. One so young should not be forced to deal with such a harsh reality. At fourteen he had lost his father, but even that terrible blow had not contained the horror of this.

Frau Bonhoeffer tried to reassure Renate that something was being done to put a stop to such atrocities. While the others talked of what could be done and of a protest already entered by Bishop Wurm, Eberhard watched Renate, who appeared to be lost in her thoughts of the victims of euthanasia.

That afternoon Dietrich went to see Hans at the Abwehr. The next day he showed Eberhard his written commission, signed by Canaris, to act for the Abwehr in East Prussia. "They tell me that gathering information for them from that frontier will counter any move the Gestapo might make against me," Dietrich said.

While they were in Berlin a job had come through for Eberhard as assistant to the director of the Gossner Mission, located in Dahlem. The director was a good man of the Confessing Church, Hans Lokies, who up to now had escaped dismissal. There was an apartment for Eberhard in the Burkhardthaus.

It was the first time Eberhard had ever had a dwelling of his own. Dietrich seemed to share his pride and appeared every day with a piece of furniture or a household item rounded up from some unknown source. How much Dietrich bought from his own pocket Eberhard never knew.

Everything had moved so fast that when the time came for Dietrich to leave for East Prussia, Eberhard was unprepared.

"I'll see you before long. Only a few weeks," said Dietrich, in a light tone that showed how well he had schooled himself for this good-bye. "Keep Lokies straight now. You can do it. You managed to keep me straight most of the time."

Dietrich gave a firm handshake and a quick direct look into Eberhard's eyes. Then he strode rapidly to his car and drove away.

28

"Subversive activity? What subversive activity?" Dietrich asked.

"That is not specified, Pastor Bonhoeffer."

"May I see the order, please?"

The police officer slid the papers across the desk. The order from the Reich Security Office read: "On account of his subversive activity, I issue against Pastor Dietrich Bonhoeffer of Schlawe, Pomerania, a prohibition against speaking in public in the whole of the Reich territory. By order, signed Roth." On the second sheet was a more sinister notation: from now on Dietrich was to report regularly to the police in Schlawe and make no move without notifying them.

Dietrich looked up and met the eyes of the man behind the desk. He realized that argument with this small-town officer would be futile. Instead he asked for a copy of the order. The man refused, but allowed him to write down the reference number: Reich Security Office IVA 4b 776/40.

As Dietrich walked to his car the inferences came into sharp focus. The order not to speak was bad, and he knew instinctively that it would become more and more burdensome as time went on. But the compulsory registration with the police in Schlawe was the greater blow—a restraint that had to be countered at all costs. That was no simple matter. Sensing that he was stepping into deep, swirling waters, Dietrich started the car and turned toward Berlin.

At the Tirpitz Ufer, Hans and Oster devised a plan to offset the restrictive order. Dietrich would become a staff member of the Munich office of the Abwehr and, ostensibly, use his ecumenical connections for the German military secret service. In reality he would be using them for the Resistance. Dietrich had come to the conclusion that he could no longer stand aside from those who were hazarding their lives in the only way that remained open, the way of conspiracy.

Dietrich did not like the word. He knew he was entering a road he would have to travel alone. He could not tell his friends in the Church what he was doing or justify his actions to them. He would be putting a strain on the trust his ecumenical friends had in him—all except Bishop Bell. He felt sure, somehow, that Bell would understand.

"How credible is it, after all, Herr Colonel," Dietrich asked, "a Confessing pastor in the Abwehr?"

Oster replied without hesitation, "The Abwehr works with everyone, with Communists and with Jews. Why not also with people of the Confessing Church?"

They chose to place Dietrich in the Munich Abwehr office, where a trusted colleague, Josef Müller, who had been negotiating with the Vatican for the Resistance, was already installed, along with a number of other reliable anti-Nazis. The job was to make a believable case that Dietrich was indispensable to the Abwehr, a maneuver that would also solve his call-up problem. But it could take months to clear up the order to report regularly to the police at Schlawe. Until that time, Hans said, Dietrich should keep out of sight. Josef Müller suggested the Benedictine monastery at Ettal in the Bavarian Alps. He knew the abbot and would make the necessary arrangements.

"But even that may take a while, and, meantime," said Hans, "you need to be away from here—somewhere in the country, preferably. Is there some place you can go where the people are reliable?"

Dietrich thought at once of an old lady, Frau Ruth von Kleist-Retzow, who since the Finkenwalde days had been a friend of his and a faithful Confessing Church member. Her main estate, Kieckow, administered by her son, and a smaller estate, Klein-Krossin, were not far from Köslin. Since the closing of Finkenwalde, Dietrich had been a guest at one or the other of the manor houses, most often Klein-Krossin, which Frau von Kleist called her "cottage." There she kept a room ready especially for him. He told Hans and Oster about the place.

Hans finally consented, although he thought it was too close to Schlawe. "Just don't leave the premises," he said.

With that settled, Hans, Oster, and Dietrich went together to Canaris for his final approval. The little admiral was in one of those acid humors that Dietrich had heard about.

"The British announce fifty planes shot down, the Germans claim fifty also. With that, Stalin books one hundred," he said. "Even if Hitler mounts the invasion, which he can't—there aren't enough ships to do the job—all it will do eventually is open up Europe to the Russians. Look how quickly Stalin lapped up the Baltic states. Hitler has never studied the globe."

"You think he cannot mount an invasion?" Dietrich asked.

"Not at all. The Navy's been trying to tell him that for weeks."

Dietrich hoped the admiral was right, but he was afraid to count on it.

"Our exalted Führer won't listen," Canaris continued. "He'll stand or fall in this struggle—he's said that many times—and annihilate anyone who is against him. Keeps himself surrounded by his SS guards. Day and night." He subsided into a brooding silence. As on previous occasions, Canaris took a pillbox from his pocket, put a flat white pill on his tongue, and turned to Dietrich. "You've been to Spain, Herr Pastor?"

"Yes. I spent a year there in 1928."

The admiral's face brightened. "Ah! I just came from there. We must get together one day and swap stories. I hated to come back, I can tell you. But I had to convince the Führer that I'd made a proper reconnoiter for taking Gibraltar from the rear. Instead, of course, I was warning Franco to be careful about Hitler's victorious chariot, if he hitched up to it he might end up over a cliff. Maybe now he won't take so readily to Hitler's wooing." Canaris smiled as if pleased that he might be living up to his reputation as the "wily Odysseus."

When he had heard the plans and approved them, the admiral stood and walked to the sideboard along the richly paneled wall. "So, shall we drink to our new arrangements?" Canaris poured brandy into four goblets on a silver tray.

Hans sat on the sofa with Canaris' two wirehaired dachshunds resting contentedly on either side of him. Oster lounged in a worn armchair near Dietrich. In the corner behind Oster a folding screen partially concealed an army cot. On the stand beside it were several books, among them *Don Quixote*.

Canaris returned with the tray and passed the glasses around. They all stood and the admiral proposed a toast: "We are thinking of the Führer—how we may rid ourselves of him."

Canaris' grim humor neither amused nor comforted Dietrich. He felt only that, as a Christian responsible to God for his actions, there was no other way he could go. To stand aside would be complicity in the ever-increasing crimes of the man Oster called "the greatest criminal of all time."

"You do not appreciate my little joke, Herr Pastor?"

Dietrich looked up, surprised at the admiral's perceptiveness. "I don't think it's a way any of us wishes to go."

"You're right. Yes, you're right." Canaris sipped the brandy slowly, then set the goblet down on the desk before him. "Ah, but we are a luckless band, my friends. It may take a hundred years for people to realize the degree of our misfortune. Should Hitler win this war, it will certainly be the end of us and also the end of Germany as we love it and want it to be. And if Hitler loses, that too will be the end of Germany, and of ourselves, for having failed to get rid of him—if indeed we do fail. Either way inevitably leads to national self-destruction. The average general can never be expected to grasp this, which means that even before the defeat of Hitler we ourselves will die, abandoned by all the world."

Dietrich looked forward to Klein-Krossin. With its well-ordered fields and woods, the small finger lake in the distance, and Frau von Kleist-Retzow's hospitality, it was ideal for rest and undisturbed writing.

From the beginning at Finkenwalde and later at Sigurdshof and Köslin, Frau von Kleist-Retzow had given money generously to the seminary and sent provisions from her country estates: a cartload of potatoes and vegetables, whole sides of meat and sausages, and bushels of fruit. On Sundays in the Finkenwalde time she had brought along to the service several of her grandchildren, who, in order to attend good schools, spent the winter with her in her townhouse in Stettin. They would bring to Finkenwalde a large basket of food and stay for lunch. Frau von Kleist-Retzow did not fit Dietrich's preconceived notions of the Junker aristocracy and constantly surprised him with her open-minded attitude. At the time of the Nuremberg Laws, she had told him how much his words impressed her—"He who refuses to raise his voice for the Jews, has no right to sing Gregorian chants"—and wanted him to repeat them wherever possible, especially to university students. "They're so indoctrinated with racial hate."

When some pastors thought they could change things from within if they joined the Church Committees, she had said, "No, if the root is rotten, even the sound twig grafted on will not help."

Frau von Kleist-Retzow told Dietrich once that she had started studying Greek. "You said, you remember, that the New Testament cannot be fully understood and appreciated without reading it in the Greek, so I've taken it up." Her merry eyes gaged his reaction. "You think that's too hard for an old woman like me?"

"I didn't say that."

"But you thought it," she said with a roguish grin. "It doesn't come easy, you're right. I'm not as quick as I once was. For a long time I've been praying about the petrification of the Church. Now I can begin to see a Christian renaissance coming, and I want to be in on it."

Frau von Kleist-Retzow had sent her carriage to meet Dietrich at the train station in Belgard. When he arrived at Klein-Krossin, she came down the steps to meet him. She walked with a cane—not because of age, she had assured him earlier, but because of an injury. Her dark dress touched her ankles, giving her short, rotund figure its best advantage.

She walked a little slower now and some of the sparkle was gone from her voice when she greeted him. The year before, one of her grandsons had been killed in the Polish campaign. But her welcome was warm and full of concern.

The servants took care of the luggage. Dietrich and Frau von Kleist-Retzow walked through the house to the vine-covered terrace at the back, where they were joined by two of Frau von Kleist's grandchildren, Max von Wedemeyer and his younger sister, Maria. As children they both had visited Finkenwalde several times with their grandmother. Max was now a splendid, young junior lieutenant on his way to join his cavalry regiment. It was taken for granted that he would serve in the Army; military service was part of the way of life for these young Pomeranian aristocrats, especially with the Fatherland at war.

Maria, now a fair, unspoiled creature of sixteen, stood poised on the threshold of young womanhood. When they all four were seated in the wicker chairs, Dietrich inquired about Max and Maria's parents and brothers and sisters. Their father, called back into service as a major, had served in the French campaign. Recently his unit had been redeployed in southeast Poland.

"Then he was home for two weeks," said Maria. Her deep blue eyes lit up with the memory of that time with her father. "That was splendid. It just didn't last long enough."

She wore a dark blue riding habit, with a velvet collar and a simple white shirt. Her hair was cut shoulder length, and a single gold clasp held the red-brown tresses back on one side. She was leaving the next day for her high school in Weiblingen, on the outskirts of Heidelberg.

"Is it a good school?" asked Dietrich.

"It's all right."

"Of course, it's a good school," said Frau von Kleist, "one of the best."

"I'd rather be in Pätzig. Or here."

"You don't like Heidelberg?" Dietrich asked.

"I don't like any city these days. There's no free air to breathe.

You have to be so careful what you say—can't trust anyone. That's so stupid. I can't bear not to say what I think."

"How true," said Max.

Maria laughed. There was a slight separation between her two front teeth, a small defect in an otherwise perfect face. "Yes, it is true," she said. "Here and at home I can be myself."

A young brother and sister from a neighboring estate came for horseback riding with Max and Maria. They invited Dietrich to ride with them, but he declined. He had not been on a horse since he was a child at his grandmother's in Tübingen, and then only a few times. Maria and Max had grown up on horses. When they left for the stables, Dietrich and Frau von Kleist moved to comfortable wicker chairs on the lawn. The grass underfoot was green after a late September rain. In the distance the vast fields of the estate stretched to the edge of a forest. A smooth sandy drive encircled both lawn and house.

For a time neither Frau von Kleist-Retzow nor Dietrich spoke, then, as if she were picking up an ongoing conversation, she said, "As long as she's in school, I don't worry too much. She has two more years. But after that—those horrible work camps."

"Yes, of course. She must be preserved from that," Dietrich agreed.

"At all costs. But it isn't easy, Herr Bonhoeffer. Almost no exceptions are allowed. And it's getting worse all the time. Our pharmacist in Tychow has a daughter in one of those camps. He and his wife are faithful members of our little congregation. The other day he showed me a letter from the director of the camp. It said his daughter and five other girls from the camp would soon 'present the Führer with a child.' The poor man was distraught."

"Yes, I've heard about that," said Dietrich, with a shudder. Himmler was sending his SS Army men to these camps for their leave time. The girls were expected to cooperate. If not, they were accused of disloyalty to the Führer and the Reich. "We'll have to do something."

"You think you can?"

"Not I, perhaps, but Hans von Dohnanyi—or someone." He explained the possibilities. "We'll work on it when the time comes."

The old lady nodded. "Ah, yes, that's good. I know you will." She instinctively touched the pearl necklace at her throat as if it were a talisman. The one diamond, suspended at the center, sparkled in the sun. It was a gift from her young husband, who had died in the twelfth year of their marriage. Dietrich had never seen her without the necklace. "Ah, me," she sighed. "Now you'll be far off in Bavaria. Just where in Bavaria is that monastery, anyway?"

"Ettal, south of Munich. Near the Austrian border."

"You see, a thousand miles away."

From the direction of the barns came the rhythmic thud of horses' hooves. The riders drew rein not far from their two chairs.

"Where do you plan to ride?" Frau von Kleist asked.

"Wherever the horses take us," said Maria with an easy laugh. "Maybe down by the lake." She leaned over and patted her horse on the neck. The sun picked up the red and gold highlights in her hair. Wind and motion would soon have it flying about her face.

"Better come along, Pastor Bonhoeffer," called Max, "it's a perfect day."

"Thanks. Some other time," said Dietrich, and with regret watched them ride away.

In the evening Frau von Kleist-Retzow's son, Hans-Jürgen, came with his family from Kieckow, where he ran the main Kleist-Retzow estate. Dietrich had not seen him since the death of his son on the Western Front. Now he seemed older and said little.

Frau von Kleist-Retzow initiated the music. First, two of the children played, then their grandmother asked Maria to play the violin.

She laughed and said, "You'll be sorry. I'm very much out of practice." She turned to Dietrich. "If Pastor Bonhoeffer will accompany me. He can cover my mistakes."

Dietrich and Maria conferred and decided on a Schubert serenade. Despite the missed notes she played with vigor and sensitivity, the tone firm and mellow. Her slender body moved with grace to the gentle rhythm.

After that Dietrich was bombarded with requests and played one number after the other. Two young officers in dress uniform, friends of Max, joined the company. One was a tall handsome fellow with dark curly hair, who stayed by Maria's side and paid little attention to the music.

When Dietrich finished, the talk turned to a hunting party Max and his friends had planned for the next day in the hunting grounds of Kieckow. One of the girls put a record on the gramophone—an American record by Glenn Miller. The young people began to dance; the officer with the dark curly hair danced with Maria.

Neither the sight nor the sound was pleasing to Dietrich. He sat with Hans-Jürgen von Kleist-Retzow and talked of the problems of storing the good potato harvest. Above the hearth hung a giant elkshead. He looked down on Dietrich with benign indifference, as if to say, my day on earth is past, and now it is given to me to hang here and look down on the likes of you.

29

When Dietrich arrived at the Benedictine Abbey in Ettal, winter had already set in. Snow covered the high mountains that pressed in on three sides of the narrow valley. In midwinter, he was told, the northern peaks blocked the sun so that for several weeks it only touched the valley floor for an hour at high noon. At the foot of the mountains, the houses of the tiny village huddled near the monastery. Suspended over all was the great dome of the cloister church.

Josef Müller had made all the arrangements with his friend Father Johannes, administrator of the abbey. With their characteristic Christian hospitality, the Benedictines made Dietrich their guest. He slept in the monastery's Hotel Ludwig der Bayer—across the winding street from the abbey—took his meals with the monks in the refectory, and had complete access to the library. Father Johannes, a tall, slender priest—made taller still by his long black habit—gave Dietrich a key of his own to the enclosure. There he showed him a small secluded room, free from all distraction, which would be Dietrich's for prayer and meditation.

"You may come and go as one of us," he said. "If it should become advisable you may, of course, stay here overnight."

Father Johannes' smile was slightly strained, and Dietrich wondered how much he knew of his problem with the Gestapo. Müller had said only that the priest was familiar with the story and was willing to take the risk.

Dietrich spent most of each morning in the library, where he worked on his book on ethics. At lunchtime, in the refectory, one of the monks read historical works in the sing-song tone of the liturgy. The food was excellent. After a nap Dietrich worked another hour or two in his room; then before supper he explored the paths that traversed the valleys, or climbed the hill behind the monastery. Finally, the monastery bells echoed their evensong against the crags, and he returned. This daily routine seemed almost dilatory after the fierce pace of the previous five years.

Dietrich sometimes attended mass in the cloister church, where the light, airy heights represented the best of baroque architecture. Despite theological differences, he found at the abbey a common fellowship of prayer and worship. Once, in an alcove overlooking the inner courtyard, he discovered a group of monks reading his *Cost of Discipleship*. The brothers extracted a promise, which Dietrich was glad to give, to spend an afternoon together discussing the work.

As required, Dietrich had registered as a resident of Munich, nominally with his Aunt Christine, the Countess Kalckreuth, who had kindly offered her address. Then followed the wait while the Munich Abwehr office applied for a cancellation of his call-up requirement and of the order to report regularly to the police. For that he had to travel once a week to Munich.

Dietrich's second-floor room overlooked the valley at the back of the hotel. He had a little balcony, which would have been pleasant in summer. A girls' school, moved en masse from Hamburg for safety from the bombing, occupied the entire two floors above him. Dietrich encountered the students frequently in the halls and on the stairs. Most of them wore the uniform of the Hitler Youth. On Dietrich's floor were a number of children from Berlin, there for the same reason. At the end of the first week, Christel arrived with her three children: Klaus, Christoph, and Bärbel. Emmi followed later with her son Thomas and daughter Cornelia. According to an arrangement with the monastery, the children were to occupy rooms on Dietrich's floor and attend school at the cloister. Christel and Emmi would divide their time between Berlin and Ettal.

Keeping an eye on five nieces and nephews, ranging in age from seven to fourteen, soon banished all dullness from Dietrich's routine. After their classes each day, the children shouldered their skis and headed for the hills. When they came back to Dietrich's room, they were usually starved and ate whatever sausages, crackers, or fruit he had on hand. Day after day they confided to him their problems, hurts, joys, and questions about homework. The responsibilities of this deputy-parenting sometimes outweighed the pleasures.

One day he was standing in the hall near the corner, where a short flight of steps led down to the main dining hall, now the classroom of the Hamburg school.

Out of sight on the stair he heard a girl's voice ask, "But what is your uncle doing here?"

And Christoph's voice in reply, "Studying theology, of course."

"But isn't he a Protestant? What would he be doing in a Catholic monastery?"

"He's a theologian. He has to know about all religions. That's his job."

"I find it very strange all the same."

"No reason. He's just doing his job. Please excuse me, I have to go to my room."

Dietrich ducked into the sitting room until Christoph passed. He watched over his newspaper, and soon the Hamburg girl followed. She was one of the older ones, who always wore her BDM uniform. He had noticed her before, casting questioning looks his way.

Christoph did not mention the incident, and Dietrich did not ask. He forgot about it until one week later, when the bellboy knocked on his door and said he was wanted downstairs.

"It's the Gestapo, Pastor Bonhoeffer," the boy whispered, his usually cheery countenance pale and frightened.

"Thank you, Rolf. Please tell them I'll be right down. And don't worry. It's all right." Dietrich closed the door and quickly checked his desk for anything that might be suspicious. A recent letter from Hans told him, in their code, of progress on his case. He tore the letter in tiny pieces, tossed it over his balcony, and watched the wind scatter it across the snow-covered valley. Then Dietrich went downstairs to face the Nazi.

The officer had ensconced himself behind a little desk in one of the sitting rooms. "You are registered in Munich, I believe?" he asked with exaggerated politeness. He read off the address.

"Yes, that is my home now."

"Then what brings you here so often?"

"My work, to be sure. Research for my book on ethics."

"Ethics?"

"Yes."

"You are not Catholic."

"No. But in this work, you see, it is important to explore all points of view. And this kind of research takes time. The very excellent library here—"

"I understand," said the tall, handsome, pure Aryan, whose interest did not seem to include the library facilities of Ettal. "How long do you expect to be here?"

"Oh, back and forth for some time, I'm sure. It's hard to set a definite schedule. Often in research one thing leads to another."

The Nazi asked no further questions and made no move to

search Dietrich's room. After he left, Dietrich wondered why the officer had come at all and decided it must have been a routine check, although the fact that they seemed to be keeping close tabs on him was not reassuring.

Father Johannes' anxiety was not so easily dispelled, and he admonished Dietrich repeatedly to be careful. The priest installed a telephone in the library stacks so that he could warn Dietrich if they appeared again, and gave him a monk's habit "in case you need to disappear."

Dietrich smiled. "I don't think it's that serious, Father Johannes."

"One can't be too careful."

The next day the nine-year-old Christoph came down with the flu, and Dietrich brought him into his room so he could look after the child during the night. In the evening as Dietrich was writing Christmas letters to the brothers, Christoph rose up on his elbow and asked, "Who's getting all those letters, Uncle Dietrich?"

"The young pastors who used to be in my seminary."

"Doesn't your hand get tired, writing so much?"

"Yes, it does. But I want them to have the letters. They are lonely in their army stations."

"Do they all get a picture, too?" asked Christoph.

"Yes."

"May I see it?"

Dietrich handed him one of the cards with the print of Altdorfer's *Nativity*. He had bought ninety of them to send the men and a larger one, framed, for Frau Niemöller, to whom he always sent something at Christmas.

"It's kinda crazy, isn't it?" said Christoph. "Doesn't look like the manger scene."

"I know. 'Christmas among the ruins.' It seemed appropriate."

The child pondered that for a moment and then asked, "Will I have to go to war, Uncle Dietrich?"

"Oh, no. It will be over before then. Soon, we hope."

"My Papa hopes so, too. But Hans-Walter—"

"Yes, Hans-Walter may have to go, if the war lasts much longer."

Christoph returned the picture, and Dietrich turned again to his desk.

"Is that why the Gestapo is after you? Because you're working with my Papa?"

Dietrich was taken by surprise. Clearly Christoph knew or guessed more than Hans and Christel imagined. "It's because they don't want me to speak in public any more and they're checking up on me, I suppose."

"But you are working for Admiral Canaris too, aren't you? Are you a double agent?"

"What romantic ideas you have. Now, turn over and go to sleep. Double agent, indeed."

Dietrich continued to write and to check off the names on the list.

"Uncle Dietrich?"

"Yes."

The child had pulled the comforter up tightly under his chin. "A girl in the Hamburg school was asking about you."

"Indeed? What did she ask?"

"What you were doing. Why you were here. I think she was suspicious."

"And what did you say?"

"I said that you were a theologian and you needed to know about the Catholic religion and that was your job. But maybe I didn't say it right, and she was still suspicious, and that's why the Gestapo came." His lips trembled and his eyes filled with tears.

Dietrich turned his chair around beside the cot. "No, Christoph. I'm sure you said it exactly right. You were very clever to say it that way, which was, of course, precisely the truth." He winked at the child and squeezed his hand. "Now, go to sleep."

There was one bright piece of news during those months. Hans was able to get Eberhard's deferment from the call-up. Hans had claimed that Eberhard's contacts with India and the Middle East through the Gossner Mission would be indispensable to the Abwehr. For the first time since Dietrich's arrival at Ettal he went skiing. He took Christoph with him.

As Christmas neared, Hans and Josef Müller came to Ettal to discuss the possibility of contact once again with the Allies. In the interval since Müller had arranged Dietrich's refuge at Ettal, Dietrich had learned a good deal about the rugged lawyer and had come to like him. Müller was the kind of man sprung-from-the-people, whom the Nazis would have liked to claim for their own but never could. He had earned his way through secondary school hauling manure behind a team of oxen—hence the nickname "Ochsensepp," which had become his code name in the Resistance.

When they met the first time Müller had said, "So, we work in a common cause, you in the Lutheran Church and I in the Catholic. I've heard about the memo to Hitler back in '36. That took courage, real courage." Müller's brown eyes—the one soft feature in a broad, uneven countenance—smiled approvingly. "So, if Hitler brings our churches together, he'll have done one good thing. One sheepfold, no?"

"And one shepherd?"

"Well—" Müller began.

"You know which one it would have to be."

Müller laughed. "We must talk about it." But there had been no time to continue the conversation. Müller had timed the present meeting to coincide with a Christmas visit to the abbey by three prelates from the Vatican. Father Leiber, who had been the go-between for Müller's Vatican exchanges the year before, was one of them. They met in the small, private dining room of the hotel. A spirit of solidarity, political and spiritual, released the constraints imposed by life in a police state and made room for free and open talk. Müller's amusing anecdotes, which he told between hearty swigs of the best Ettaler beer, furthered the infectious gaiety of the group.

"I arrived at the Abwehr that first time," Müller said, "expecting to meet Canaris. That was the summons. But it was Oster and

Dohnanyi here who received me. Oster had hardly begun the conversation before he said, 'We know a great deal more about you than you do about us.' You can imagine my surprise. They knew everything. Everything. Well, almost," Müller said with a grin.

"One story they had is not true, unfortunately. I had to disabuse them. They'd heard I was married by Pacelli—years ago, of course, before he was Pope. But it was another priest. I don't always correct that story. It has a nice ring—married by the Pope. But I knew I'd better level with these Abwehr fellows." Müller laughed retelling the tale. "Now Heydrich has the notion I'm a disguised Jesuit, given a special dispensation by the Pope to have a wife and family as a cover for my work for the Church."

Everyone laughed uproariously. Even Hans, who rarely showed his fun-loving nature outside the family, seemed relaxed and cheerful.

Late in the evening and with obvious reluctance, the company turned to serious talk. During all the revelry Dietrich had observed Father Leiber and wondered what a man so close to the Pope was really like. A whisper of a priest in his black cossack, Leiber had revealed little of himself behind a modest and retiring smile. So his firm reaction came as a surprise when Hans made overtures to him for a renewal of contacts with the British.

"I regret to say that is not at all possible. I cannot speak about it to His Holiness again," Father Leiber said in a soft but clear accent.

"That's because we failed him," said Müller. "We led him to expect too much."

"Perhaps, but no more than you yourselves expected. His Holiness is aware of that. Your accurate warnings about Norway, and later the Low Countries, proved your sincerity. You understand, my friends, that I and the Holy Father also went too far that time. We cannot do that again."

The finality of Father Leiber's tone made no further pressure possible. Behind the priest's kindly smile Dietrich sensed his assessment that the Vatican could not again involve itself with plans—no matter how honorable or morally imperative—where the power for their implementation was not assured. He did, however, clear up one mystery: he confirmed that the warnings to the Low Countries had been passed on and received on the other side.

Hans asked, "Then why were they not acted upon?"

"I'm not sure," the priest replied. "Perhaps the whole thing seemed to them too incredible. I did hear the Belgian ambassador say that no German would do a thing like that." He turned to Müller. "I think he assumed you were either a traitor, and therefore not to be trusted, or else sent by Hitler to try to mislead them."

"Ah, me," Müller said with a shake of his head.

When Father Johannes and his guests from Rome had retired to the abbey, Müller poured himself another glass of beer and drank half of it down in gloomy silence. "Well," he said with a heavy sigh, "what next?"

"We'll have to keep trying to get through by other channels," said Hans. "Dietrich's friend, Bishop Bell, is one of them." He turned to Dietrich. "What are the chances there, do you think?"

"I might be able to contact him through the ecumenical people in Geneva, but I'd have to go there to find out. I don't know if that's possible."

"Yes, it's possible. We would have to file a report when you return—make up something—to show you'd collected information for Military Intelligence. That won't be too hard."

Double agent, indeed! "How soon?" Dietrich asked.

"As soon as possible. As soon as we can clear up all this stupid business with the Gestapo."

Dietrich relished the thought of being part of the action at last.

30

At the Swiss border the train slowed to a standstill. Dietrich's pulse quickened, and he rubbed his sweating palms on his knees. He did not look at the others in the first class compartment but kept his eyes on the window. Snow was falling on the wide expanse of harshly lit concrete where the border guards and the SS, who sometimes accompanied them, moved to board the train. A short distance beyond, other policemen paced up and down with dogs on leashes, a sight that sent shivers down Dietrich's spine.

The trip had presented an opportunity to help Sabine and Gert in London. So before he left Dietrich had drawn two thousand marks from the account that Gert had made over to him and distributed the bills in "pockets" that he slit in the uncut pages of two new, uncontroversial books. One he had packed in his suitcase, the other in his briefcase.

Suddenly he heard a commotion at the far end of the car. He watched through the window as two policemen dragged a man from the train and shoved him across the platform. Dogs on either side barked and snapped as they strained at their leashes. Dietrich glimpsed the pale, frightened face of the man as the SS men pushed him into the station.

Without warning the patrol officer appeared at the door of the compartment. He gave an abrupt Hitler salute and held out his hand for the passports. From his briefcase Dietrich took his passport and the courier pass, which the Munich Abwehr had prepared for him. The other occupants of the compartment made ready their papers also. The officer looked at the passes and at their faces, then went through the luggage, piece by piece. He turned through some of Dietrich's papers, then picked up one of the books with the money. Slowly he leafed through it. Dietrich did not move a muscle. He wondered briefly if Nazis, like dogs, could smell fear. But the officer did not look up and asked no questions. He put the book back, returned their passports, and with another curt salute moved on.

The train began to move slowly forward. Ten minutes later they arrived in Basel. Dietrich walked to the shortest check line, anticipating no problems. There had been some difficulty getting a visa, but in the end the Abwehr had managed it. At the desk he presented it with his passport.

The clean-shaven, young Swiss official seemed skeptical. "And what is your business in Switzerland, Herr Bonhoeffer?"

"Church business. I will be meeting with ecumenical leaders in Geneva."

"I wasn't aware that your government permitted representatives to such meetings."

"This is a private meeting, having to do with purely interfaith matters."

It was clear that the man did not believe him. There were Germans behind Dietrich who could hear every word. He asked to speak with the top official.

In a small inner office Dietrich faced an older man, who was also immediately skeptical. Without being specific, Dietrich explained to him that his purpose was to reopen lines of communication between the churches, whose task was to work for Christian brotherhood and peace in spite of war.

The man smiled. "You expect me to believe the Nazis would let you out for that?"

"Certainly not. They think I have a different mission."

As Dietrich talked, the man, who had been drawing on a pad, grinned. "All rather vague, Herr Bonhoeffer. Have you no credentials from your church?"

"It would be impossible to get out of Germany with such papers. You perhaps understand that?"

"Perhaps. The truth is, you are simply asking me to take your word." Obviously the official was not inclined to do that.

"Look, ring Karl Barth here in Basel. He knows me," Dietrich said.

Without further questions the official excused himself and went into another room, closing the door behind him.

Dietrich was sure that Karl Barth would stand up for him, although they had not been in direct communication for several years. The eminent theologian, more than any other, had influenced Dietrich to enter the field of theology; he read everything Barth wrote. They had met in 1931, when Dietrich returned from the United States and spent three weeks in Barth's seminar in Bonn. In the first session Dietrich had quoted Luther: "The curses

of the godless sometimes sound better in God's ear than the halle-
lujahs of the pious." That had delighted Barth, and since that time
their friendship had been one of complete frankness and sometimes completely frank disagreement.

When the official returned, he smiled and held out his hand.
"You must forgive me, Pastor Bonhoeffer, but the Gestapo is constantly trying to slip undercover men into Switzerland. We have to
be careful."

Barth removed his black-rimmed glasses and began wiping
them with his handkerchief. His rugged face still showed skepticism. "I hope you realize that this totally impossible story is going
to be doubted in Geneva. If I didn't know you, I'd have trouble
myself."

There had been plenty of trouble already here in Barth's book-
lined study. It had taken a good deal of explaining to persuade him,
even with Dietrich laying out in general terms the whole truth of
the Resistance.

"Yes," Barth continued, "with the Swiss you'll find it difficult.
These days they doubt everybody and everything that comes out
of Germany."

"I suppose so."

The professor was not enthusiastic about efforts to overthrow
Hitler. He feared that such a move would result in another nationalistic and repressive regime, with militarism remaining predomi-
nant. "Prussia was born from a cannonball, like an eagle from an
egg," he said. Barth especially distrusted the generals. His probing
questions forced Dietrich to admit the wide political differences
among the people of the Resistance and the difficulties in getting a
working consensus on a future government.

"We're not leaving that work undone," Dietrich said. "In fact, a
great deal of our discussion concerns the future government. But
the overriding prerequisite is to get rid of this criminal regime."

Barth smiled and drew on his pipe, which filled the room with
the aroma of sweet tobacco. "Perhaps when you come back by,
you can persuade me," he said.

"I'd rather talk theology," said Dietrich. He looked again into the friendly face of the professor, who was twenty years his senior. He longed to stay several days with this man and talk about the essential thing, theological existence. But now there was no time.

In Zurich Dietrich's old friend from Union Seminary days, Erwin Sutz, gave him a months-old message from Bishop Bell, in which Bell assured Dietrich of his unchanged Christian fellowship and told him that Franz was doing well. That alone was worth the trip to Switzerland.

Through Emmi's sister, Lore Schmidt, who lived near Zurich, Dietrich had news of Sabine, now in Oxford. During the fall and winter months, when England was under constant attack from Göring's bombers, there had been no word from Sabine and Gert, and no knowledge of their whereabouts. Lore told of Gert's internment as a German national for several months early in the war, and of Bishop Bell's help in gaining his release. Dietrich wrote Sabine a long letter and sent her the two thousand marks. He also wrote Bell and thanked him.

In Geneva there were difficulties, as Barth predicted. But thanks to W. A. Visser 't Hooft, the general secretary of the reorganized World Council of Churches, and a small group of ecumenical colleagues, Dietrich was able to accomplish his mission. His ecumenical friends, upon whom he must depend for contact with the Allies, accepted his report of the church situation in Germany, but it was hard for them to imagine a resistance operation centered in the heart of German Military Intelligence. Patiently Dietrich explained the Resistance movement to them, giving as few specifics as possible and no names. Finally he was able to convince them. Visser 't Hooft agreed to give a detailed report of their talks to Bishop Bell, and they began notes for a memo—intended for the British government—on Christian peace aims in the event of a successful overthrow of the Nazi regime. Guided by Bell's reaction, they would expand those notes when Dietrich returned and use them as a basis for further communication. Dietrich requested assurance that the Allies would suspend military operations during the revolt. He made clear that in order to succeed the resisters must have the cooperation of several strategically placed generals, and that without this assurance from the Allies, that was not likely.

For Dietrich, the spirit of universal Christian brotherhood was healing. He drank in the talk about the life of the churches in the world, of Christ taking form in His Church across the events of the times, and of the policy the churches should follow in the present circumstances. Hungry for reliable, uncensored information, Dietrich stayed up late each night and devoured periodicals and papers of the past two years; then the next day he peppered his friends with questions.

Too soon the four weeks ended, and he had to leave. Refreshed and invigorated, he crossed the border and headed once more into the tempest.

At the Abwehr in Berlin Dietrich took the sheet of paper that Colonel Oster handed him. It was a copy of an order from the Führer's headquarters to be issued two months hence on June 6, 1941. It was entitled "General instructions on the treatment of Political Kommissars," and the preamble read: "The war against Russia will be such that it cannot be conducted in a knightly fashion. This struggle is one of ideologies and racial differences and will have to be conducted with unprecedented, unmerciful and unrelenting harshness. All officers will have to rid themselves of obsolete ideologies. I insist absolutely that my orders be executed without contradiction." One paragraph in the general instructions jumped out at Dietrich: "Political commissars of the Red Army will be shot at once, whether captured during operations or otherwise showing resistance. German soldiers guilty of breaking international law will be excused."

The order went on to state that all guerrillas were to be "shot down without mercy" and any suspicious movement by enemy civilians "crushed immediately by the most stringent measures, including summary execution."

"This means that now the Army will be expected to do what the

SS did in Poland?" Dietrich asked. With a sense of horror he thought of his former seminarians, many of them in Army units now poised on the Russian frontier.

"Right," Oster replied, "that's exactly what it means."

"But surely the commanders won't stand for such a thing."

Oster smiled thinly. "That remains to be seen. Many of them are upset, but Brauchitsch won't go against Hitler."

"He'll stay in his post? Halder, too?" Dietrich asked.

"They say so, 'to prevent something worse.' To try to miti-gate—"

"But will it? Will they be able to prevent any of this?"

"Some, maybe. They may save a few lives by special order, but not enough. No, not enough. They're sacrificing the honor of the German Army, and we and our children will bear the stain of it." Oster took the order back and put it in his desk drawer. "The 'Little Greek' wishes to see you. He has read your report—both the 'official' one and the one for us. Also, he agrees that you can stay in Berlin for the time being."

"What does he think of this order?"

"Exactly what you would imagine," said Oster.

The admiral's dachshunds greeted them noisily, but the "Little Greek," as Oster called Canaris, was not in the room.

"He's feeding the birds," said Oster.

On the balcony a bundled figure sprinkled birdseed from a green box onto a tray on the railing, then turned again to come inside.

"Ah, Pastor Bonhoeffer, it was good of you to come." The ad-miral advanced into the room and shook hands. Although it was late April and not bitterly cold, he wore a greatcoat, so long it almost touched his shoe tops. The dachshunds stood expectantly on either side of him.

"Ah, Lollo, Spitze, it's your turn, is it? Yes, you know it is." He took two dog biscuits from his pocket and gave one to each of them, with a pat on the head, then watched approvingly as they took their appointed places beside his desk. "Dogs have all man's good qualities without possessing any of their failings," he said, as he hung his coat on the halltree. "My dachshunds are discreet. They'll never give me away."

Canaris asked few details of Dietrich's trip, but was interested in Bishop Bell and impressed that Bell was a member of the House of Lords. "Does he know Churchill?" he asked Dietrich.

"I'm not sure, Herr Admiral. He knows many people in high places."

"Churchill is a great man and Britain the essential aircraft carrier to save Europe from both plagues—Nazi and Bolshevik. You're aware that our initials are the same, Churchill's and mine?"

"Yes." Dietrich smiled. Wilhelm Canaris, yes, but he had never thought of it.

Canaris waved them to a seat and sat down heavily in a worn armchair. "Yet it is my job to try to bring him down. The 'master spy,' as they call me, must preside over all these strategems—fifth column, sabotage, suicide missions—to bring Churchill and his people down. That's my job," he said with a gloomy smile. "You see, one day I have to contend with criminals like Heydrich and Schellenberger and court the danger of being reduced to their level; the next, I talk with men like you about how to get rid of this regime." Then he added, without dropping a beat, "You know Martin Niemöller, I believe?"

"Yes, I do," Dietrich answered.

"And do you know how he is faring?"

"As well as can be expected, I believe. I spoke with Frau Niemöller just before I left home to come here. He is cheerful and sound in health and faith."

"A brave man. What is it now—four years?" Canaris asked.

"Almost."

"A brave man. I've been attending his church sometimes in Dahlem." With that surprising assertion, the admiral sighed. "But I'm not sure how much use it is to strive against one's destiny."

"Not much, I think, if that means the time and place in which one has been set down," Dietrich replied.

"An evil time and place it is, too. So why struggle? That seems a legitimate question, don't you think?"

"Not if you believe, as I do, that God can and will bring good out of evil, even out of the greatest evil."

Canaris looked at Dietrich as if recounting his experiences in the hope that somehow he could believe that.

Dietrich added, "For that purpose He needs men who make the best use of everything."

It was impossible to know what Canaris was thinking. After a time he asked, "Have you ever been to Argentina, Pastor Bonhoeffer?"

"No."

"Lovely country. Wide open spaces. A place to dream about, though I'd settle for a Grecian isle just now."

Oster flicked his cigarette impatiently.

Canaris continued, "Why did you come back here? Why didn't you stay in America?"

"Because I could not divorce myself from the destiny of my people."

"Ah, yes." His eyes flashed, but he made no further comment. "You know of this infamous new order?"

"I showed it to him," said Colonel Oster.

"Ah, yes," said Canaris. "If that order is not countermanded, it will blight us forever."

"There's only one way to countermand it," said Oster. "We're sending Hassell to Witzleben in France with a plan. When Hitler goes to Paris in May to celebrate the anniversary of the fall of France, we hope to strike—"

"Spare me the details," said Canaris. "Just get on with it." He leaned over and touched the head of one of the dachshunds. "We don't want to hear the gory details, do we, Lollo? No, we don't." With a sigh the admiral leaned back in his chair. "The German armies, commanded by lunacy in person, will bleed to death on the icy steppes of Russia. Hitler is ignorant of Napoleon and Charles XII."

It struck Dietrich as odd that his niece would confide in Eberhard first and not to her parents or Dietrich himself. "And who is this girl?" he asked.

"A girl at school," Renate answered. "I thought she was my friend. We're the elected spokesmen for the class, so we work together." She brushed her honey-gold hair from her cheek and looked at Eberhard, then back down at the piano. The Debussy was open at the place she had been practicing. She played a soft triad.

"Why would she threaten to report you?" Dietrich asked.

"I thought she should know all these terrible things that are going on. So I told her."

"What did you tell her?"

Eberhard answered for her. "She told her about the euthanasia and about the concentration camps and what they're doing to the Jews."

Renate lifted her head in a gesture of self-command, but her chin trembled slightly as she spoke. "She is—she seemed a nice girl. Her father is a Nazi, but she's been very nice to me. I thought— she appeared to be a reasonable person. And so, I thought she should know, you see."

"Yes, of course," said Dietrich.

Dietrich's niece was a different person from the child he had left in the fall. Even then he had begun to notice the always enchanting metamorphosis that takes place when a girl becomes a young woman. Now, after six months away, he found the change remarkable. The simple schoolgirl dress—the crisp white shirt collar that peeped over the round neck of a blue sweater, the pleated skirt which fanned out over the piano bench, and the white socks— could not hide the change. It was most evident in her bearing, in the lift of her head and the maturing lines of her face, which showed a new awareness of who she was. Dietrich had heard already of a boyfriend or two—one especially, who was a friend of her brother and recently called into the military.

Renate continued, "I thought she was a reasonable girl, and should know it. But she got very upset and said I couldn't go around telling such things or she would have to report me. She said it was her duty, you see, with a war going on. And now I'm afraid she really will, and I don't know what to do."

"Have you told your parents?" Dietrich asked.

"Not yet."

"Don't you think perhaps you should?"

"But they'll be terribly worried. Everyone would be in danger, wouldn't they, if she did that?"

"I can't imagine that she would really want to hurt you," said Eberhard gently, "if she's your friend."

"I don't think she wants to, but she thinks it's her duty."

"Maybe she'll try to find a way out—to think of something." The tenderness in Eberhard's voice and eyes made Dietrich look twice, but Eberhard seemed unaware of the scrutiny.

"I don't know—maybe," said Renate. "But she's very strong on duty—what she thinks is her duty."

"She has a duty as a friend, too," said Eberhard.

"Yes, but—"

"I should think that would be more important to her." She looked at Eberhard and back down at the piano keys, as if that were too much to hope for.

"Just go on being her friend," said Eberhard, "but don't argue any more, don't try to convince her."

"No, I won't."

For the moment Eberhard and Renate seemed to have forgotten that Dietrich was there.

Later, when Eberhard and Dietrich were alone again, Eberhard appeared unable to rest and kept pacing the floor. "It's terrible not to be able to do anything to help her," he said, "to see her at the mercy of someone completely out of our reach."

"Maybe you're right, and the girl has a decent streak underneath that Nazi indoctrination."

"Do you think that's possible?" He did not wait for an answer. "I don't know, I don't know. I was grasping at straws."

"I think for the moment there is nothing to do but wait."

Except for a sigh, Eberhard was silent.

"You two seem to have become quite good friends," Dietrich said.

"Yes," said Eberhard with a half-smile. "Your family—they're all my friends, you know. With you gone, of course, Renate's been my accompanist."

"With your flute?"

"With the singing, too. She's very good, you know."

"I know. How's the flute coming?"

"Well enough, I think."

"Well enough to tackle the 'Müllerlieder?'" Dietrich asked. "Shall we try it?"

"Renate and I have been working on them already."

"Have you, really?"

"We were thinking of doing one or two on Saturday."

"Splendid. It seems I've been gone longer than I imagined." Dietrich could not entirely squelch his disappointment.

The next few days nothing changed. The girl at school had said no more, but the level of Renate's anxiety seemed to rise. At the Saturday Evening Musical she and Eberhard played two selections from the "Müllerlieder." Their ensemble performance and Eberhard's proficiency on the flute impressed the whole assembly, especially Dietrich. It became clear that Renate wanted to continue working with Eberhard on the music.

Two weeks passed and though Renate's schoolmate had not carried out her threat, Renate still seemed worried. One day Dietrich suggested that he and Eberhard attend an upcoming symphony concert.

"Good!" said Eberhard, "Renate mentioned that concert yesterday. I think she would like to go. Perhaps we could invite her to join us?"

The music was superb. Renate sat between them on the second row of the first balcony. At the breaks Eberhard focused his attention on her in an apparently successful attempt to cheer her up.

Late the next afternoon as Dietrich and Eberhard relaxed in the

April sun and discussed Eberhard's work at the Gossner Mission, Renate approached from next door, her face beaming.

She sat down on the edge of the lawn chair that Eberhard pulled up for her and turned to him. "You were right," she said. "She has come up with an idea so she won't have to report me. She wants to convert me."

Eberhard laughed aloud. "You see, what did I tell you."

"Yes. Tomorrow she will bring Hitler's *Mein Kampf* and some other material she has at home, and show me that I'm wrong— make clear to me that those things I told her couldn't be."

"And you, of course, as a good actress, will be convinced."

"Yes."

They all laughed. It occurred to Dietrich that not once in the weeks since he came home had he heard Renate say, "Uncle Bethge," as she had called Eberhard all these years. Nor had she said "Eberhard." That would have been a little shocking; after all, she was not yet sixteen.

One cold November day Nils Ehrenstrom, an ecumenical emissary from Geneva, brought Dietrich news from Bell in England. There had been some interest in Dietrich's memorandum, and Bell was making copies for a few people. He hoped to send a considerable reply before long.

Dietrich had arranged to meet Ehrenstrom in the Gossner Mission, a reasonably safe place; and when the visitor left, he went to see Eberhard in his upstairs apartment. They tried to find encouragement in the nebulous phrases, "copies for a few people" and "a considerable reply," but without much success. Finally, Dietrich took off his shoes, propped up his feet, and tried to forget the whole worrisome evening.

After a while Eberhard said, "I wanted to ask you something."

"Good or bad?"

"I don't know. That's why I'm asking."

Eberhard's smile was so sheepish, Dietrich could not help but laugh. "Well, fire away."

"You know, Renate's birthday—"

"Oh, yes, it's soon, isn't it? Next week?"

"Friday."

"Friday? Hmm, I haven't thought what to give her."

"Well, that's what I wanted to ask you. I've found something I'd like to give her. In fact, I've bought it already. But I'm not sure—I mean, I'm wondering if it's quite proper or so for me—" A slow blush spread over his face. "I mean, it's quite nice, and I think she'd like it, but I'm not sure."

Dietrich realized suddenly that this was by no means a trivial matter for Eberhard. He had noticed half-veiled hints of Eberhard's growing attachment for Renate, but had dismissed the idea as improbable. This would be Renate's sixteenth birthday. He wondered what Ursel and Rüdiger would say, and if Renate herself was ready to return such a serious regard.

Eberhard had moved restlessly from his chair and waited, with his hands on the back of the wooden settle. "Could I see it?" Dietrich asked. "You said you'd bought it already."

Eberhard went into the other room and returned with a brown paper package. He opened it up on the tea table. There were four large elegantly bound volumes, old folksongs of the fifteenth and sixteenth centuries, arranged for four voices. Tasteful baroque scenes surrounded the music on each page. Dietrich knew how much Renate would appreciate the gift, and how much the whole family would enjoy singing the songs. He also knew that Eberhard, normally so frugal, could not have paid less than forty marks for them, a good chunk of his monthly salary.

"Lovely," said Dietrich, as he leafed through the first volume. "You have excellent taste. They'll make a marvelous birthday present."

"Then you think it's all right?"

"Yes, it's all right. It's fine. She'll be very pleased."

Dietrich was in Munich for several weeks and missed the birthday party. The day after he returned, Eberhard came with a face so radiant that Dietrich asked, half joking, whether Renate had promised to marry him.

"Yes, she has."

"You're serious? Yes, I can see you are." That news, with all its ramifications, would take some adjustment. "It seems rather sudden," Dietrich said.

"It's not so sudden, actually."

"No, I guess not."

"The truth is, I didn't know if I should speak to her at all, if I dared to do that. I thought about it a lot. Then she—it turned out she was thinking the same way." Eberhard smiled as if he still could not believe it was possible.

It was not so remarkable, after all. For all his thirty-two years, Eberhard was still boyish in both manner and looks, and possessed a fresh and happy charm. "I'm glad, very glad," said Dietrich, "and I hope it works, though it might not be easy. Have you talked to Ursel and Rüdiger?"

"Not yet."

"I see. You may run up against some problems there, since Renate is so young."

Eberhard said he knew that, but no obstacle was insurmountable. Renate loved him. That was enough for the time being.

The next afternoon Eberhard came to see Dietrich with a despairing look on his face. "Renate told her parents," he said. "Last night her father called me in and asked me not to see her for six months. Six months! Can you believe it?"

"Well, that does seem a little extreme," said Dietrich.

"Extreme? It's terrible. Totally unreasonable. This is the twentieth century. Not see her? Can you imagine what that means to me?"

Dietrich had never seen him so upset. "Try to understand. Any such thought is too much for Rüdiger to handle right now. Father's are like that with their little girls."

"She's not a little girl. She's very mature for her age. Very."

"I agree. But couldn't you go along with him for a while? Give him time to get used to the idea. He'll likely change his mind before long."

"I don't know. He sounded adamant."

"Maybe. But give him time." A little time wouldn't hurt Renate either, Dietrich thought to himself.

Eberhard showed little sign of being consoled. When he was gone Dietrich sat by his window and studied the house next door like a gypsy reading tea leaves. It revealed no fortune.

31

It had seemed incredible when, at the end of 1941, Hitler dismissed Brauchitsch and took over himself as supreme commander. Just when Brauchitsch had at last agreed to support the resisters. After Christmas, as the conspirators were trying to regain their footing, Klaus suggested that they bring together representatives of the different Resistance groups and try to come to a consensus about what must be done next. Hans agreed and offered as a meeting place his recently purchased house in Sakrow on the western shore of the Havel. He insisted, though, on limiting the participants to key people, and Dietrich was to be one of them.

Adam von Trott zu Solz, one of the young resisters from the Foreign Office, arrived early. He lit one cigarette after another, as if they were not as scarce as gold, and devoured every word. He belonged to the circle forming around Count Helmut von Moltke, a group critical of the Resistance leaders in the Abwehr—especially Goerdeler, whom they considered too reactionary.

Justus Delbrück, Emmi's brother and Hans's assistant in the Abwehr, came with his cousin, Ernst von Harnack, who represented the group of Social Democrats and former labor leaders with whom Klaus had been meeting. General Beck was too ill to attend, but Carl Goerdeler, generally accepted as Chancellor in the new

government, arrived late from another meeting. Dietrich had met
him once before at Klaus's house and had immediately liked him.
The tall, rugged, former mayor of Leipzig in his soft gray hat,
billowing overcoat, and carrying a gnarled cane, looked the part of
the "circuit rider"—first a nickname and now his code name in the
conspiracy. Goerdeler's missionary zeal was legendary in the ranks
of the Resistance. In 1937, when the Nazis destroyed a statue of
Mendelssohn in Leipzig, Goerdeler had resigned in protest. Since
then he had stumped the country, all of Europe, and even the
United States, preaching his word that "a tyrant can never create
anything but a tyranny." He had called for the diplomatic isolation
of Hitler and an embargo of raw materials against Germany and
Italy. At the same time he had earnestly appealed to the Allies for
rectification of the wrongs of the Treaty of Versailles. Dietrich had
heard him say once that things could be changed by the common
sense and clear argument of a man of integrity.

For that reason Dietrich felt akin to him. "The optimism that is
will for the future should never be despised," Dietrich had told
Hans and Klaus, "even if it is proved wrong a hundred times."

Since the war began Goerdeler had added to his arguments an
insistence that Germany expiate her wrongdoing and bring every
Nazi criminal to justice in German courts of law. For that Dietrich
respected him all the more. Why the Gestapo had not already arrested the intrepid Burgermeister was a mystery. Klaus had said,
"They must believe a dog with so loud a bark could not possibly
bite," but Oster's contacts inside the Gestapo held a more sinister
view; they thought Himmler was far more interested in discover-
ing Goerdeler's many contacts than in stopping his "fanciful" activities.

Early in the evening, the resisters discussed the future government. Adam von Trott insisted that there must be no monarchy of
any kind and no "gentlemen's club." It would drive away the labor
people, he said. "We can't afford to give the impression of an aristocracy defending indefensible positions." Those remarks were addressed particularly to Goerdeler, who had gone along earlier with
the idea of bringing in Prince Louis Ferdinand as one who could

effectively give the signal for revolt. The Social Democrats in the group agreed with von Trott.

The question came around to assassination. To arrest Hitler was no longer a viable option; he now spent most of his time in his closely-guarded military stronghold, Wolfschänze, and was present in the Chancellery only rarely and always at unscheduled times. The "last resort" was upon them. Everywhere in all directions, were increasing numbers of victims and would-be victims of this man: the Jews, being deported in ever more alarming numbers; the casualties of war on all fronts; the retarded in the euthanasia scheme; the young girls, like Renate and Maria von Wedemeyer, being threatened with sexual abuse in the name of babies for the Führer.

As soon as Oster broached the subject, Adam von Trott said the leader of his group, Count von Moltke, was against it. "He says murder is always a crime. If we fight evil with its own methods, we will corrupt and eventually destroy the very principles we are fighting for."

"What does he propose we do, then?" asked Oster with quick acidity, "leave it to the Allies?"

"Maybe so. He believes there's one advantage in allowing Hitler to face the consequences of his crimes. The lesson to the German people would be unmistakable. They could not again claim that Germany's defeat was due only to internal treachery."

"So, our task is to teach the people a lesson while thousands, if not millions of innocent people die at the hands of this criminal," said Oster.

"Moltke is aware of that dilemma, I assure you. But he believes very strongly that we ought not to begin a new government with a new crime. Others in our group are less certain. I, for one. I know it may have to come to that—as a last resort."

"It's come already, my dear sir," said Oster. "Time is running out for us. Unfortunately most of the generals think only with an eye to that red stripe down their trouser seams. After it's done—successfully—they'll join us."

In his booming voice Goerdeler said, "Let's not be so hard on the generals. They have problems we can't even conceive. And there are still a goodly number who will work with us, if we create the right conditions."

Dietrich exchanged glances with Hans. Goerdeler seemed to have an unfortunate habit of forgetting unpleasant realities.

Hans leaned forward in his seat and spoke with quiet emphasis, "I'm afraid, Sir, there are no possible 'right conditions' left."

"Count von Moltke is right, I think," said Goerdeler. "Assassination goes against Christian conscience."

No one said anything. Dietrich was aware that all eyes were upon him.

"Is that not true, Pastor Bonhoeffer?" Goerdeler asked.

"Perhaps so, if we set up an ironclad rule and say: This is true for all times and places; I cannot deviate from it."

"It's not something we set up. It's God's commandment," said Goerdeler.

"Yes, that makes it especially easy, doesn't it?" said Dietrich. "We can say it's God's commandment, and that relieves us of responsibility. We don't have to make the hard decision."

"I'm not sure what you're driving at," said von Trott. "I don't profess to be a very devout Christian, but the commandment seems quite plain. 'Thou shalt not kill.' Period."

"It is certainly God's commandment," said Dietrich, "but isn't Jesus Christ the only period we can put to it?"

Dietrich noticed the quickening interest in Oster's usually skeptical face and wanted to respond to it with complete honesty. It was unbearable to Dietrich that a century of failure of the Church to be the Church of the Gospel had moved Oster and others like him—Klaus and Emmi, Dietrich's father—to set themselves beyond the reach of Christ. As for the problem, Dietrich had spent many a sleepless hour seeking God's guidance. "I believe the commandment of God is meant to be obeyed," he said. "It leaves no room for interpretation—only for obedience. But for the Christian isn't it—and doesn't it always remain—the commandment of

God which is revealed in Jesus Christ? If we accept that, then it cannot be a static thing we put a period to. It's the living God speaking to us in our dilemma here right now, permitting—even bidding—us to make the decision, put it behind us, and go on. We don't have to stand forever at the crossroads like Hercules."

"You think we can kill this man and not be guilty of breaking the commandment?" asked von Trott.

"I see no way to kill him without entering into guilt. We have to accept that. But I believe it is worse to be evil than to do evil." That seemed too abstract for them so Dietrich tried again. "For instance, it is worse for Josef Goebbels to tell the truth than for me or you or another lover of truth to lie." Now there were nods of assent. "The question is: Should we set our own personal innocence above our responsibility to the Jews and all others who are suffering and dying at this man's hand? What is the reality here? Are we not in fact killing when we fail to stop his murders in the only way left to us? Wouldn't that incur an even more irredeemable guilt than killing him?"

"Exactly," said Oster. "If we do nothing, if we allow ourselves to settle on our lees, we become one with the whole evil vintage. Afterward, when it's all over, the sediment may be thrown out, but no amount of decanting will change the essence." The colonel leaned forward on the edge of his chair. "We must not lose the moment. If we let it slip from our grasp because we're hamstrung by our inhibitions, it may be gone forever."

Goerdeler sighed and shook his head, with its profusion of white hair. "I can't be comfortable with assassination. I can't. Neither can Beck—nor Canaris."

Dietrich again exchanged glances with Hans. It was this inability to grasp the real necessity and unite behind it that was the major weakness of the Resistance.

With a wry smile Goerdeler added, "Maybe in the last moment there'll be a ram in the bushes."

"Please, Sir," said Oster, "we aren't talking about an innocent child here."

"I know, I know. But before we resort to assassination, let me say that I'm ready to do all I can to get an interview with Hitler. I would say to him what has to be said—that his withdrawal is a vital necessity for the nation."

Dietrich was surprised and sad. Goerdeler was as brave as he was naive.

Goerdeler continued, "Don't suppose, as I see you do, that it would of necessity be a total failure. There might be surprises, but the risk should be taken."

Oster's eye circled the group. He spoke softly. "Herr Burgermeister, we all know your fearlessness and your integrity, and are grateful, but I believe even Moltke would agree you shouldn't try that."

When Goerdeler saw that everyone in the group agreed, he said, "Well, we'll do what we have to do. As Canaris says, 'just get on with it.' But you'll report all this to General Beck?"

"Tomorrow, sir," said Oster.

The need remained for assurances from the Allies of a less hostile attitude. Goerdeler asked both Dietrich and Adam von Trott, who also had important connections in England, to continue their efforts. He also authorized them to give to the Allies more precise information, including the names of the leaders of the conspiracy and the planned set-up of the new government.

After everyone had left, Dietrich, Hans, and Oster sat at the table and assessed the evening's work. The course they had chosen would be criminally irresponsible if great care were not taken to ensure its success. Following the assassination, mass support for their actions would be crucial. This could come only if a carefully planned new government were ready to step in immediately and in an orderly fashion begin to restore healthy conditions. No one present that evening minimized the difficulty of this task, given the degree to which the masses were nazified.

The major question now was: How could the assassination be carried out, and who would be willing and able to accomplish what was certain to be a suicidal mission? As security had tightened around the dictator, the number of reliable men who had access to Hitler had greatly diminished. Hans and Oster reviewed possible names. The number seemed pitifully small, and there was no assurance that any of them would be willing to make such a sacrifice.

"I don't know about access, or how it could be arranged," said Dietrich slowly, "but if it fell to me to do it, I would be ready. I would first have to resign from the Church. I couldn't expect—nor would I want—the Church to shield me, even if that were possible."

"You would be willing to do that?" asked Oster softly.

"I'm afraid I know nothing about guns or explosives. I was never a hunter, but I suppose you could teach me."

Hans said nothing. It was impossible to read his thoughts.

Oster tamped out his cigarette in the crystal ashtray. In the hall the clock struck ten forty-five. "I've always known you were with us, Pastor Bonhoeffer. Your willingness to go so far is heartening, indeed. So don't think I'm taking your offer lightly—I'm not, I assure you—but, the truth is, we need you where you are. There are so few who can make useful contacts with the Allies, and we need every one of you. In fact, your next trip to Switzerland is most important. We'll soon be ready for it."

It was eleven-thirty when Dietrich knocked on Eberhard's door. In his telephone call Dietrich had apologized for the lateness of the hour, but Eberhard had told him to come on. Now, in his nightclothes, Eberhard put water to heat on the little two-burner stove, while Dietrich told him what had transpired at the meeting.

Suddenly the question poured forth: "Tell me, Eberhard, what do you think? Can a Christian receive absolution for assassination of a tyrant?"

"It has come to that, then?"

"Yes."

For a long time Eberhard said nothing, but stirred the ersatz coffee into their cups. At last he replied, "Jesus himself broke the commandment in order to help those who were suffering. Not once but several times. I remember you said one time that the

Church cannot merely gather up the victims from under the wheel, it must prevent the wheel from crushing them."

"I remember."

"And that time in the Temple. I can't imagine the Jesus who drove out the money-changers with a whip standing by and doing nothing in the face of this situation. Can you?"

"No, I can't. That's the thought I cling to." Dietrich sipped the bitter drink. He told Eberhard of his offer to Oster and Oster's answer. The response in Eberhard's face went from surprise to awe to relief; but no condemnation. "I'm still as much a part of it as the man who does the actual deed. I could no longer be a pastor."

"You think not?"

"No. Not possible. It sets a precedent, you see. Luther himself would have justified opposition to a ruler who defies law and constitution, but the Lutheran Church today has forgotten that."

They talked far into the night and, although no certain answers came from it, Dietrich found comfort in being able to share some of the burden with Eberhard.

It was mid-May when Dietrich found himself again in Geneva. This time his mission was two-fold. In addition to his work for the Resistance, he had a special assignment for a mission called Operation 7. Some time earlier Admiral Canaris, anxious to save a few Jewish friends, had given Hans the task of arranging their escape into Switzerland on the pretext that they were being used as agents by the Abwehr. When Hans asked Dietrich to help through his ecumenical connections in Switzerland, Dietrich had agreed immediately. The Swiss had closed their borders to Jews, and only those with special permission were allowed in. Hans called it "Operation 7" because at first there were seven people on the list, but over time the number of Jews had increased to fourteen.

This time, before Dietrich left for Switzerland, Hans and Oster gave him new and more detailed instructions in the art of spotting and dodging the Gestapo. When Eberhard took him to the train, Dietrich pulled from his pocket a sheet of paper on which he had written his last will and testament.

"Nothing to be taken too seriously, of course," he said. "I've no intention of getting caught or anything so stupid. But keep it safe, will you? No use to worry the family with it."

At the World Council of Churches office in Geneva, Dietrich discovered to his dismay that Visser 't Hooft was in England. Ehrenstrom was also out of town. They were not expected back for several weeks. He traveled then to Zurich to meet with Alphonse Koechlin, president of the Federation of Swiss Churches, to seek his help for the Jews of Operation 7. Dietrich had known him for years in ecumenical circles. On a number of occasions since 1934 Koechlin had given concrete support to the struggling Confessing Church. This time Dietrich was not disappointed. Koechlin promised to intercede with the government and obtain the necessary permission for the Jews to enter Switzerland as refugees. With that assurance Dietrich returned to Geneva and waited there in the hope that some useful communication would become possible.

One afternoon Dietrich explored the shops along the Rue de l'Eveche in the old part of the city, looking for things that were impossible to buy in Germany. On the street there were no flags, no propaganda posters, no blaring loudspeakers, almost no uniforms. Carefree couples with well-fed, laughing children strolled the avenue, their faces relaxed and unafraid. A light breeze blew in off the lake. The chimes in the old cathedral rang out, and over his head a clock doll leaned out from her window. He felt as if all the evil and darkness had receded behind the snow-covered Alps and he had dropped by umbrella into a fairyland.

An hour and several streets later Dietrich became aware that he had seen the man, lounging now at a sidewalk table, several times before. He wore an ill-fitting, dark gray suit, and had a face that never would have inspired a second glance. Dietrich emerged from the candy store and passed the stranger without glancing in his direction.

In the next block Dietrich turned into a coffee shop and, sitting back from the window, watched the sidewalk outside. Soon the man appeared, passed the coffee shop, and at the corner crossed the narrow street; then he took up a position in the shadowed entrance of a theater and waited.

Dietrich's first impulse was to shake him, then he realized the man must already have his hotel staked out. He decided it was best simply to go on his way, acting as if he suspected nothing. The rest of the week he walked with the stranger as his shadow. The fairyland magic had evaporated.

Invitations came for evenings with several acquaintances of former years. One evening, as Dietrich sat with friends at Visser 't Hooft's home, he overheard someone say, "But then, Bishop Bell is in Sweden just now."

Dietrich, seated on one of the loveseats, turned his head. Frau Visser 't Hooft near the piano was speaking to one of the theology professors.

She continued, "I hope my husband caught him before he left England."

It was not until the other guests had left that Dietrich could speak to her privately and learn the particulars. Bell was in Sweden for three weeks. He had arrived there May 11, the same day Dietrich had left Berlin.

At first Dietrich felt dejected by such a cruel twist of events. If he had known, he would have gone to Sweden instead of Switzerland. It occurred to him that it might not be too late. The Abwehr would have to set up a trip to Sweden. He did not know how long that would take or whether they would approve.

He left Geneva the next afternoon—unhurriedly—so that his ever-present sleuth would have no cause for suspicion.

In Berlin everything moved with dispatch. By Saturday Dietrich was on the flight from Tempelhof to Stockholm. At home no one but Hans knew his destination, not even Eberhard.

32

After a bumpy flight, and with the queasiness it always induced, Dietrich arrived in Stockholm at ten-thirty the next night. With the aid of an agile cab driver he reached the small hotel confident that he had not been followed. He spent half the next day, which was Whit Sunday, trying to locate Bishop Bell, and finally learned that he was in Sigtuna, thirty miles north, at the Nordic Ecumenical Institute. Dietrich arrived there at three-thirty in the afternoon. He paid the taxi driver, took up his one small bag, and looked both ways before stepping out of the taxi. No one was in sight, and he dashed to the door.

When he asked for Bishop Bell, the maid led him down the hall to a small low-ceilinged study. There were two others in the room, but Dietrich saw only Bell directly across from him.

The bishop rose in astonishment. "Dietrich!"

"My lord Bishop."

"I can't believe my eyes. Is it possible?"

"I was in Switzerland and heard you were here."

"Switzerland, yes. Visser 't Hooft told me you had been there." Bishop Bell's face gave the impression of holding back a stream of questions. He turned and introduced the other two men, then suggested that he and Dietrich speak privately together. The host, a tall Swede named Harry Johannson, led them across the hall into a small sunroom and left them alone. A warm western sun streamed through the windows on his old friend's face. Dietrich was unable to speak.

Finally the bishop said, "It's indeed a miracle, hard to believe. How could you do it?"

Dietrich told the bishop of his position in the Abwehr and the Resistance group there. He showed him his courier's pass and gave him a brief rundown of what had happened since the start of the war—the final shutdown of the seminary, the prohibition against his speaking and publishing, and the gradual capitulation of the Church. "The churches, like the generals, have done their duty by the devil. They are afraid to call sin by its name. Clergymen who long since should have smelled the rottenness are walking through this pigsty with handkerchiefs over their noses." At Bell's questioning look he added, "Yes, the Confessing Church, too."

Dietrich and the bishop sat down at a little wrought-iron table. They talked quickly, fully aware of the pressure of time. Dietrich asked about Sabine and Gert and gave Bell a letter for them, written in the hotel the night before.

They were fine, Bell said, doing well in Oxford—a safe place, away from the bombing. Bell kept up a correspondence with Gert, depending on him for a clearer understanding of events in Germany. Franz was also well and more at home in England. He still worked almost full time with the refugees. From Bell's modest words Dietrich was able to conclude how much the bishop had done for Sabine, for Franz, and for many other refugees.

They spoke of Dietrich's secret memorandum to Bell the previous summer and Bell's efforts to get it into the hands of influential people in England. "I'm afraid they didn't take it seriously," Bell said. "They refused to believe that anti-Nazi forces in Germany could become effective, except after a major military reversal."

"But the resisters can succeed. They will succeed, if given half a chance." Dietrich gave a rundown of the present state of affairs and reiterated the need for some kind of assurance from the Allies of positive peace aims. He laid out the resisters' peace plan: "We offer—foremost, of course—the ouster of Hitler and all Nazi leaders, but also the evacuation of the occupied territories, and willingness to disarm, even willingness to accept temporary occupation, if necessary."

"That is certainly reasonable enough," said Bell "Now, can you tell me the names of these Resistance leaders, Dietrich? I think it might help. Especially the names of those who will form the new government."

Dietrich, armed with permission from Oster and Beck, did so without hesitation and explained in detail who they were. He outlined the aims and plans for the coup d'etat, including the assassination of Hitler. He rose and turned away to the window. Word piled upon word as he revealed to his friend the horror of all that was happening.

Dietrich told what he knew about the deportations of the Jews. "They're cramming them into railway cars and carrying them away to the East, some to Poland, some to Czechoslovakia. Out there, they're killing them systematically." He turned back to the bishop, who looked as if he could not grasp the idea of such an atrocity. "It's true. There are whisperings of it in the corridors of the ministries. They're killing them by the thousands, by the hundreds of thousands. My country is doing this! We're all guilty— the Church, too—guilty of the deaths of the weakest and most defenseless brothers of Jesus Christ." Dietrich's voice faltered.

The bishop did not move or speak, but Dietrich could feel his compassion, and composed himself. "It goes back for generations—ill will, prejudice, envy. Contamination in the ground water. We're guilty, all of us. Especially those of my class who should have seen what was coming and stopped it while it still could be stopped. We've taken our privileged life for granted. We've put too much stock in obedience to commands from superiors and robbed our people of the ability to make responsible decisions. Now it's too late. There's no way left but to kill the tyrant. To be brought to this pass—to be forced to do this awful thing— is part of the punishment, I think."

"Oh, but my thought is the danger, the immense danger to you," said Bell.

"The danger doesn't matter. I hardly think of it. After the suffering my country has brought on others, how could I shrink from it myself, if any good could come of it?" Dietrich sat down again at the little table. "You see why I pray for the defeat of my country? That is, if we fail. If we cannot bring this madman down."

After a time Bell broke the silence. "I'll do everything I can to help. I believe I can get to Eden, if not Churchill. But I must warn you. Churchill doesn't want any discussion of peace."

"Yes, I heard that in Zurich. But for heaven's sake, why not?"

"He sees it as a distraction from the great push to win the war."

Dietrich was silent. He sighed. "That's the inherent tendency of war, isn't it? To break through all reason and assume its own unconditional form."

"So there's no turning back," Bell added. "Even talk of the future after the war, of justice and a new order for Europe, has no place. But especially talk of peace. That might be dangerous."

"Dangerous?" Dietrich asked.

"With Russia. It's a bad time, you see. Stalin's angry because there is still no second front in the West. If he got wind of British negotiations with Germans—any Germans—it might hurt the alliance. The slightest risk of losing Russia as an ally would be frightening."

That was a sobering thought, one the leaders of the Resistance had not taken into account.

"No," Bell continued, "our leaders speak only of 'victory' and 'survival' and 'liberation' of the vanquished nations. Some of us have introduced the question of just peace aims in a number of forums, including the House of Lords, but to no avail. By now I'm not very well liked in the top echelons of the government. Eden calls me 'that pernicious priest.'"

Bell's habitual manner of understatement made Dietrich wonder how serious the consequences really were for the bishop. In Switzerland he had heard that Bell was generally acknowledged as the most likely candidate to be the next Archbishop of Canterbury. "I shouldn't think that would enhance your future in the church," Dietrich said.

Bell smiled, "But that's not terribly important just now, is it?"

Dietrich said nothing. Then he asked, "You think this information might make a difference?"

"I hope so. I pray so. I'll do my best to convince them," Bell promised.

They worked out a code by which Bell could send a reply. Dietrich looked at his watch. They had been there two hours. Reluctantly, they stood to go.

"I will be grateful for your prayers," said Dietrich.

Bell took his hand. "I'll pray for you and for your family. And always for your safety. That's important to me. And not just to me. The world needs you, Dietrich."

In Berlin Dietrich made his reports for the Abwehr, conferred at length with Oster and with General Beck, gave the news of Sabine and Gert to his grateful parents, and within three days was on his way again to the peace and quiet of Klein-Krossin. He had been there three times so far in 1942, and the year before, three restful weeks in November, when he was recuperating from pneumonia. Since then Frau von Kleist-Retzow had lost two more grandsons at the front and was still dealing with her grief for them. Dietrich had seen nothing the past year of the young Maria von Wedemeyer.

In the months since his last visit had come the sinister rumors of what was happening to the Jews. Now on the train he tried to combat it by reading *Don Quixote*, his present spare-time companion. The faces of the other passengers showed neither resignation nor resistance, but rather a tired indifference. They half-dozed in their seats, as if disengaged from all life about them.

In the afternoon the train entered the lake country beyond Stargard. Dietrich put aside his book and watched as they wound through steeply forested hills with long ribbons of glacial lakes beside them. At Gross-Tychow Frau von Kleist would have a carriage to meet him.

The thick square tower of the village church came into view. By the time the train rolled into the station a peppering rain had set in. On the platform Dietrich raised his umbrella and looked about him. There was no sign of Henryk, Frau von Kleist's Polish driver.

"Pastor Bonhoeffer!"

Dietrich turned. It was Maria von Wedemeyer.

"Henryk is bringing the carriage around," she said, as she ran toward him and took refuge under his umbrella. "Whew! It's coming down, isn't it?"

"Yes, let's get inside."

Beside the baggage counter Maria undid her scarf and shook off the raindrops. She wore a simple blue dress with a narrow belt encircling her waist. "I'm glad you weren't waiting," she said. "I almost didn't make it in time. There was a long line at the apothecary."

It would have been worth the wait, Dietrich thought. "You didn't lose your place in line, I hope?"

"No, No. I got through, thank you. But can you believe it? An hour and ten minutes for a bottle of aspirin and a box of boric acid. Next time, I'll bring a milkmaid's stool and my knitting."

Dietrich laughed.

Halfway to Klein-Krossin the rain stopped, and far away to the West a patch of blue appeared on the horizon. As they drew alongside the lake that bordered the Kleist property, Maria asked Henryk to stop. "Shall we walk the rest of the way?"

Dietrich's feet were on the ground before his answer was spoken. The clip-clop of the horses' hooves receded around the curve as he and Maria turned to the trail along the lake.

She walked beside him with an assured, carefree grace. The gladness he had begun to feel since Maria's appearance on the train platform took up audacious residence in his breast.

In the carriage Dietrich had asked Maria about her present life and discovered that she had finished school at Weiblingen and taken her Abitur. She had spent a week at home in Pätzig, she said, before coming to be with her grandmother. Next to Pätzig, she loved Klein-Krossin best of all places on earth. She and her grandmother were kindred spirits. "Grandmother says I remind her of herself when she was my age—a little wild. That's why I like it here. Mother isn't so tolerant. You know how mothers are. They don't like their daughters to be tomboys who do crazy things. Father's different. He just laughs at me."

Her father was at the front on the Donets River, she said, and Max was with the Center Army somewhere beyond Smolensk. There was hard fighting on both fronts. Sometimes two or three weeks would pass without word from either of them. As she spoke a shadow fell over her face and she was silent. Dietrich knew she was thinking of her two fallen cousins.

"Now that you've finished high school what are your plans for the future?" He dared not ask the question that had worked its way into his thoughts—was there a young man in her life.

"I hope someday to continue my studies in mathematics," she said.

That seemed already an answer.

"But then college is impossible for the duration of the war," she added. "Eventually, I might go for Red Cross training, but I'm not anxious to start anything new at the moment. It would suit me just fine to divide my time between Klein-Krossin and Pätzig. With all the men gone off to war, I am needed in both places."

They walked for a time in easy silence. Presently Maria said, "I was sorry when grandmother told me they shut down your seminary. That happened twice, didn't it?"

"Yes."

"That must have been awful for you."

"It was bad, yes."

"I remember the first time I went with grandmother to Finkenwalde. You beat me at table tennis, remember? I was impressed. I thought I was pretty good."

Dietrich smiled but said nothing.

The distant estate house had come closer as they talked; then, suddenly, to Dietrich's sorrow, the driveway was there before them. The house was small by Junker standards. It was a long, solid structure, with many white-shuttered windows across the front and dormers set in the sloping roof. The old lady waited in a lawn chair to greet them.

That evening the three of them sat on the terrace and talked of mathematics. Although Dietrich knew little about the subject and had never been particularly interested in it, he found the conversation enchanting.

The routine he usually followed at Klein-Krossin kept coming unravelled. The power of complete concentration on his work had always served him well. Now he found himself at times suspended in mid-sentence, his ear tuned to the sounds in the house, to a particular footstep and a lilting voice. Often he surveyed the landscape outside his window for a glimpse of Maria as she went about her duties or flew across the fields on her favorite mare.

Sometimes Dietrich gave up altogether and walked out to the stables or down by the lake or to the copse on the other side of the hill, where he "accidentally" found her.

Life at the country house was relatively spartan. Under the burden of strict rationing Frau von Kleist-Retzow saw to it that nothing was wasted. She carefully slit open envelopes and turned them inside out to use again. She washed foil and rolled it up for another time. Once at the lunch table she asked Dietrich what he thought the mock chocolate soup was made of.

He tasted carefully. It had a slightly scorched flavor that in no way resembled chocolate. "Browned flour?"

"How did you guess?" asked the lady, with a twinkle in her eyes.

Maria laughed and made a face. "It's awful," she said with abrupt honesty. But Dietrich ate it without complaint.

The entire household directed its primary attention to the burning problems of the eastern front and their men stationed there. Often someone known to the family appeared on the daily casualty lists. "One's whole life is made up almost entirely of waiting," said Frau von Kleist.

After lunch one day Dietrich tarried in the hall and studied the portrait there of the youthful Ruth and her husband, Jürgen. He was struck for the first time by the resemblance of Maria to her grandmother, the same eyes and nose, the same assured lift of the head.

"Those were simpler days," said Frau von Kleist-Retzow, who had quietly entered behind him. "He was mine for only twelve years but I wouldn't change it for a lifetime with any other man."

Dietrich studied the serious-faced young man, whose arm the young Ruth held. Behind the prodigious moustache was a good, strong face.

The sound of unfamiliar music came from the veranda.

"That's Maria," she said, with a smile and a little turn of her hand. "She's put on one of her American records. I hope it won't disturb you."

"No, certainly not."

"Well, I must leave you. I have to check with the cook about supper," she said and, leaning heavily on her cane, moved off toward the kitchen.

"You see," said Maria, "it's simple. You just make a box. Step out, and slide, then up. Across and slide, then back. See! Then repeat. When you get that down, you can turn any way you want with the music. Try it!"

Dietrich had not danced in a long time, but even though both the music and the step were unfamiliar, he felt on sure ground here. Dancing school had been a part of his upbringing, as were the elegant balls his mother used to give. The rhythm of this "Moonlight Serenade" was simple, almost too simple, but he allowed himself to be taught by this engaging creature.

Her nearness, the fragrance of her hair, the touch of his hand upon her waist, was more than enough pleasure for him—pleasure and confusion. His feet would not obey him! They laughed together when he made a misstep. When it ended they turned the record over and continued the dance.

"You know, I can't do this in public," Dietrich said.

"Why not?"

"It's just something pastors aren't supposed to do."

"That's silly."

They put on a waltz and whirled all around the tiled floor.

It had to end; the dance, and the time at Klein-Krossin. He was due to go with Hans to Rome on business for the Abwehr. It had been eleven days; he counted them. He had spoken no revealing word to Maria and wondered if her feelings in any degree parallelled his own. He dared not guess and was afraid to hope.

33

It was the end of August before Dietrich was able to go back to Klein-Krossin. The driver, Henryk, met him at the train and told him the bad news. "The Fräulein Maria has lost her father," he said.

"She's here?"

"Yes, Herr Pastor. She got here the day before yesterday. The news came this morning."

It seemed the three-mile ride would never end, yet it ended before Dietrich was ready. Frau von Kleist-Retzow was waiting for him.

"Where is she?" Dietrich asked.

"Out at the stables," Frau von Kleist replied. "You know, her father loved horses as much as she."

"Yes, I know."

"Go to her, Dietrich. She needs you."

He hesitated, fearful of intruding upon her privacy.

"Yes. You can help her."

Dietrich found Maria at the fence that separated the barnyard from the pasture. Her horse, Scarlett, reached across and nuzzled her neck, as if she understood her grief. Maria lifted her head as Dietrich approached. Her eyes, deeply wounded, turned to him.

He took her hand and held it in both of his. Neither of them spoke. Her head drooped and she leaned her forehead against his shoulder.

For a long time they stood silent, then she said in a voice strained and weary from weeping, "Oh, this hateful war! I don't understand how God can let such things happen."

"I know. Your father was a good man. It seems God is letting himself be robbed of his best people at a time when the world needs them most."

"Why? It doesn't make any sense. None of it makes any sense."

"I wish I could answer that. There are some things we can't understand—may never understand—and that is hard to accept."

Her sigh fell somewhere between assent and a sob.

"But one thing is sure. God loved your father, and we know your father loved Him. He showed it by his deeds."

"I know he did." With her finger she wiped the tears from her cheeks. "They say it's God's will. I have to accept it because it's God's will. I can't do that."

"No. This was not God's doing."

Her eyes, full of questioning, turned up to him. "No," Dietrich repeated, "it was not. God is on the side of life. It was hate and folly that killed your father. All you can think of right now is that your father is gone. That's terribly hard. It would be wrong to try to deny that."

She said nothing, but a look of gratitude passed over her face, as if she had not expected anyone to understand.

"After a while, when the hurt begins to go away, you'll remember something—that for your father God makes this not the end, but the beginning of life."

She stood straight and stroked the nose of the docile mare. After a long while she said, "I was going for a ride. Will you come with me?"

All Dietrich's inhibition about his horsemanship left him. In that moment he was simply grateful that he could be there for her.

The next day Maria returned to Pätzig. Frau von Kleist went with her. That evening Dietrich wrote to Maria's mother and to Max at the front. At the end of the week he returned to Berlin to prepare for scheduled trips to Switzerland, Italy, and the Balkans. While he waited for a new passport, Hans returned from Switzerland with an answer from Bishop Bell. The cable, sent six weeks earlier to Visser 't Hooft, said: "Interest undoubted, but deeply regret no reply possible." They pondered every word. If there was undoubted interest, why was no reply possible? Could it be that a final decision had not been reached? They held on to that slender hope. Hans also reported that the fifteen Jews of Operation 7 had arrived safely in Bern. Consul Wilhelm Schmidhuber of the Munich Abwehr office had been able to smuggle out the required American dollars for their temporary support.

The final arrangements for Dietrich's trip were to be made with Josef Müller at the Munich Abwehr. When Dietrich arrived there he discovered that Consul Schmidhuber was under investigation by the War Court. A man had been arrested in Prague for smuggling a substantial quantity of American dollars across the border from Germany. He had done this, the man testified, on behalf of Consul Schmidhuber. In the course of the questioning the officials had asked Schmidhuber about currency transactions for Operation 7. The consul admitted to a similar arrangement in that case.

"How much does he know?" Müller asked.

"I was going to ask you that question," said Dietrich.

Between them they established that, in addition to the currency transfers for Operation 7, Schmidhuber knew about the illicit passports for the Jews. Besides that, he had been in on the Vatican exchanges over the past two years and knew something of Dietrich's contacts with the British.

"How much detail, I'm not sure," said Dietrich.

"Enough to pop the lid off everything, I'll wager," said Müller, and chomped on his cigar. Müller began pacing the floor, leaning forward, with his hands crossed at his back. In a gravelly voice he said, "There's no telling where it'll end, unless we can get Schmidhuber out of the country before the Gestapo takes a hand. They will, of course," he added morosely. "Then we're in for it. They're just looking for an excuse to go after the Abwehr."

Dietrich knew this was true. Keitel's permission was necessary for the Gestapo to break the seal of secrecy over the Abwehr offices, which Canaris so jealously guarded. A mere charge of currency irregularities would not be enough. But if the Gestapo could get more than that out of Schmidhuber—.

"Schmidhuber's a weak man," said Müller. "I've heard him say he couldn't stand up under the Gestapo's brand of persuasion."

As it turned out, the investigation ended without formal charges. Within a few days Müller managed to get the consul and his wife into Italy and under the protection of the Portuguese ambassador.

"There'll be no trips for you now, I'm afraid," he said to Dietrich, "not until this is cleared up, if it ever is. You might as well go back to Berlin."

When Dietrich arrived in Berlin he found a letter from Frau von Kleist-Retzow unopened on his desk. She would be in Berlin for an operation on her eyes, and Maria would be staying with relatives in Charlottenburg, so she could be with her. Dietrich checked the date and realized with a start that they were already there. At the Charité!

Immediately he put on his coat again and brushed his hair. On top there remained only one meager wisp growing near the front. The face that looked back from the mirror was no longer boyish, but leaner than a few years back. Since the beginning of the Russian campaign the year before, with its accompanying scarcities, he had lost twenty-five pounds. He was thirty-six years old, a fact that he rarely took into account. Twice Maria's age, lacking two months. It had been six weeks to the day since he had seen her.

He brushed his shoes and straightened himself to his full vigorous height. He was a powerfully built man. None of his strength had diminished, so what did it matter if he was twice her age?

Downstairs he explained the situation to his mother.

"But you just got here! Don't you want to rest a while first?"

"No, I think I ought to see how she is." Despite her mystified look, Dietrich did not tell his mother that Maria was there also.

The British air raids had been heavy while he was away, and in Berlin there was new devastation right and left. Beyond the Zoo Station the train slogged around the wreckage of some of the tracks. Nearby in the Tiergarten young schoolboys, fifteen and sixteen years old, frantically repaired installations at one of the giant antiaircraft towers. It had taken two years' labor around the clock to build this concrete and steel monstrosity and the companion tower one hundred feet back in the woods.

At the Lehrter Station he bought a bouquet of roses then skirted the northern shore of the Humbolt Harbor. Beyond lay the grounds of the Charité. The eye clinic was the nearest building.

"Roses! How nice! She can enjoy the fragrance, even if she can't see them."

"How is she?" Dietrich asked.

"Just now she's asleep, I'm happy to say. She's had some pain, but she won't admit it. You know my grandmother. The worst for her is not being able to see."

"How long will that last?"

"Two weeks with the eye packs," Maria answered. She explained that her grandmother had to lie perfectly still, with sandbags on either side of her head so she could not move. "I've been reading to her, and if today's any indication, I'll be well read by the end of two weeks."

Dietrich followed her to the nurses' station, where Maria asked for a vase for the roses.

He asked about her mother.

"She's trying to be strong, but it isn't easy for her. She and my father were very close."

The question he most wanted to ask slipped gently to the surface. "And you, Maria?"

She sighed and touched a rose petal. "I've had difficulty believing it is true," she said softly. "Sometimes I think I hear him driving up, or in the stable, talking to his horse. I have to force myself to face the truth. That's hard."

"I'm sure it is."

When they got back to Frau von Kleist-Retzow's room, they found her awake. She inhaled the fragrance of the roses and held Dietrich's hand. "Now that you're here, I'm bound to get well," she said.

He came every day to the hospital. As Frau von Kleist improved, there was more time for Maria, aided and abetted, he soon perceived, by her grandmother. Often she would send them out into the hall. "I need the nurse now," or "I want a nap so why don't you two take a walk. Maria gets tired cooped up in here."

Every day confirmed that this was not a passing infatuation. Maria's outlook on life was in tune with Dietrich's own, though some of her views were different. He did not like reminders that they were not of the same generation, but sometimes it was obvious. They laughed at the same things and disliked many of the same things, especially sham in any form; both were dedicated to life and found intolerable any desecration of it.

Dietrich enjoyed taking Maria to lunch at a few of the good restaurants still left in Berlin. Once he took her to the "Alois," a restaurant in the Wittenbergplatz owned by Hitler's brother. When she expressed surprise, Dietrich laughed and said, "No safer place to talk." They ate ambrosia, one of the delicacies unavailable anywhere else, and talked of former times.

They rarely talked of theology or the Church, but once she mentioned that she was reading his *Life Together* to her grandmother. She did not remember too much about it, but one thing stuck in her mind. He had written: "A pastor should not complain about his congregation, certainly never to other people, but also not to God." She liked that and said with a smile, "You, of course, follow your own precept."

"Of course."

"I recall once you were praising a student for a good sermon—I can't remember his name—but you criticized him that he didn't give it from memory. Remember?"

"No."

"Oh, yes. You claimed you had learned your first ten sermons by heart. At that point I slipped out of the room, I remember, for fear you might be tempted to prove your point."

Dietrich laughed aloud and the people at the next table turned to look at them. It was no wonder they continued to stare; she was enchanting. Her puckish lack of awe and the strength of her independent spirit enamored him and at the same time made him fear rejection. That, and hesitation about declaring himself so soon after her father's death and without her mother's permission, kept him silent.

At night, awake in his bed, uncertainties nagged him. He wondered if indeed he had a chance at all. He had seen the way the young striplings in their snappy uniforms looked at her. He wondered, also, about his work, provided the time came when he could preach again. Would she be happy as a pastor's wife? Then there was the uncertainty of the future. Had he the right to involve her in the web of conspiracy that held him fast, with the outcome so questionable?

Over the days he told her in general terms a good deal of what was going on. She already knew more than he imagined. She had heard talk between her father and her cousins, Henning von Tresckow and Fabian von Schlabrendorff, about their conspiratorial schemes in Army Group Center and their connection with the Oster group. One day as they sat in the hospital waiting room she told him that her father could not go along with the conspiracy; it went against his conscience.

"Was he wrong?" she asked.

"Each person has to be true to himself—to his own understanding of what is right."

"But you think he was mistaken."

He could not lie to her, and said gently, "There are honest mistakes, based on a lifetime of seeing things from a particular perspective. One can forgive an honest mistake."

Before Maria returned to Pomerania, Dietrich wanted to introduce her to the family. He asked Renate, who, with Eberhard, had met Maria one day at the hospital, to invite her to the Saturday Musical Evening. He hoped to keep down speculation; only Eberhard knew of Dietrich's interest in Maria, although he doubted Eberhard had been able to keep it from Renate.

Maria came and, as Dietrich had expected, captured the imagination of everyone. The men capitulated instantly. In an aside Klaus said, "Where have you been hiding her?" Dietrich stayed at her side almost the entire evening and did not take his usual respite in his room. Maria, too, seemed at home and happy in the midst of his family.

Eberhard drove as they took her home—Renate with him in the front seat, Dietrich and Maria in the back. They wound slowly through the darkened streets, with the eerie blue lights at every other street corner. Only at the door of her uncle's house, when

Dietrich said good-night to Maria and she slipped inside, did the real world close in again. She was leaving for home the next day.

Later that night, alone with Eberhard, he asked, "What can I do? What would you do?"

"I'd tell her how I feel."

"It's not that simple."

Eberhard laughed. "Of course it is."

"I'm twice her age."

"Tell me something new."

"It's not just that. It's the whole situation—her father's death, her mother left alone. Besides, these people hold very much to the old traditions."

"Then go to see her mother and lay your case before her."

Dietrich was silent.

"It wouldn't hurt anything," Eberhard added.

"Maybe not."

"Believe me, it will work out. In the end, it'll work out."

Dietrich looked at Eberhard's smiling, confident face. That was indeed true for him. He and Renate had already crossed many hurdles. The previous month, with her parents' blessing, Renate had gone with Eberhard to Kade to visit his mother. It had turned out well, and now they were pressing for an open engagement. This was helped by the fact that after her final school exam, Renate would be subject to call-up for the War Helping Service, something only marriage could prevent.

Before Dietrich could make a decision, a call came from Frau von Kleist-Retzow in Klein-Krossin. Max von Wedemeyer had been killed at the front.

"Oh, no."

"Yes, Dietrich, yes. It is too much for me. The father—and now the son. Five grandsons now. It is too much. I'm an old woman, and it's too much for me." Her voice broke and a low keening came over the wire.

"I know it is, Frau von Kleist."

"I want to go to Pätzig with Maria, but she says I shouldn't try—

too much jostling for my eyes, she says. I want to be with my daughter. She is devastated."

"I know you do, but perhaps Maria is right. Why don't you talk to your doctor?"

"Yes, I will, I suppose."

Dietrich did his best to comfort her and after a while asked to speak with Maria.

Maria's strength and composure surprised and touched him. He knew how fond she was of her older brother. Her concern now was for her grandmother. He made a quick decision. "I'll come to Klein-Krossin and stay with her a few days. Do you think that will help?"

"Oh, yes, yes. If you can do that. Thank you very much, Pastor Bonhoeffer. It will mean so much to her."

He stayed four days with Maria's grandmother and while he was there wrote a letter to Maria at Pätzig, in which he expressed his fondness and appreciation for Max and, more directly than was his habit, his sorrow for her sake.

When Dietrich returned to Berlin a serious crisis had developed. The military authorities in Munich had forced Schmidhuber's extradition from Italy and brought him back in handcuffs for further interrogation. Nobody knew what information he had given, but the discovery that Dr. Manfred Roeder, a judge in the Luftwaffe judiciary, had a hand in the proceedings alarmed Hans. "A bloodhound!" he said to Dietrich. "He'd love to get the credit for uncovering something at the Abwehr." The Gestapo also had picked up Josef Müller for questioning.

Hans hoped Müller would put them off the track. "I want you to go back to Munich and see what you can find out," he said. "Wait around 'til you can see Müller. He might know something. At least, I hope so. But be careful about it."

34

It was walking distance from the Munich Abwehr to the Europäischer Hof, where Abwehr personnel usually stayed. A call had come from Admiral Canaris while Dietrich was in Müller's office. The admiral was at the hotel, having arrived from France earlier in the day, and wanted to see Müller immediately. When he heard that Dietrich was there, he had asked that he come too.

A light snow was falling, early for the first of November. As they walked Müller continued his account of his interrogation.

"I was lucky, I guess, to have Sauermann. He didn't think much of Schmidhuber—was skeptical of his insinuations of treasonous activity in the Abwehr. Schmidhuber's a damned coward. He dished up all kinds of lies. Even accused Canaris of trying to have him silenced. Not a bad idea, come to think of it." Müller chewed angrily on his cigar. "He also hinted that Canaris planned a coup in '39 and '40. I convinced Sauermann that such notions were ludicrous. I said those rumors were flying around everywhere at the time, even in British newspapers, and certainly must have come to the Führer's attention. I asked, 'Would he have left the admiral in his post these two years if there'd been a breath of truth in it? Do you think the Führer so naive?' Of course, he couldn't say 'yes' to that."

"Were they flying around everywhere?" Dietrich asked.

"How should I know?" he said with a sly lift of his eyebrows. Much more serious was Schmidhuber's claim that all his currency transactions, which turned out to be numerous and included jewels as well as money, were on behalf of the Abwehr.

"He'd been lining his own pockets, to be sure," said Müller. "But he alleges all this smuggling was known to both Dohnanyi and me."

"He named Hans?" Dietrich asked.

"You, too."

Icy alarm. Dietrich looked sharply at Müller.

"Yes. I was sitting in the next room and heard it clearly."

"In what connection?" Dietrich asked.

"I couldn't tell. Just your name. But probably the same thing—Operation 7."

"Will this jeopardize the refugees in Switzerland?"

"It's possible."

Dietrich and Müller had arrived at the hotel and crossed the lobby to the foot of the curving stair, where an archway led into the restaurant. Three SS officers sat at a table facing the arch. One of these, taller than the rest and with a long scar down his cheek, looked directly at Dietrich and Müller as they passed.

"Kaltenbrunner," Müller whispered, when they were halfway up the marble stair. "You saw him, didn't you?"

"Yes," said Dietrich. He had seen pictures of the man who had replaced the assassinated Heydrich as head of the SS.

Vice Admiral Brückner, Canaris' deputy, met them at the top of the steps and led them to the admiral's suite.

Canaris rose from his chair and shook hands. Before he could say anything, Müller asked softly, "Have you seen Kaltenbrunner? He's downstairs in the restaurant."

Canaris shook his head and immediately began to examine the wall with light slaps of his hand. He took the pictures down and scrutinized the area behind them with special care, then ran his hand under the edge of the two tables and the chairs. The others stood perfectly still without a word during this procedure.

Apparently satisfied that there were no hidden microphones, Canaris laid his coat gently over the telephone and said, "Please be seated, gentlemen."

The admiral did not sit down, but paced up and down in front of Müller as he questioned him in a low voice on every small detail of the interrogation. He passed lightly over the allusion to his own part in a proposed coup and asked, "What about your files?"

"We purged them before Sauermann and his men arrived. They found nothing."

"Good."

Canaris was concerned about the money Hans had turned over

to Schmidhuber for the Operation 7 people in Switzerland. "How much?"

"I don't know that. Dohnanyi handled it," Müller answered.

"100,000 reichsmarks," said Dietrich. Hans had shown him the receipt, signed by Schmidhuber. That act of restitution to those Jews had given them both a singular degree of satisfaction.

"One wonders how much of it they saw," said Canaris.

That had already occurred to Dietrich, and he asked himself whether they had been dealing with a swindler as well as a coward and a liar. But they had the receipt, and the delivery could be verified by Koechlin in Switzerland.

The admiral stopped pacing directly in front of Dietrich. "How will it turn out, Pastor Bonhoeffer? Are we lost, or not?"

"I have no divining rod, Herr Admiral, to predict the future." Dietrich was aware of the coolness in his voice. He knew the admiral's superstitious tendencies and hated the insinuation that because he was a pastor, he might have some inside track to a higher power. Then he saw the very real anxiety in Canaris' face. "I don't have an answer, I'm afraid, Sir. It depends. If the Gestapo takes over—"

"Then we're jinxed," said Canaris. "If we openly try to keep it out of their hands, we'll be giving them more rope for their sinister weavings. Kaltenbrunner already has his net out, we may be sure, but he'll wait until he's certain he has the big fish before he pulls it in." He took a turn around the room and stopped again in front of Dietrich. "These coup plans don't amount to treason against country, do they?"

Müller broke in. "Admiral, that kind of talk's no good. Our glorious Führer puts treason against country and high treason on the same level. He *is* the country, you know! So we're in the soup either way."

Canaris continued his pacing, then stopped suddenly and said in a loud voice, "This criminal! He sacrifices millions of lives without blinking an eye, just for the sake of his own miserable ego!"

"Please, Admiral," Müller whispered frantically.

Brückner stepped to the door and quickly opened it. There was no one in the hall.

"Forgive me, gentlemen." The admiral sank into a chair and muttered, half to himself, "This constant strain. My nerves are shot."

The next day, before Dietrich left for Berlin, he went by Müller's office and found him gazing out the window.

"Ah, Dietrich. I was trying to call you to tell you the scene has shifted. Now it's in your theater. The Gestapo just took Schmidhuber away. Destination: Prinz-Albrecht-Strasse."

At eight o'clock Paula arrived at the greengrocers, and found there was already a long line of glum-faced housewives, curving back around a bomb crater. The three-inch snow of the night before softened the piles of debris on the street. She prepared for a long cold wait. Lately the grumbling in the lines had turned bitter. Since the Americans had landed in North Africa, the mood in the city had darkened. Besides that, lack of hard news from Stalingrad had increased the fear that a catastrophe was building there; that and the increasing numbers of little black crosses that appeared in the papers beside the names of fallen soldiers.

She kept hearing Christel's words of the day before: "It's a race against time, Mama." Earlier Christel had told her that Hans and Dietrich were being tailed in the street. Paula had guessed as much. She had seen Dietrich's extra precaution in every movement. "Canaris is on a bed of nails," Christel had said. "He'll try to cast doubt on Schmidhuber's credibility, but I don't know."

Everything Paula heard showed how desperate the situation was. On orders from Beck, Oster had moved all the Resistance documents, including Hans's "Chronicles," to a steel file cabinet in one of the deep cellars in the Army Headquarters in Zossen, fifteen miles south of the city. That these incriminating documents existed at all was an alarming fact of life that Paula had to live with. Besides the "Chronicles" they included Oster's detailed coup plans, Hans's proclamations to the people, and records of the peace negotiations—including those with the Vatican, and Dietrich's discussion with Bell in Sweden. So far as Paula knew, there was nothing that compromised Karl and his panel of psychiatrists.

Paula stamped her feet to keep them from freezing. Up ahead two women were talking about the new government order that mothers and widows of fallen men would be given extra clothing coupons so they could buy mourning clothes. The reaction was one of derision and disgust. One woman began to laugh hysterically and to scream, "He thinks that will compensate," until her friend frantically drew her away.

It was a quarter to nine when Paula finally got inside, where she found that potatoes were still in short supply. She was allowed two pounds, not even enough for one meal for her increased family. There was no rice; there had been none for months. She bought a white cabbage that seemed reasonably fresh and a few onions. At the next shop there was another long wait, but this time she managed to get a pound of lard. There was no butter, even for preferred customers. She refused to buy the substitute fat, made by filtering table scraps and other garbage in a special machine that all restaurants were required to install in their kitchens.

"A race against time." A sense of foreboding descended upon her as she turned toward home. A showdown was bound to come—and soon—with danger either way to those she loved.

When she got home she found that Karl had received a visit from his old colleague, Dr. Sauerbruch. He had been called in to see Hitler the day before and wanted to talk with Karl about the dictator's mental state. "Sauerbruch thinks Hitler is out of his mind."

"That's nothing new."

"No, but he is convinced he is insane. Said he found him looking old and broken and mumbling all kinds of disjointed phrases, like: 'I must go to India,' and 'for one German killed, ten of the enemy must die.' Sauerbruch was afraid he would go into convulsions when he spoke of the generals, whom he blames for everything. Sauerbruch wanted my opinion."

"What did you say?"

"I told him I agreed. He hinted that something should be done, but I, of course, gave no inkling—" He looked at her face and immediately broke off. "Enough of that. Let's go to something more pleasant. Dietrich is going to Pomerania."

"Yes, I know."

"But not to Klein-Krossin. To Pätzig."

"Pätzig! So! Well, I can't help but wonder a little about the girl."

"Don't worry. The girl is lovely."

"She doesn't seem to be quite his type."

"Were you my type?" Karl asked.

She looked at him in surprise and then laughed. "No, I suppose not."

"Then don't worry."

The train, thronged with recruits both younger and older than ever before, proceeded cautiously over the bridge at Küstrin. Dietrich had stopped trying to read; his mind was too much occupied with the coming interview with Frau von Wedemeyer. Never in his life had he felt so unsure, so uncertain of how to handle a situation or what to expect.

He still had not declared himself openly to Maria, though when he had seen her again in Klein-Krossin for two short days he had sensed a deepening warmth and esteem in her manner. She had lingered at the table or in the living room, instead of going off to her own pursuits. The second morning she had invited him to accompany her on her rounds of the estate and on a sick visit in the tiny village. He had watched her dealings with these simple people: her firmness, her generous spirit, her bright good humor. Clearly, she was a favorite with all of them.

Since his return to Berlin he had written to her three times and each time received a cordial and friendly answer. Her handwriting was large and free, as if she were talking on paper and giving just the time necessary for writing, but no more. She still addressed him as "Pastor Bonhoeffer." She remained in Klein-Krossin unaware of Dietrich's visit to her mother.

After two train changes and an hour's ride in the von Wedemeyer carriage, the imposing facade of the manor house, with its high gabled entry, came into view through the trees. The seventy-five miles from Berlin had taken seven hours.

Frau von Wedemeyer's eyes revealed the recent desolation of her inner forces. Dietrich had felt it at the supper table with her four younger children. She had not seemed surprised at his request. He had no notion whether that should alarm or encourage him. She was a tall, large-boned woman with an expressive face, whose irregular features were saved from plainness by a warm kindly smile. She held herself erect, as if she were fortifying herself for a coming skirmish.

Dietrich noticed little of the second-floor sitting room to which she had brought him except that it seemed dark; there was one lamp on the table beside his chair and the smell of burning wood on the open fire. At their feet a wolfhound stretched himself luxuriously on a bear rug.

"You have spoken already to Maria?"

"No, Frau von Wedemeyer. I did not feel I had the right, with all that's happened."

"That was very good of you. I would not have expected less." She spoke rapidly in a low, musical voice, but with the natural assertiveness of one used to authority. "I appreciate the honor to Maria and to our family. I do appreciate it. I'm aware of my mother's high regard for you, Pastor Bonhoeffer, shared, to be sure, by all of us. But my first duty is to my daughter, as you must certainly realize." She made a quick, decisive movement with her hand. In a lower voice she added, "I feel it now more than ever."

"That is understandable."

"First of all, she is too young. I know she has a mind of her own, she always has. But just the same, she is impressionable. I don't think she is able to assess—adequately—all the implications of such a marriage."

"I'm not sure what you mean."

"I mean particularly your involvement with this—conspiracy."

"I've made clear to Maria the extent of my involvement. I've kept nothing from her."

"Perhaps not. I didn't think you would. No. But there's a difference. Please don't misunderstand me. I don't hold it against you. I can't know or decide what should be binding on you, though my husband could not see his way clear to join such activity. Even though he was always firmly against the Nazis, so much so they tried more than once to smear him. My cousins, too, have taken that step, the same as you—Schlabrendorff and Tresckow—but you know them."

"Yes, I know."

"So you see," she sighed and clasped one hand in the other, "my husband felt himself bound by his oath—his personal oath, given on his honor as a gentleman. And the country at war. He felt a responsibility—not to Hitler—but to the country."

Dietrich said nothing. All argument died before it reached his lips. Yet his eyes must have said something, for she quickly added, "I know all the arguments, Pastor Bonhoeffer. All of them have been spoken around our table. But there is a point beyond which some could not go. Because of it they are dying in Russia. And the instinct that compelled them to do it I consider honorable. So you see, I—and Maria—belong to these frightful events in a way perhaps different from you."

"Different, yes, in a manner of speaking. But not in a way that need divide us. It certainly has not divided us. And we have talked about it."

"Perhaps so. How well she understands it is another matter."

Dietrich was sure that Maria understood more than her mother thought, but he did not press the point.

"But that's not the main thing," she continued. "If she were a year or two older, she might be ready for such a decision. She is only eighteen."

"A mature eighteen."

"She looks up to you, of course."

Dietrich had no answer to that, being uncertain himself as to the extent of Maria's regard for him. He did not feel called upon to divulge his uncertainty to Frau von Wedemeyer.

"And she feels very deeply the loss of her father and Max."

"I'm aware of that."

"I have to try to think what my husband would say. He would want her to have plenty of time, time to be sure of her own mind and not to be swept away by the force of emotion and events."

"That's why I have waited this long."

"This long? Three months, since her father's death, and one since Max? Ah, but it all runs together for me. Time has little meaning."

A servant boy came to put fresh wood on the fire. After he left Frau von Wedemeyer stared for a long time into its flames. Finally she turned to him and said, "Yes, she must have time. I think you must stay apart for a year."

"A year! Do you know how long that is, in this day and time? It could be the same as five or ten years. A year? My dear Frau von Wedemeyer—"

"Yes, a year. She needs a year."

The shock was so profound that Dietrich did not speak. At last he said, "I recognize your right—the right of the mother over the daughter. I understand that. However, the present circumstances—which are certainly unusual, I think you'll agree—may render such a restriction impractical. I think so."

"I'm sorry. To me it seems the only correct course."

There was nothing more to say. Soon he bade her good-night and went to his room. For a long time he stood at the window and looked out over the moonlit landscape.

He felt that he might talk her round if he tried hard enough, yet he hesitated. It seemed wrong to him to take advantage of her present weakness. If her husband had been there, he could have presented his arguments as forcefully as need be. It was some time before he could compose his disappointed feelings and go to bed.

The next morning at the breakfast table nothing was said of the evening's discussion. She asked him to stay and lead their morning devotion, with the four younger children and all the servants together. Afterward, as he prepared to leave he said to her, "I hope when you have time to reflect, you will be disposed to relent."

She smiled but said nothing.

"At any rate, when the time is right—and I hope it won't be too long—I'll come again."

As the horses pulled the wagon down the tree-lined drive, Dietrich looked back. Frau von Wedemeyer waved from the veranda, sadly, it seemed to him, and a little uncertainly. He would come back soon.

35

The betrothal party was a success. Despite all the difficulties— the shortages, the restrictions on travel, the dark mood of the city—Ursel had managed to get everything accomplished.

At the center of attention the young couple shed their radiance over the entire proceeding. Renate, in the simple blue dress that her mother had remade, was more beautiful than Paula had ever seen her. Through all the introductions of Eberhard's family to hers, through the many toasts and the good-natured teasing, she had conducted herself with graciousness and restraint.

It was Dietrich whom Paula had watched throughout the evening. He had kept his frustration well hidden, and had joined the laughter when Klaus warned Eberhard that his life would never be the same with this new disturbing element—a wife. And at Karl's rejoinder, "Wives *should* disturb!" But Paula had seen Dietrich's weary smile when Eberhard said to him, "Your day will come."

The party was to break up about nine-thirty, so that everyone could get home safely before the air raids began. Near that time, as Paula was walking up the hall, the voices of Dietrich and Hans stopped her. They were standing beneath the stair, partially hidden by the tall clock.

Hans was speaking. "Can you come by the house when this is over? We need to talk. Himmler's trying to get approval for our arrest—yours and mine. He wants more comprehensive investigations and he wants the Gestapo in on them. Of course, that bloodhound Roeder has no objection to working with them."

"Any idea when?" Dietrich asked.

"As soon as they think they have enough to go on. It's a race against time, Dietrich. Our only hope is to pull off the coup before they get us."

Paula passed them and went on as if she had not heard. Later, at home in bed, she kept hearing the phrase "a race against time." Finally she got up, slipped downstairs to the kitchen, and put a kettle of water on the stove. At a quarter-to-one she heard Dietrich at the door.

He seemed determined to be cheerful. "A good evening, wasn't it?" he said. "There was something hopeful and healing about it. It seemed to say, 'Claim the future for yourselves and your children. Don't abandon it to the forces of evil.'" He stretched out his legs and leaned back in the chair, his hand behind his head. "Of course, that's not easy. Some people—some of the church people, even— only want to forget the present or escape into dreams of the Second Coming. I can't do that. It may be that the day of judgment will dawn tomorrow. In that case I'll gladly stop working for a better future. But not before." He smiled. "I think I got that from you, Mama."

"You think so? Maybe. But sometimes, when it comes right down to it, it's not easy to be brave." Paula told him what she had overheard beneath the stairs. "I couldn't help but listen."

Dietrich was silent for a moment, then said, "We shouldn't be surprised, should we? We've lived with this possibility for a long time."

"But to know it is planned. Isn't it wise to get away while you can?"

Dietrich smiled. "I tried that once."

"It's not the same."

"Almost. Except that now there would be real danger to the families left behind. I can't do that, Mama."

Paula searched her mind for some alternative, but on every side came up against a wall.

Dietrich continued, "It's not a matter of heroics. The real question is how little Walter and Andreas, and the children of Renate and Eberhard are to live."

"What good can you do in prison?"

"Let's not assume that will happen. There's still hope we can carry out our plans. They're almost complete. They look good, in fact. But if we're picked up beforehand, you mustn't worry. It would probably be temporary."

"But the Gestapo—"

"For now they don't have jurisdiction. Hans and I worked out a plan so our stories will harmonize—we are rehearsing every detail. But the coup will work this time, Mama. We'll have the cooperation of at least one field commander and some units near the city. When the full story of Stalingrad comes out, it shouldn't be hard to enlist the support of the people."

"I hope you are right," Paula said with a sigh.

Later, as Dietrich lay in bed, he wondered if he had given his mother false assurances. The field commander he had spoken of, Field Marshal von Kluge, commander-in-chief of Army Group Center at Smolensk, had indicated to Goerdeler in November a willingness to cooperate. That sounded fine until Dietrich heard that shortly beforehand Kluge had accepted a gift of 250,000 reichsmarks from Hitler.

Dietrich tried to look at the positive side. A number of officers at Kluge's headquarters were actively planning to get rid of Hitler one way or another, even without Kluge's help. The two cousins that Frau von Wedemeyer had spoken of, General von Tresckow and Lt. Fabian von Schlabrendorff, were the chief plotters and had been in touch with the Oster group for many months. Schlabrendorff was the liaison between them and came often to Berlin to consult with Resistance leaders. The plan was to lure Hitler to the headquarters in Smolensk, where there was a better chance to penetrate the heavy security around him. Immediately following the assassination, the Berlin group would swing into action.

Despite the feverish activity of those weeks, Dietrich never ceased thinking of Maria. He learned from Frau von Kleist-Retzow that she had gone for training as a Red Cross nurse. It had been two months since he had seen her. With great difficulty Dietrich restrained his desire to contact her directly. Even Eberhard agreed that he should wait awhile.

The new year—1943—came slowly around. On a day in mid-January, after a planning session in Hans's office, Dietrich started home, followed by his ever-present shadow from the Gestapo. When he turned onto the Marienburger Allee, Dietrich glimpsed the man rounding the curve on the Soldauer Allee.

In the foyer Dietrich spoke to his mother and flipped idly through the mail on the table. Under a long envelope there appeared suddenly, as if by magic, a letter addressed to him in a handwriting he immediately recognized. He stared at the letter as if he expected it to vanish, then snatched it up, excused himself and, with a semblance of calm, moved up the steps. When he had turned the corner and was out of sight, he took the steps two at a time, all the way to his attic room.

Inside, he leaned against the door, the letter in his open palm, until he recovered his breath, then walked to the desk, opened the letter with the penknife, and sat down to read.

Maria began with "Dear Pastor Bonhoeffer" and still used the formal address, "Sie." Her mother had told her of his visit and his request, which had come as a surprise to her. She was grateful, however, for his kindly feelings toward her and for the honor that his request bestowed upon her. At the proper time she would, indeed, be happy to become his wife.

Dietrich jumped up from the chair with a cry of disbelief, turned the letter to the light of the window, and read the words again. At the proper time she would, indeed, be happy to become his wife. She had waited to write to him because she wanted to be sure that her first feelings were true and lasting. The more she had thought about it the more certain she had become. Yet Maria agreed with her mother that they should not rush into an engagement, but should give themselves time and, in fact, abide by the separation her mother wished. Maria also asked Dietrich to tell no one except his parents, out of respect for the mourning period for her father and Max. The rest of the letter told of her training at the hospital and the work with the wounded in the wards. She asked about Dietrich's work and family, and sent special greetings to Renate and Eberhard.

That was all. Yet it said more than ten pages could have said. Dietrich read the letter through again, and again a third time. He opened the window just as Ursel came out onto her terrace below.

"Hello, Ursel! Beautiful day, isn't it?"

She looked up in surprise. Before Ursel could answer, Dietrich closed the window, put on his hat again, and—with the letter carefully folded in his breast pocket—went downstairs and out onto the snow-covered street. After an hour of tramping through the forest, Dietrich returned home and told the good news to his parents. They were not so surprised at his great good fortune as he would have imagined. They shared his happiness, but were less sanguine about the chances of changing Frau von Wedemeyer's dictum.

That night Dietrich wrote an eight-page letter to Maria. He had decided against calling. The telephone was no instrument for intimate conversation. With more liberty than usual he poured out his gratitude, his love, and went into every argument he could think of against the unnaturally imposed separation. He must see her. Anything else was insane. If she thought it would help he would go again and talk with her mother.

Two days later Dietrich received an answer—a longer and more detailed letter. Maria asked him to be patient. In two weeks, when she went home on leave, she would talk with her mother.

After that Dietrich and Maria exchanged letters every few days. One day Dietrich called her. The sound of her voice made him want to see her all the more. Her mother, however, held her position, and Maria would not go against her wishes.

"You don't want that, I'm sure," said Maria.

"No. I want her wishes to change."

"So do I."

That simple affirmation contented him for two days. After that he began to plan ways to mount an offensive—a gentle offensive—against the good mother's old-fashioned ideas.

The events of the next two weeks alternately lowered and raised Dietrich's expectations. A joint communiqué from the Allied heads of state, meeting in Casablanca, demanded "unconditional surrender," which cast a shadow over the hopes for a negotiated peace after the overthrow. This was bound to heighten the generals' fears of a new Versailles. Shortly afterward, the official announcement of the loss of Stalingrad increased the sense of urgency for a coup, and made the prospects for success more promising than at any time since 1938. All that was needed now was to get Hitler to Smolensk.

"Anything definite?" Dietrich asked Hans one day in late February.

"Nothing's ever definite with Hitler," said Hans. "But we hope he can be persuaded to pay a visit to Army Group Center. Tresckow is working on it. He knows Hitler's adjutant personally and has told him how much the visit is needed to boost morale. When it looks promising, we'll go to Smolensk to coordinate our actions with Tresckow."

"We're going to Smolensk," Hans said one evening three weeks later. "Canaris has arranged a general intelligence conference as a cover. Even Canaris is going; Oster, too."

In Sakrow the night before Hans left, Dietrich saw the explosive device his brother-in-law was taking with him in his suitcase. Dietrich was surprised at how small it was—about the size of a compact pocket Bible. It was a British bomb, called a "clam," one of many dropped by parachute for French resisters to use in sabotage. Some had fallen into German hands and had been turned over to the sabotage section of the Abwehr.

"German explosives are not suitable," said Hans. "Their fuses make a hissing sound that would give them away." He pulled the pencil-shaped fuse from the clam. "This one works with an acid capsule, see. When punctured, it eats through this wire holding back the striking-pin with a spring. That sets off the detonator."

"How does Tresckow expect to use it?" Dietrich asked.

"It will depend on the situation. If they can't do it before, they'll try to smuggle it aboard Hitler's plane as he leaves."

"What about danger to innocent people?"

"That's a factor. We're trying to minimize the bloodshed. But that gets in the way." Hans shook his head. "We aren't cut out for this kind of thing, Dietrich. Too many scruples. If we fail, no one will ask or care about our motives. We'll have only condemnation." He stared at Dietrich as if searching for some kind of comfort.

"We can't help that. We have to try anyway, don't we, whether we succeed or not? As for our motives, God knows it is done in the name of life."

Hans sighed and walked to the window. "I need somebody to take me to the train. But not you."

"Perhaps Eberhard? I think he's free tomorrow."

The next day Eberhard took Hans to the station, but Dietrich did not tell him what he carried in his suitcase.

When Hans returned two days later, the plan was set. Hitler was due in Smolensk that Saturday. Talking far into the night, Hans, Schlabrendorff, and Tresckow had settled on the details of communication between the two groups, including code words for every possible contingency, so that action in Berlin could follow immediately after the assassination. The plotters alerted key people all over the city and commanders in Cologne, Munich, and Vienna. With Hitler dead, the generals at the front would no longer withhold their support.

The strictest secrecy was in order. In the family, only Dietrich, Hans, and Christel knew of the plan. When Saturday came, Dietrich found that study was out of the question. After lunch he went to see Christel in Sakrow.

Christel seemed glad to see him, but had no news. With their phone tapped Hans would not dare try to tell her anything, even in code. The two boys were there, and Dietrich initiated a game of cards. Normally a consummate bridge player, Christel made numerous mistakes. Christoph laughingly took several tricks that should have been hers. Soon the boys tired of the cards and went outside to play in the snow.

Dietrich asked, "Should we turn on the radio? Just in case."

Christel silently turned it on. There was nothing but martial music, interspersed with the usual propaganda. "It's too soon," she said.

They went over the plan, and Christel seemed relieved to talk about it. Dietrich stressed the hopeful possibilities.

"No use to paint it better than it is, Dietrich. We're taking a terrible chance. If one little thing goes wrong—. I try to prepare myself, but the truth is—if Hans—"

She did not need to say more. It was written on her face. Dietrich said, gently, "We can bear more than we think we can, Christel."

"Perhaps so. But I know—I know how it would be."

The afternoon dragged on. Finally at six-fifteen Hans appeared. He looked at them and shook his head. "Something went wrong. We still don't know what. Schlabrendorff alerted us in mid-morning that the 'flash' was imminent, then at two o'clock, a second call: the operation had been set in motion." Hans slumped into a chair and leaned sideways, his cheek on his hand. "We waited for two hours," said Hans. "Not a word. Then Schlabrendorff called again. The attempt had failed, but, of course, he couldn't tell us why."

Christel sat unmoving at the table, her hand over her mouth and her eyes closed. Dietrich could not tell which was uppermost— relief or disappointment.

The answer came two days later, when Schlabrendorff arrived in Berlin. Dietrich was in General Oster's office to consult with him about a new threat of call-up. The day before, Dietrich had received an order from the Munich recruiting station to report in one week with all of his papers. Oster assured him that at this time, and especially after the coup, he would need Dietrich more than ever for negotiations with the Allies. He would use all his authority to get Dietrich released from this order.

"We must dream up some valid-sounding reasons for sending

you to Rome," Oster said, "possibly in the next two or three weeks, as a preliminary step in this direction. Dohnanyi and I will work on it."

At that moment the tall figure of Fabian von Schlabrendorff appeared in the door. Oster called in Hans from the adjoining office; and Schlabrendorff, his smooth bespectacled face showing little emotion, told the story of the failed coup attempt.

"The bomb simply failed to go off. I myself handed it to Lieutenant Colonel Brandt as he boarded Hitler's airplane just before takeoff. I had crushed the acid capsule with a key just two minutes before. Brandt knew nothing, of course. He thought it was a gift of spirits to General Stieff in Rastenburg. The two bombs wrapped together looked like a bottle of Cointreau. I watched the plane until it was out of sight. Well, we waited. And after two hours we called Rastenburg. The plane had landed already—safely."

"And Colonel Brandt?" asked Oster.

"He had not delivered the package. And he didn't suspect anything, thank God. Yesterday I retrieved it and took it to an empty railway car where I defused the bomb." The young lieutenant spoke as matter-of-factly as if he were talking about a flashlight with a bad battery. He took a package from his briefcase and opened it on the desk. The two clams, containing enough explosive to blow them all to bits, nested one atop the other on the brown paper. Schlabrendorff undid the fuse, wrapped separately, and showed it to them. "You see, the acid ate through the wire, and the striker hit the detonator cap, just as it was supposed to." It had burned the cap, and the detonator was black on the outside. "But the explosive didn't ignite. I don't know why. Tresckow and I tested it several times and it worked—once just the day before."

Just then a call came to Schlabrendorff from Tresckow in Smolensk. When he put down the phone, he quietly announced, "Well, gentlemen, we have another chance. One of our officers had offered to do it himself here in Berlin this Sunday. Now he will go ahead." He looked around at their puzzled faces. "Heroes Memorial Day, March 21. Our Army Group Center is scheduled to present an exhibition of captured war matériel on this occasion. That gives Colonel Gersdorff an excuse to be on hand to answer Hitler's questions as he reviews the exhibition. Gersdorff is prepared to blow himself up with Hitler. His wife died a year ago, and he feels that in view of what it would accomplish, his own life is not too great a sacrifice."

No one spoke for a long time. Oster broke the silence. "Wrap up your clams, Herr Lieutenant. We'll have to report this to the admiral."

Paula opened her eyes and realized she had been asleep. It was the first time in two weeks that she had been able to sleep at nap-time—not since the brave Colonel Gersdorff failed in his sacrificial attempt to get Hitler. She had tried to live one day at a time, as Karl repeatedly admonished, but that was hard. It was plain to her that Dietrich feared the worst, although he was trying to hide it from her.

She looked at the clock. Three-thirty. Quietly she got up, put on her shoes, and went upstairs to Dietrich's room. He was not there. Probably next door, but she had not heard him leave. As she came downstairs again, the doorbell rang. When she opened the door two men stood there—one in a gray suit, the other in the uniform of the Gestapo. With all the strength at her command she held herself straight and made no sound.

"Dietrich Bonhoeffer, please," said the man in the gray suit. "We have business with him."

"He is not here," she said, forcing calm into her voice.

"Then, of course, you must fetch him. We will wait. In his room, if you please."

Paula did not move.

"Perhaps you don't understand," said the man, harshly. "Your son—I presume he is your son—is under arrest. Take us to his room immediately."

At that moment Karl came down the stairs and, when he had heard the demand, led the intruders up the steps to Dietrich's attic. Paula followed, but was unable to make it all the way. She leaned against the wall with Hans's words tolling in her ears "the Gestapo will try to get jurisdiction—torture—doing their worst—"

When she heard Karl coming back, she stood straight and went before him to the foyer. "What can we do?" she whispered.

"There's nothing we can do. I'll go and get him."

Paula watched from the window as Karl and Dietrich returned across the lawn. She met them at the back door.

Dietrich took her hands in his. "Mama, you're not to worry. I'll be all right."

Paula could not speak. All she could think was that she must not break down and make things worse for Dietrich than they already were. She listened to his words of reassurance—he had known they were coming and put everything in order—they wouldn't find anything important. "Really, Mama."

It was an hour and a half before Dietrich came down the stairs again with his captors. The sight of the handcuffs almost undid Paula. Without speaking—she did not trust herself to speak—she kissed her son. Standing beside Karl, she watched the Nazis put him in the back seat of their car. As they drove away Dietrich turned once and waved with bound hands from the rear window.

36

As the night wore on the prison cell grew colder, but Dietrich could not bring himself to use the filthy blanket. Toward morning he began to doze. He slid down on the mattress, curled into a ball and, cold and hungry as he was, slept.

The shouts of the guards woke him.

"What do you expect, you damned swine. Bring your bucket to the door. Can't you move, you blockhead!"

Dietrich heard the key turn in his door. It opened and the guard, silhouetted against the harsh light, threw something into the cell.

"Your bucket, bring it here," he said.

Dietrich stood up and took the bucket to the door.

"Set it there." The guard pointed to the floor outside the door. Dietrich put it down. The guard shoved a cup into Dietrich's hand and filled it from a large coffee pot. When Dietrich did not move, he barked, "Well, what are you waiting for, you dolt? You have your bread, get back inside."

Dietrich stepped back and the door slammed in his face. He turned and in the dim light saw the piece of bread on the floor, where the guard had thrown it. His first thought was that he could not eat anything that had touched that floor, but severe hunger pangs soon overtook his squeamishness.

Dietrich put the cup of coffee on the bench and picked up the bread. With the clean handkerchief from his pocket he brushed off the bread, then spread the handkerchief on the bench and laid the bread on it.

Dietrich sat on the low stool with his long legs crossed. Automatically he began to say grace, but stopped himself in the middle and prayed, instead, an earnest prayer that God would help him to be thankful even for that poor meal.

The bread was hard and dry. He ate slowly so it would last longer. The coffee, if it could be called coffee, was bitter, but he drank it all.

Soon the guards returned and marched Dietrich out with the other prisoners, five in all, into a courtyard in front of the building. It occurred to him that the cell of the night before might not be his permanent lodging. He had noticed only a few cells on that short hall, and the front part of the building consisted of offices.

"March, you goddamn blackguards!" the guard bawled, as they stepped out into the daylight. "Now, halt!"

It was a scraggly lineup of men with tired, young faces, three of them in dirty, wrinkled uniforms.

"Would you mind taking up a military attitude, you beggarly tramps."

The line straightened and the men stood at attention.

A sergeant major in a crisply pressed green uniform appeared from the opposite building and reviewed the line. He asked the first man his occupation and why he had been arrested.

So the others were also new arrivals, thought Dietrich, sure now that their lodging was indeed temporary. The sergeant major pressed answers from one after the other. One was accused of stealing, two of insubordination, the last of desertion. The sergeant major berated each one with vile oaths. The deserter he cursed uncontrollably. The young man stood next to Dietrich. His eyes were weary and tormented, and he said almost nothing in his defense. He had been at the front in Russia all winter. He did not know why he had run away, it had just happened. After twelve hours he had collapsed in the snow, and there they had found him.

"So you left your comrades in the lurch, cowardly bastard, while every decent man is giving his life's blood for the Fatherland. Well, just wait, we'll show you."

The sergeant major came to Dietrich. "And you?" he asked with a sneer. "Why are you here?"

"I don't know," said Dietrich.

"You don't know? You don't know why you were arrested?"

"No, I don't."

"Ha!" said the man. "You'll find out soon enough, by God! I see you're one of our civilians. What are you, then?"

"I am a pastor."

"A pastor? He's a pastor. Well, now, isn't that a hell of a note. Now we have a pastor. What will they send us next?" He turned to the guard. "Get them assigned, and get them cleaned up." Then facing the prisoners again, "We keep a clean place here. Don't you forget it."

The guard saluted. Then the sergeant major added, "The pastor goes into isolation. Orders from the commandant."

They were marched back into the building and through various offices, where clerks took more particulars and the prisoners underwent medical examinations. Twice, while Dietrich waited in line, noncommissioned officers who had learned that he was a pastor stopped to talk with him. Immediately the guards ordered them away. No one was allowed to speak with him, the guards said.

In the first office a new guard—big and burly, with a countenance not entirely unpleasant—returned Dietrich's bag, billfold, and watch. The bag seemed lighter. Curious, Dietrich opened it. "My Bible isn't here," he said.

"You'll get it back soon enough," the guard said.

"What do they want with it?"

"Everything has to be checked."

"What for?"

The guard laughed. "Who knows what you've hid in its pages."

The man led Dietrich outside, and they followed a walkway beside the building, past the entrance of the center prison house and around the corner. A hundred feet or so down the path was another prison house, equally vast, its high walls lined with little barred windows.

The guard's keys jingled as they walked. Beside them sandy paths criss-crossed an enclosed prison yard, but the clerk had told Dietrich he would not be allowed the daily half-hour walks or any mail until further notice. Isolation. Orders of the commandant. Dietrich looked once more at the blue sky before the guard unlocked the heavy door.

Inside, the stone passageway was wide, with steel doors at close intervals along each side. Overhead, three upper floors rose to the ceiling. On all three levels cell doors opened onto bannistered walkways, which ran the length of the building and were joined by an occasional steel catwalk.

The building was in the shape of a cross—four arms joined at a central well, with guard stations on each level. Dietrich's escort led him quickly to a metal stairway on the far side. Their footsteps echoed along the open passages as they climbed the steps to the top floor. There the guard turned to a cell a few feet away. He had said nothing the whole time.

When the guard unlocked the door, Dietrich looked him straight in the eye. "I would like to have my Bible."

There was a glimmer of decency in the man's broad red face. "I'll see about it."

"Thanks."

The door closed and locked behind Dietrich. The cell was the same size as the other, but cleaner. There was a small, high window, and through it he could see the sky. Even isolation could be bearable, he thought, if one could see the sky.

The desperate sobbing, accompanied by clanking chains, had persisted for hours. Several times the prisoner banged frantically against the masonry partition between the two cells. Once Dietrich tapped gently on the wall and for a moment the sobbing stopped, but soon resumed, more violently than ever. There was no way to reach the man, and no one else seemed to notice. Dietrich wondered if in this corner of purgatory such sounds were a nightly occurrence. During the long day, with the repetition of murderous curses from the guards, Dietrich realized that he was lodged with condemned felons. Rest was impossible, although he was utterly weary from loss of sleep the night before.

This cell was not as cold as the other. The blanket did not stink, but it felt so greasy that Dietrich draped it only over his feet. All night he felt something crawling on him, but it was impossible to see. Yet he must have slept some. In the half-light of early morning the abrupt banging of heavy doors and abusive shouts of the guards hurled Dietrich from his blessed dreams to the hellish clamor of Tegel. The sorry ritual began: carry the bucket to the door, eat the meager breakfast slowly; wash in a basin of cold water and dry with a small dingy towel; then, when his turn comes, shave in the presence of a guard and without a mirror. When he washed he noticed several itchy bites on his arms and around his trunk. With some curiosity he began to examine the mattress and soon, in one of its folds, he discovered a flat reddish bug. He had never seen a bedbug, but remembered when he was a child one summer at Friedrichsbrunn, his mother had burned a mattress in horror and then disinfected the entire house. He continued the search and found two more of the little bloodsuckers, which he dispatched without regret.

By eight o'clock the morning routine was finished. There was nothing left to do. The long day like the one before it stretched before him. Work had always been the water of life for Dietrich.

Now there was not even a scrap of paper to write on. On the wall over his bed was a sentence scribbled by a former inmate: "In a hundred years it'll all be over."

The third day, Dietrich's Bible was returned to him. Until then the only persons he had seen were the guards who brought his meals and took his bucket. Mid-morning the key turned in the door and the same young man who had brought him there the first day stood with the Bible in his hand.

"You've brought my Bible. Thanks very much."

"It's nothing. You would have got it back anyway."

"They found no saw, or razor or—"

The young guard smiled and turned to go.

"Herr Corporal, is there a library here?" Dietrich asked.

"Yes."

"Do you think you could bring me a newspaper and maybe a book or two?"

The young man hesitated. He looked again in Dietrich's face. "Well, I'll see. I don't know."

"Thanks. Thanks very much."

Late in the afternoon the corporal came again with the *Deutsche Allgemeine Zeitung*, a newspaper that still hinted here and there at views opposed to the Nazi line, and two books—Gotthelf's *Geld und Geist* and letters by an obscure preacher from a trip through Palestine. Dietrich sat on the corner of his bed and buried himself in the Gotthelf. Even the pleasure of reading lost its taste after a while. He laid the book aside and stared at the gray wall. Again he saw his mother's face as the Nazis took him away. He longed to speak to her, to assure her he was all right, and to tell her how sorry he was to cause her so much pain. The vision shifted to a sunny meadow and a girl in a blue dress. Ah, Maria! He longed for the sight of her, for a time to nurture the tender shoot that had sprung up so miraculously between them. Or if he could talk with Eberhard, even for an hour.

Day followed day. Gradually Dietrich gathered strength and found comfort in prayer and meditation.

One night the air raid siren woke him up, and the smell of fear, like hot tar, filled the prison house. Locked helplessly in his cell like all the other prisoners, Dietrich watched from his window. He could see little of the main action to the southeast, but heard the roar of the fighters taking off from the nearby field, and soon the "hrrrmmp" of bombs exploding in the city. Overhead lights from the antiaircraft batteries crisscrossed the night sky. No bombs fell near the prison, and an hour later the all-clear sounded.

Dietrich's sixth night at Tegel came and still no word from anyone. Each morning he had dressed in coat and tie in case he was summoned for interrogation. He had no idea what questions might be asked or how to prepare, and that uncertainty was worse than all else put together.

The next morning at eight o'clock two guards opened his door, clamped handcuffs on his wrists, and led him out. Dietrich hated facing his interrogators in a dirty shirt and wrinkled suit.

The Supreme Military Tribunal sat in a gray stone building on the familiar Witzleben Strasse. To be back in the vicinity of his childhood softened the dread of the impending encounter. The guards ushered him into an anteroom on the second floor and turned him over to uniformed court officials. A door opened into the brightly lit hearing room. In the center of the room was a heavy polished table, behind which were two empty chairs. A secretary entered and sat at a stenographer's desk.

Suddenly there was a commotion at the rear door as Judge Advocate Roeder burst in, followed by the SS man Sonderegger. Clearly the Gestapo had gained some kind of jurisdiction in Dietrich's case. Roeder sat beside Sonderegger with an air of satisfaction and laid aside his hat. An officer's uniform of colonel's rank encased his rotund figure. The court officials removed Dietrich's handcuffs and stood him before the table.

"Well, Herr Dr. Bonhoeffer, we meet again," said Roeder, sarcastically. "I hope the intervening days have convinced you to be cooperative. I'm sure you agree with me that the authority of the government must be upheld at all costs." Roeder spoke with a slight lisp, and his eyes blinked expectantly behind his rimless glasses.

"Certainly, Herr Colonel." Dietrich forced the words out.

Roeder continued, "And that Germany would be inconceivable without the Party?"

"That is true." Again Dietrich lied.

In Roeder's smile there was a cynical set of the mouth, the mark of years of self-indulgence and rank ambition. "Then I see no problems ahead for us," he said. "I must inform you that Dohnanyi and Müller are in our hands, along with Dohnanyi's wife— your sister, I believe."

Christel arrested! Dietrich swallowed hard. "Frau von Dohnanyi is my sister." The words began evenly enough, but almost immediately the inner turmoil broke free. "To arrest her was senseless! She knows nothing of the Abwehr."

Roeder's eyes flared. "Criticism of this court is not your prerogative. What's more, their confessions—his and hers—confirm Herr Consul Schmidhuber's information about treasonous activities in the heart of the Abwehr."

Dietrich said nothing.

"You are not going to be so foolish as to deny that," said Roeder.

"I have no knowledge of treasonous activities in the Abwehr."

"We know better. Your brother-in-law named you as an accomplice."

Dietrich glanced at Sonderegger's narrow inscrutable face and turned again to Roeder. "That's impossible. My brother-in-law is not a liar."

"Are you implying that I am a liar?" Roeder shouted.

"I am implying nothing. I know that Herr von Dohnanyi is not a liar."

Roeder took a sheet of paper from his briefcase and laid it before Dietrich. "I suppose you'll say you know nothing of this piece of treason!"

It was the carefully worded memo that Dietrich and Hans had sent to General Beck for his approval. It outlined, in disguised language, the proposals Dietrich was to present in Rome. Beck had signed it with his code initial "O" and penciled a note at the bottom instructing Bonhoeffer and Müller to report back to him upon their return. The memo read:

> From clerics in the German Protestant Church to representatives of the Catholic Church in Rome:
>
> −We request your help in this war to bring about a just and lasting peace and to construct a social system based on Christian foundations.
>
> −We are aware that British, American, Dutch, Norwegian and French Protestant Churches are devoting keen consideration to these questions and believe it would carry great weight if all Christian Churches adopted a concerted approach to the problem of arranging a peace when the time comes.
>
> −We are aware of the basic peace aims enunciated by the Pope in his last two Christmas messages and believe a consensus on all essential points is possible among all the churches.
>
> −We intend to prepare universally intelligible leaflets, explaining these peace aims, to be made available to the public when the occasion arises.
>
> −It seems extremely important and desirable that a German Protestant cleric be enabled to hold discussions on this subject with representatives of the Catholic Church in Rome and with worldwide Protestant Churches in Geneva.

"Even a fool could see the treason lurking there," Roeder hissed, "and I'm no fool. Dohnanyi admitted that he wrote it with your help and that Oster initialled it. There's no use denying it."

So they took the "O" for Oster's initial. And Hans had gone along with that. Or had he? "I don't deny it. You're simply misinterpreting it. It means the opposite of what it says."

"How interesting. I'm supposed to believe that?"

"According to my brother-in-law, that's common practice in the Abwehr. Directives that are to cross the border are often coded in that way. What appears as an overt proposition to the Vatican was in fact to serve as my credentials."

"Are you trying to confuse me?" Roeder asked.

"Certainly not. If the Vatican authorities believed what it

seemed to say, they might more readily divulge the important information we were seeking. In Rome I would pretend to be talking about peace aims, when in fact I would be learning where the Allies were weak, and something of their plans."

A puzzled frown crossed Roeder's face. Dietrich hoped Hans had given the same version or something near it. They had no agreement on what to say about this particular memorandum, but there was a general understanding among the Oster people that any such paper—if it fell into unfriendly hands—would be called "coded language," not to be taken literally.

"Your fabrication is clever, but not clever enough, Herr Bonhoeffer. If your story were true, why would General Oster have attempted to hide that piece of paper?"

Dietrich quickly answered, "I can't say, since I don't know the circumstances."

"The Herr Kommissar caught General Oster in the act," said Roeder, nodding in Sonderegger's direction.

A smile spread over the SS officer's thin bony face, as if he relished the recollection. "Yes," Sonderegger said, "Oster tried to whisk it from Dohnanyi's desk and slip it into his back pocket, but I was a bit too fast for him."

"General Oster's finished," Roeder continued. "He won't be back at the Abwehr. I'm going to clean the whole place out from top to bottom. Schmidhuber spoke of a 'clique of generals.' I expect you to give me their names."

"I can't help you there," said Dietrich. "In the first place, I was not in a position to know very much. I was merely a pastor, who happened to have ecumenical connections that the Abwehr thought might be useful to the war effort. I considered it my duty—a privilege, in fact—to serve in this manner. But this work never brought me into the inner recesses of the Abwehr. I was not important enough for that, so, of course, I know no names."

"Why, then, would General Oster be so concerned as to try to snatch this paper away?"

"I have no idea," Dietrich answered calmly.

Roeder looked him up and down. "I doubt that." He put the

paper back in his briefcase and stood up. "Be assured, Herr Bonhoeffer, I intend to get to the bottom of this, whatever it takes. There are other methods for extracting the truth from you. If need be, I'll ask the Führer personally to give me permission to use them." To the guards he said, "Take him away."

37

"He who does the truth comes to the light." Dietrich's Bible lay open at that verse in the Gospel of John. He had come back to it over and over all afternoon as he struggled with the question: What is telling the truth? He had thought about it a great deal since he and Hans had worked on the diversionary testimony. But until that morning Dietrich had not fully come to grips with it. Lying did not come easy for him. He could not accept the idea that if the situation demanded, one could lie oneself out of a difficulty. Yet it was inconceivable that, in this instance, God's truth could mean betraying his co-conspirators into the hands of the Nazis. He remembered what he had said to Adam von Trott: "It is worse for a liar to tell the truth than for a lover of the truth to lie."

By eight o'clock the lights were out and Dietrich could not see to read his Bible. As was his habit at night, he began to pray from memory one of the Psalms—this time, Psalm 11: "His searching gaze scans all mankind. . . . Yahweh is righteous, he loves virtue, upright men will contemplate his face."

"Upright men will contemplate his face," he repeated aloud.

The morning brought new resolve—he would set himself a strict ordering of the day: up by six and a cold wash-down before breakfast came around; after that, Bible reading, beginning with Genesis, in a plan for reading it straight through; memorize a new passage of Scripture; then prayer and meditation; next, calisthenics. The rest of the time he would divide between reading and walking up and down the cell. That left him with two hours of free time after supper, which was at four o'clock.

By evening Dietrich was tired of trying to pretend he was busy. The time had crawled, but he was determined to stick to the regimen and find something to fill the long hours.

The next day the guards came for him again, and once more Dietrich found himself before Roeder and Sonderegger.

"You will please note that you are accused of high treason and treason against the state," was Roeder's salutation.

"There are no grounds for the charge," said Dietrich.

"The grounds are fast appearing. Oster denies knowing anything about that document."

"That seems strange. You said he tried to hide it," Dietrich countered.

"He denies he signed it. He does not use 'O' as his signature. And he has no knowledge of the coded language you claim was agreed upon. Oster said you would not have been dispatched to Rome as an agent. The Central Section is not even authorized to maintain agents of its own."

"Not officially, perhaps, but I have been an agent of the Abwehr Foreign Bureau since September 1940," said Dietrich.

"And your function?"

"I told you, my work for military intelligence was to gather information through my ecumenical contacts. That was the whole point."

Roeder leaned back and cocked his head to one side. "You'd do well to confess the truth, Herr Bonhoeffer. It would save us all a lot of grief and pain."

"I cannot confess to something that isn't so."

"It's your word against Oster's."

Dietrich's brain whirled. What was the matter with Oster? "My commission came from Admiral Canaris himself. If you'd ask him, I'm sure he would be able to clear this up."

The interview ended as abruptly as it began.

In one of the books from the prison library Dietrich found a sheet of paper, yellowed and torn. On it he wrote a letter to his parents, hoping that it would slip by the ban on his mail. He tried to put the best possible face on his situation. In a round-about way he asked them to share the letter with Maria and suggested that they invite her to visit them in Berlin. When the young guard—the only one who had shown Dietrich any degree of decency—appeared with his supper, Dietrich asked him to mail the letter.

"It's forbidden."

"But would you try? My aged parents need to hear from me."

"Well, I'll take it to the sergeant, but I doubt if he will go against orders."

"Thank you very much. May I ask your name, Herr Corporal?"

"Knobloch. Hans Knobloch."

Dietrich held out his hand. "I am Dietrich Bonhoeffer."

Shyly Knobloch shook hands.

"Have you been here long?" Dietrich asked.

The corporal sighed. "Almost a year."

"I dare say you had no choice."

"No. I was wounded. They had to put a steel plate in my head. I can't go back."

"That must be hard for you."

Knobloch shrugged and a bitter smile crossed his face. "Are some of the prisoners soldiers?" Dietrich asked.

"Most of them."

Dietrich told him of the weeping of the prisoner next door.

"Yes. He's condemned. The other, too, on this side. Condemned to death."

"What for?"

Knobloch drew himself up as if he suddenly realized what he was doing. "I must go. I'm not supposed—" He turned quickly to the door.

"Thank you, Herr Knobloch—the letter—thank you."

After the guard left, a terrible feeling of helplessness crept over Dietrich. He doubted his letter would get outside the building.

Dietrich marked Friday, April 16th, 1943, on his homemade calendar. He had been nearly two weeks in that hellhole. Soon afterward the guards fetched him for the third interrogation.

"Now, we've made a thorough search of Abwehr files," Roeder

began with a satisfied smile, "and do not find your name listed in the agents' card index or on the payroll."

"That's true," said Dietrich, "I was not on the payroll. I considered this a service due—"

"What's more, you had not sworn the customary oath of secrecy."

"In my case it was not required."

"All quite irregular. So irregular that we might decide your case should be placed in other hands," Roeder added with a pointed look at Sonderegger. "Admiral Canaris conceded that your exempt status was irregular."

Dietrich's emotions veered from alarm at the implied threat to relief that he had talked to Canaris after all. "The admiral nevertheless confirmed it as a fact, I'm sure," he said.

"He was incensed—or pretended to be incensed—to learn that you have been under Gestapo surveillance for years, with travel restrictions and various prohibitions." He turned to Sonderegger. "True, Herr Kommissar?"

"True," said Sonderegger.

Roeder continued, "Why do you suppose Dohnanyi kept that from the admiral? Or is the admiral holding back too? We know he's been sneaking Jews across the border on improbable pretexts and tossing the taxpayer's money after them."

Dietrich ignored the last remark and said, "I don't know that Dohnanyi kept it from the admiral, but if so, it was because such restrictions were unwarranted. I myself wrote a letter to the Reich Security Head Office, explaining—"

"Never mind," said Roeder.

Dietrich turned to Sonderegger. "Perhaps the letter is still in their files. It would help to clear this up."

"That's not necessary," said Roeder. "We have enough evidence now to make a charge of treason, so you might as well come clean."

"There's nothing to come clean about."

"You're lying! You've been lying all along. Don't try to hold out against me. I'm not a fool. Don't you see there's no one left to cover up for you?"

Dietrich said nothing, and Roeder, red-faced and spluttering, stalked out of the room.

After breakfast the next morning one of the guards appeared and announced that Dietrich was to be moved to another cell.

"Why is that?"

"Orders of the commandant, Herr Doktor."

It was the first time anyone had addressed Dietrich as if they knew who he was. How peculiar, he thought, as he packed his few belongings into the small bag. When he was ready, the guard held the door and offered to carry his bag, an unprecedented action.

The new cell—on the same floor but in the adjoining wing— seemed larger than the other, and cleaner. The smell of disinfectant lingered, and the blanket and sheets were clean.

"If you will come with us to the guardroom, there is a package for you," said the guard.

After twelve days of isolation the sight of a parcel from home and letters from his father and Ursel brought Dietrich close to tears. He was grateful for the diversion when the sergeant in charge asked him to check the contents of the package against the list his father had made on a laundry slip. It was dated April 7, ten days earlier. The bread was already molded, but there was a small sausage, a box of cookies—made, he was sure, by Ursel—and a package of dried apples, a blanket, his brown woolen vest, a clean shirt, clean underwear, and warm socks.

"Your letter to your parents has been sent on to Judge Advocate Roeder," said the sergeant, a man of small stature, who appeared to be about Dietrich's age. He had a limp in his left leg, and Dietrich wondered if it was from a war wound. Most of the staff seemed to be made up of men who, for one reason or another, were unable to perform front line duty.

"Thank you, but why to him?" Dietrich asked.

"All your mail must go through him. Those are his orders."

"I see." He had expected censorship, but not by Roeder himself.

"I would like to write also to my fiancée."

"I'm sorry, Herr Doktor, the Judge Advocate's orders are that you may write only to your parents, once every ten days. Also, you may receive a parcel and send your laundry once a week, a privilege not every prisoner has. The corporal will give you a yellow flag, which you may put through the opening in your door in case of emergency. Not to be used indiscriminately, of course. I will assign a prisoner to clean your cell each day. I hope you'll be more comfortable in the new quarters. If I had known—" The sergeant paused and rearranged the papers on his desk. "I was not aware of your relationship to the city commandant."

So that was it. Dietrich's Uncle Paul had intervened.

At midday he was allowed his first half-hour walk in the exercise yard. At first he walked briskly, breathing deeply the fresh air, until finally he slowed his pace and took notice of the signs of life about him: two lime trees with the first traces of green and a titmouse flitting from one tree to the other. He looked up to the top of the building and, counting from the corner, determined which was his cell window. Too soon the guard stepped forward to take him inside again. The attitude of this guard and of all the others had completely changed. The next day, Palm Sunday, several of them came to apologize. "We didn't know," they said.

In the afternoon a guard came with a bouquet of blue and yellow primulas. When Dietrich asked who had sent them, the guard said it was a girl named Maria. Dietrich arranged the flowers in his tin cup, and all day when he looked at them joy and amazement filled his heart.

On Monday Dietrich was driven to the court again and at once, without warning, brought face to face with Hans. They stared at one another across the open space, laden with all the questions they could not ask.

"Well, say something," Roeder barked from behind the table. "You do know each other, I believe."

"Good-day, Hans, I hope you're well," Dietrich began.

"Well enough, thank you, and you?"

"I'm all right," Dietrich answered. Hans looked as if he had not slept for days. Dietrich knew how tortured he must be, knowing that Christel was also in prison.

"Well, now," said Roeder with a smack of his lips, "I think we can get down to business. It's obvious to us that you're both lying. We assume, Herr Bonhoeffer, that this trip to Rome was not meant to be a pleasure trip. Since you're not a bona fide Abwehr agent and since General Oster denies your claim that he ordered it, we can only conclude that you were working for someone else whose intent was treasonous, as this slip of paper clearly shows. Who is it? That's all I want to know. If this 'O' is not General Oster, who is it?"

"General Oster was the one who had the authority," said Dietrich, not daring to look at Hans, but hoping desperately that he was on the right track, "and, as I told you, that paper was to camouflage my real—"

"Answer my question. Who was it?"

"I can't imagine, if not General Oster. As to my status in the Abwehr, that was something I left up to the officials. But I did understand that an official status would have damaged the disguise, which was absolutely necessary for my journeys."

Roeder turned to Hans. "Your brother-in-law pretends not to know who 'O' is, but you know, and you'll do well to tell me."

"I've said over and over that it is Oster."

Dietrich breathed a sigh of relief.

"So he's lying, you say," said Roeder.

"General Oster naturally feared that you might misinterpret that document and so he felt he must deny knowledge of it. It's a normal reaction."

"Well, if the Abwehr's officers are of such weak character and are so careless as to harbor men who are not even agents—"

"Don't you understand?" said Hans. "The ecumenical people would not have trusted anyone officially connected with the Abwehr."

"You make a pretty argument, but it doesn't convince me." Roeder stood up. "I presume you both care something about the welfare of Frau von Dohnanyi. Please be advised, so long as you refuse to tell us what you know, we cannot release her."

"You devil!" said Hans.

"Take them away."

As they came to the door, Hans's eyes met Dietrich's. His lips formed the words "Well done."

38

"We can't accept that," said the control guard and pushed the jar of plum preserves back across the table.

"Why?" Paula asked and looked at Emmi.

"No glass allowed and no tins." With cold indifference the guard continued his check: slippers, shoe polish, writing paper and envelopes, ink, shaving cream, needle and thread, and the brown suit. He marked off each item on the list Paula had made and put it into a cardboard box marked C3–10.

"Since our request to see my son is refused, may I not at least send a message to let him know we are here?"

"No message," the guard answered. "Go back to the waiting room. I'll see if the prisoner has something for you."

Paula waited with Emmi for forty-five minutes before their number was called again. There was a bag from Dietrich. Once more the control guard examined everything—the empty box that had held Ursel's cookies, the carefully folded paper bags and the wax paper, the dirty linen, and the suit to be cleaned. There was a scrap of paper on which Dietrich had written in uncharacteristically clear handwriting—for the benefit, no doubt, of the control officer—a list of things he needed: the brown boots with laces; his hairbrush; a pipe with tobacco, matches, and cleaners; and two books, Schilling's *Morals Vol. II* and something by Stifter. There was no greeting and no signature.

Emmi carried the bag as they walked out. On the sandy path they turned back and Paula looked up at the rows of barred windows. It seemed inconceivable that Dietrich was behind one of them, a caged bird.

"Come on, Mama," said Emmi. "It's best if we leave now."

When Paula reached home she found that Karl had not yet returned. Lotte, the only servant left now, had taken her afternoon off to visit her sister. And next door Ursel and Renate were immersed in preparations for Renate's wedding, less than a week away. In accordance with Dietrich's express wishes, they had decided not to wait. With a cup of ersatz coffee in her hand Paula sat alone in the living room.

The four weeks since the arrests had been a nightmare. At first the appearance of the SS man brought the terrible fear that the prisoners were in the hands of the Gestapo, especially when he came again the next morning to Ursel's door with more questions. It was not until the second day that Rüdiger found out through his colleague Dr. Karl Sack where they had been taken: Dietrich to Tegel, Hans to Lehrterstrasse, and Christel to the women's prison in Charlottenburg. Immediately Paula had called her cousin Paul von Hase, the Commandant of Berlin, but he was out of town. When she finally got him, he said he would do what he could, but he could do nothing to secure their release. That was in other hands. Karl had written to Dr. Roeder and requested permission to visit them, but it was denied. Writing letters and taking parcels, with no assurance that they were being delivered, was all the Bonhoeffers could do.

After an hour Karl came home. Paula made him coffee, and they sat together on the sofa. Sack had spoken to Keitel about Christel. Now they would have to wait for results. Visitation was Roeder's prerogative.

"Oh, Karl, I want to see them, to see with my own eyes that they're all right." Paula sank back against the cushions. "You know what today is?"

"Today?"

"Today, yes." She sighed deeply. "Twenty-five years ago today we lost Walter."

Karl took her hand in his. She could not look at him.

Two mornings later, after the children had gone to school, Christel suddenly appeared on the doorstep, pale and hollow-eyed. She would not go near anyone until she had bathed from head to foot with disinfectant soap and had Lotte boil her clothes. Afterward, wrapped in Paula's robe, she ate hungrily the breakfast Lotte prepared for her and learned all Paula knew of Hans. When she heard it was the day to take him a parcel, Christel said she would have to get a message to him.

"They won't allow it," said Paula.

"We'll have to smuggle it in. He has to know somehow that I am out."

Christel asked for two empty paper cups with lids and took the bottom from one to make a false bottom in the other, then wrote a note, hid it between the two bottoms, and filled the cup with bread pudding.

"How will Hans find it?" Paula asked.

"Do you have some red ink?"

Paula produced it and Christel drew a red flower on the lid of the cup. "In our code red means 'look for a message'," she explained.

By then Ursel and Renate had come, and they all sat together as Christel told of her prison experiences. Every detail poured out—the filth, the cold slop they gave her for food, the noise, the harshness of the guards, and the relentless interrogations. "Roeder is a devil," she said. "I pretended to be stupid and flighty, and to know nothing. It worked, I think."

Paula left that afternoon with the parcel. At the prison in the Lehterstrasse, the parcel passed the control officer without question.

A week later, when Thursday came around again, Christel took a parcel to the prison. On her return she immediately retrieved the empty paper cup and found a message between the two bottoms. Hans had torn pieces of paper to fit and stacked them one on another. When she had read them, she passed them silently to Paula.

Paula held the rounds to the light and read the tiny closely written words: "Oster was present when I was arrested. There was a memo on my desk about Dietrich's trip to Rome, signed by Beck with his 'O.' I signalled Oster to warn you, but he misunderstood and tried to slip the memo into his pocket. Sonderegger caught him. Then Oster denied it was his signature. He's still denying it. Someone has to prevail on him to acknowledge it. That is crucial to our defense."

"I can't figure out how to get to Oster," said Christel, after a long silence.

"You certainly can't go yourself, with his house staked out," said Paula.

"I know that, Mama. Neither can Justus, or Dr. Sack, or any of his friends."

"Perhaps I can go," Paula suggested.

"No, it's too dangerous."

"It's simple. I'll go to town first, where I can shake off anyone who might be following me, then come back to Oster's. They're not likely to suspect a woman my age."

That afternoon Paula entered the public library without a backward glance at the man who had been following her. The great lobby looked gaunt and bare without its paintings and sculptures, which lay stacked now in the safety of subterranean vaults. As Paula turned in the door of the "Ancient History" room, she glimpsed the plainclothesman coming up the stairs. Moving quickly past the tables to the door on the other side of the room, she crossed the hall and entered "Biography." The next hall over there was a rest room, where she exchanged the brown hat on her head for the blue one in her shopping bag, then draped the long blue silk shawl over her shoulders. She left the old shopping bag, with the brown hat in it, in the corner. No one was in the hall. She walked to the side entrance, opened her handbag for the guard to check, and quickly left.

Forty-five minutes later, after nudging her way through the weary, impatient crowds at two subway changes and enduring the jerky rides between—a mode of travel she would never get used to—Paula sat in General Oster's sitting room.

Oster seemed genuinely glad to see her. He felt isolated these days, he told her. His wife was staying in the country, and he rarely had the pleasure of a visit from a friend. He was thinner, and his countenance bore signs of frustration and worry. Oster was one of the select few for whom Dietrich had written and given as a present the past Christmas an essay entitled "After Ten Years." "Oster is a brave man," he had told her then, "imprudent sometimes, but I'll take him any day over these all-too-cautious characters."

They came quickly to the matter on both their minds. Oster was delighted at Christel's release, but anxious about the others.

"It's the worst thing that could have happened," he said.

"All is not lost, Herr General, if the truth can be kept from the interrogators. Hans and Dietrich are trying very hard to do that."

"I know. Thank God they seem to have been successful so far."

"But they need your help."

"How can I help? I'm almost as much a prisoner as they."

She told him about Hans's secret message to Christel. "About the piece of paper with the 'O'—Hans thinks you misunderstood him."

"He wanted me to get rid of it."

"No, no. He wanted you to get a message to Christel."

In Oster's eyes there dawned a realization of what had happened. "I thought he said—"

"No, his real intention—seeing they were bound to find it and suspect it—must have been to acknowledge it then and there and—"

"And pretend it was an official document in coded form," he whispered with despair.

"With your signature."

"Oh, my God, I seem to have played the fool." The general covered his face with his hands, but looked up again almost immediately. "We have to remedy it, but how?"

"Hans wants you to acknowledge it as yours—the 'O' as your signature. It's the only way."

"Yes, yes, I see that. But it won't be easy. I've denied it so vigorously." He stared at the wall beyond. "God help us," he said.

"But of course you can do it. You can make up something."

"Canaris will have to back me up."

"He will, won't he?"

"I think so. Yes, yes, he must. I'll have to get a message to him." He must have seen the look on her face, for he quickly added, "Don't worry, I have ways. I'll be careful, very careful."

Paula stood to go, and Oster accompanied her to the door. "My dear lady, you took a chance to come here. We all owe you thanks."

"Oh, but it was simple." Paula described the episode at the library.

"Ah, you're a first-class agent yourself. I should have had you in the Abwehr."

At that she laughed. He bowed and kissed her hand as they said good-bye. She arrived home exhausted, after eluding another sticky follower, this time in the labyrinths under Westkreuz. Soon after supper she went to bed, but despite extreme weariness, she could not sleep. Playing the agent, she decided, was meant for younger people.

"There is a letter too, Herr Doktor," said Corporal Linke, as Dietrich put the contents of the parcel in his bag.

The handwriting was his mother's. "Thank you, Herr Corporal. And your wife? I hope she is better?"

"Much better, thank you. We did as you said with the hot compresses, and it seemed to work wonders."

"I'm glad." Dietrich rested the bag on the table. "If you have the time, could you come by to see me a few minutes sometime this afternoon? It's something rather important."

The face of the guard lit up. "Yes, Herr Doktor, I have the time. I'll be there."

Back in his cell Dietrich read the letter from his mother. It was filled with plans for Eberhard's and Renate's wedding, now only three days away. She closed with the words, "As you said in your letter, it's amazing how both joy and sorrow can have a place side by side in heart and senses."

On the day of the wedding Corporal Linke came as planned and took the wedding sermon Dietrich had written for Eberhard and

Renate and money for a wedding present: a pewter soup tureen Dietrich had seen months earlier in the little antique shop near the Nollendorfplatz. He gave the corporal exact directions.

Weeks passed and turned into months. In the interrogations Roeder was still fulminating against him. If Dietrich did not reveal the names he knew, he would have no other choice but to turn the investigation over to the Gestapo. Dietrich reminded him again and again that since he was a member of the Abwehr, the Wehrmacht alone had jurisdiction over his case.

One morning, after two hours of trying to trick Dietrich into implicating both Canaris and Oster, Roeder said, "I'm sure you know that I have the power to hold anyone for investigation that I deem useful, including wives, like Frau von Dohnanyi and Frau Müller. You, I understand, have a young fiancée."

"You wouldn't dare!"

"You do not tell me what I dare and what I do not dare!" Roeder shouted.

"She is from the Grenzmark and knows nothing of any of this. She hardly knows my family."

"Bring her in," Roeder said to the guard.

The guard opened the door on the far side of the room. Beyond it sat Maria on a bench. Dietrich shuddered from head to foot. He could not move or speak.

With head erect and the steady movement of one who wasted no time in fearful imaginings, Maria came toward him. As she neared, Dietrich recovered enough to take one step to meet her.

"Hello, Dietrich." Maria's voice was calm as she extended her hand toward him. He crushed it within his own as though it were his only link to life. He had not been allowed to hear from her directly, but through his parents she had sent greetings and contributions for the parcel—a week's ration of butter (her own, he was sure), a small bag of coffee beans, and a packet of Turkish cigarettes.

Maria's eyes assured Dietrich that she was undaunted by the poisonous air around them and would not be tempted to say the wrong thing.

"I'm sorry—" Dietrich began.

She shook her head slightly and her lips formed the words, "Are you all right?"

"I'm all right," Dietrich said, "and what of you?" He asked about her work in the Red Cross hospital and about her mother, and found that her mother was with her in Berlin and they were staying the night with his parents. So, Roeder's ploy was just that, a ploy, and would not work. Dietrich wanted to ask about Eberhard but dared not bring him to Roeder's attention. Partly for Roeder's benefit he asked about her cousins on the African front and on the Russian front.

"So far as we know they are safe."

Then Roeder's harsh voice cut in. "That's enough. You may say good-bye to your lady love. If you hope to see her again, you will begin to cooperate."

Dietrich looked into Maria's eyes. Neither of them spoke. In the next moment she was gone.

39

Dietrich walked the sandy paths of Tegel prison's courtyard and savored his first letter from Maria, folded now in his shirt pocket. The letter was a wonderful surprise after the threats of the week before. She told him she had requested permission to visit him at the prison, but it had been denied. She would keep trying, she said. He longed to write her directly, but would have to content himself with answering her letter through his parents.

At the edge of the path Dietrich stooped and observed a colony of ants he had watched for several days, then turned to the alcove of the prison house. He had been following the progress of a pair of titmice as they built their nest among the sullen leaves of a short, spindly tree. Until it was time to go in again, he watched the mother minister to her young.

At the control desk a book, Stifter's *Nachsommer*, was the last item in the parcel. Dietrich tried to appear unconcerned as he opened the cover. His name was underlined. That meant a message was spelled out in dots under specific letters. In his cell again he turned quickly to the plank desk and opened the book to the back. The last page revealed no sign of a dot under any letter. But on the next to the last page a dot appeared under a letter "y." The third page, the letters "o" and "u." The next seven dots at two-page intervals completed the words "yours recvd." The code had worked. His parents had deciphered his message in the book he sent back and knew now the gist of his defense before Roeder. The dots were faint and sometimes he had to search the page twice, but the final message read, "O. now officially acknowledges Rome coding card."

The next week Dietrich received another coded message stating that Canaris backed Oster's statement.

When the interrogations resumed soon afterward, Roeder did not mention the memorandum but focused instead on Operation 7. Dietrich truthfully represented himself as having been only peripherally involved. He admitted responsibility for introducing Schmidhuber to Koechlin in Switzerland to facilitate the travel arrangements. Answering the question of the date of this introduction, Dietrich made a vague reference to the spring of 1942.

"So! Just as I suspected. An attempt to sabotage the government's policy of deportation," Roeder shouted, triumph in his eyes.

Dietrich realized his mistake. "Not at all, your honor. I may be wrong about that date, it was so long ago, and a great deal was happening at the time."

Dietrich carefully prepared for the next session. He professed to having confused two separate operations and stated definitely that the meeting between Schmidhuber and Koechlin had taken place in the early fall of 1941, well before the deportations of the Jews began. After much argument Roeder appeared to accept that new version.

Dietrich left the courtroom that day handcuffed and with a guard on either side. As he turned down the stairs, his parents came into view, their eyes fixed upon him. Dietrich took the steps slowly to prolong the time. At the bottom he said, "Hello, Mama, Papa."

His mother reached out and touched his manacled hand. "Are you all right, my boy?"

"I'm all right, Mother."

"You've been getting all the parcels?" his father asked.

"Yes, Papa. Thanks for everything."

The guards immediately intervened, "This is not allowed. Come along, now."

Dietrich's parents followed him out of the courthouse and from the curb waved to him as the car carried him away.

The long stretches between letters dragged on, dull and joyless. In Tegel there were no sounds of laughter, only the lonely tramp of prisoners in their cells. Toward the end of June Dietrich was writing one morning when Knobloch opened his door and announced that he had a visitor.

Dietrich stood to his feet in astonishment. "Who is it?"

The corporal smiled and handed him a folded piece of paper. Inside was written, "Maria."

Dietrich hurriedly washed his hands and face in the enamel basin and combed his hair, covering the bald spot the best he could. With one hand he buttoned the top button of his shirt and with the other grabbed his only tie from the nail on the wall. It seemed an eternity before he could make a proper knot. He preceded Knobloch out the door, donning his coat as they clattered down the steps.

The visitation cell was near the entrance of the prison house. Through the half-open door he caught a glimpse of Maria. She turned quickly as Dietrich entered and held out both hands to him. He took them in his own and for a moment gazed into her upturned face, until the realization that they were not alone dispelled the enchantment. He turned with her to the plank seat along the wall directly across from the desk of the attending officer. Dietrich still held her hand in his.

"Thanks for all the good things you've been sending in the parcel," he said at last. "But you shouldn't have deprived yourself of your own ration of butter. You need it yourself for your strenuous work. It seems to me an Army hospital is the most difficult service you could have chosen."

"But, of course, it is a privilege."

Again Maria was staying the night with Dietrich's parents and gave him news of them. They no longer trusted the dirt walls of the air raid shelter in the garden, she told him, and had sealed off a room in the basement instead.

"You think it's safe?" he asked.

"I think so. Except for a direct hit. Nothing would be safe then. What about you?"

Dietrich shook his head. "No shelters here. Every prisoner stays in his own cell. Not a very pleasant state of affairs, but there's nothing we can do," Dietrich added, especially for the ears of the officer behind the desk. "I can't believe I'll be here much longer. There's no reason whatever for them to keep me, and after almost three months I think they are beginning to see that." He looked into her eyes. "Each day I think what a hard school God has led you through this past year. And now this—because of me—"

"You mustn't think like that, Dietrich. You can't help it." She smiled, her eyes warm and tender. "I have good news. Mother has given permission to announce our engagement. She and I are making my wedding dress."

Dietrich smiled, unable to speak. Finally, he said, "Remember what Jeremiah told his people to do when things looked darkest?"

"What was that?"

"'Still buy houses and acres in this land.' That's important—not giving up on our world with pious longings for heaven. You're doing what Jeremiah says and it rubs off on me." He smiled. "You know, people who stand with only one foot on earth also stand with only one foot in heaven."

Her smile made a future for them seem possible.

Soon it was time for her to go.

"You must not think I'm pining away in my cell," he said as they stood up. He looked into her eyes. "I have much to be grateful for."

From the door Dietrich watched as Maria walked the long hall to the prison entrance, where she turned and waved good-bye. He rushed ahead of Knobloch up the stairs to his cell. At the barred window he fixed his eyes on the gatehouse until at last she emerged. He watched until she had passed beyond his view.

At noon the next day he took his walk as usual. When he reached the alcove the nest was gone from the tree. He looked down quickly and saw it on the ground, torn asunder by rough hands. Scattered in the dust beside the nest the three baby birds lay dead. Dietrich turned and saw two guards laughing and joking as they walked away. "Damned savages!" he cried aloud. Sickened, he stooped down and lifted one of the birds in his hand. It was still warm, but there was no life there.

In the hot arid cell beneath the prison roof Dietrich searched page after page for dots. Slowly they spelled out the message: "Sack has persuaded Keitel to order treason charges dropped." It seemed a miracle. Roeder had indeed been concentrating lately on Dietrich's Abwehr exemption from service and on his helping other pastors to do the same, rather than on his foreign travels. That seemed to indicate that Roeder was still in the dark as to the true facts of the conspiracy.

At the next interrogation Roeder told Dietrich he would be laying a charge of antimilitary conduct against him. That seemed serious enough in itself, but not insurmountable. Dietrich looked forward, with more confidence than he had felt since his arrest, to a quick trial and possible release.

But the processes of law ground slowly. So Dietrich waited— for the law and for everything else. Letters sometimes took two weeks to reach him. Visits were allowed only once a month, so his parents and Maria had to take turns. He waited for the parcel every Friday. So far, it had arrived without fail.

The prison psyche feeds on rumor, Dietrich learned. The trick was to distinguish between fact and wishful thinking. Thus it was some time before he believed the rumor that the Allies had landed in Sicily and, soon afterward, that Mussolini had fallen. During the first week of August terrifying tales of Allied air attacks on

Hamburg spread through the prison. The whisper went, "If it happened there today it could happen here tomorrow."

One bright moonlit night the expected attack hit Berlin. Dietrich watched from his fourth-floor window as thousands of searchlights streaked the sky. With a steady drone the incoming bombers propelled their high impersonal menace. For a few minutes, time seemed suspended on an icy thread; then suddenly, from every side, pandemonium erupted. Tracer shells fanned upward, incandescent rockets flowered into giant Roman candles, and red and green "Christmas trees"—the British target finders—floated earthward. The bombs began to fall and the antiaircraft batteries rent the dome of the sky. Sometimes they caught their target in coned beams of light, and a plane disintegrated in orange flame. Fires sprang up all over the city. The tallest landmarks defied the odds: church spires everywhere, the Victory Column beside the burned out Reichstag, and, at the edge of Dietrich's line of vision, the radio tower near his home. Air battles raged between the fighters of the Luftwaffe and the giant four-engined bombers. One of the bombers fell on a slant close by the prison. Two engines dropped from the flaming wing, one after the other, before the plane nosed straight down beyond the Borsig iron works.

The explosions came closer and closer to the prison until one came so near that Dietrich fell to the floor and pulled the mattress on top of him. When the explosions receded, he was drawn once more to the window. By the light of battle Dietrich read the time on his watch: 1:10 A.M. Suddenly far to the right, a rain of phosphorus bombs exploded in rapid succession, glowing green along the rooftops of Charlottenburg, where Dietrich's parents lived. Soon the entire area was ablaze. The raid ended shortly thereafter, and Dietrich had to wait out the night for news of his family. The next morning he went with Knobloch to Captain Maetz, the commandant, and asked if he might call to see if they were all right.

"I cannot do that, Herr Bonhoeffer, but I will call them for you." Ever since the captain learned that Dietrich was a relative of his boss he had shown him special favor, even, accompanying him sometimes on his daily walk. Now he called and conveyed to Dietrich the news that they were all safe.

Soon after the raid Captain Maetz appointed Dietrich medical orderly for his section. The new appointment meant many hours in the sick bay. There he played chess with the attendants and listened to the radio, even the BBC, which the NCOs heard regularly with an openness that Dietrich found astonishing. During the next week there were two raids, and Dietrich spent the time attending hysterical prisoners.

One day in September the coded message from Dietrich's parents said, "Promising new plans. K. and R. involved." At their next visit Dietrich noticed that the strain of the past five months was beginning to show—tension around his mother's eyes and deepening lines at the corners of her mouth.

"They say war years count double," she said. "I have the feeling they count fourfold."

She had lost weight and, for the first time in Dietrich's memory, the bone structure of her face was clearly discernible beneath the smooth fair skin. His father also looked tired and harassed. They were at last staying the nights with Christel at Sakrow and told Dietrich that Renate and Eberhard were there too, because of bomb damage to their new flat. The children of the family were in the country.

"But it's you I worry about in these air raids," Dietrich's mother continued. "Ah me! When will it ever end?" She stroked the worn leather handbag in her lap.

As they were leaving his mother said, almost as an afterthought, "Then there's poor Renate."

"Poor Renate? What's wrong?"

"Well, with Eberhard called up—and a baby on the way."

"Called up? When did that happen? Why didn't you tell me that before now?" Dietrich had heard the word "baby," but the icy "called up" froze it out.

"I'm sorry, we didn't think. There was so much."

The presence of the attendant cut off the questions that scrambled for answers. The specter of the Russian front, where Dietrich already had lost thirty of his seminarians, came immediately to his mind. "Where is he assigned?"

"Nowhere yet. It will be another two weeks, he said."

"I hope—" Dietrich could not say in front of the guard that he hoped the family somehow would be able to keep him out of Russia.

"We hope so, too," said his mother. As they left, she added, "Renate is fine. The baby is due in February. In everything God works for good with those who love him. Remember that."

40

In their bombed-out flat Eberhard and Renate surveyed the damaged rooms that had been their home in Berlin for a few short months. Only the piano was left. All their other possessions were scattered wherever someone had room for them. Renate walked to the piano, lifted the flannel cover, and ran her fingers over the keys. "They are beginning to stick. It's the dampness. Eberhard, we have to get it moved out of here." They were holding the piano in trust for a Jewish acquaintance who had fled the country, and Renate took the care of it seriously.

"We will, sweetheart, as soon as possible." But that would not be easy. The few trucks still in the city had orders backed up for weeks. "We'd better go. We've done all we can for now."

"I suppose so."

"Things will get better soon," Eberhard assured her.

"But they'll get worse first. They're bound to, you know." Renate brushed a speck from the collar of his overcoat. "They'll send you far off somewhere and you won't be here when the baby comes."

Eberhard wished he had some definite word that would comfort her. Justus Delbrück, still in the Abwehr, was trying to get him assigned to a military intelligence unit in Italy. But that took time.

"Let's not think of that now," he said. "We have two weeks. Let's enjoy them."

At the end of the first week Eberhard and Renate came to the Schleichers on the Marienburger Allee for a few nights, and the Bonhoeffer grandparents returned to their house next door. The first night one of the worst raids yet caught them all by surprise. In the crowded basement shelter Rüdiger read Goethe to the family until the din overhead became so intense and the bombs so shook the foundations of the house that he blew out the lamp.

Suddenly, there was a deafening crash and the whole house shuddered. Falling plaster and broken glass peppered the ceiling above their heads.

Renate's mother was the first to come out of the hypnotic state into which the brush with death had plunged them all. "Mama and Papa! It may have hit them! They're alone over there!" She groped her way to the door.

Rüdiger turned on his flashlight. "Wait, Ursel. You stay here. I'll see about it."

He came back almost immediately. "The house still stands. It's bright as day out there, with all the flares. We'd better not go out yet."

After the all-clear they found the grandparents unhurt. The bomb, which apparently struck one of the tall pines and exploded above the ground, had damaged the roofs of both houses and broken most of the windows facing the garden. By daylight it became clear that the houses needed extensive repairs. They would have to go back to Christel's in Sakrow.

Another severe raid followed in Berlin two nights later. Christel, as usual, went the next morning to the prison in Moabit to see if Hans was safe. Before long she returned to Sakrow with long-dreaded news. Hans's cell had been struck by incendiary bombs. He was badly injured.

"Did you see him?" her father asked.

"No, they wouldn't let me."

"What kind of injury? Did they tell you?"

"A head injury. No details. He's in the sick bay, they said. But, Papa, he'll die there. We have to get him to a hospital."

"I'll go to Dr. Sack. Eberhard can drive me," her father told her.

"I'll go, too."

"No, you must stay here."

"I want to go, Papa."

Gently Christel's father reasoned with her. "My dear, you should not be seen in the Bendlerstrasse. I don't know if we can get him out, but success will depend on how quietly it can be done. If Roeder gets wind of it, there will be no chance. We'll try to move him to Sauerbruch's clinic in the Charité. Then you can see him."

When Christel was calm again, Eberhard and Dr. Bonhoeffer left. The old Horsch was the only car remaining in the family, a privilege for doctors only. Over and again it was necessary to detour around rubble-clogged streets. But finally they arrived at the Army Headquarters on the Bendlerstrasse, around the corner from the Abwehr. Eberhard waited in the car, while the doctor went inside.

It was an hour before he returned. "An Army ambulance will move him to the Charité," he said, as he closed the car door. "We'll go there and wait."

Although the prison was only a block from the Charité, it was an hour and a half before Eberhard and Dr. Bonhoeffer heard the ambulance arrive. From the door of Dr. Sauerbruch's office Eberhard watched as the stretcher-bearers carried Hans down the hall. His face was pale and he showed no response to anything around him. Dr. Bonhoeffer followed with Sauerbruch, his old friend and colleague, who had agreed to take personal charge of the patient.

After three hours, Dr. Bonhoeffer returned and hurried Eberhard to the car. "Christel was right, he would have died in that prison," he said as they drove away. "It's a brain embolism. After we worked on him a while, I'm thankful to say, he regained consciousness and recognized me. I think he will make it. Sauerbruch is excellent."

Two days later while Eberhard and the Bonhoeffers were replacing window panes on the veranda, Christel arrived from a visit to the hospital to see Hans. Her face was pale and her eyes dark and frightened. "Roeder is trying to get Hans away," she burst out. "He came this morning and demanded that Sauerbruch turn him over."

The doctor turned from the window. "Surely Sauerbruch didn't do that, did he?"

"No, but Roeder will try again. I know he will. Hans is his prize fish. He'll do anything to keep him in his net." With her hands in her coat pockets, Christel walked up and down the veranda. "Dietrich's trial will have to be postponed. A separate trial would be dangerous."

"You really think so?" her mother asked. "It's such a trivial charge."

"We can't be sure they would limit it to that. There's no telling what they might drag in. Dietrich doesn't know the ropes like Hans, and he might be tricked into saying the wrong thing."

"He's nobody's fool."

"I know that, Mama. But all the intricacies at the Abwehr are so impossible. If he loosed the wrong thread, the whole thing could unravel. Even one string left hanging—the Gestapo would pounce on it like a cat on a ball of yarn. We can't risk it. Not as long as Hans is in the Charité, and I want him to stay there as long as possible. Maybe before then the coup—"

"Who's going to tell Dietrich?" Frau Bonhoeffer asked.

"Does it matter?"

"Christel, he's going to be terribly disappointed. I would hate to tell him."

Eberhard's eyes met those of Christel's father, who paused with a piece of broken glass in his gloved hand but said nothing. Eberhard continued his work in silence.

"Then let the lawyers do it," said Christel.

"That doesn't seem right," said Frau Bonhoeffer.

"Certainly it is. They'll know better how to explain it."

"That's true, Paula," said Dr. Bonhoeffer. "I think we must let them explain it."

While Hans remained under Dr. Sauerbruch's care Christel was able to visit him. One day she told Eberhard that Hans was worried about his "Chronicles" and other Resistance papers hidden in the cellar of the Army Headquarters in Zossen.

"He begged me to prevail on General Beck to have them destroyed," said Christel. "Beck answered that they must be kept, 'to prove to the world that we did not merely start acting when everything was lost, but in those early days, when the world still believed in Germany's military victories.' Those were his words."

"That seems a valid reason," said Eberhard.

"To some people, maybe. But to Hans every sheet of paper there constitutes a death sentence." Christel closed her eyes and with a shake of her head added, "Of course, if they ever found those papers, it would be not just Hans, but Beck too, and all the others before it was over. Beck knows that." She sighed in resignation and said no more.

Justus Delbrück succeeded in getting Eberhard assigned to an Abwehr support unit in northern Italy—not as an agent, but as a clerk, a private in one of the command posts. One day while Eberhard waited for orders he received a long letter from Dietrich, brought in person by one of the prison guards, Corporal Knobloch. The corporal had agreed to be the go-between for a clandestine correspondence between them and gave the address of his brother's bakery in Wedding as the pickup and delivery point. It was Eberhard's first direct word from Dietrich. On the envelope were the words: "Under two eyes." This letter was more candid about his actual situation than the ones addressed to his parents. Still, there was a tranquil tone that relieved some of Eberhard's anxiety. Two days later he received long sought permission to visit Dietrich.

In the visitor's cell at Tegel there was one desk and two straight chairs. Eberhard could not sit still and kept going back and forth to the door. Several times he heard the clatter of footsteps on the steel stairs, and at last he saw Dietrich coming down the long hall, followed by the guard.

"Well, so it did come off, at last," said Dietrich, with a firm handshake. He introduced Eberhard to the guard, Corporal Linke, whom Dietrich referred to as his trusted friend. The guard shut the door and locked it behind them. Dietrich was smiling broadly, but he looked much thinner in his brown tweed trousers, hanging in loose folds from a belt pulled notches tighter.

"How can we be alone in the cell?" Eberhard asked.

"You're a special case," said Dietrich, smiling. "Actually, I insisted. I knew we had to talk. Captain Maetz does what he can for me." He pulled the chair from behind the desk, offered it to Eberhard, and inquired about Renate and the rest of the family. Then, leaning back against the desk, he said, "The spring of my intellectual life was about to dry up. Your letter brought the first drops of water for a long, long time. That may sound like an exaggeration—"

"No. I felt the same with yours."

Dietrich smiled and questioned Eberhard for a time about army life. "Well, so now it's northern Italy?" he asked.

"Justus thinks so."

"Good. But prepare yourself for very cold days. And learn Italian properly. You can do it in eight weeks."

Eberhard laughed. "You may have learned it in eight weeks."

"You can too. It's chiefly a matter of a good ear, and you have that." He asked about Hans and seemed relieved to hear that he was still in Sauerbruch's hospital. When Eberhard told of Hans's worry about the "Chronicles" and Beck's decision, Dietrich said quickly, "Yes, Hans should be worried."

"You think so?" Eberhard asked. "Who knows the 'Chronicles' are there? I didn't know it."

"Just one or two others besides Oster and Beck."

"Who has a key to that file?"

"No one at Zossen. At least, not six months ago." Dietrich sighed. "Well, there's nothing we can do about it. But I have to admit, I've been uneasy too. I keep hoping—. The dots told me there was a new plan? Is that true?"

"There was one, but an Allied bomb destroyed the equipment— a new assault pack or so—that Hitler was to inspect. I don't know

how soon they'll try again. Klaus is pretty tight-lipped about it."
Eberhard sensed how much Dietrich's hopes hung upon another
coup and added, "But they'll keep trying. You can be sure of it."
Eberhard did not have many details, but told Dietrich about the
young officer, Colonel Count von Stauffenburg, who had taken
over the reins of the Resistance and seemed determined to accomplish the task.

Dietrich fell silent for a time, then said, "It appears I won't be
out of here by Christmas."

"Who says so?"

"The lawyers. I have a feeling the family knows it and doesn't
dare tell me. I wonder why. Do they think I'm so easily upset?"

"I don't think—"

"Or that it's kinder to lull me from day to day with empty
hopes? The English have a suitable word for this sort of thing—
'tantalizing.'" Dietrich stood straight and walked around the desk.
"Eberhard, tell me what's going on."

"They think your trial should be held in conjunction with
Hans's."

"I know that, but why?"

"The fear that the Gestapo might bring up something new."

"And I couldn't handle it?"

"Well, not exactly."

"What else? With God's help, I think I could handle most anything they might throw at me. But I guess they don't give me that
much credit. Besides that—oh, well." Dietrich sighed. "I sometimes think enemies are less dangerous than good friends." He
threw himself down in the straight chair. "Well, we'll see what
happens. The lawyers think it will be February now. I can wait that
long. I have no choice." Dietrich stared straight ahead in silence,
then turned to Eberhard. "I'm going on and on about my problems, when it is you who will soon be facing a bad situation."

Dietrich gave Eberhard addresses of people he knew in the Vatican and Bell's address in England, "in case you're ever captured by
the Allies. But we'll celebrate Easter again in peace," Dietrich said
in a voice that, despite his obvious efforts to sound cheerful, be-

trayed his anxiety. "Why does Old Testament law never punish anyone by depriving him of his freedom?"

Eberhard had never thought of that before and had to admit it.

Predictably the topic turned to Maria and Dietrich's wonder that she wanted to marry him. "Can you believe that since our engagement we haven't spent even an hour alone together. When her short visits end, we're torn apart again, yet she bears up with such self-control. I don't know why she has to put up with so much hardship. Do you think I'm asking too much of her?"

"No, Dietrich, no. I don't think so."

They heard the key turn in the lock. Eberhard looked at his watch—an hour and a half had already passed.

They both stood up and Dietrich said, "I haven't for a moment regretted coming back in 1939—nor any of the consequences, whatever they may be. I wanted you to know that." He shook Eberhard's hand. "Read Proverbs 18:24 when you get home. Don't forget it."

Back in Sakrow Eberhard looked up the verse first thing. It read: "There are friends who pretend to be friends, but there is a friend who sticks closer than a brother."

41

The young NCO studied the board, then looked up questioningly. Dietrich remained noncommittal. The fellow would never learn chess if he did not figure it out for himself. The other NCO, an older man named Schmidt, sat on the stool beside the examining table and silently watched the game.

In the passageway outside the door a gruff voice complained, "Shut up, crybaby, I've heard enough of your whining. You're here now. Get inside."

As Dietrich turned, a broad-shouldered guard shoved and kicked a man through the door. The prisoner, pale, disheveled, and clutching his side in pain, staggered to the table, where the NCOs came to his aid. Swept by an uncontrollable fury, Dietrich stood and faced the guard. "Have you been ordered so to mistreat a defenseless man, or is it your own practice?"

The guard let drop his jaw, but did not answer.

"I should think your duty would be to help a man in obvious pain, not make it worse."

The guard muttered something indistinguishable, which ended with a peevish, "I brought him, didn't I?" and left.

It turned out that the prisoner had acute appendicitis and had to be taken to the military hospital. When it was all over and the young NCO took Dietrich back to his cell, he stood for a moment at the door and said, "I'm glad you told him off, the bully." Then he added, "Pray for us, Pastor, that we may have no alert tonight."

Dietrich smiled and said gently, "I will pray that God will be with us whatever happens."

The young man seemed assured and turned back downstairs. A year ago such deference might have engendered in Dietrich the old feelings of disdain. Now the demons were gone. It was as if they recognized that he was no longer their target. His hands, once strong and active, were bound. He belonged to a band of men with no ground under their feet. There came to him a vision of a tow-haired boy in the corner of the garden, hiding a laurel wreath under dry leaves. Now, at last, in his prison cell, Dietrich could forgive that boy and feel free to bring the laurel wreath from its hiding place.

Maria came to visit the day before Christmas with a great Christmas tree. Dietrich laughed and said if he stood up throughout the season, he might get the tree in his cell. In the end they had set it up in the guardroom. As a present she gave Dietrich her father's wristwatch. That affected him deeply and saddened him, too, because he could not give her anything.

"I want to give you a ring, but not until I am free again and can give it to you myself," Dietrich told her.

"Of course." She understood.

When Maria was gone and darkness descended, Dietrich stretched out on the cot and listened to the night voices of the prison—the uneasy creak of plank beds, the sighs, the chains, the brisk step of the guards, their shouts, the evil howl of dogs within the compound. From beyond the prison wall came the sound of singing in the street, and distant secret laughter. In his longing for God Dietrich crossed himself, something he had never done before.

He tried to "listen" to a Paul Gerhardt hymn, with the lines, "Thou art a Spirit of joy" and "Grant us joyfulness and strength." With deliberate effort he had trained himself over the months to concentrate so intently that he could recall whole sections and then whole pieces of music. In that silent repertoire was the Bach B Minor Mass, which he could "hear" almost in its entirety. He could manage some portions of "The Art of the Fugue." The very fact that it was a fragment gave him hope. He told himself that if his life—even here, in Tegel—could be but the remotest reflection of such a fragment, he would not bemoan it but rejoice in it.

It occurred to him that he might write of some of his deep, abiding questions in letters to Eberhard and get the feedback he needed. That idea gave new courage for his work. He made it a New Year's resolution for 1944.

Late one moonless January night, the three up and down shrieks of the early warning went off. Soon after came the sound of running feet, as the prison staff hurried out to the shelter, leaving the prisoners locked in their unlighted cells.

Dietrich stood on the stool beside the window and watched as the pathfinders dropped their "Christmas trees" to mark the targets for incoming bombers—the green one beyond the Borsig works, the red to the west of the airfield. He waited for the other two to make the four corners of the "carpet," but they did not appear. Then he realized the other two markers must be to the north and east, beyond his view. That would put Tegel in the middle of the "carpet"!

The key turned in Dietrich's door and the young NCO from the sick bay whispered, "Come quickly, Herr Pastor. We'll need you."

As they entered the infirmary the crescendo of the approaching planes reached a deep-throated rumble. The first bombs shattered all the windows and ripped loose the blackout curtains.

"Get the lights!" someone yelled. In the dark Dietrich and Schmidt tried to replace the curtains, but the whistle of more high-explosive bombs drove them to the floor. Dietrich shielded his head with his hands as bottles and medical supplies from the cupboards crashed down. The orderly, Hemplemann, crouching beside him in the dust and debris, moaned over and over, "Oh, God! Oh, God!" Normally Hemplemann was flippant, sometimes cynical. Dietrich could not bring himself to offer a word of Christian comfort now. It seemed wrong to force religion down someone's throat at such a time. "It will be over in ten minutes," Dietrich assured him.

The next bomb demolished the prison wall a few yards away and rocked the building. From their locked cells the prisoners began to scream and beat wildly on their doors.

Dietrich got to his feet. "We must help them," he said. "Find the first-aid kits."

They rummaged among the debris until they found them. Then Schmidt sent the NCO and Hemplemann along one passage, while he and Dietrich took the other. The bombs kept falling, and in the general tumult it was impossible to tell where all the wounded were. Not until the all-clear could they bring the most severely wounded to the sick bay for treatment. It was two-thirty when they finished all the bandaging. Back in his cell, Dietrich collapsed on his cot and fell immediately into a sound sleep.

The next day he wrote a poem and called it "Who Am I?"

Who am I? They often tell me
I step from my cell's confinement
calmly, cheerfully, firmly,
like a squire from his country-house.

Who am I? They often tell me
I talk to my warders freely and friendly and clearly,
as though it were mine to command.
Who am I? They also tell me

I bear the days of misfortune
equably, smilingly, proudly,
like one accustomed to win.

Am I then really all that which other men tell of?
Or am I only what I know of myself,
restless and longing and sick, like a bird in a cage,
struggling for breath, as though hands were compressing my throat,
yearning for colors, for flowers, for the voices of birds,
thirsting for words of kindness, for neighborliness,
trembling with anger at despotisms and petty humiliation,
tossing in expectation of great events,
powerlessly trembling for friends at an infinite distance,
weary and empty at praying, at thinking, at making,
faint, and ready to say farewell to it all?

Who am I? This or the other?
Am I one person today, and tomorrow another?
Am I both at once? A hypocrite before others,
and before myself a contemptibly woebegone weakling?
Or is something within me still like a beaten army,
fleeing in disorder from victory already achieved?

Who am I? They mock me, these lonely questions of mine.
Whoever I am, thou knowest, O God, I am thine.

In the sick bay the NCOs tuned in the BBC at ten o'clock. The British announcer spoke in emotionless tones: "The Allies have landed at Anzio, south of Rome. A firm beachhead has been established and the drive inland begun." No one spoke, but the anxiety was unmistakable. Dietrich thought instantly of Eberhard, who was north of Rome. But how long before he would be in the middle of the fighting?

That night Dietrich found himself praying over and over again for God to keep Eberhard safe. He recalled a verse from Psalm 50: "Call upon me in the day of trouble; I will deliver you, and you shall glorify me."

On her next visit Maria told Dietrich the exciting news: Eberhard and Renate had a baby boy on February 3 in Sakrow, the day before Dietrich's birthday. The child's name—Dietrich. That night

Dietrich wrote to Eberhard in Italy, "You realize you've promoted me to the third generation."

The weeks dragged by. Maria wrote to Dietrich that his parents were in Pätzig. They had finally accepted her mother's invitation. A week later another note came from her. She had just arrived in Berlin from Pätzig and would visit him in Tegel the next afternoon. Dietrich put out his flag and paced up and down the cell until Corporal Knobloch appeared. In a manner as offhand as he could make it, Dietrich explained what he wanted. Yes, Knobloch said with a smile, he thought he could arrange for the Herr Doktor to see the Fräulein Maria unattended.

The door closed behind them. The key turned in the lock. For the first time since their engagement Dietrich and Maria were alone. Neither of them moved, then Dietrich opened his arms and she came into them. He pressed his face into her soft brown hair. Gone was the dank and stifling air of the gray enclosure. From her he breathed the sun-warmed fragrance of Klein-Krossin and all the free and open places dear to him. The pain that accompanied most of his waking hours gently loosened. Strength and joy returned.

They sat down side by side. Dietrich, always adept with words, could find no word now for what he wanted to say. He held her hand, turned it in his own, and lifted it to his lips.

"What an engagement ours has been," he said at last. "Who could imagine it?"

"Who, indeed?"

"It has been hard for you. I wish it could have been different. I wanted—I should have spoken sooner."

"Yes, and to me, maybe?" She smiled. "I wouldn't have minded hearing about it first."

"But you must have known."

"How could I? You gave me no signals. None of the kind I'm used to."

He wondered what kind those were, but did not ask. "The truth is, I didn't know how to handle it."

"Now, Dietrich—"

"No, I'm not exactly a ladies' man, you know. Oh, there were girl friends—a few—in high school. And later, only one." He told her a little about Elenore.

"It sounds like she waited for you a long time. Did you leave her in the lurch?"

"No, nothing like that."

"I bet—"

"No. She married soon afterward."

The conversation was not going at all as he had planned. "You said you went to Pätzig. I hope you found your mother well."

"Yes. And your parents too." She told how she and her mother had made a celebration for his father's birthday. Dietrich knew how much joy such a spontaneous act of friendship must have brought his parents.

"Was she pretty?" Maria asked suddenly.

"Who?"

"Elenore."

"Yes. She was pretty."

"And she could discuss theology with you."

"Well, yes—" he said.

"I'm reading your book."

"Are you? Which one?"

"*Sanctorum Communio.*"

"Oh, that one. What do you think of it?"

"The truth is I don't understand much of it," Maria answered.

He laughed. "My darling, it's not you. It was my first work; I thought I had to use all that theological verbiage. You might read *The Cost of Discipleship*. But, then, maybe you should wait until we can read it together, you and I, and talk about it."

"It won't be much longer, will it?"

"I can't honestly say. They keep postponing the trial. These jurists are incapable of sober judgment and action. It's out of their range."

"But you won't let it get you down."

He shrugged. "Oh, I'm all right. One gradually becomes part of the furniture."

"Do you get enough to eat? You look thinner."

"Not always," he admitted. He did not tell her how hungry he actually was most days.

She told him she had brought some of the food from his father's birthday dinner and left it for him at the control desk.

They discussed future plans and agreed to marry immediately after his release if there was time before his call-up. Dietrich asked all about the Berneuchen wedding tradition. A nuptial mass in the morning, she told him, followed by the wedding breakfast, then at noonday the bridal procession back across the lawn to the church for the wedding; again in the evening the blessing for the journey. Dietrich visualized their wedding in the beautifully painted little church her father had built in Pätzig.

"I hope it will be soon," she said, "before the Russians get there."

"They seem to be on the move. If it comes to it, we could be married in Friedrichsbrunn."

"But I hope—maybe it won't be much longer," she said.

Maria stood up and laid her folded coat over the telephone, then moved with him as far away from it as the small room would allow. In a low voice she told Dietrich about a distant cousin who was the latest to offer his life in an assassination attempt. The father, Ewald von Kleist, was one of the conspirators. Dietrich often had visited him on his estate in Further Pomerania.

"But he failed, Hitler did not show." She sighed. "That's been the story, hasn't it?"

"Yes. But we mustn't give up hope," Dietrich said.

"There are new plans, your father says."

"I know. So we'll keep hoping." They were talking fast, almost in whispers.

The time had come, the inevitable good-bye. He took her hands and gazed into her eyes, as if by sheer power of will he could defy the passage of time. With a groan he clasped her to him. He knew not what the future held for him; but here, now, she was warm and real, and he steadfastly refused to know anything else. To him Maria lifted her face, fresh and open as a flower. Dietrich studied every line to stamp its lineaments indelibly upon his memory. His mouth brushed her eyelids, a tender seal of his devotion, and at last he kissed her lips.

The key turned in the lock.

He kissed her again quickly, before the guard could open the door.

"I'll come again soon," she whispered, and was gone.

Within a week a message came from Sack that Dietrich should no longer expect the trial. The theory was that it might do more harm than good; it could draw the attention of the Gestapo, who were already too much interested. Besides, Josef Müller—who had conducted his own trial successfully, but had not won release after all—was now locked up in Sachenhausen. Hans von Dohnanyi, back now in prison, was still physically unable to stand trial. It was best, Sack said, to let the case "run out of steam."

The news was hard to take. In the end Dietrich turned to the theological questions that had been stirring and began to write them in letters to Eberhard. He worked steadily through the months of May and June, with frequent interruptions from daylight air attacks. The flow of work stopped momentarily when he heard on the BBC that the Allies had landed in Normandy. That and the Allies' rapid advance through Italy brought a mixture of hope and anxiety. In late June Dietrich received a surprise visit from his Uncle Paul. Paul von Hase was now working with the coup planners and said that, as commandant of Berlin, he would be in charge of securing and sealing off the government buildings. The Home Replacement Army would supply the troops. It would be soon.

Then one evening in July in the sick bay, the music on the radio broke off and an announcer spoke: "There has been an assassination attempt on the life of the Führer, but he is not seriously injured. I repeat, he is not seriously injured. No details are available at present."

Dietrich almost dropped the flask into which he was pouring hydrogen peroxide.

"My God, did you hear that?" said Schmidt.

"I can't believe it," said Hempelmann, "someone tried to kill Hitler? I can't believe it. Who would do such a thing?"

"Criminals, that's what," said Schmidt, "nothing else. It's a foul act to stab him in the back like that."

"But he's all right. That's what the announcer said. He's not hurt bad, he said. Isn't that right, Herr Doktor?"

"That's what he said." Dietrich spoke without knowing what he was saying. He set the flask down automatically with the vague feeling that it would break in pieces if he held onto it. By the round clock on the wall it was 6:38 P.M.

The same announcement came every fifteen or twenty minutes until nine o'clock, when the announcer ended with the promise that the Führer himself would speak to the nation shortly. It was 1:00 A.M. before the raspy voice of the dictator came over the airways.

My German comrades,

If I speak to you today it is first in order that you should hear my voice and should know that I am unhurt and well, and secondly, that you should know of a crime unparalleled in German history.

A very small clique of ambitious, irresponsible and, at the same time, senseless and stupid officers have concocted a plot to eliminate me and, with me, the staff of the High Command of the Wehrmacht.

The bomb, planted by Colonel Count Stauffenberg, exploded two meters to the right of me. It seriously wounded a number of my true and loyal collaborators, one of whom has died. I myself am entirely unhurt, aside from some very minor scratches, bruises and burns. I regard this as a confirmation of the task imposed upon me by Providence . . .

The circle of these usurpers is very small and has nothing in common with the spirit of the German Wehrmacht and, above all, none with the German people. It is a gang of criminal elements which will be destroyed without mercy.

When the speech ended, Dietrich looked at the calendar. The day was July 20, 1944.

42

Dietrich laid down his pen. The *Losungen*, which Eberhard had given him at Christmas, lay open at the place: "The Lord is my shepherd, I shall not want" and "I am the good shepherd; I know my own and my own know me." He turned back the page to the reading for the day before, the fatal day of which he still knew nothing, except that the plot had failed disastrously: "Some boast of chariots, and some of horses; but we boast of the name of the Lord our God" and "If God be for us, who can be against us?"

Dietrich had awakened from a meager sleep with a sense of urgency; first of all, to write to Eberhard while he still had Knobloch to send mail secretly for him; then to begin putting his accumulated papers and books in order to give to his parents for safekeeping before the Gestapo came for him. He turned back to the letter, in which he was trying to sum up what he had wanted to say to Eberhard in his last few letters.

> I'm still discovering right up to this moment, that it is only by living completely in this world that we learn to have faith. We must completely abandon any attempt to make something of ourselves, whether it be a saint, or a converted sinner, or a churchman (a so-called priestly type!), a righteous man or an unrighteous one, a sick man or a healthy one. By this-worldliness I mean living unreservedly in life's duties, problems, successes and failures, experiences and perplexities. In so doing we throw ourselves completely into the arms of God, taking seriously, not our own sufferings, but those of God in the world—watching with Christ in Gethsemane. That, I think, is faith; that is *metanoia;* and that is how one becomes a man and a Christian (cf. Jer. 45!). How can success make us arrogant, or failure lead us astray, when we share in God's sufferings through a life of this kind?
>
> I think you see what I mean, even though I put it so briefly. I am glad to have been able to learn this, and I know I've been able to do so only along the road that I've traveled.

He quickly finished the letter and spent the rest of the morning and part of the afternoon going through his papers, listening all the while for Knobloch to turn the key in the lock. As he flipped through some of his books his eye fell on a sentence from Jeremias Gotthelf: "While the servant of God may be held in bonds and chains, the Word of God, which proceeded from his mouth, remains free. Even when death closes his mouth, the Word he proclaimed remains free and alive. Death has no power over that; it cannot be locked up in the grave."

Comforted, he closed the book and gathered together into one packet the various fragments he had written for his *Ethics*. There would be no time now to finish them or assemble them with the other chapters in his room at home, some of which were also incomplete. He would trust Eberhard to put them into some kind of order. The same with the fragmentary probings he had written in his recent letters to Eberhard. He had hoped to develop all those thoughts into a unified work. Now he gave them over to God.

In the evening Knobloch arrived. He had waited, he said, to find out as much as possible about what had happened. "I kept finding excuses to stay around the captain's office," Knobloch said. "He was getting calls from all over—Alexanderplatz and Unter-den-Linden. It's not just the little 'clique' of military men Hitler mentioned. They're arresting top people." The corporal stared incredulously. He seemed in no hurry to continue.

Dietrich suppressed his impatience. "Their names? Do you know?"

"I wouldn't a' believed it. The city commandant himself—" Knobloch broke off. "I'm sorry, Herr Doktor. They got him."

"I see."

"Captain Maetz couldn't believe it. He kept saying, 'That bastard!' Rumors are flying wild all over. Nobody knows what happened. Late in the night, in the Bendlerstrasse, they say, there was a quick trial—a court-martial—somebody said it was the ringleaders. They shot 'em right afterward in the courtyard. Firing squad. Could be rumors, though. Nobody knows anything for sure."

"Did they tell the names? Of these ringleaders?"

"Count Stauffenberg, General Beck, General Olbricht. There

were some more, but I can't remember." Knobloch looked around the cell at the stacks of papers and books.

"Could you get some boxes for me, Herr Corporal," said Dietrich, seeing as he spoke the pale, sensitive face of General Beck. "I need to pack these things up to give to my parents."

"You don't think they're comin' after you, do you?"

"One never knows." Dietrich removed his gold signet ring with the Bonhoeffer coat of arms, a lion with a beanstalk in his paw, and held it out to the corporal. "In any case, I want you to have this." Knobloch looked astonished. "Here, it is yours."

Knobloch held it in his palm and looked at it with awe. "I'll take care of it for you."

"No, my friend, it is yours. Put it on your finger."

The corporal put it on and gazed at it on his finger. "I never had anything so costly! But I won't wear it in the prison." He took it off and put it in his pocket, then removed his cap and ran his fingers through his curly hair. "You know, it wouldn't be too hard for you to get out'a here."

"How do you mean?"

"Escape. You could do it. I'd help you."

"You would do that?" Dietrich asked.

"Sure I would."

"You would be taking quite a chance, wouldn't you?"

"Everything's takin' a chance these days. If it's worth anything, that is." Knobloch's eyes shone with modest devotion.

Dietrich opened the cover of a book lying on the desk and stared unseeing at the title page. At last, he looked up. "I'm very grateful, Herr Knobloch, that you would think of that—that you would offer to take such a risk for me. I think, however, we should wait and see. They may not be able to prove anything against me, or even suspect anything. After all, I've been locked up in here all this time."

"But we could be thinking about it and making some plans, couldn't we, just in case?"

"Yes, I suppose we could do that."

It seemed to be daylight behind the closed curtains. Paula realized she must have slept some after all. Awake now, the happenings of the night before flooded back to her mind.

Following Hitler's speech Paula and Karl had stayed up and listened for Klaus to come and tell them what had happened. At last he arrived at 2:30 A.M., but had known little more than they. His colleague, Otto John, had called Klaus in his office at five o'clock in the afternoon and said Hitler was dead. John had been summoned to the Bendlerstrasse, where the conspirators were in the process of taking control of the government. John said he would keep in touch by telephone.

"I waited," Klaus had said, "but John didn't call back. From my window I saw our troops cordon off the government sector. Everything seemed fine. Then came the claims on the radio that Hitler was not dead, and I realized that our people did not have control of the broadcast centers. In the street there was a lot of milling around and confusion. Finally, about nine o'clock, I noticed SS units among the troops. There was no shooting—no resistance that I could tell. But I knew something was terribly wrong. About that time an announcement came on the radio that Hitler was going to speak to the nation."

Karl had cut off Klaus's bitter speculation about what had gone wrong and said they should all go to bed, it did no good to speculate.

Now Paula turned and saw that it was 7:30 and Karl was not in his bed. At the same moment she heard a car door slam out front. She sprang up, grabbed her robe, and ran down the hall to the front window. It was the same black car that had taken Dietrich away. Coming through the gate was the SS officer who had come with Roeder that day. She had seen him at the War Court and knew he must be the one Dietrich called Sonderegger. Her first thought was that he had come for Karl.

She slipped quickly down the steps and stopped just before the landing. Karl had opened the door. Their voices were near and distinct. She leaned against the wall out of sight.

"Do you know Hans von Dohnanyi?" the strange dark voice asked.

"He is my son-in-law," Karl replied.

"Ah, yes. Then you know of his connection with General Oster."

"General Oster?"

"General Hans Oster."

"I don't know General Hans Oster."

"Of the Abwehr? Dohnanyi worked with him, did he not?"

"My son-in-law did not discuss his work with me."

"Not at all? Come, Herr Professor!"

"That was sensitive intelligence work for the military. I never would have questioned him about it."

There was a pause. "Then perhaps your daughter will be able to help me. She lives in Sakrow, I believe?"

"Yes."

"I'll go there. Good day, Herr Professor."

"Good day."

The door closed and for a moment all was quiet. Then Karl said, without raising his voice, "You can come out now. He's gone."

Paula turned onto the landing and ran down the last steps into his arms. "Oh, Karl," she said with a shudder, "I thought he had come for you."

"I knew you would think that. I heard you run down the hall." He kissed her gently. "Now, I must call Christel."

"Be careful."

"Yes."

That afternoon Christel came and told Karl and Paula how Sonderegger had tried to dig information from her about Oster, but she had pretended to know nothing.

During the next week Klaus and Rüdiger reported to them the arrests of many men connected with the conspiracy, beginning with Admiral Canaris and General Oster. The newspapers named only a select few, vilified as the lowest of traitors. They would be tried in the People's Court and dealt with as such traitors deserved.

Among them were Paul von Hase and General von Witzleben. Family members were arrested too in accordance with Hitler's edict against the "kith and kin" of the traitors. Paul von Hase's wife, Deta, was among them.

Visits to Hans were denied Christel; but Karl, as a doctor, was allowed to see him. Karl reported him in a lamentable condition, paralyzed from the diphtheria and unable to walk. The self-infection with diphtheria had been the lesser of two evils—it had been either that or the Gestapo tormentors—but it seemed a terrible price to pay. Paula had said so earlier, when in a smuggled letter Hans asked for the diphtheria culture and Karl provided it. Christel had hidden it in a food parcel. "You don't know the Gestapo's methods, Mama," Christel had said. "It's just as well not to know." That had infuriated Paula, as if she could not face reality.

It was impossible to piece together all that had gone wrong on July 20. The family knew that after the bomb blast the communications between the conspirators in Rastenburg and the conspirators in the Bendlerstrasse had failed. No one knew exactly why. By the time Stauffenberg reached Berlin, still believing he had killed Hitler, almost four critical hours had been lost. The conspirators finally got their troops on the move, but by then some of the Nazi leaders had recovered and alerted commanders loyal to Hitler. It was only a matter of time before the coup collapsed. Similar events took place in other cities of the Reich, as well as Vienna, Prague, and Paris.

A week after the failure Paula and Karl were allowed to visit Dietrich. It was hard to tell how much his circumstances had changed. The guard behind was unfamiliar; and although he appeared busy with his papers, Paula sensed that he was listening. Dietrich did not look as if he had lost sleep, and his voice was firm and strong. He asked questions about the family as if nothing had happened. Karl told him about Hans's illness.

"We must remain hopeful," Dietrich said. "One never knows what good may come out of such trouble—all kinds of trouble."

From Dietrich's look Paula knew he was referring to the fact that so far he was not suspected and that his long imprisonment might save him. "Yes," she said, "man proposes and God disposes."

"By the way," said Dietrich, "I've begun work on a new book."

"Have you?" said Karl with immediate interest. "What about?"

"About the Church and—." He paused and glanced at his father as if to determine how far his interest went. He seemed reassured by Karl's look and continued with undisguised eagerness, "—and what it means to live the Christian life. I want to ask what do we really believe? I mean, believe in a way that we stake our lives on it. As for the Church, there's not much the Church can say right now that anyone will listen to. We've lost our credibility. Nothing will help but to do as the prophet says: 'Do justice, love mercy, and walk humbly with your God.'" He looked at his father with an almost shy smile. "I want to say to the Church: Give all your property away to those in need. Let the clergy live solely on the free-will offerings of the congregations. No help from the State. That's only a beginning, of course."

"It sounds good, Dietrich," said Karl. "It needs to be said." If Karl had doubts that such reforms could be realized, he did not voice them. During all the years Paula had never said a word to her husband about his lack of enthusiasm for Dietrich's calling, but she knew instinctively how much Dietrich had felt it.

Dietrich went on to talk about the new travel restrictions, brought on by the great press of refugees, mostly from the East. "That might mean some people can't come to see me if they have to come a distance." He looked hard at them as if to make sure they knew who he meant. "By the way, Papa, do you have a new receptionist yet? I don't see how you can manage without one."

Karl had not had a receptionist for months.

"I know one young lady who might be interested in the job," said Karl. "She lives in Pomerania, but she might consider it."

Dietrich smiled that ready and radiant smile of his. "That would be splendid."

The next week Karl and Paula made arrangements for Maria to come live with them and register with the authorities as Karl's receptionist. Since the Allied invasion of Normandy and the subsequent letup in the air raids, they had been staying home in Berlin full time, and Paula wanted to keep it that way. She had had enough of traveling back and forth to Sakrow.

All that week the newspapers were full of the trials in the People's Court and the executions that followed immediately. There were pictures of the prisoners as they appeared one at a time before their judge, Roland Freisler, the Nazi who years before had tried so hard to get Hans thrown out of the Justice Department. The prisoners' faces revealed the horror of their ordeal at the hands of the Gestapo. They had been deprived of every dignity and stood before their accuser unshaven and without neckties. Nevertheless, in the picture, Paul von Hase held his head high. The once-proud Field Marshal von Witzleben looked old and broken. He held on to his trousers to keep them from falling, which made him appear befuddled and unprepared, the intent, no doubt, of his captors when they took away his suspenders.

That Saturday evening the family gathered in Paula's living room for the usual music-making. She hoped they would all find some consolation in it. Klaus arrived late, his face grim and inscrutable. He mumbled greetings but did not sit down. Paula watched as he wandered about the room.

"What's wrong, Klaus?" Karl asked. "You may as well tell us."

"It's too shameful. I never heard anything so shameful in all my life."

"What is?"

Klaus stopped at the piano. His hands gripped the back of the chair and his voice trembled as he spoke. "Hitler had moving pictures made of the hangings so he could see his victims' agony—and revel in it." He turned aside. "Oh, God."

"Who told you that?"

"It's all over the Air Ministry. Goebbels told Göring. He was there last night, at the Chancellery, and saw the films himself."

There was no music that night. Everyone left early. It was just as well. At midnight the air raids began again in earnest.

A few days later Maria arrived. It seemed a terrible time for this innocent girl to come into the family. Everyone was weighed down with burdens of their own and had no time to give her the welcome she deserved as Dietrich's future bride. Paula, tired as she was, made only token protests as Maria took over one responsibility after another. Maria had brought great bags of fresh produce and cheese and sausages from Pätzig, some of which went into Dietrich's and Hans's parcels. From the rest they ate better for two weeks than they had in many months.

Karl liked Maria particularly and, in one of his rare compliments, told her how brave she was during the air raids, when she would stretch out on the boxes of books in the cellar shelter and sleep through the bombings.

According to Dietrich's carefully written instructions, Ursel and Rüdiger were to meet Corporal Knobloch at the gardener's hut in the fourth allotment past Berlin-Niederschonhausen and give him the package. Renate was going along with her parents to make it look like a Sunday family outing.

With trembling hands Paula folded the blue mechanic's coveralls and put them in the paper bag. She hoped they would fit Dietrich. She had washed them and left them wrinkled, so they would not look so new.

"Wait, Mama," said Ursel. "Why don't we put the coupons and the money in the pocket? Wouldn't that be better than wrapping them separately?"

"Maybe so."

Ursel folded the 200 reichsmarks in one handkerchief, the special traveler's food coupons in the other, and slipped them into the breast pocket of the coveralls; then put the package in the basket under the sandwiches. Rüdiger had secured enough special coupons to last four days. Paula had hoped for twice that many in case Dietrich ran into trouble getting to the border. For two months now, with an aroused populace to help them, the Gestapo had relentlessly combed the country for every suspect. Besides the arrests Paula had heard of many suicides. Yet, if anyone could manage an escape, Dietrich could. He was clever, nimble, and a careful planner. Besides, he had many faithful friends in Pomerania, the direction she believed he would take.

The church bells were chiming evensong when Ursel and the others returned from the East side. Knobloch had taken the package and told them he would come to the Schleicher's house soon to discuss final plans. Meanwhile the family should obtain two false passports and have them ready.

It was the end of the week before Rüdiger, by various stratagems, managed to get the two passports. That afternoon Paula decided to take Ursel some of the potatoes and apples that Maria had brought from Pätzig. As she approached the back terrace, she saw Klaus beyond the lattice fence, walking rapidly toward Ursel's front gate. Inside Paula deposited the produce in the kitchen and turned toward the hall, where she heard the voices of Ursel and Klaus.

"How do you know that, if they're not in uniform?" Ursel asked.

"It's their car. I know their cars. They're sitting there waiting for me to come home."

"Maybe you're mistaken."

"I'm not mistaken, Ursel."

"It seems stupid. Wouldn't they know you'd see them and run away?"

From the doorway Paula asked, "What is it?" even though she knew.

"The Gestapo. They're waiting for me at my garden gate." A hunted look flared from Klaus's eyes. "I can't stay here. They'll come here next."

"What are you going to do?" asked Paula.

"I'm going to Herr Dickmann's. They won't think to look there."

It seemed logical. Most small businessmen were above suspicion; they made up the backbone of Hitler's support. Herr Dickmann had repaired their shoes for fifteen years. He was a reliable man, who shared their anti-Nazi views and had always been especially fond of Klaus.

Ursel offered Klaus supper. "My God," he said, "who could eat at a time like this," and left again immediately.

Half an hour later the telephone rang in the hall, and Ursel went to answer it. Her voice was clear and precise. "No, I don't know where he is. I haven't seen him today."

While Ursel was speaking the doorbell rang, and Paula went to see who it was. On the doorstep stood Herr Corporal Knobloch. She let him in and closed the door just as Ursel hung up the phone. "You have come about the escape plans," she said.

"Yes, gnädige Frau."

Paula looked at Ursel. "I'm afraid it's a bad time, Herr Corporal."

"Yes," said Ursel. "That was the Gestapo. They're looking for my brother, Klaus." She told the corporal what had happened. "They shouldn't find you here."

"I think you're right, gnädige Frau, but what should I tell Herr Dr. Bonhoeffer?"

"Tell him the truth, and that you should come back tomorrow, or, better still, Monday."

"Your pardon, but what should I tell him about the passports?"

"Tell him they are ready."

"We are grateful for what you are doing," said Paula, "and all you've done for my son in the past."

The corporal bowed, first to Paula then to Ursel, and took his leave.

Back in the kitchen Ursel decided that Paula should go home, since the Gestapo would most likely search there as well. When Paula opened the back door to leave, Klaus was standing on the veranda.

"I couldn't stay there. Herr Dickmann was afraid," Klaus told them.

"Well, come inside."

Klaus did not move. "He has a wife and children and was afraid—"

"Come in, Klaus. Don't stand there. Quickly, quickly, and shut the door."

He closed the door behind him. "I went home again, but they were still there, before the gate."

"We think they might come here," said Paula, and told him about the telephone call.

Without a word Klaus turned again to the door.

"Wait," said Ursel. "Where would you go? Wait, now. We have to think. Where can you hide?"

"Not here. Not in this house, not in either house."

Paula looked out the window. The hedge between the two houses was thick near the back line. "In the hedge. Hide there and see if we can see you from here. Hurry, Klaus, hurry! I'm going home in a minute, I'll let you know as I pass."

Paula watched until Klaus disappeared beneath the mass of shiny green leaves. Then whispering "God be with us," she slipped through the door. At the hedge, she paused and said softly, "All's well. Keep out of sight."

Paula and Karl ate supper in silence, their eyes fastened on the house next door and the hedge. Prison would be hard for Klaus. As a child he had hated school. He could not bear to be forced together with inferior people and stupid teachers, and had rebelled in various ways. Once, as punishment Paula and Karl had taken away his microscope. "Then I'll not be a doctor after all," Klaus announced. Much to Karl's sorrow, Klaus had stuck to his pronouncement.

"We never should have taken away his microscope," Paula said, half to herself.

"What?"

"His microscope, remember?"

Karl frowned and put down his fork. "Paula, such talk will do no good now."

She sighed, "No, no, it won't, will it?"

The sight of the car stopped Paula cold. She laid her hand on Karl's arm and they watched as the two plainclothesmen got out and went to Ursel's door.

Thirty-five minutes later the Nazis came to their door. Paula and Karl sat side by side in the living room and listened to the Nazis' heavy footsteps as they searched the house. After forty minutes they left without a word. When their car moved out of sight around the corner, Paula and Karl went to the window and, in the twilight, watched the hedge. They did not dare use the telephone. On the corner a strange man took up his station by the lamppost. Full darkness came, and there was still no movement in the hedge. At last the shadowy figure emerged and moved cautiously toward Ursel's house, beyond the Nazi's line of vision. The back door opened immediately and closed behind him.

Ursel came over early the next morning. Her beautiful eyes were sad and ringed with dark circles. "He's asleep, I think—I hope. We talked half the night. It's terrible. He doesn't know what to do."

"They'll come back," said Karl.

"Yes, oh, yes, they'll come back. Klaus said Emmi could hide him in Holstein with a fisherman she knows. He won't do that for fear of reprisals against her and the children, or against you. He talked of taking his own life—"

"No!" said Paula.

"I think I have dissuaded him—we talked a long time. 'There's nothing left,' he said, 'but to let them come and get me.'"

Paula and Karl went back with Ursel to keep the vigil. At ten o'clock that morning, while the church bells were ringing, the Gestapo came and took Klaus away.

43

"You were right, Herr Doktor. I thought he would get away, but you were right. He must'a come back last night n' stayed there. The Gestapo come and got him about church time. I watched from the lane."

"I see," said Dietrich. In his mind he knew already what he must do. "You didn't go to the house, then?"

"No. I did just as you said and come straight back here. Nobody saw me."

"Good." Dietrich moved to the stool and looked out on the broken city. The plan was set. For days he had carefully thought out all the details. Now it was ready. In the evening, disguised as a mechanic carrying his toolbox, Dietrich would walk with Knobloch out of the prison to Knobloch's flat in Pankow. There he would prepare the corporal's disguise. In the early morning hours they would leave separately and meet again in Stettin. Fritz Onnasch's uncle plied a freighter between Stettin and Ystad, Sweden. Dietrich was sure Fritz would help the two of them ship aboard as hands. His own disguise was ready. He was good at disguises; he had had enough practice in his youth for his mother's fancy-dress ball. Knobloch had brought the materials for the moustache and the hairpiece to wear under the mechanic's cap. He closed his eyes and imagined the ship at anchor in Stettin harbor, waiting to bear him north to freedom across the Baltic. He sighed. Now he knew how Moses felt as he looked out from Mount Nebo onto the promised land.

Dietrich turned back to the narrow cell. "Ah! Herr Knobloch, I've kept you standing. Forgive me." He stepped down from the stool. "I think we must give it up."

"I was afraid of that. I was afraid when I saw 'em take your brother away. I said to myself—but I still hoped." The corporal turned aside, his head down, the back of one hand rubbing and patting the inside of the other. In time he lifted his head. "You sure it wouldn't be all right, Herr Doktor? It's your only chance, and that's the God's truth."

"Maybe so. But didn't you tell me they arrested Herr Goerdeler's family when he ran away, and still have them, even after they found him? No, my friend. Sometimes the only way to keep one's freedom is to give it up."

The corporal pondered that paradox but did not contest it.

"But we won't give up hope, even so," Dietrich continued. "God is still in charge of His world, no matter how dark it looks. Now, you'll need to go back tomorrow and tell my family the plan is off. You'll do that, won't you?"

"Yes, I'll do that."

That night in his cell Dietrich wrote a poem, which he called simply "Jonah."

> In fear of death they cried aloud and, clinging fast
> to wet ropes straining on the battered deck,
> they gazed in stricken terror at the sea
> that now, unchained in sudden fury, lashed the ship.
>
> "O, gods eternal, excellent, provoked to anger,
> help us, or give a sign, that we may know
> who has offended you by secret sin,
> by breach of oath, or heedless blasphemy, or murder,
>
> who brings us to disaster by misdeed still hidden,
> to make a paltry profit for his pride."
> This they besought. And Jonah said, "Behold,
> I sinned before the Lord of hosts. My life is forfeit.
>
> Cast me away! My guilt must bear the wrath of God;
> the righteous shall not perish with the sinner!"
> They trembled. But with hands that knew no weakness
> they cast the offender from their midst. The sea stood still.

Knowing that his time might be limited, Dietrich worked diligently all week on his new book. On Friday, parcel day, he went outside at noon with Knobloch. He knew that either Maria or Susi would bring the parcel about that time of day. As they rounded the corner, he saw Maria's young figure on the sidewalk near the entrance. She appeared to be examining the wheel of her bicycle. Halfway down the path, two guards stood talking.

As Dietrich and Knobloch approached, Maria spoke to them as strangers. "Oh, I'm so glad you came along. My tires have both gone flat. I have a pump, but—"

"It's all right, Maria," said Dietrich softly. "This is Corporal Knobloch. He's entirely trustworthy. We can talk."

She handed Knobloch the pump and the two valves, which she obviously had screwed off herself.

Assuming an unconcerned look, Dietrich spoke without moving his lips. "What of Klaus? Where is he?"

"Lehrterstrasse Prison."

Dietrich was relieved that it was not Prinz-Albrecht-Strasse.

"Emmi is home from Holstein. She left the children with relatives." Maria spoke across the bicycle, her eyes on Knobloch, as if giving him advice about the tires. Dietrich knelt and pretended to help the corporal.

Maria continued, "Worse has come, though. Rüdiger's arrested—Wednesday, in his office. Ursel is devastated, as you can imagine."

"And Mama?"

"Mama isn't at all well. She gets upset easily. I have to be careful."

Dietrich looked quickly into Maria's face and saw the stress there. He dared not address her directly; the guards had turned toward them. Still on his knees, Dietrich said softly, "Thank you for taking care of them. It means a great deal to me that you are there."

When Dietrich stood again, there were tears in Maria's eyes. She took the pump from Knobloch and turned the bicycle around. Ostentatiously, as if they were strangers, she shook their hands and breathed a soft "Goodbye, Dietrich." Without looking back she pushed the bicycle down the path, past the two guards, and through the gate.

Three days later the Gestapo came for Dietrich. It was no surprise. He had set all his affairs in order, as far as possible. With him he kept a few essential possessions—Maria's letters and her picture, a picture of his parents, and the small snapshot from Italy of Eberhard in his uniform. Of his writings only the new work remained with him, along with a small store of blank paper and writing materials. As he packed his things he caught an occasional glimpse of Knobloch's anxious face outside the door. When he was ready, the SS man fastened the handcuffs on Dietrich's wrists. Dietrich looked once into the faithful warder's eyes, a wordless farewell that he hoped conveyed his thankfulness. Knobloch had already given his assurance that whatever happened, he would get word to Dietrich's parents.

The devastation of the city was more extensive than Dietrich had imagined. At frequent intervals the car stopped, while Labor Service crews—mostly old men or wounded veterans—cleared a passageway with their shovels. When they reached the Stettin station, the clock showed six-thirty. It had taken an hour and a half to drive the five miles from Tegel. It took another hour to cross the city center.

The car swung around the old Trinity Church—where Dietrich had preached in a time long past—circled the Kaiserhof Hotel, drove by the Air Ministry, and turned into the short block dominated by the Gestapo Headquarters.

Inside, two SS men, with guns at his back, herded Dietrich down the steps to a small room and ordered him to strip. When he protested, one of them—a giant with an artificial leg—struck him across the face. "You don't ask questions here." At the touch of their searching hands Dietrich concentrated with all his might on the heavy door beyond. Finally it occurred to him that they were looking for poison. They ordered him to dress, replaced the handcuffs, and led him down more steps to a low-ceilinged basement and a corridor lined on either side with cells. At Cell 19 they removed the handcuffs and pushed him inside.

The cell was much smaller than the one at Tegel, at least two feet shorter and so narrow Dietrich could stand in the middle with fingers touching each wall. The only furnishings were a small table, a stool, and a bed, that folded up against the wall to make room to sit at the table. There was no window, but there was a fan-shaped grill over the door; and in the door a small grate with a ledge. One bulb in the ceiling cast a harsh light over the barren cell.

Dietrich put his suitcase on the floor and on the table arranged his Bible, the Goethe, and the small store of writing paper. To one side he set up the pictures of his parents, Maria, and Eberhard. He had missed the evening meal at both places, but made a supper from the last of the bread and dried apples he had received the previous week from home.

Before Dietrich finished his meager dinner, the air raid alarm went off. Immediately doors were opened, and up and down the hall urgent voices ordered, "Out, out!" The key turned in his door. A guard clamped handcuffs on his wrists and motioned him out into the hall. Up and down, SS men with machine guns reinforced the guards as they marched the column of prisoners through the hall. No one spoke or turned around, but Dietrich thought he recognized Canaris and Oster up ahead. Outside, in the smoky blue light, they crossed a courtyard to a large concrete bunker about sixty feet away. The SS men waved them down the steps with their machine guns, then followed close behind. The shelter was brightly lit and larger than Dietrich expected. The passage opened on to a square hall with doors to other rooms, one of which was apparently open to the general public. People, among them women and children, streamed in from outside. The handcuffed prisoners crowded together in the passageway. The guards forbade them to speak to one another. Besides Oster and Canaris, Dietrich recognized Josef Müller, Karl Sack, Carl Goerdeler, and, close by, Maria's cousin, Fabian von Schlabrendorff—all men of the Resistance, gathered together in one place like characters in the last act of a comic opera. Dietrich had not seen Schlabrendorff since his abortive attempt to put a bomb on Hitler's plane. When their eyes met, Schlabrendorff appeared alarmed, but Dietrich made no sign of recognition.

The seemingly endless raid proceeded with familiar sounds overhead and an occasional tremor of the wall behind him. The handcuffs became torture. After a long time he noticed that Oster, at the end of the line, was trying to get his attention. Standing beside a heavy steel file cabinet and, with his eyes on Dietrich, Oster rubbed the edge of the cabinet lightly with the back of his manacled hand, opened his fingers wide, then lifted his hands slowly and laid one finger against his mouth. Dietrich could not figure out what he was trying to say and looked away, then back again. Oster repeated the movements exactly, then flicked his head and raised an eyebrow. He seemed to be asking if Dietrich understood. With a slight motion Dietrich shook his head. This time Oster put his finger to his lips first—secret. Then he touched the file cabinet—secret cabinet. Then Oster opened his fingers wide—secret cabinet opened. Zossen! The SS had found the papers that would incriminate them all.

The night was long. The mattress was thinner than at Tegel, but at last Dietrich slept.

The next morning he was led with Oster to the washroom. There were four toilet seats across one end, but no chance to talk there, since a guard paced up and down in front of them the whole time. But in the showers, which were ice cold, they managed to whisper, their words drowned out by the spray of water.

"Zossen?" Dietrich asked.

"Yes. Someone led them straight there. They have everything. They're waiting to kill us until they can wring everything possible from us, especially names. We must string them along—false leads—anything to drag it out. What of the Allies? Any hope there?"

"They're moving fast. Almost to the Rhine."

"Not fast enough, I'm afraid."

Dietrich and Oster discovered they were neighbors. Oster occupied Cell 20. On the way back to Cell 19, Dietrich met Canaris. The two guards had some business with one another, and for a moment Dietrich and the admiral were face to face.

"This place is hell, Herr Pastor," Canaris whispered.

Canaris, always slight, now looked emaciated. His eyes, dark-circled and sunken, glowed like the last live coals amid gray ashes. Dietrich put all the heart he could into the one word, "Courage," before the guards separated them again.

Breakfast, passed through the grate in the door, consisted of a mug of ersatz coffee and two slices of brown bread spread with a gummy substance, which was supposed to be jam but had little fruit flavor. Dietrich turned then to his Bible and an hour of meditation and prayer.

Suddenly, in mid-morning there were frightful cries from an upper floor. Dietrich instinctively crossed himself. The screams continued for a long time, each more terrible than the other, then changed into whimpers and moans. When he thought they had ended, the cries became loud again. He had heard the stories of torture in this place, but no amount of prior knowledge could have prepared him for this.

The next morning Dietrich was beside Schlabrendorff in the shower. Shocked, he noticed puncture marks up and down Schlabrendorff's legs and red and black welts on his back. "You've been tortured," Dietrich whispered.

"Yes," said the tall lieutenant. "I haven't given anything away. Not yet. But I don't know how much longer—" His voice choked up.

A guard approached, and they scrubbed in silence.

When the guard moved away, Schlabrendorff whispered, "Pray for me, Herr Pastor."

"I will—every day."

As he was led back to his cell, Dietrich noticed a bright light flooding Cell 14, which was across the hall and down from him. The figure slumped in the chair was Canaris—chained hand and foot. Outside the door stood a special SS guard, armed with a machine gun. Next door, Cell 13 was also open and brightly lit, but Dietrich could not see the occupant.

The next few days he learned who most of the other prisoners were. Goerdeler was in Cell 13, and to Dietrich's left in Cell 18 was Josef Müller. Up the hall, Dr. Sack occupied Cell 8. At various times in the washroom Dietrich managed whispered conversations with each of them. Müller had given nothing away. So far he had not been physically tortured, but was kept handcuffed all the time, with a bright light in his cell night and day to make sleep difficult. Before his arrest Sack had burned papers relating to Dietrich and Müller and told the Gestapo they had been lost in an air raid. Canaris was denying his own complicity, and trying to throw the Gestapo off the track of the others.

"But Oster's a fool," Canaris said. "He's admitted too much. It's those Zossen papers. He should have destroyed them long ago. A fool he is. But even they need not be fatal." Canaris looked at Dietrich with his dark-rimmed eyes, his toothbrush poised in his right hand. "Don't give away anything. Keep them guessing. They don't know everything, by a long shot." When the guard moved out of range Canaris whispered again. "Himmler has put out peace feelers to the Allies. Göring too. This can help you. Use it."

Goerdeler, who had already been condemned to death by the People's Court, told Dietrich that he had confessed openly the purpose and scope of the opposition. "I wanted them to know it. No names, of course, no names. And only insignificant details, to throw sand in their eyes. Now they have me writing, writing all day long—my ideas of government—all that sort of thing. Maybe something I say will persuade Hitler to reverse his policy. I'm hoping he'll ask me for an interview, or Himmler, at least."

Dietrich said nothing to shatter his illusion.

One night a loud shouting awakened Dietrich. He watched from his grilled hatch as an SS man cursed and threatened Goerdeler. They would carry out the death penalty immediately, the SS man said, if Goerdeler did not reveal the names of the men picked for the new government.

"Then carry it out," said Goerdeler. "Do you think I'm afraid to die?"

The man's threats failed to budge him.

More often than not the sounds of men being tortured filled the morning hours with terror. Schlabrendorff was in a pitiable condition from the continued tortures. After a week Dietrich was moved to Cell 24, next door to him. It was Wednesday, and Dietrich's first parcel from home arrived—clean linen, dried apples, bread, and two cigars. He wrapped some of the food and one cigar in paper and, when the doors were open that evening for the trips to the washroom, he slipped the package to Schlabrendorff through the slits between the hinges. The next evening at the same time Schlabrendorff whispered to Dietrich that a conspirator, Kurt von Plattenburg, had jumped from a third-floor window to his death.

"Your father is a doctor, isn't he?" Schlabrendorff asked.

"Yes."

"Ask him, please, to send some poison in the next parcel—a little vial—it wouldn't be hard to hide. I don't think I can hold out much longer. Please do that for me."

The desperation in the lieutenant's voice touched Dietrich to his inmost being. He whispered, "I'll do what I can, but it might not be possible. Don't lose heart, my friend. The only fight lost is the one given up. Remember that when the hard times come." The words rang hollow in Dietrich's ears. He had not experienced the horrors. That night he wrote out on little slips of paper words of hope and comfort from the Bible, more real and sure than his own. When there were opportunities, he passed them one at a time to Schlabrendorff.

The next morning an SS man came for Dietrich and led him, handcuffed, down the hall to an elevator. The folding grill was padlocked. Far up the shaft the cables rattled and screeched, shifting victims from one circle of hell to another. Suddenly the car swooped down and stopped at the grill. The guard opened the lock with a key, pushed Dietrich inside, and locked it again. At the third floor they got off and walked down a long hall to an anteroom, where a guard with a machine gun stood by the door. Inside, the SS man told Dietrich to wait; he would be summoned.

It was a small room, brightly lit. Dietrich sat in one of two straight chairs along the wall. After a long time the high double doors to his right opened and Dietrich heard a familiar voice, "Take the bastard out." A prisoner, his arms manacled behind his back and his feet bound, hopped to the door. His shoes had no laces. He was bent almost double, and Dietrich could not see his face.

"Out, damn you!" The guard kicked the prisoner from behind so that he almost lost his balance.

Dietrich sprang to his feet. As swiftly, the guard shoved him down again with a shout, "No meddling, bastard!"

When Dietrich lifted his head he was looking into the bruised face of his friend and Confessing Church colleague, Justus Perels.

In that brief encounter Perels' eyes conveyed deep pain and warning.

From the double doors a guard's voice crackled, "Prisoner Bonhoeffer."

In the other room Dietrich found himself standing before Franz Xaver Sonderegger.

44

In a gravelly voice and without looking up from his papers, Sonderegger spoke. "You saw your friend Perels. Unless you cooperate, you'll find yourself in the same shape." He leaned back in the chair, his narrow face turned slightly to one side. "That bastard is your friend, isn't he?"

"Herr Doktor Perels is an acquaintance of mine," said Dietrich, trying desperately to control his rage. "Whatever the case, he does not deserve such vile treatment."

"He brings it on himself when he refuses to tell the truth. I have a job to do—serious work that has to be done—and I'll use whatever methods are necessary."

Dietrich remembered Sonderegger's twangy, low-German accent and the avid look on his face. His spotless uniform showed how prestigious he considered his position as an officer in the Gestapo. It made him one of the new elite.

Sonderegger's crafty eyes turned on Dietrich. "You were very clever before—you and Dohnanyi—but I knew something was up. I knew damn well there was a nest of traitors around Canaris. Now I can prove I was right. Yes, we know what you and your friends have been up to. There's no use denying it."

"I've been up to my theological writing—what little I could do in Tegel prison."

"Before that, before that. You know what I'm talking about. I want to hear about this circle you were moving in."

"Circle, Herr Kommissar?"

"Beck, Goerdeler, Oster, Dohnanyi, and, of course, Canaris."

"I know of no such circle."

"I say we have proof of it. You'd best not deny it. Now, Beck, first. What do you know of him?"

"Beck? I don't know a Beck."

"General Ludwig Beck."

"A general? Oh, yes, I've heard of General Beck. But that must have been quite a while back. I haven't seen his name in the papers lately."

"Enough of that. You were taking orders from him."

"I was taking orders from Admiral Canaris."

"Canaris, yes. But I say Beck too. Beck too."

"That's impossible. I don't even know the man."

A secretary scribbled furiously. Sonderegger took from a drawer a bulging folder and laid it before Dietrich. "You should read this before you make any more stupid denials."

Dietrich looked at him. "Have you tried turning pages with these things on your wrists?"

The Kommissar motioned to the guard to remove the handcuffs. The first papers in the folder were the proclamations written by Hans for Beck and Goerdeler. Next were Oster's handwritten plan for the coup d'etat and Müller's reports from the Vatican exchanges. There was no sign of Dietrich's reports of his meetings in Switzerland and Sweden. Dietrich was aware of Sonderegger's avid gaze, but—thanks to Oster's warning—he was able to show no emotion. "I never saw any of this before in my life," he said.

"You were working with all these men."

"Only Müller—and my brother-in-law."

"Who is a proven traitor. A proven traitor! I have his full confession."

"You don't expect me to believe that, I'm sure."

Sonderegger threw Dietrich a calculating look and, without pursuing it further, asked him about Oster.

"I met General Oster only a few times in the Abwehr."

"And you knew he was deep in a conspiracy against the Führer."

"That would be surprising indeed. I didn't know him very well but I seriously doubt—"

"And you were there for the same reason," said Sonderegger.

"You surprise me, Herr Kommissar. As you know I came to the Abwehr in the first place because my brother-in-law knew of my ecumenical contacts and believed they could supply helpful information for the Wehrmacht."

"There's more to it than that—more to it than that. We have reasons to question your loyalty. Do you think your prohibition from speaking and writing was for nothing? You evaded military service and helped others do the same. Your two houses—your parents' and your sister's—have been visited by people wearing the star. It all fits together, clear enough. Clear enough." Sonderegger bared his gums in a mirthless grin. "Wouldn't it be better just to tell the truth and avoid the consequences? We have ways, and I can tell you this, we don't have to ask anyone's permission."

"I've told you what I know. You heard it all in the War Court."

"Would you like to see your parents behind bars here?"

Dietrich recoiled in horror and spoke with difficulty. "Why do anything so cruel when it wouldn't get you anywhere at all?"

Sonderegger's eyes turned rancorous. "You'll thwart me once too often, Bonhoeffer. Once too often. Think about it." To the guard he said, "Take him away."

Three weeks after Klaus's arrest Paula learned that the Gestapo had ordered Eberhard's arrest in Italy and had taken him to the Lehrterstrasse Prison, where Klaus and Rüdiger were. Renate joined her mother and Emmi in preparing daily meals for their men. They wrapped the hot food in newspapers and pillows to keep it warm and left it with the guards at the prison, then waited until the guards returned with the empty utensils. Paula and Maria asked to do the same for Dietrich, but the officials at Prinz-Albrecht-Strasse refused. A parcel once a week was all they could send.

In the year and a half since Dietrich's arrest Paula had become very fond of his young fiancée. Since Maria had come to live with them in August, Paula had turned over the management of the household almost entirely to her. Maria made it easy; she handled everything with the least possible fuss and bother.

Over the weeks Maria and Emmi became fast friends. Emmi often stopped by to see Maria on her way home from the prison. One afternoon Paula happened upon them in the kitchen. Emmi was crying, her face contorted with rage.

"They're beasts—evil, vicious beasts!" she cried. "No. That's unfair to the beasts. They aren't so cruel as men." Then Emmi saw Paula in the door and quickly stuffed a piece of clothing back into a bag on the table.

"What's the matter?" Paula asked.

"I'm sorry, Mama, I thought you were next door."

Paula moved to the table. On it was the valise Emmi used to carry Klaus's laundry back and forth. "What was that you put back in the bag? Tell me, Emmi!"

"I didn't mean for you to see—"

"I have to see."

Silently Emmi opened the bag and took out an undershirt. The back of it was covered with bloodstains. A pair of socks also had stains. Paula looked at Maria and then Emmi. She did not move. Then, trembling, she picked up the undershirt and held it to her breast. For a long time she held the shirt there, then handed it back to Emmi, and walked blindly out of the room.

The weeks dragged on. One evening in early December when Emmi was there to visit, she asked Maria to walk partway home with her.

"Please be careful," Paula said. It was almost nine o'clock and she did not like Maria walking back alone. A half-hour passed, and Paula began to watch for Maria at the door.

"My dear," said Karl. "Come and sit down. Watching won't bring her back any sooner."

Paula came and sat on the sofa. The time crept by more and more slowly, and Maria did not come. Unable to sit still, Paula again walked back and forth between the door and the window in

Karl's office. Ten o'clock came and went. Finally, she heard a footstep outside the door. The door opened and Maria entered.

"Oh, you're here," said Paula, almost sobbing. By this time Karl was by her side.

"Yes," said Maria. She looked from one to the other, as the realization dawned on her face. "I'm sorry, am I late?"

"Yes," said Karl, "it's been a very long time. Why did you do this to Mama? Didn't it occur to you that she would be worried?" Karl had raised his voice, something he never did.

"I'm sorry," said Maria, "I didn't realize—we were just talking and forgot the time."

Paula wanted to reach out and touch her, to reassure her, but she could not speak. She could barely stand.

"I'm sorry—," Maria said again, then turned and went quickly up the stairs.

That night there was no air raid, and from sheer exhaustion Paula slept. After breakfast the next morning, she said to Maria, "I hope you slept well."

"Yes, thank you. And you?"

"Very well. The Americans stayed away."

"They must have a cold, or something," Maria said, smiling.

After a while Paula said, "I think you must love Dietrich very much."

Maria seemed surprised. "Yes, I love him."

"It cannot be easy for you here."

"It's not easy for anyone, wherever they are."

"But you might wish to go somewhere else? Or home to Pätzig?"

"No. I want to stay here." Maria smiled and lifted the used tea leaves from the teapot onto a tray, scattering them with a fork.

"Why do you love him, Maria?"

"My mother asked that same question. I don't know—we have fun together. He laughs at my jokes. It's always nice when someone laughs at your jokes. And he likes me the way I am. I don't feel like he wants me as a trophy. That's rather nice, you know." Maria looked directly into Paula's eyes. "I want to be the mother of his children."

Paula watched as she put the tray on the radiator so the tea leaves could dry for another time. All reservations she had had about Maria melted away.

The two months of interrogations had been long and tedious, but Sonderegger had not threatened Dietrich's parents again. One day he had suddenly confronted Dietrich with the report of his trip to Sweden, written in disguised language. Dietrich had been able to explain that report away. Now, for the first time, Sonderegger asked specific questions about Dietrich's talks with Bishop Bell.

"If this was, as you said, on the orders of Canaris, what was your commission? What were you supposed to find out?"

"As much as possible about British plans. For instance, how things stood between Britain and the Russians, what they thought of Russian power at that point."

As Dietrich expected, Sonderegger pricked up his ears. For quite some time the interrogations had been leaning in this direction, and Dietrich—remembering Canaris' hint about peace feelers by Himmler and Göring—had spent many hours in his cell planning how he would reply, to gain time without harming anyone.

"And what did you learn?"

"A good deal, actually. Some members of the British government thought they were underestimating the power of Russia."

"Who was that?"

"Sir Stafford Cripps, for one. He feared that no power, not even England, would be in a position to stop the Russians from advancing as far as the Brandenburg Gate."

Alarm appeared in the Kommissar's eyes.

Dietrich continued, "The consequences of that—for England—were unforeseeable, he thought."

"And that's all you learned?"

"Well, Cripps said Lord Beaverbrook had gone to Switzerland earlier and talked with German industrialists about the possibilities of negotiating peace and then forming a common front between the Western powers and Germany against Russia."

The Kommissar leaned forward. "What German industrialists? Who were they?"

"The Lord Bishop didn't know that."

For a time Sonderegger said nothing, then he asked just who Bishop Bell was. Dietrich described the bishop as a man of peace who favored mutual understanding, and an outspoken friend of the German people. "For that reason Bell was not named as successor to Archbishop Lang of Canterbury, as had been expected."

"You reported all this?"

"To the Abwehr, yes."

"You would have done better to give it to us. To us here, instead of those degenerates."

"But they were my superiors, you understand."

In the anteroom the secretary had a transcript of the previous interrogation. As usual, Dietrich had to read it and sign all seven carbon copies.

One night as he lay awake on his cot, Dietrich heard footsteps in the corridor. He got up and watched as an SS man entered Goerdeler's cell.

"All right, wake up," the rough voice sounded. "I want to know about your brother."

"My brother?" came Goerdeler's voice, stupified with sleep.

"He knew about these plans for July 20, didn't he?"

"Yes, he knew—". He seemed to realize suddenly what he had said. "But it was because of me, because I told him. He never would have known—he had no interest in that business—it was because I told him, like brothers talk, you know."

"That's all I wanted to know," said the SS man, and left.

Two days later in the washroom Dietrich saw Goerdeler weeping. "What is the matter, Sir? What has happened?"

"They killed him. They executed my brother, and it's my fault." Goerdeler told Dietrich what had happened in the middle of the night. "You see, I betrayed him."

"But weren't you half asleep? You didn't know what you were doing. They tricked you into it."

Just then the guard turned their way, and there was no more chance to talk. Back in his cell Dietrich wrote on a slip of paper the words from Psalm 116: "The death of the devout costs Yahweh dear" and "He bends down to listen to me when I call." On the evening trip to the washroom he slipped the paper into Goerdeler's hand.

That night the reading was from Philippians. The Apostle Paul, himself a prisoner, wrote: "My one hope and trust is that I shall never have to admit defeat, but that now, as always, I shall have the courage for Christ to be glorified in my body, whether by my life or by my death."

After the last interrogation, Dietrich received the long-sought permission to write to Maria. He tried to reassure her and, through her, his parents that he was well and not being mistreated. A few days later he finally received a letter from her, the first real letter he had been allowed. He read it over and over until he had memorized it.

Soon afterward Sonderegger snuffed that little candleflame. "You tell us what you know or we'll bring Maria in tomorrow," he threatened. "Tomorrow! There are plenty of women in these cells, so don't think it's an idle threat."

Dietrich tried to speak firmly. "I've told you what I know."

"That doesn't seem to be the case. I've thought so all along. Now one of your fellow traitors has named you."

"That is not possible, unless someone perjured himself at the hands of your bullies."

"You think your friend, Perels, would lie?"

The vision of his colleague's tormented face filled Dietrich with alarm. Perels knew a great deal. Before July 20 he had served as an emissary between the imprisoned conspirators and General Beck, even risking a visit to the beleaguered Oster on Dietrich's behalf.

"Herr Doktor Perels is not a liar."

"Good," said Sonderegger. "Then you'll admit your participation in a traitorous meeting in Freiburg in 1942, along with Perels and others."

"Freiburg? In 1942? I have no recollection of a meeting in Freiburg."

Sonderegger opened a file and turned to the last page, pointing to Perels's signature. It was Perels's part of the memoranda from the week-long Freiburg discussions on the future of a Germany without Hitler. Dietrich had persuaded the Brethren Council to let him, along with Perels, represent the Confessing Church at the meetings. Dietrich's own formulations on the future relationship of Church and State had not been included in the final document.

"I'm not familiar with this," said Dietrich, "although I don't find it surprising that Dr. Perels was trying to heal the broken Church so it could better serve the Fatherland." The words came with a facility that surprised Dietrich.

"Goerdeler was also there." Sonderegger kept his eyes on Dietrich. "He confessed that the plans were for a government following an overthrow of the Führer."

"I know nothing of such plans."

"It's clear you are lying. Very clear." Sonderegger took up his pen. "I'll give the order to bring the young Fräulein in."

"I don't know what you want of me. I've told you of my assignments at the Abwehr. Often they asked me for addresses, introductions, advice—mostly about ecumenical people." Dietrich sought desperately for some harmless piece of information that might satisfy the man. "Sometimes I helped with the internal information service."

"What internal information service? That is the province of the SS. Or didn't you know that?"

"I knew there was some kind of division of responsibility, but naturally it was not my place—"

"Who ordered this?"

There was no alternative. Dietrich could not imagine that a violation of the "Ten Commandments" would hurt very much now. "It was for Admiral Canaris. He wanted only what was needed for better military intelligence, he said, to find every possible way to overcome the difficulties of conducting the war."

Much to Dietrich's relief, Sonderegger left it at that and turned again to the peace initiatives of the Britons. "You spoke of Lord Beaverbrook and his peace feelers. Do you think there are others in England who would welcome some kind of common front with us against the Russians?"

"I don't know. That was a long time ago—1942—but there may be. It seems logical."

"This Bell is a good friend of yours?"

"A good friend, yes."

"And he has lots of influence with his government?"

"I would say so."

"Very well, you may go now."

All the way back to his cell Dietrich tried to determine the significance of Sonderegger's last questions and his change of tone. There was no connection with the matter of the internal information service.

Christmas came and went with one round of carol-singing from the darkened cells, begun spontaneously by Dietrich. The voices filled the basement, like Paul and Silas in their dungeon. On the twenty-eighth, Dietrich asked permission to write his mother a birthday letter, and Sonderegger, softened of late, granted it.

During January the air raids intensified, and the prisoners were herded to the bunker two or three times a day. One day at the end of the month a near-miss broke the water main and spread mud and debris all over the prison floor. The guards set Canaris and Josef Müller to scrubbing it up.

As the two prisoners neared Dietrich's cell, the guard, his machine gun over his arm, said to Canaris, "Well, sailor-boy, you never thought you'd be scrubbing floors one day, did you?"

When the guard passed, Canaris whispered to Müller, "He doesn't know what a favor he's doing us."

Dietrich observed their secret exchanges as the two men moved on hands and knees down the corridor. Just then two guards entered from the other direction, carrying someone on a stretcher.

Dietrich watched in horrified recognition as the guards deposited their burden in Cell 10, diagonally across from him, then came out again and left the door open.

Walter Huppenkothen, the head of interrogation into the July 20 assassination attempt, had followed them into the corridor.

"Who's going to look after him?" one of the stretcher-bearers asked. "He can't do for hisself."

"Let him croak in his own shit," said Huppenkothen, with a malevolent look into the cell. "Then we'll see if he decides to talk."

Dietrich stared through his grill at the open cell and the guard with his machine gun pacing up and down. Only the foot of the cot was visible, but the man lying there was Hans.

45

"Where's Klaus? Where's Dietrich?" Paula could hear herself speaking the words. She tried to focus on the dim faces hovering over her.

"She's coming out of it." Karl took her hand. "Paula, it's Karl. Are you feeling better?"

She looked from Karl, on his knees beside her with his stethoscope around his neck, to Maria at the end of the sofa—her own sofa in her own living room. Paula slowly lifted her hand to her head. "What happened?"

"You just blacked out for a little while," Karl assured her.

"Fainted?"

"Something like that. But you're going to be all right now. Rest is what you need."

Maria brought a cold cloth for her head, and Karl pulled a chair beside her and sat down. Paula tried to recall what had happened. They all three had been sitting around the dining table, reading Dietrich's letter—the third letter since he had been in the Gestapo Headquarters. The first two months he was there they had heard nothing, then a letter had come for Maria. At the end of December there was a birthday letter and poem for Paula. Now, a month later, this letter. Dietrich asked for some books, and Karl had said he would go that afternoon to the library and try to find them. Paula could remember nothing else. It was the second time since Christmas that this had happened. Worrying Karl distressed her more than anything else. She reached out and touched his hand. "I'm sorry," she said.

"Ssh! It's all right. Don't try to talk."

She rested on the sofa until suppertime.

The next day a call came for Maria from her mother, asking her to come to Pätzig to take her younger brothers and sisters to safety in the West. They could hear the guns of the Russians in the distance, she said, and there was no time to lose.

"It's a terrible time to leave you," said Maria. "Are you sure you're all right?"

"I'm all right. You must go. We'll be able to manage."

"We'll have to come by horse and wagon, mother says. No refugees are allowed on trains coming West. Even wagons are forbidden—Hitler's new orders. There'll be sentries at all the bridges across the Oder. But don't worry, I know the back ways."

That same day a letter came from Klaus in the Lehterstrasse prison. His trial in the People's Court was set for February 2, two days hence. In Paula's mind that meant only one thing; there were no acquittals by the infamous Judge Freisler. In his letter Klaus was preparing them for the worst. He never wanted to see the faces of those men again, he wrote, "so much depravity. I've seen the devil and I can't forget it. In this ride between death and the devil, death is truly the nobler companion. The devil suits the times." For a long time Paula sat motionless with the letter in her lap. Later in the day Renate came and told her that her father's trial was to be the same day.

On Friday they waited in the anteroom of the court: Paula, Karl, Emmi, and Ursel. Finally, at seven o'clock, the great double doors opened.

Karl asked one of the officials, "What was the verdict?"

"Death, what else did you expect? They are traitors."

Paula forced herself to remain erect. She dared not look at Ursel.

Karl took her arm. "We must go to the side door quickly, if we hope to see them."

Outside by the curb stood the Grune Minna waiting for the condemned men. The cold moonlight cast brittle shadows on the sidewalk. Soon the door opened and the closely guarded prisoners emerged, all of them handcuffed. Rüdiger was first.

He went straight to Ursel, kissed her, and said, "Be of good courage."

A guard struck him on the shoulder and shouted, "Get on, you!"

For Klaus there was no such chance, but on his face was an expression so tender as he looked at Emmi and at her that Paula almost broke down. Justus Perels and Hans John followed and, with their guards, entered the rear of the van. The door closed and the Grune Minna carried the victims away.

Early the next morning Ursel set out for the city to appeal for mercy at the court. Paula and Karl left a little later to deliver a birthday parcel and letter to Dietrich. Emmi offered to accompany them before making her own appeal for Klaus. When they arrived at the Anhalter Station the full alarm was already sounding. No one was allowed to go up to the street.

For two hours Karl, Paula, and Emmi huddled on the floor of the underground station, while the blockbusters struck one after another. The faces of the Berliners around them—hardened from months of air attacks—showed not so much fear as a fatalistic rigidity, a dogged resolution to hold on, whatever the odds. The all-clear finally sounded and they came up again. Outside the air was so dense with smoke and ash that they could hardly breathe. The nearby buildings were in ruins, many of them burning. Paula looked through the haze toward the Gestapo Headquarters; the back corner should have been visible in the next block. Instead, half a wall stood there amid smoking rubble.

"Karl, look! It's been hit! It's been hit!" With her handkerchief over her mouth, Paula started across the rock-strewn street. Karl and Emmi caught up with her, and together they made their way around the block to the front of the building, part of which was still standing. A civilian defense official prevented them from going near the entrance.

"We have to clear out unexploded bombs," he said.

They waited for an hour, but still were not allowed inside.

"Come back tomorrow," the officer said.

"But we can't leave without knowing what has happened to our son," said Paula.

"There's no help for it, meine Dame. Come back tomorrow."

All train and streetcar service was out. For two miles they picked their way through the ruins. People in the way stumbled along like sleepwalkers. In the air was a peculiar smell, the sick sweet smell of bodies not yet dug out. At the Zoo Station Emmi parted from them to see about Klaus and the others in the Lehrterstrasse. It was late afternoon before they all came together again at Paula's house, assured of the safety of all but Dietrich. Now Dietrich, if he were still alive, would have to spend his birthday in that awful place without any word from them.

Dietrich awoke early and his mind leaped immediately to Hans, so near and yet so far. For two days Dietrich had been trying to communicate in some way with his brother-in-law. Twice he had caught Hans's eye as he passed his cell, and once had covertly tossed onto his cot a tightly wadded paper on which he had written a few words of greeting. "I am diagonally across from you," he wrote, "and pray for a chance somehow to see you."

Dietrich knew that since the next day was his birthday, his parents might try to deliver a greeting to him. He hoped not. He did not want them in town for any reason. Intense hunger, an almost constant accompaniment of his days, made him listen for the breakfast cart. Instead, from the distant hall came the firm stamp of two pairs of boots. Something in the tone of those footsteps touched a nerve, a warning of sinister intent. How such intent was translated into the way a guard walked Dietrich did not know, but over the months he had come to recognize the walk.

The clamp of the boots entered their corridor and passed his door. Two-thirds of the way to the washroom they stopped, and the voices of the two guards began to bellow. "Get up! Come on! Come on!" Dietrich threw his blanket over his shoulders and stepped to the door. Through the hatch he watched as the guards led the disheveled and bewildered Goerdeler from his cell. As Goerdeler walked between the guards, the realization of what was happening seemed to dawn upon him. He lifted his head and walked erectly. At their hatches across the way the faces of the other prisoners appeared, alert and silent. In the next moment Goerdeler was gone.

The siren went off early that morning, while Dietrich was still reading his Bible. As the prisoners jostled one another in the corridor, Dietrich stepped back one step and in a lightning move slipped into Hans's cell. He ducked down on the other side of the table and listened until all the prisoners and guards had filed out. Even then he was afraid to speak. He simply looked at his brother-in-law, whose dark-circled eyes gazed into his own. Hans's pale face was unshaven and his hair long and matted. The nails of his emaciated hand on the cover were dirty and untrimmed.

Hans spoke first. "Sorry, I stink like hell, but it suits the place, doesn't it?"

The stench was indeed almost unbearable. "I heard what Huppenkothen said. Have they really done nothing for you?"

"Nothing."

"I'll carry you to the washroom. Are you well enough for that?"

"Yes, oh God, yes!"

"How about clothes?"

Hans pointed to the floor at the foot of the cot. "In the suitcase there."

Dietrich found underwe r, trousers, and a shirt, then helped Hans sit up.

"I think I can stand on my feet, if you hold onto me. I'm not quite as sick as I let on to them." A smile flickered across Hans's weary face. "My only weapon, you know."

Dietrich held Hans on his arm, and they walked slowly down the corridor past the empty cells. The rumble of the planes overhead vibrated the whole basement.

"Our friends are out in force," said Hans. "It's music I like to hear."

In the lavatory Dietrich helped Hans undress and while Hans rested on one of the toilets, he flushed out the soiled underwear and put it to soak in the sink. He quickly threw off his own clothes, so he could stand with Hans in the shower and help him bathe.

All the while bombs rained down with hellish fury. By the time they were back in Hans's cell the building was shaking and plaster was falling. Hans collapsed exhausted on his cot. After he hung the wet clothes on the back of the chair, Dietrich sat on the floor beside Hans's head.

"If we die now, it will be good," said Hans.

"I think you are right."

"Yes. We'll die in the end, so it would be better this way. They've discovered everything, you know, absolutely everything. I can't think who has betrayed us."

"Does it matter, Hans?"

"No, not really. More than one, probably—a vicious circle of statements. With their winding sheet of incrimination, the Gestapo can bide their time and carry us off one after another, like Goerdeler."

"You saw that?"

"How could I not?"

Dietrich was silent. "I told one thing. Sonderegger was threatening Maria. He was going to bring her here. Lock her up here in this hell."

"What did you tell?"

"That I had helped with the Abwehr's internal information service."

"And that's all?"

"Sonderegger asked who gave the order. I had to say Canaris."

Hans mulled that over. "Well, they probably knew it anyway. I wouldn't worry too much. It's not crucial."

In the brief lulls between the crashing bombs Hans and Dietrich rapidly compared notes and found that on the whole they had kept their stories in harmony. Hans had never made a genuine confession, although there were some things he could not deny, because they were written in his own handwriting.

"But I haven't named anyone. When things get too hot I simply pretend to lose consciousness. As long as I'm in this shape, they won't put me up for public trial." Hans raised up on his elbow. "But I can't keep pretending much longer. I need more diphtheria culture for a new illness."

"Isn't that dangerous? You're so weak already."

"I have nothing to lose. It's the only way. We have to gain time." Hans sank back again on the pillow. "Only one thing would completely finish me off. That's if anything happened to Christel. I pray for her safety every day and night. The children, too."

The din overhead drowned out Hans's voice. One after another the dealers of destruction whistled earthward, each nearer than the other. When the next bomb struck, the whole basement rocked.

"That hit the building somewhere," said Hans.

Dietrich wondered about the strength of the ceiling, if the whole structure crashed in upon it.

"This place'll hold. It's practically a bunker itself." Hans lay with his arm under his head, and when the noise above abated, he said, "What I fear most is being moved from Berlin. I want to stay as near to Christel as possible. Sometimes—because of her—I think I must after all, win out. No one has a wife like her. Those long months in Sachsenhausen, when she couldn't visit me—all that time, I knew she was with me. It's really strange—that awareness. You know what I mean?"

"Yes. I know."

"If you survive and I don't, you must tell her that."

"I will, of course. But we aren't giving up yet."

"Oh, but they have us in the hollow of their hands. Remember what you said about Matthew 26: 'All who take the sword will perish by the sword.'"

"I remember."

"I keep thinking about it."

"I've thought about it sometimes too. The deliverance comes when we put it in God's hands and remember his promise of forgiveness." Dietrich looked into his brother-in-law's eyes. "He knows our hearts."

"I hope so."

"You can believe it, Hans."

"Do you believe what we did was right? Will it make a difference?"

"I don't know how much difference it will make, but I think it was right."

"Only, too little, too late—" Hans's voice trailed off, then he turned and looked at Dietrich. "Do you sometimes wish you had stayed in the United States?"

"No. My place was here and I knew it. I've never regretted it. For a long time—especially since July 20—I've felt sure of God's guiding hand. That is liberating. It's helped me accept all this as an extension of our action—a completion of freedom—no matter how it ends."

"Freedom? I don't exactly see this as freedom," said Hans.

"But they really can't touch us, can they? In our inmost being? We are the ones who are free, not they."

Finally Hans said, "I think of 'The St. Matthew Passion' sometimes and hear snatches of the music. But the words. I want to hear the words. And Dietrich, I want to receive the sacrament. Is it possible in this place?"

In his cell Dietrich opened the earthenware bottle of wine he had brought from Tegel. His mother had sent it almost a year before; now there was very little left. He poured it into his tin cup. From the Wednesday parcel he took out a clean handkerchief and the bread. With these and his Bible, he returned to Hans's cell. Dietrich laid the handkerchief on the table and placed the bread and the cup upon it. From his seat on the floor he read in Mark's Gospel the words of Jesus at the Last Supper: "And as they were eating, Jesus took bread, and blessed, and broke it, and gave it to them, and said, 'Take, eat; this is my body.' And he took the cup, and when he had given thanks he gave it to them, and they all drank of it. And he said to them, 'This is my blood of the new covenant, which is poured out for many.'"

Kneeling beside Hans's cot, he prayed the prayer of thanksgiving for the Lord's sacrifice. Hans leaned on his elbow as Dietrich broke the bread and with the words, "This is the body of Christ, broken for you," gave it to him. Then Dietrich offered the cup and said, "This is the blood of Christ, shed for you." Hans drank from the cup and Dietrich asked, "Now, will you do this for me?"

"Is it permitted? A layman?" Hans asked.

"Yes."

Hans, with trembling hands, administered the sacrament to Dietrich. Afterwards they sang together the Eucharist hymn "Gott sei gelobet."

There had been a lull in the attack. Now a new wave of bombers started dropping their load directly on the Prinz-Albrecht-Strasse. Another hit shook the building. A crack appeared in the ceiling and water began to drip through from broken pipes overhead.

"Get under the table," Hans shouted.

"You first." Dietrich helped Hans up, wrapped the blanket around him, and lowered him to a sitting position under the table. He folded himself beside Hans—his head bent onto his knees, his feet straddling the leg of the table. Almost immediately another crashing bomb shattered the glass in the window and sent splinters cascading onto the cot. The lights went out. Dietrich put his hand to the floor; it was covered with water.

"Well, you can't sit here," Dietrich said. "Weak as you are you'd get pneumonia."

"Fine," said Hans. "Better than diphtheria."

Dietrich got up and shook the glass from the bed; then lifted Hans back into it. The bombing began to subside. Dietrich turned his watch toward the meager light; it was eleven o'clock. The American visit had lasted two hours. "I think it's about over. Do you have paper and pencil?"

"On the table there."

Dietrich found them and wrote the words from 1 Peter 3:14:

"But even if you do suffer for righteousness' sake, you will be blessed. Have no fear of them, nor be troubled." He folded it and put it beside Hans's pillow. "You might find this helpful. I have."

"Thanks, Dietrich. Thanks for everything." Hans rose on his elbow. "You know, of course, they got Eberhard."

"No! Who told you?"

"Sonderegger."

"What did he say? Where is he?"

"I don't know. He wanted to know why Eberhard had stayed in our house. I just said that Christel was Renate's aunt."

"Do you think it was because of me? I was always careful in the letters—"

"Sonderegger never mentioned you," said Hans. "I don't think he suspected any connection. It must be because of Rüdiger."

"When was this? How long ago?"

"I can't remember. Sometime before Christmas, I think."

The all clear sounded.

"The building must be wrecked," said Hans. "I wonder what they'll do with us?"

"I don't know. We'll just pray we can stay together."

When he heard voices in the hall, Dietrich reluctantly said good-bye and returned to his cell. As the other prisoners shuffled in, Dietrich sat in the dark and thought about Eberhard.

With water, electricity, and heat knocked out the cell soon became cold. No food was brought the rest of that day. Dietrich parcelled out two prunes and a crust of bread from his food packet. Half of the bread he had left with Hans. In the evening the guards brought a kerosene lamp and hung it from the ceiling of the corridor, then opened the doors for the trip to the washroom.

Through the crack Schlabrendorff whispered, "He's dead. The scoundrel is dead!"

"Who?"

"Freisler. A beam hit him on the head. My trial was due next when the siren went off. Now the fiend is dead. Ewald von Kleist was on the stand just prior to that. He said he had always fought against Hitler with everything he had. He had never made a secret of it, believed it to be in accordance with God's commandment. Freisler erupted into a towering rage and condemned him straight out. Then the siren went off. I was supposed to be next. Now, thank God, the fiend is dead."

With no water to flush the toilets, the place soon smelled like a cesspool. Later on the prisoners were taken to a freshly dug latrine in the courtyard with a log set up across it. Rumor made its way around the basement that the Russians were advancing rapidly and would soon reach Berlin. The next morning, when Dietrich was sitting with Oster and Müller on the latrine, Müller said, "Don't be fooled. The guards have orders to shoot us in our cells if the Russians cut off Prinz-Albrecht-Strasse. I heard it just now."

Dietrich was worried about Hans and mentioned it to several of the guards with whom he was on good terms.

They said, "Orders. Nothing we can do."

"You might bring it to their attention all the same. Maybe the orders could be changed." The guards promised to try. Dietrich asked all week for permission to write his parents and let them know he was safe, but none was granted. On Wednesday the food parcel arrived as usual. In it Dietrich found some little birthday cakes from his mother, Plutarch's *Lives* from Karl-Friedrich, and a letter from his father. As he suspected, they had tried to come on Saturday with a birthday letter and were caught in the raid. The other disquieting news was that Maria had gone to bring her younger brothers and sisters from Pätzig to the West. From all Dietrich had heard, Pätzig could be behind the Russian lines by now.

Toward evening a guard opened his cell and told him to get ready immediately for a journey.

"A journey? Where?"

"Never mind," the guard said, and went on down the corridor, opening other cells.

Dietrich packed his things, including the manuscript on which he had been working since his arrival four months before. When the guard's back was turned, he managed to toss a note onto Hans's cot, saying, "I'm being moved. Destination unknown. God be with you."

In the courtyard among the ruins stood two Grune Minnas, and before each one a group of prisoners with their luggage. On all sides stood SS men with machine guns. The last weak rays of the sun, visible now because so many of the surrounding buildings were gone, filtered through the smoke and ash.

An officer beside the first van read from a list of names. Last he called, "Prisoner Bonhoeffer." Among the others were Josef Müller, General von Falkenhausen, a Count Bismarck, and Ludwig Gehre, a colleague of Müller's whom Dietrich had seen on occasion in the basement. Gehre had tried to kill himself before his arrest, Müller had told Dietrich, but succeeded only in destroying one of his eyes. At the other van stood Canaris, Oster, Sack, Halder, and a man Dietrich recognized as the former Austrian chancellor, Schuschnigg.

Before they boarded the van, Huppenkothen ordered handcuffs for Dietrich and Müller.

"Why handcuffs?" asked Dietrich. "We aren't going to try anything."

"Don't ask questions," said Huppenkothen.

"No use to resist," said Müller, as they climbed aboard. "Let us go calmly to the gallows as Christians."

Gallows, perhaps, thought Dietrich, as he took a seat in the crowded Grune Minna. But if that were so, it seemed unlikely they would have their luggage.

Two SS guards took their places among the prisoners. The motor started, and the van began to move over the bumpy street away from the Gestapo Headquarters. Despite fears for Hans, left behind, and the uncertainty of what lay ahead, Dietrich was relieved to be rid of that evil place.

46

Maria leaned on the arm of the chair and sipped the black coffee Paula had brought her. Across from her, Karl peeled and divided an apple from those she had brought from Pätzig.

"It was already dark when I got there," Maria said. "I could hear the Russian cannons in the distance. Once, as we came over a little rise, I saw the flash of gunfire on the horizon. Mother already had the men preparing the wagon. They had made a wooden frame and covered it with a rug, then a tarp. We spent the whole night packing. Once, when the dumbwaiter came up from the kitchen with a tray of silver, I flipped it over into my suitcase, without thinking." She smiled and put the cup down. "But we didn't bring much of that sort of thing—maybe we should have. We were thinking of necessities mostly—food, warm clothes, hay for the horses, and firewood in case we got stranded somewhere and needed it to keep warm. It turned out we didn't need very much of the wood. We always found a place to stay, even after we ran out of estates where we knew people. Folks were very kind, all along the way."

"But weren't some of them fleeing too?" Paula asked.

"No. Not yet. Most of them didn't realize what was happening. Even the first house before we got to the Oder. They had no idea. They were out of earshot of the Russian guns, you see. It was bitterly cold that first morning, close to zero. Mother made us take every fur coat in the house."

"You and the three children?"

"No, there were eight of us. Two elderly ladies—refugees from Berlin—and another lady with her baby. So there were eight, a wagon-full. Plus our driver."

"And your mother?"

"I tried to get her to come, but she wouldn't. She couldn't forsake her people, she said."

Karl's face showed the misgiving Paula was feeling, but they kept quiet. Paula asked how she got across the river.

"On the ice. It was scary," Maria said with a half laugh. "When we got there we could hear the ice cracking. The driver and I decided we had to try anyway. We lightened the load—some of the firewood and other extra baggage. I sent the ladies on across with the children. Then the driver and I walked with the wagon. In the middle of the river, with the ice cracking under our feet, I panicked. But we made it. After that, it wasn't so bad. Sometimes, when we had to put up in a refugee center and there was no barn for the horses, I slept in the wagon. I was afraid someone would steal them."

"Didn't you freeze?" asked Paula.

"Oh, I had a fur coat. I never took it off after that. When we got toward the West the Allied planes began to strafe the roads. Once, the bullets came right through our wagon. After that I decided we had to travel at night. We cut branches from the trees and camouflaged the wagon by day. The kids thought that was great fun. I was so glad to get to my uncle's in Oberbehme."

The next day Paula, Karl, and Maria went to the Prinz-Albrecht-Strasse. The devastation in the city center was even greater than the week before. There was nothing left of the Gestapo Headquarters but a broken wall with one recessed door. A guard took them down some steps to an alcove, where they waited for an hour in the cold and damp.

When Paula thought they had been forgotten, the guard returned and said, "Prisoner Bonhoeffer is no longer here."

Paula sprang to her feet. "No longer here! Where is he?"

"I don't know. He's been gone a week."

Karl, at her side, steadied her with his arm. To the guard he said, "You must have some idea where they took him."

"No. No idea." The man was short, with no mark of military smartness about him. He spoke with a tired whine. "All I know is they took a whole string of 'em away."

Then Maria spoke. "I'm Dr. Bonhoeffer's fiancée. Please take me to Herr Kommissar Sonderegger. He knows me."

"That's impossible, Fräulein. He's a very busy man."

"He'll want to see me. I have important news for him. Tell him

I just came from the eastern front and can give him information he needs to know."

The man looked at her for a moment then, without a word, turned and left. In a few minutes he came back and said, "This way, Fräulein."

Shortly, Maria returned. The prisoners had been taken south to a concentration camp. Sonderegger claimed he did not know which one.

Maria stayed in Berlin with Paula and Karl, and in the following weeks they tried every avenue to learn Dietrich's whereabouts. No one knew anything. At the same time, Maria tried over and over to call Pätzig, but the phone lines were down. One day, two weeks later, her mother called from Oberbehme. With the Russians threatening from all sides she had fled Pätzig in the snow.

A few days later Maria went back to the Gestapo Headquarters in the hope of seeing Sonderegger again. Paula was doubtful, but when Maria came back she had found that it was one of three concentration camps: Buchenwald, Dachau, or Flossenbürg.

The next morning Maria set out to look for Dietrich. It was her own idea, and Paula did not try to dissuade her.

"Don't worry, Mama. I'll do my best to find him. And I'll keep you informed the best I can. But it may take a long time. You know how the mail is."

Over the next three weeks of anxious waiting the letters came from Maria, all with the same answer—Dietrich was not there. At Buchenwald, Dachau, and Flossenbürg the clerks had checked the prisoner lists, or at least had gone through the motions. They could find no record of him.

Dietrich awoke early. The smell of burning flesh was stronger than ever. He had never gotten used to it in the almost two months since his arrival at Buchenwald. Sometimes, when the wind blew from that direction, it exceeded the usual stench of death and human excrement. The loudspeaker droned off the roll call. It sounded near, though the camp proper was some distance down the hill. Then orders began to blare out for the formation of work parties. General von Rabenau, in the bunk below, was still snoring. Dietrich sat up, his head bent to avoid touching the ceiling, and looked outside the tiny window, which was just above ground level. The yellow building next door blocked any distant view, but if he leaned forward he could see the street and the western hills beyond. The American lines were over there somewhere. The West and freedom.

It had stopped raining, but water trickled down the white-washed wall from a crack near his bunk. Everything would be mildewed again. The tramp of the prisoner slaves in their wooden-soled shoes drew near. They soon came into view, looking so emaciated that Dietrich wondered how they could work. Dietrich himself was always hungry. Sippach, the head guard of their special prison, had said, "Food's scarce. We can't get enough to feed so many. Thuringia's flooded with refugees fleeing from the Russians."

Dietrich shivered in the damp, penetrating cold. There had been heat in the basement only twice during March, and with April's arrival they could expect only what seeped through from the guardroom stove. Not wanting to wake the old general, Dietrich slid back under the blanket. Rabenau had been moved into Dietrich's cell some weeks earlier, and this first experience with a cellmate had proven more agreeable than Dietrich expected. The general was unobtrusive and considerate and, because he was a theologian of sorts, they had had some interesting discussions. When Rabenau had retired in 1942 as head of the military archives, he had gone back to the University of Berlin and studied theology. He was in prison because he was a friend of Goerdeler. Since 1940 he had been a liaison between Beck and some of the leading generals.

"The greatest failure of my life," Rabenau said. "I could not bring them around. Blind men!"

The old man suffered severely from the cold, and Dietrich had given him his extra blanket.

"It's warmer up here, you know. Heat rises."

"What heat?" Rabenau had shot back with a grim smile.

For three days now, since Easter Sunday, they had been hearing a muffled roll in the distant West. This morning it seemed closer. The first time they heard the guns, another guard, Dittman, had said with a swagger that he would never surrender. "You'll never leave this place alive. None of you. We'll see to that. If you go anywhere, it'll be on foot." Could that mean execution in the woods? Unless—unless—by some miracle—Payne Best's plan for a mass escape succeeded. But that seemed unlikely. It rested too much on Sippach's nervous whim. A Nazi could not be trusted, especially a nervous Nazi. And all the guards were nervous. Every day they asked General von Falkenhausen, who occupied Cell 5, to interpret the Wehrmacht report and show them on the map the American and Russian positions. Buchenwald was located in an increasingly narrow corridor between the two armies. Sippach had admitted to Dietrich that when the time came he was planning to bolt the camp at night. "The Russians would tear me limb from limb," he said.

On their daily walk in the corridor Dietrich had told that to Payne Best, a British Secret Service captain, in the cell across the corridor. Best had stopped, adjusted his monocle, and said, "Well, now, there's only one direction Sippach can go. It seems logical that he would need some insurance, in case the Americans got hold of him. Wouldn't you think so?"

"A British captain, perhaps?"

"Right. And a German pastor. And other prisoners of the Nazis." They turned at the end of the corridor and started back. The other fourteen prisoners also promenaded back and forth before the open cell doors, busy with their own conversations. The guards were playing cards in the guardroom. Best continued, "We'll have to persuade the others to join us. The more the better. We'll say to Sippach: Lead us to the American lines and we'll promise protection for you. Now, Bonhoeffer, you speak to Müller and Rabenau, I'll start with Falkenhausen."

Since Best arrived shortly after Dietrich, this tall, seemingly fearless Britisher had been giving orders as if he owned the place. He often succeeded, and life for the prisoners had improved. Dietrich enjoyed the captain's stories of derring-do. He had been captured at Venlo in 1939 in a sensational Gestapo intrigue, which Dietrich remembered.

That same morning Dietrich had sought out Müller, who was all for the plan, but Rabenau was leery. "Too risky. They'd be after us with dogs."

Best had gotten a similar response. They had said that Sippach wouldn't dare. It would be better to wait it out. Liberation was near in any case. To Dietrich, Best said, "Cowards all! The three of us will have to risk it then. I'll speak to Sippach tomorrow."

But Sippach did not appear. On their walk in the corridor Best said, "He'll be here in the afternoon." It was nine o'clock at night before he came and with him the camp commandant, who ordered the prisoners to be ready for departure in an hour. When Payne Best questioned Sippach, all he would say was, "Orders from higher up."

At ten o'clock the guards led them out of the basement to an ancient wood-burning prison van at the curb. With all sixteen prisoners seated around the sides there was not an inch of room to move. Dietrich, in the rear of the van, had his manuscript, wrapped in brown paper, on the seat behind him. The luggage was piled on the floor in the middle, so there was little room for their legs. Next to him was Payne Best and on the other side the Russian, Wassili Kokorin—a nephew of Molotov, who had been teaching Dietrich Russian. Josef Müller and his cellmate, Ludwig Gehre, sat on one side with the former ambassador to Spain and his wife. At the front, next to the wood, sat Dr. Rascher, an SS doctor. No one knew why he was a prisoner. Dietrich had avoided him in the prison.

All night they bumped along over rough back roads, never more than fifteen or twenty miles an hour. Sleep was impossible. About noon the next day they reached Neustadt above Weiden, where the road turned off for Flossenbürg. The van rolled to a stop.

"Flossenbürg!" said Rascher. "Extermination camp. No one leaves there alive." Dietrich and the others waited in anxious silence, while the guards went into a building that Müller, beside the door, said was the police station. Presently they returned and one of them said to Müller, "We'll have to go farther. They can't take you here. Too full."

Dietrich was not surprised when, a few miles beyond Weiden, two motorcyclists pulled alongside the van and ordered it to stop. Every eye turned toward the door. Not a word was spoken. The key scraped in the lock and the door creaked open.

A rough voice called out, "Müller and Liedig, get your things and come with us."

Dietrich was sure the new orders had come from Flossenbürg. He drew back in the shadow and listened for his own name, while Müller and Franz Liedig, a former member of Canaris' staff, dug out their luggage from the pile. Suddenly, Ludwig Gehre, Müller's cellmate, found his bag and jumped out even though his name had not been called.

When the door was shut again and the van started up, Dietrich sat back on the hard seat and tried to comprehend what had happened. Gehre obviously did not want to be separated from Müller. But why had the Gestapo taken him, when they had called out only two names? The suspicion that he himself was the intended third person wormed its way into Dietrich's consciousness.

At dusk they arrived in Regensburg. They stopped at the state prison next to the courthouse. There the warders grumbled that they had no room, but finally put them on the second floor, five to a cell. Even the corridors were accommodating prisoners, many of them—Dietrich soon learned—relatives of Resistance leaders.

The next twenty-four hours were astonishing: for supper, a passable bowl of vegetable soup with a large hunk of bread; a sleep of exhaustion, stretched side by side on straw mats with Rabenau and three others; a morning with cell doors open and an atmosphere in the corridors more like a reception than a criminal prison, with greetings and introductions and exchanges of information. There were wives, children, brothers, and sisters of some of the resisters: Goerdeler, Stauffenberg, Halder, Hammerstein, Hassell, and others. In the afternoon Dietrich was able to tell Frau Goerdeler of the last weeks of her husband's life.

At five o'clock it ended. The guard from Buchenwald ordered the thirteen back into their fume-filled, wood-burning van. It was raining. They had not gone far out of town when the van gave a lurch and came to a stand-still. The steering had given out. The guards sent a passing motorist back to Regensburg for a relief vehicle. Hour stretched into hour and no car came. At dawn the guards let them out to stretch their legs, then herded them back inside for more waiting. At last, about eleven o'clock, a bus drove up, with windows and upholstered seats. The nine or ten SS guards on the bus, machine guns at the ready, hustled the prisoners aboard.

At two o'clock that afternoon they approached a town set on a ridge, dominated by a white church with a tall spire—Schönberg. Near the church the bus took a sharp left and stopped before a large square building of cream-colored stucco. Over the door were the words: *Mädchen Schule.*

The guards escorted the prisoners inside the girl's school and up a flight of steps to a large room with windows on three sides. Feather beds with bright green and yellow coverlets lined the walls, and in the center stood a long table. The air was fresh and clean with the fragrance of lilacs. Smiles lit up faces that had been lined with fatigue.

"Well, now," said Payne Best, turning his monocle, as if he could not be sure it was working, "beds, real beds. Everyone choose one and put your name on it."

The prisoners settled in the unexpected accommodations. Although the door was locked, Dietrich was out of sight and sound of his enemies.

It appeared there would be no food. The town was choked with refugees, the guard said, and the mayor refused to divide their dwindling supplies. But when the ambassador's wife, Frau Heberlein, told the housekeeper they had not eaten for twenty-four hours, the housekeeper said they must have food. Later two large basins of boiled potatoes arrived. Dietrich and his comrades stood around the table eating them with their hands and licking their fingers.

The next day was Saturday. Still no sign of the Gestapo. The day passed pleasantly, beginning with the men lining up for a shave with Payne Best's electric razor. There was lively conversation, marching around the table for exercise, potato salad and bread from the villagers, and a feast of beauty from the windows. No Gestapo. Dietrich entertained the thought that Flossenbürg was indeed behind him.

Sunday morning was Low Sunday, the first Sunday after Easter. One of the prisoners, Dr. Pünder, came to Dietrich and suggested that he hold a worship service for the group. The thought of taking part in a service once more was attractive, but Dietrich knew that more than half the group were Catholic and might not feel comfortable with a Protestant service. And there was the Russian, Kokorin.

Dietrich pointed this out to Dr. Pünder. "They might feel themselves a captive audience, especially Kokorin."

But when they all urged him to do it, even Kokorin, Dietrich consented. The prisoners sat on their beds, and Dietrich stood at the head of the table. They sang one verse of "O Bone Jesu," and Dietrich offered a prayer of praise and thanksgiving. Then he spoke quietly to them of the unjust suffering they had known and of the good that had come in spite of it: the help and friendship they had found in one another; the appreciation of even the smallest blessing; the greater understanding of God's purposes for them and for the world. He then read from the reading of the day, Isaiah 53:5: "'But he was wounded for our transgressions, he was bruised for our iniquities: the chastisement of our peace was upon him; and with his stripes we are healed.' This prophecy points to the suffering of Jesus," said Dietrich. "We hear his words from the cross, 'My God, my God, why have you forsaken me?' We understand them better than before. Every Christian asks this question at sometime, when everything is going against him, when all earthly hope is smashed, when he feels completely helpless in the hands of his enemies. But whoever has found God in the cross of Jesus Christ knows how mysteriously God hides himself in this world, how he lets himself be pushed out of the world and on to the cross.

God calls us, like the disciples in Gethsemane, 'Will you not watch with me one hour?' He calls us to share his sufferings at the hands of a godless world, not in the first place thinking about our own needs, problems, sins, and fears, but allowing ourselves to be caught up into the way of Jesus, a way of powerlessness, a way of suffering, a way of love and forgiveness of our enemies, thus fulfilling the Scripture, 'with his stripes we are healed.'

"Then, with confidence and hope we can look at the other reading, 1 Peter 1:3: 'Blessed be the God and Father of our Lord Jesus Christ. By his great mercy we have been born anew to a living hope through the resurrection of Jesus Christ from the dead.' If we want to learn what God promises and what he fulfills, we will listen to his Word in the life, sayings, deeds, sufferings, death, and resurrection of Jesus. It is certain that we may always be close to God and in the light of his presence, and that such living is an entirely new life for us; that nothing is then impossible for us, because all things are possible with God; that no earthly power can touch us without his will, and that danger and distress can only drive us closer to him. It is certain that we can claim nothing for ourselves, and may yet pray for everything; it is certain that our joy is hidden in suffering, and our life in death; it is certain that in all this we are in a fellowship that sustains us. In Jesus, God has said Yes and Amen to it all, and that Yes and Amen is the firm ground on which we stand."

Dietrich offered a prayer of thanksgiving and closed with the words: "If it is your will once more to give us joy in this world and the splendor of its sun, then help us to reflect and learn from these hard experiences, that henceforth the whole of our lives may belong to Thee. But let us receive whatever comes thankfully, without wavering, from your good and loving hand. Amen."

Dietrich looked up. His comrades seemed reluctant to turn away from the moment. In that stillness came the sound of heavy footsteps in the hall. The key turned in the lock and the door was flung open. Two men in civilian clothes entered. The entire group froze. For Dietrich it seemed the inevitable playing out of the last scene of the drama.

One of the men spoke, "Prisoner Bonhoeffer, get ready and come with us."

Without a word Dietrich packed his meager belongings, except the Plutarch, his manuscript, and his Bible. In the Plutarch he wrote his name and address in large letters in the front, the back, and the middle, and left it on the table. He wrote it also on the manuscript and gave it to General Rabenau. "If you can get this to my parents, I will be grateful," he said.

"I'll do my best," said the general, his eyes filled with tears. Dietrich shook his hand, then the hand of each of his comrades, last of all, Payne Best.

Drawing Best aside, he put the Bible in his hand and said, "If you get back to England—and I pray you will—would you please give this to the Bishop of Chichester and tell him that for me this is the end, but also the beginning of life—"

"But my dear Bonhoeffer, this may not be—." The incorrigible Best seemed to be searching for some reason to offer hope.

Dietrich merely shook his head and continued, "Tell him also that with him I believe in our Universal Christian brotherhood, which rises above all national interests, and that our victory is certain."

The tall Englishman appeared greatly subdued. "I'll tell him. I'll tell him what you said."

"And tell him that I have never forgotten his words at our last meeting."

He shook Best's hand, then turned and went out with his captors.

47

And with his stripes we are healed. The words of Isaiah came again to Dietrich's mind as the car sped north on the narrow road. The two men, grim and silent, sat in front. Dietrich, handcuffed in the back seat, hardly noticed them. In the face of death, Dietrich thought, a man tries to arrange his affairs. For him there were left the affairs of heart and spirit, and these could be arranged through prayer alone.

During the four days' passage from Flossenbürg to Schönberg, the fate of Müller, Gehre, and Liedig never had been far from Dietrich's thoughts. He thought of them now as he struggled to restore his equilibrium—to regain, with some degree of humility, acceptance of what lay ahead. Dietrich kept his eyes on the landscape outside the window. Green fields sped by, interspersed with patches of fir and a few birches. Time was losing its relevance.

And with his stripes we are healed. He is despised and rejected of men, a man of sorrows, and acquainted with grief. Beyond Regen, high on the left, an ancient rock bridge came into view.

"Come with me, Hörnchen," the little boy says. The bridge is long and the black water of the Spree swirls beneath.

"What will the other children think? You're a schoolboy now, Dietrich."

"Then you walk over there, on the other side of the bridge. But come with me!" It is still scary and a long way across to the school on the other side of the river. But she is there.

Beyond Regen the road curved through a damp forest of tall firs. Here and there the slender white trunk of a birch snaked its way upward through folded layers of dark green fir, as if reaching for the life-giving sun. Once through the trees a small lake glimmered—on its surface a single white swan.

"But, Papa, he accused us of trying to steal the eggs," says Walter. "I told him we loved animals, we'd never do that."

"We were just hiding in the bushes," Dietrich says. "We didn't go close. Honest we didn't. We were waiting for the mother swan to come back so Walter could take a picture of her on the nest. He showed his camera to the forest ranger. It didn't make a bit of difference. He's a bad man."

"Go to him, Papa, and tell him. Explain."

Their father lays his hand on Walter's shoulder and shakes his head. "No, my boy, that is the way of the world. Many times you will be misunderstood. It's good that you learn this. Better now, early in life."

He was oppressed and he was afflicted, yet he opened not his mouth: he is brought as a lamb to the slaughter, and as a sheep before her shearers is dumb, so he opened not his mouth. Below the road a river wound its way through the valley, flanked on the other side by a railroad. Eventually the curves straightened out, and up ahead a farmer herded his sheep across in front of them. The car came to a halt, and the man at the wheel—the one with the close-clipped hair—cursed impatiently.

"Dietrich, don't you have a song for your brother?" His mother's face is pale, and a shadow flickers over it when she looks at Walter who is leaving the next morning for the front. Dietrich hopes his song will cheer her heart, though he had arranged it especially for Walter. Nun zu guter Letzt geben wir dir jetzt auf die Wandrung des Geleite. *Now, at the last, we say God speed you on your way.*

Surely he hath borne our griefs and carried our sorrows: yet we did esteem him stricken, smitten of God, and afflicted. Beyond a rock quarry the hills parted into a wide valley. In the distance were three church steeples—one yellow, one an onion dome, and one with twin spires.

"Why would you choose the Church?" Klaus argues, "that's the line of least resistance. A poor, feeble, boring, petty bourgeois institution."

"If the Church is feeble, I shall reform it," Dietrich answers, half joking. But in his heart he means it.

The wide valley continued beyond the town and gave forth now the pungent smell of manure. At a crossroad stood a small wayside crucifix made of wood, with a little pointed roof to protect the figure of the broken Christ. *All we like sheep have gone astray; we have turned every one to his own way; and the Lord hath laid on him the iniquity of us all.*

At Neustadt the car turned right onto a narrow asphalt road. It was the road to Flossenbürg. Through tiny villages the car sped on until, on the highest hill of the eastern horizon, a jagged ruin appeared, ghost of a time long past, when this remote valley was guarded by its own Bürg. In the next village—Floss, the sign read—a tiny railroad station nestled beside the rails. It was the end of the line.

He was cut off from the land of the living: for the transgression of my people was he stricken. Dietrich remembered the words he had said to Payne Best—for me, the beginning of life. But the passage to that life—that last dark station on the way. Dietrich closed his eyes and listened. *If he offers his life in atonement he shall see his heirs, he shall have a long life and through him what the Lord wishes will be done. His soul's anguish over, he shall see the light and be content.*

That was the promise.

Suddenly the Bürg was there. The car roared up an incline, past clustered houses and a little church. The camp—the closely set barracks, the barbed wire, the watchtowers—was spread across the saddle of the hill. In front was a large gray stone building where the car pulled to a stop.

The two guards hustled Dietrich inside to a spacious, well-furnished office. The SS officer behind the desk was waiting for them.

"We found him."

"Good," said the officer, and to Dietrich, "Your name is Dietrich Bonhoeffer?"

"Yes."

"You thought you had escaped our vigilance?"

Dietrich said nothing.

To the others the officer said, "The trial is in progress. Take him first to the bunker. He will be called."

The guards marched Dietrich along the arched gateway, which ran through the center of the main building, and out into the drill yard. At his feet, beside the stone building, withered moss and twisted, dust-covered brambles struggled for life. A scattering of ragged, emaciated inmates watched with dull curiosity as Dietrich, handcuffed and flanked by the two men, was led between the long barracks. At the second row they turned right onto a cobbled road, which led a short distance to an iron gate. One of the men unlocked the gate, and they stepped into an unpaved yard, beyond which stood a long, low building.

Inside, the two men turned Dietrich over to the guards. "The lost sheep. We found him. Keep him fast," one of the men said.

From the guardroom a corridor extended in both directions the length of the building. The men took Dietrich to the right. On one side windows, spaced at intervals, looked out onto the dirt yard. On the other, cell doors lined up side by side. In Cell 24 the guards chained Dietrich by wrist and ankle to the wall and left him, locking the door behind them.

This space was not unlike the other cells Dietrich had known, except more barren—no table, just a plank bed and a stool. The only sound was the occasional clanking of chains. He stood still in the middle of the floor.

The fact that a trial was going on was no cause for hope. Dietrich had glimpsed the license plate of the car before they left Schönberg. It was from Berlin. Once or twice during the drive the SS men mentioned the name "Huppenkothen." The head of the investigation into the July 20 plot would not come to Flossenbürg without orders from high up, and such orders could have one purpose alone. Any trial was a farce. The subterfuge was over. No need to cover up.

It was dark when the guards returned for Dietrich. They traversed the same cobbled road to a large white building near the center of the camp. The room inside was long, with the near end brightly lit. Sinks, wash tubs, and canvas hampers confirmed that the camp laundry had been converted into a courtroom. Black shades covered the windows. Harsh light bulbs hung from the ceiling, and beneath them were two tables set at right angles and a small desk with a typewriter. Walter Huppenkothen sat at the table on the right. Behind the other was a heavy-set man in a judge's robe. Standing beside him was Stawitzky, the one-legged giant Dietrich knew for his cruel treatment of the prisoners in Prinz-Albrecht-Strasse—a monster of the Nazi system. A secretary sat at the typewriter. There was no defense counsel.

In the Gestapo Headquarters Sonderegger had handled Dietrich's case for the most part, but Dietrich had stood before Huppenkothen a few times and knew his manner of feigned reasonableness. Cool and urbane, Huppenkothen's hardened features gave the impression of a machine with a mind, although on a few occasions there had been violent outbursts.

After the mock formalities of an opening court session, the

judge, whose name was Otto Thorbeck, asked Stawitzky to read the charges—high treason and treason in the field during wartime. Stawitzky did this with perverse satisfaction.

After a sarcastic remark about the cat being back in the bag, Huppenkothen, who had been introduced as the prosecutor, said: "We know and have known for a long time of your complicity in these plots, which up to now you have been foolish enough to deny. Do you still deny it?"

"Exactly what plots do you mean?" asked Dietrich.

Huppenkothen waved a weary hand at Stawitzky, who read from a handwritten paper detailing Oster's plans for the coup d'etat in 1938.

"You knew of this?" asked Huppenkothen.

"Yes."

"Ah! And what was your part in it?"

"No part. But I approved it."

Stawitzky, in a lightning move, struck Dietrich in the face.

"That's enough," said Huppenkothen.

The Kommissar, his face filled with a mixture of hate and sadistic glee, stepped back.

Huppenkothen then cited Dietrich's trips to Switzerland and Sweden and his part in Operation 7.

Dietrich admitted the true purpose for all of them, but made no attempt to defend or justify his actions. He tasted the blood that had run down from his nose, but did not try to wipe it away.

"And all under the orders of Admiral Canaris, I believe you testified."

This gave Dietrich pause. He was unsure how much they knew of Canaris' involvement. "He signed my orders, but may not have known their real intent."

"We'll see about that." Huppenkothen turned to the guard. "Bring Oster and Canaris again."

The wait was long. When Oster and Canaris finally came, Dietrich was shocked by the admiral's appearance. A bruise covered half his face, and his nose appeared broken. His pale gray suit was crumpled, and on his tie and shirt were splotches of blood. Oster, also battered, but with a defiant look in his eyes, nodded a greeting to Dietrich.

"Now," said Huppenkothen, "perhaps you two would like to hear what your chief has been telling us. He denies that he was one of you and insists he worked only for the good of the Reich. What do you say to that?"

Oster looked at Dietrich, but Dietrich said nothing. Then Oster turned to Canaris. "Sir, it's no good. We're done for, you know. They'll kill us whatever we say. There's no use to deny anything."

With a desperate look Canaris said, "But everything I did was for the good of the Fatherland, don't you understand? I am not a traitor."

"You had nothing to do with these plots?" asked Thorbeck.

"I am not a traitor," Canaris repeated.

"What do you say to that, Oster?"

"I've already told you what I know."

"Tell us again."

"We were all in it together." He looked at the admiral. "I can only say what I know. It's too late to lie."

Canaris cast a despairing glance in Dietrich's direction. Dietrich said nothing, but tried with a small nod to convey his encouragement.

Thorbeck spoke to Canaris. "So, do you say General Oster is falsely incriminating you?"

Canaris bowed his head and said in an almost inaudible voice, "No."

One at a time the judge read out the sentences: death by hanging at dawn the next day.

His watch read 10:25 when Dietrich arrived back in his cell. He dragged the chain and stood at the window. On the hill beyond the barbed wire fence the firs drooped their dark arms to the earth. Dietrich listened for some comforting night sound. There was nothing but brooding silence. He could hear the beating of his own heart. Holding the chain in his hand, he walked the few steps to the bed and sank to his knees. O, Righteous Father, be with me now. In the stillness he heard the word he had so often given fellow-sufferers in the Gestapo cellar: "But even if you do suffer for righteousness sake, you will be blessed. Have no fear of them, nor be troubled. Simply reverence the Lord Christ in your heart."

Dietrich begged forgiveness for his sins and the sorrow he was bringing to his parents. He prayed that God would comfort them, then prayed for all the others—beginning with Eberhard and Maria. The prayers brought visions of times past and thanksgiving for the people God had given him. Peace and comfort descended. All night the Psalms spoke to him out of the storehouse where he had laid them up over the years.

Near morning Dietrich rose up with a start at the loud barking of guard dogs outside. It was a sound designed to strike terror in his heart—he had a latent fear of dogs. It seemed a device of Satan to defeat him. He was still on his knees and realized he must have fallen asleep there, leaning on the cot.

Loud voices in the cell block shouted, "Out, out you come!"

The key turned in Dietrich's lock and the door opened. Two men stood there, one a guard. "Come, come along. It's time."

Dietrich arose and picked up the Goethe, the only book he had left. He wanted to leave it where someone might find it and know that he had been there. He walked ahead of the guard down the corridor. From the other direction came Karl Sack and Ludwig Gehre. Canaris and Oster were already in the guardroom. The guards herded them into the washroom and ordered them to undress. In silence Dietrich took off his clothes.

> Naked I lay on the floor when I came,
> When I drew my first breath;
> Naked I shall depart again
> When I shall flee this earth, a shadow.

He laid his things with the Goethe on the guardroom table. Canaris, too, laid a book beside it.

Dietrich took the admiral's hand and said softly, "God be with you, Sir."

Canaris, pale and sorrowful, nodded his thanks.

Silently Dietrich shook the hands of the others. To Oster, no word was spoken. The look between them confirmed their common bond.

They were lined up in the corridor, Dietrich third in line behind Canaris and Oster. Soon the door opened and, as the cold April air rushed in, the guards took Canaris. The vicious barking intensified. *Thou wilt keep him in perfect peace, whose mind is stayed on Thee.* The time was long. How could it take so long, he wondered? Again the door opened. They took Oster.

This time it was not long. The open door, the glare of the arc lights, on one side Huppenkothen, Stawitzky, a man with a stethoscope, and on the other guards with dogs on the leash. Dietrich wondered for what purpose. Why did they need dogs? He looked at the faces of the men—by their folly, malice, and unbridled ambition they had taken up arms against their own humanity. He heard the words of Jesus from the cross, "Father, forgive them for they know not what they do."

Beyond them a wooden roof projected from the wall, and from its supporting beams hung three nooses. Below each stood a platform with three steps.

O, my God. But Dietrich's lips did not move. He looked squarely at the instrument of his death and measured the distance—twenty paces. *Lord, my encircling shield, you help me hold up my head.*

The executioner, wearing an SS uniform, waited for him. Dietrich looked him straight in the eye until the man, at last, turned his eyes away. At the foot of the scaffold Dietrich knelt and with his finger traced in the trampled earth the sign of the cross. He rose and surrendered his life into the hands of the Father.

The executioner clamped Dietrich's hands behind his back, then motioned him to the steps. Dietrich lifted his head, stood erect, and mounted the three steps. There he turned. Beyond the lights, beyond the men and the dogs, beyond the far wall on a distant hill the dawn lit up the trees. The sun was rising.

Afterword

On April 20, eleven days after this predawn execution, American soldiers liberated Flossenbürg Concentration Camp. Meanwhile, Josef Müller and Fabian von Schlabrendorff, who, on April 10, learned of the murders outside their prison the previous morning, were moved to Dachau Concentration Camp, near Munich. Eventually Müller and Schlabrendorff escaped with other survivors, including Martin Niemöller, into Italy and American custody. From there they sent word of Dietrich's death to Visser 't Hooft, general secretary of the World Council of Churches, in Geneva. Through him, Sabine, in Oxford, England, learned on May 31 of her brother's fate. At that time no communication with her family in Berlin was possible.

The manuscript that Dietrich left behind in Schönberg has never been found. A few days after Dietrich's death, General von Rabenau was taken to Flossenbürg and executed.

In late July, Bishop Bell, assisted by Franz Hildebrandt and Julius Rieger, ·held a memorial service for Dietrich in the Church of the Holy Trinity in Kingsway, London. It was broadcast in Germany by the BBC. Dietrich's parents in Berlin, who up to then had no certain knowledge of what had happened to him, heard this broadcast, and their worst fears were confirmed.

Hans von Dohnanyi was kept in the Gestapo basement for almost six weeks after Dietrich was taken away. He came under the care of a prison doctor, Dr. Tietze, who had him removed to a hospital and kept there under guard. With the doctor's help, he was able to see Christel once more. On April 6 Sonderegger transferred him to Sachsenhausen concentration camp. Before Walter Huppenkothen started on his murderous mission to Flossenbürg, he went to Sachsenhausen by a "special order of the Führer" and set up a hasty court-martial in which Hans, lying half-conscious on a stretcher, was condemned to death. The Nazis hanged him on April 9, the same day as Dietrich. When Christel asked Sonderegger about him, he merely handed her Hans's clothes. The final

confirmation came when Sonderegger appeared before Allied authorities. Hans's "Chronicles of Scandals" were never found. It is
assumed that they were destroyed by the Gestapo.

All through March and into April the family continued its efforts to save Klaus and Rüdiger. Eberhard was in the same prison
with them and was sometimes able to communicate briefly with
them. On Sunday night, April 22, the Russian artillery shelling
became so intense that the prisoners, now numbering about fifty,
were taken to the basement. Although Rüdiger and Klaus, along
with fourteen other condemned prisoners, were in a separate
room, Eberhard managed to get across and speak with them
briefly. About midnight he went back to his own room and went
to sleep. The next morning he learned that the sixteen had been
taken away in the night. The SS guards had also disappeared and
left their uniforms. It was two days before the remaining prisoners
persuaded the other guards and the prison commandant to let
them go. By then Russian machine gun fire could be heard in the
streets.

When the prison gates finally opened, Eberhard invited another
prisoner, a Russian Jew who had no place to go, to accompany him
home. They walked to Charlottenburg, where the Russians were
guarding the bridge at the Schloss. They managed to get through
safely. Later, when Russian soldiers came to the Schleicher house,
where they were all staying in the basement because of the shelling, the Russian Jew explained that they were anti-Nazi and probably saved all of their lives.

It was Eberhard who learned the facts of the deaths of Rüdiger
and Klaus. One of the sixteen prisoners, Herbert Kosney, had escaped death that night and, later, Eberhard talked directly with
him. An execution detachment from Prinz-Albrecht-Strasse had
arrived about one o'clock in the morning and taken the condemned prisoners out, on the pretext that they were being transferred to another place in order to be released. There was one SS
man for every prisoner. After they had walked about a hundred
yards into an area near the Lehrter Station, the SS men—on com-

mand—shot the prisoners in the back of the head. Kosney turned his head at the moment the shot was fired and the bullet went through his neck and cheek. He collapsed and pretended to be dead. After the Gestapo left the scene, he crawled away. The fifteen, including Klaus and Rüdiger, were buried in a bomb crater nearby. Later the families of the men held a memorial service at the spot and erected a monument in their honor, which stands there today.

Sabine and Gert Leibholz returned to Göttingen, West Germany, in 1951, where Sabine still lives. Gert, who made significant contributions to the constitution and the justice system of the new West German government, died in 1981. Paula and Karl Bonhoeffer continued to live at 43 Marienburger Allee. The father died in 1948 and the mother in 1951. Christine von Dohnanyi (Christel) never fully recovered from her terrible sufferings but, nevertheless, was able to give important testimony after the war to Allied investigating authorities. She died in 1965. Ursula Schleicher (Ursel), devastated at first by her husband's death, emerged from her despairing grief and turned her thought and action to caring for her children and those who needed her. She lived near Hamburg at the time of her death in 1983. Emmi Bonhoeffer, on one of those first days after war's end, swam the Elbe to escape the Russians and walked to Schleswig-Holstein to join her children. She died in 1991, as did Dietrich's younger sister, Susanne Dress (Susi). Karl-Friedrich died in 1957. After the death of the parents, the church bought the house at Marienburger Allee as a student center. The plan is to make it a Bonhoeffer Museum.

Franz Hildebrandt never again returned to Germany. He eventually married and served in Britain as a Methodist pastor. For several years he taught at Drew University Theological School in Madison, New Jersey, before returning to Edinburgh, Scotland. He was one of forty Protestant clergymen worldwide to be invited to attend the Vatican II Council. In 1984, though failing in health, he traveled to Vancouver, British Columbia, and gave an address at the Fiftieth Anniversary Celebration of the Barmen Declaration of the Confessing Church. In November of that year he died, leaving his wife, Nancy, and three children.

After the war, Maria von Wedemeyer studied mathematics at Göttingen University, married a young German, and they emigrated to the United States. They had two children, both boys. For a number of years Maria held a responsible position with Honeywell, Inc., in Boston, Massachusetts. In 1977 she died of cancer. Her ashes are buried in the Black Forest in Germany.

Peter Hoffmann, in his book, *The History of the German Resistance*, states that "based on files captured after the war, the British estimate that 4,980 people were executed for participation in the 20 July 1944 conspiracy alone." Although this figure may include some executions not connected with July 20, it is probably low, because it does not include many deaths from starvation and torture, nor does it include those conspirators who committed suicide rather than face arrest by the Gestapo. Some of the most moving documents to come out of World War II are farewell letters of the condemned conspirators to their wives, children, and parents, among them, letters from Hans von Dohnanyi and Klaus Bonhoeffer.

During the war Renate buried some of Dietrich's letters from prison in gas mask cases in the garden of her parents' house at Marienburger Allee 42. Others were kept by Eberhard's mother in Kade. In 1951, after the first difficult years of recovery from the devastation of war, Eberhard submitted the letters for publication. In a short time this book, known in English as *Letters and Papers from Prison*, became world famous, with translations into many languages.

Thus began the labor of love that was to become, with Renate's assistance, Eberhard's second vocation. In the years since then he has edited many of Bonhoeffer's works, including the *Ethics* and the six-volume *Gesammelten Schriften*. Over a period of twenty years he wrote the great definitive biography, *Dietrich Bonhoeffer: Man of Vision, Man of Courage*. Eberhard and Renate have assisted in the new sixteen-volume *Dietrich Bonhoeffer Werke* now appearing in Germany. A translation project is underway for an English-language edition of this work.

In their travels around the world and from their home near Bonn the Bethges have made themselves available to help all those who want to learn more about the life and work of Dietrich Bonhoeffer. We all owe them a debt we can never repay.